SEED
OF
DOUBT

SEED OF DOUBT

OF

DOUBT

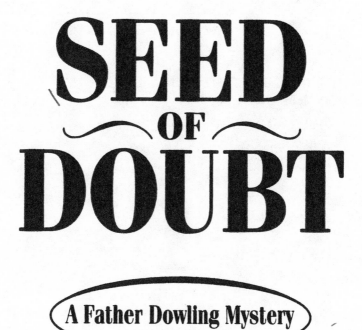

A Father Dowling Mystery

Ralph McInerny

St. Martin's Press, New York

Design by Karin Batten

ISBN 0-312-09381-0

For Beth and Paul Hark

SEED
OF
DOUBT

Prologue

The old woman sat in a brocade chair in her room on the second floor of the house in which she had lived all her widowed life. Her hands were joined in her lap, her eyes were lowered, her lips moved in prayer. She had just received Jesus Christ in the form of consecrated unleavened bread. *My Lord and my God.* She said this over and over. Her First Holy Communion had been over eighty years before, and she had frequented the sacraments all her life, but she felt a great distance between herself and God. She told Father Dowling this.

"Feeling and faith differ, Margaret."

He did not offer her false consolation and she had learned to like that. Her mind always seemed clearer when she talked with him. Before he left, he blessed her and said he would be back next week, but the old woman did not think she would see next week. Beside her stood the oxygen on which her life depended.

"It's always right here," Honora said brightly. Margaret did not trust her nurse. Honora was constantly slipping out of the room.

"To the kitchen," Dolly said.

It was an old story, romances among the help. But what could any man, even Regis, see in Honora?

The old woman fell asleep in her chair. When she wakened there was a strange man looking at her portrait on the wall. Was this another of the nurse's admirers? Where was Honora? Margaret did not like the nurse hovering about her, but neither did she care to open her eyes and find a stranger in the room with her. The man turned, then went away. She drifted off again and awoke to find the man still there. No, this wasn't the same man. Like the other he wore a beard and for a moment she thought it was Terry. Terry had been in earlier. She did not know this man.

"Where is the other painting like this?" he asked.

"There is only one."

"There's another! A portrait of Bridget."

He was right, there was a portrait of Bridget, but she could not remember where it was. Her memory was no longer reliable.

"Where is it?"

He leaned his face into hers and looked angrily at her. Margaret was frightened and her breath began to come in gasps. Instinctively she reached for her oxygen but the man snatched the mask from her and tugged at the apparatus, wheeling it out of her reach. She was unable to breathe. She felt a terrible pain in her chest, as if her lungs were in revolt. The bearded face loomed before her, talking, talking, and then the plastic mask settled over her nose and mouth and the sweet flow of oxygen began.

"Where is it?"

She tried to focus her eyes on him. Where was Honora? The man removed the mask so abruptly her seizure resumed. Opening her mouth wide, she tried to gasp in air, but could only choke. A darkness enveloped her, growing progressively deeper, and a black pain gripped her chest. When she stopped trying to breathe her head became light and she began to fall through air cold as night with the smell of rain and the sea in it, into the past, into the future, out of the present.

It had been so long since Margaret Sinclair was able to come to mass that not even Marie Murkin could remember it. The wealthy old woman at Fairview was now the last stop on Father Dowling's weekly round of sick calls and, after giving her Holy Communion, he often stayed to talk.

"What is a near-death experience, Father Dowling?"

He gave a very short explanation, suspecting that Margaret already knew as much as he did of the accounts people gave of having been at or, as some of them insisted, through death's door, only to return to life.

"I've been near death for decades, Father."

With anyone else he might have said that we are all near death, all men are mortal, the call can come at any moment, reducing the undeniably true to platitude. But not with Margaret. Her dependence on oxygen was an added reminder of mortality.

"I'd be dead without it, Father."

"So would we all."

3

She liked it when he made her lot seem the common one, no matter that she was in her tenth decade.

"Long life is a blessing, Margaret."

"A mixed one, Father. I can prepare for death, but I also have to remember all the silly things I've done. The wicked things."

The first time Margaret Sinclair made such a reference to her past life, Roger Dowling suspected her of a not uncommon fault of the aged, the half-romantic wish to portray oneself as a great sinner. From what Father Dowling knew of the condition of the old woman's soul, it would take excessive scrupulosity for Margaret to turn up dramatic misdeeds in her past.

On the wall of the room where she spent her days was a striking portrait of a young lady. He had tried to suppress his surprise when she first told him that she was the subject of the painting.

"How old were you?"

"It was done during the summer before my wedding."

A very long time ago. Amos Cadbury had told Roger Dowling that for him one of the joys of visiting Margaret Sinclair was to be someone's junior again.

"She still thinks of me as the young lawyer she met long ago."

"Have you ever had your portrait painted, Amos?"

The lawyer was silent until he had found some meaning in the question. "Ah. Hers is a striking likeness, is it not?"

Suggesting that when Amos first met Margaret, she still resembled the painting.

For Margaret, Roger was a priest, neither young nor old, ordained to fullfil a function, possessed of an impersonal competence, a gift. He could absolve her sins and bring her the Eucharist.

"I've not been a good Catholic, Father."

"Don't brag."

"I think a long life is a kind of purgatory."

There was something biblical about Margaret. From this frail woman had come a vast family: only one son, Henry (known in the family as Henry VIII because of his girth), but nine grandchildren and countless great-grandchildren.

"She's strong as an ox," Honora assured Father Dowling. On Margaret's instructions, the nurse always came with him to the door. Honora's skin was almost as white as her uniform. Her penciled brows competed with the wrinkles in her forehead.

4

"Dull work for you?"

"All nursing is dull."

Besides Honora, there was only the chef, Regis, and an arthritic housekeeper named Dolly. A widow who had been with Margaret Sinclair for twenty years, she supervised a cleaning service that came once a week. Like her employer, she spent her day in a chair in her room, but unlike Margaret, Dolly watched television. Father Dowling visited with Dolly after giving Margaret communion, letting the older woman have some minutes for thanksgiving.

"If you'd like, Father," Dolly said when he asked if he should bring her communion. "But I'm not Catholic, you know."

If Margaret liked to talk of her impending death or of the distant past, Dolly was curious about what was going on about her. Her imagination was aflame with the soap scandals she watched on television.

"That nurse has a man," she whispered to Father Dowling.

He supposed she meant Regis, the chef. Regis was a huge man made taller by the starched mushroom of a hat he was seldom without. Raisin-like eyes looked sadly from the unbaked dough of his face as he spoke to the priest about Honora. "She is an angel, Father Dowling. Mrs. Sinclair is lucky to have found her." But it seemed clear that Regis wished the good luck were his own. Father Dowling discouraged Dolly's speculation about the nurse and the chef.

"Why do we need a chef, Father? He cooks for the nurse, not for us. Mrs. Sinclair eats like a bird, and with my stomach . . ." Her eyes rolled toward the ceiling.

Thanks to the advice and stewardship of Amos Cadbury, Margaret had retained the bulk of the Sinclair wealth in her own control. The base was real estate but there were investments of variety as well as fecundity.

"And a modest collection of art. Some was given to the Fox River museum, the rest is in the house."

"Her portrait?"

"She keeps that for sentimental reasons."

Perhaps Amos meant vanity. When Roger Dowling asked Margaret who the painter was, she spoke of how much Fairview had changed since she first saw it, but any changes it had undergone would have been under her direction, the most dramatic being the

5

reduction of staff. Now there was only Dolly and Regis and, of course, the nurse. But then there was only Margaret to look after.

"Fairview has become an impossible luxury. No one will be able to keep it as a residence after I'm gone."

She had discussed her will with him and Roger Dowling understood from Amos that all the old woman's wishes were unequivocally set down. Amos had written the will and he obviously intended to see that it was carried out, jot and tittle.

"It's been a long wait," Roger Dowling said.

"The heirs? Terence Sinclair suggested that she make a living will."

"He said that to her?"

"In his darker moments, he might have suggested the Hemlock Society."

Despite Margaret's valetudinarian tone in their conversations, Roger Dowling was almost surprised when the end came. Marie Murkin took the call and rushed into the study.

"It's Fairview, Father. Margaret Sinclair."

Her expression said it all. Roger Dowling put down his Dante and rose to go. He read the *Divine Comedy* through at least once a year. He had just finished the first canto of the *Paradiso*.

2

The dean was sorry to hear of the death in Peggy's family but became matter-of-fact when told it was her great-grandmother.

"She must have been very old?"

"In her nineties."

Miss Agate sighed. "It is a cruel mercy, to prolong life beyond any reasonable purpose."

Peggy said nothing. Clearly the dean thought she was crazy to go home for the funeral of so ancient a relative only weeks before final exams in the second semester of her senior year.

"When did you last see her?"

"At Easter."

Through the windows behind Miss Agate's desk a scene of springtime exuberance was visible: flowering dogwood, magnolias in blossom, lilacs too, and on the well-mown lawns Peggy's fellow seniors disported themselves with the languor their role required. The temperature in the dean's office was artificially controlled, the only scent the musky one created when Miss Agate stirred. Her prematurely gray hair looked combed rather than brushed and her eyes, when she removed her glasses, took a while to focus on Peggy.

"Surely her death was expected."

By Margaret? Longed for might be more accurate, although Peggy had learned not to assume she knew what her great-grandmother thought. Margaret was docile with her nurse, although she dismissed Honora when Peggy visited. Sometimes while they spoke Margaret took oxygen from the contraption that was always beside her chair. Emphysema. She had never smoked but said she came by the ailment naturally.

"People once prayed to see their children's children," the old woman murmured. "They saw them and rejoiced." She looked at Peggy. "But you don't know the Bible."

"No."

"People knew it better when it was chained." A sly smile. "Have they raised you Catholic? I told Father Dowling they had."

Peggy nodded, trying to imagine that this ancient woman had once been her own age.

"It's a punishment, not a reward, Peggy."

"Being Catholic?"

"I meant a long life, but you may be right." The skeletal hand with its mottled skin closed over Peggy's. How slippery smooth the old woman's palm was, like the sole of a foot. "But I've lived to know you. And that's a blessing."

They had become close, the young woman and her great-grandmother, two Margarets. Peggy had heard the story of the wedding trip many times from others but had been unsuccessful in getting Margaret to talk about it. There was no photograph of the dead husband in the room where the old woman spent most of her days. There were no photographs at all, only the portrait in oil of Margaret painted just prior to her marriage.

"Who painted it?"

"A man named Ford."

In the catalogues it would be described as oil on canvas, 24″ × 36″, and the Ford was indeed the Clayton Ford Peggy had heard of in Art Appreciation. Known mainly as a landscape painter in the grand manner of Constable, Ford had also done some portraits, and if he lived at all it would be because of these. So at any rate said Professor Gearhart Glockner, the scruffy, bearded, overweight art historian

8

who minced back and forth before them speaking with the absolute authority of someone certain he is not being overheard. Michele's description. Michele intended to be a writer.

"Oh, it can't be, can it?" Michele asked, when Peggy told her of the Ford portrait of her great-grandmother.

The dates were right, there was certainly a similarity if not identity of style, but the portrait was not mentioned in the catalogue Professor Glockner brought out with a sigh from the messy shelf behind his desk. He began shaking his head almost before looking.

"Margaret Sinclair? Nope."

"Is there more than one Ford? I mean painter."

"Does the painting seem professional?"

His manner changed and Peggy regretted asking him. She shrugged. Professor Glockner pointed out that Ford had lived most of his life in Italy, going there quite young and almost never returning to his native land. "Still, it's an intriguing possibility."

"He became quite successful," her great-grandmother said. "He went abroad to Italy."

"Before your wedding?"

Her eyes seemed to look right through Peggy. "He didn't attend. Perhaps he was already gone."

In the end, Peggy didn't care whether the painter was regarded as important, in however minor a way, by Glockner and his ilk. Her contempt for the professor did not lessen when he gave her an A. B- was the lowest grade. He wanted desperately to be popular.

It was eerie when visiting her great-grandmother to compare the frail old woman with her oxygen supply forever at hand, drifting in and out of mental clarity, with the beautiful young woman in the portrait. The young Margaret leaned forward, as if she could not see clearly, and her lips were slightly parted, a young woman on the very threshold of life, curious, naive, vulnerable.

"Tell me about Clayton Ford."

The old woman cocked her head and cast a lidded look at Peggy. "I believe you are angling to get possession of that picture."

Peggy pulled her chair closer and took the old woman's hand in hers. "It's because it's all so romantic! Your portrait painted by a man who would become famous, then you marry and go off to Europe . . ."

A shiver of pleasure went through her as she thought of the

9

contingency of her own existence. If Margaret Sinclair had not returned pregnant as well as a widow from her honeymoon, the remote possibility of Peggy's ever being born would have been removed.

Margaret and Matthew Sinclair had honeymooned on the Amalfi coast and one night in their hotel in Maiori, with a storm raging outside, her husband had gone out onto the balcony of their room and never returned. His body was found on the road below.

Michele told Peggy she had a patriarchal hangup.

"I think of it as matriarchal."

Because the line went back to her great-grandmother as the ultimate source, at least so far as Peggy's interest was concerned. It could become an obsession, Michele was right, but so what? Peggy longed to learn as much as she could of that long-ago tragedy that had made her great-grandmother an almost sacred figure in the family.

"I want my life to be like yours," Peggy had said to Margaret.

Tears stood in the old woman's eyes. Embracing her was like hugging a golf bag.

"God forbid."

She seemed really to mean it. Peggy had thought the old woman was overcome by joy, flattered, whatever. Her hand was held by the skeletal one.

"I'll pray that you don't."

"I don't believe you're really this modest."

"Do you pray, Peggy? No, I don't suppose you do. You're already like me. I didn't pray when I was your age."

"When you were my age you were a widow."

The old woman was genuinely shocked. "That can't be true."

Margaret had been orphaned at eighteen and sent by train to Illinois to be a burden on her distant relatives, the Protestant Sinclairs. Only she hadn't been a burden, and she immediately caught the eye of the scion of the house when he came home from Princeton.

"He said that from the moment he saw me he wanted to marry me."

But he had deputized his mother to tell her. Margaret said this without a note of criticism. That remote drama had unfolded in the very house in which Peggy was told of it. Once Fairview had

10

swarmed with servants—the upper story contained their empty rooms—and ancient automobiles had stood under the porte cochère even as horses were ridden in the vast area behind the house. The low roof of the horse barn was visible in a fold of hills. Unchanged, but like the house itself, inhabiting an alien world now.

The old woman said, "This house overwhelmed me when I first saw it. You remind me of myself as a girl."

Peggy couldn't very well ask her if she had ever needed arguments not to sleep with a boy, as if the presumption was all on the side of doing it. She knew the answer. Her great-grandmother could not possibly imagine what it was like to be young at the end of the twentieth century. Peggy doubted that Margaret had been so much as passionately kissed before the wedding and then nothing happened, really, until that hotel room in Maiori. Once, twice? Then the terrible accident, and that was the end of her great-grandmother's sex life. Peggy was enough of a child of her time to feel that this was terribly unfair, but what she had never managed to do was think of the old woman as thwarted and diminished by the lack of sexual activity. Still, it was shocking.

"Victorian," Michele observed.

"Yeah." Peggy lit a cigarette she did not want. "So why do I wish life was still the way it was then?"

"Because you don't really know what it was like?"

Looking from the windows of Fairview, the old woman had remarked on how unfamiliar the scene now seemed to her.

"It might be Timbuktu, Peggy, so far as my ever going around the place is concerned."

"Nuts. You want to make a tour, I'll take you."

"A tour of my own house!"

"No. Of Timbuktu. How long has it been since you've been around the grounds?"

"My dear, there are places in this house I haven't seen in half a century."

The house could wait. "Do we have to bring your oxygen?"

"Heavens, no."

"How long can you last without it?"

"Let's find out."

Honora pretended to disapprove of Margaret's being without her oxygen, but agreed that whatever risk it meant was worth it. Maybe

11

she wanted a little relief from her responsibility. "It will give her time with Regis," Margaret whispered. Peggy wheeled the old woman out to her car, helped her in, and got the seat belt buckled. Margaret was visibly excited by the prospect of being driven around Fairview and within moments treated the excursion as her own idea, directing Peggy to take her along the pasture fence to a point where they could see one of the three guest houses put up by Peggy's late grandfather, Henry VIII, a financier who had taken a tidy fortune and multiplied it many times. He had wanted these houses for his children when they visited with their families. Only four of his children had remained in the vicinity: Maud and Bunny, William and Terence. Dennis, the youngest, was Peggy's father.

"We used to come along this road in a little pony cart, Bridget and I."

"The maid who went to Italy with you?"

"She was as much my friend as my maid. Our backgrounds were similar."

But she said no more. On the way back to the house, she asked Peggy to go by the stables and then on to a barn that dated from the time when a portion of the land had been farmed.

"That is where he painted."

She knew immediately that the old woman meant Clayton Ford. "In the barn?"

"In the loft. On the north side are two doors to let in the light."

They went around and looked. The double doors on the second story of the barn were shut, of course, but it was easy to imagine them swinging open to reveal the romantic figure of an artist about to go to work. One more piece of lore to conceal from Professor Glockner, who had become something of a pest about the Ford portrait Peggy had mentioned. He was difficult to deflect now that his interest was engaged.

"It isn't signed," Peggy said.

"He never signed his portraits."

"Did he ever live in Illinois?"

Glockner made a face. "That's the clinker, all right. I'm working on it. What year was this supposed to be?"

"I don't know," Peggy lied. "1890?"

"Ford was only a boy in 1890."

"Well."

12

"Why do you say 1890?"

Peggy wished she had said 1066. She wished she had never mentioned her great-grandmother's portrait.

"Is this where he painted your portrait?" she asked Margaret.

"At first he brought his things to the house, then we came to him here."

"So this was his studio?"

"He did one very large painting of what he could see from those open doors."

Peggy realized she had seen it. It was one of the paintings Margaret had given to the Fox River Museum.

That tour of the grounds had invigorated Margaret. Could her lungs restore themselves? Honora tucked in her chin and arched her drawn-on brows.

"Weird," Michele now said, pushing her glasses up on her nose. She lit another cigarette. They had taken up smoking, in defiance, out of boredom, because they were young enough to regard a threat to their health as improbable. Michele meant to make her life meaningful by becoming a great writer. "I sinned in another life, Peg. That's why I'm here."

"Here" was Hathaway Hall, founded in the nineteenth century by Beatrice Hathaway as a seminary for young women when this Indiana valley had been the back of the moon and even the cultural efforts of Beatrice could be regarded as an improvement. Improbably, it had prospered. It had remained exclusively female. Muriel Phonsinac, the current president, had no intention of diluting the wine of Hathaway Hall with the water of male students, as she had once infelicitously expressed it at assembly.

"She doesn't want to install urinals," Michele commented. ("Don't pee in my chablis," lyrics by Michele, was censored out of a student production.)

"You are souls awaiting your bodies," Phonsie told them enigmatically. She had written a dissertation on the Platonic Ideas. Her own odd Platonism crept into her pronouncements to the school, leading to Michele's arcane explanation of why she herself had ended up here, in Hathaway Hall.

"What if Margaret Sinclair had never gotten pregnant?" Peggy said, launching a thoughtful smoke ring across the room.

"You'd still be a soul looking for a body."

"Michele, that old woman is the most interesting person I know."

"Painted by Clayton Ford," Michele murmured.

No need to tell Michele how close she had been to telling Professor Glockner it was indeed a genuine Ford.

"Remember, you're sworn to secrecy."

Today her father had telephoned to find out what exactly he and her mother were expected to do on Commencement Day.

"Sad news, by the way. Grandma died this morning."

Miss Agate took fifteen minutes and a phone call to Phonsie before giving Peggy permission to go home for the funeral.

3

The Willa Keeler exhibit had arrived, and had been unpacked and hung. Added security for the duration of the exhibit was in place. The museum director crept to his office and collapsed.

George Frederick Mason had come to the Fox River, Illinois, gallery as its director seven years before. At the beginning of his tenure in this outpost he had, at professional meetings, joked about his position in a way that would rightly have annoyed members of the museum's board of directors.

"George!" a colleague would cry. "Where have you been? Europe?"

"My dear fellow, I'm in Illinois." He pronounced the name of his adopted state as if he were an intrepid *voyageur*. "Eel-a-nwah. Fox River, Eel-a-nwah."

A preemptive strike, of course. At least when he spoke to old friends face to face, his directorship of the Fox River Museum was a shared joke. Only then did he mention the "handful of Fords" in the collection.

"Landscapes?"

"For the most part."

"You have Ford portraits too!"

"His landscapes are still the thing, my dear fellow."

The locally owned Fords on loan to the Fox River Museum had certainly weighed heavily in favor of a positive decision. But it had also been a way to put Marjorie and her impossible daughter forever behind him. It's bad enough to marry one woman; he had married two, the at-the-time attractive divorcée and her unutterably spoiled child, Ginger. It had been years since he had so much as spoken to Marjorie on the phone.

"Isn't that a long commute?" had been her reaction to the Fox River search committee's wire.

"From where?"

"From here." Here being Manhattan, where George had been doing less than well as an art dealer. Not on his own, as he had hoped he might, when Marjorie, furred, bejeweled, afloat on a cloud of expensive perfume, came into his life. Dear God, what a fateful day.

"I'll understand if you don't want to come," George had said to Marjorie.

"What are you saying?"

"Perhaps we've reached the point you reached with Ernest."

Ernest had been Marjorie's first husband, the father of the now nubile Ginger. On this one occasion, Marjorie had praised Ernest, comparing him to George as Hyperion to a Satyr. "At least Ernest was capable of fathering a child."

"There are necessary presuppositions to having a child."

"That's what I'm saying."

"Like being sober enough to make love, for instance!"

It had been without contest their worst argument, fittingly enough, since it had been their last. Oh, the hatred that lurked beneath the veneer of their presumed love for one another. George Frederick Mason set out for Illinois looking for a new life and the recovery of self-esteem. Now, to such disfavor had he come that snagging a Willa Keeler exhibit was almost a coup. Keeler was one of the dozens of workaday women painters benefiting from the dulled critical sense induced by feminism. Yet he had fought for the three-week stay of those mediocre paintings in his museum. Better to think of the Fords.

Mason's early paper on Clayton Ford's portraits had made a stir and led to the job with Gabbiano, a shrewd and successful art dealer. Then and now, George firmly believed that Ford was far and away the best American landscape painter, male, of the first quarter of the twentieth century. But he had become an ungrudging admirer of Ford portraits as well. That daubs and brushings of oil-based pigments on a canvas surface could give an insight into the soul of the subject was a mystery that would never be penetrated. The difference between a Ford and a good or competent portrait was all but infinite. Mason was himself an artist of sorts, but long proximity to the works of the great had made him feel uneasy at an easel.

Now his eyes drifted to the picture mounted on a large blank wall opposite windows that looked out on the museum patio. A patio in Illinois! But it was a lovely place in spring and fall, a place where visitors could pause and refresh themselves, spiritually and with food. The painting had been kept in the vault by his predecessor, who doubted that it was a genuine Ford and had not listed it as such. Mason had brought it out and hung it on his wall not because of doubt as to its genuineness but out of pure selfishness. For years he had met the eyes of the woman in the portrait, communed with her. Unlike the subjects of authenticated Ford portraits, this woman was no patrician. Indeed, she was scarcely a woman, more a girl, her face and wary eyes conveying a sense of the poverty of her origins, yet there was a fresh natural beauty in the face that haunted the observer.

Who was the young woman in the portrait? It scarcely mattered. A portrait survives its subject, acquires an existence of its own, ceases to be thought of as *of* someone. Ford had been a reluctant portraitist and did not sign these works. But in the Ford canon, the similarity of technique, the use of color, the eyes, always the eyes, were as good as the signature he never attached. Ford's name appeared only on the landscapes which the artist considered to be his serious work. Margaret Sinclair's assurance that Ford had painted the picture on Mason's wall would not have carried weight in art circles, despite the fact that she owned six Ford landscapes as well. All but one of Margaret Sinclair's Fords, her portrait, were on loan to the museum and had been for years. Mason had a recurrent bad dream of the Sinclairs coming to reclaim their loaned paintings. But sometimes he dreamed a wilder dream. The Sinclair family would think the paintings had been outright gifts. Madness, of course. Less mad was the speculation that they did not know of this portrait on his wall.

"Bridget Doyle," the old woman said when he asked who the subject of this hitherto unknown Ford was.

"And who was Bridget Doyle?"

"Was? As far as I know she still is. She was my maid. Ford painted us both."

"Ah."

"I have kept only myself here." She referred to the portrait on the wall of her sitting room.

"Mrs. Sinclair, I think the museum should make your generosity known."

"What do you mean?"

"An exhibit, with acknowledgment of your decision to share these treasures . . ."

"If there is any publicity whatsoever, I will take them back! Just let them hang there on the walls so people can look at them. Isn't that what pictures are for?"

Thus had died Mason's plan for a publicity campaign to tell the world about the Fords on view in his museum. The landscapes were known to Ford buffs, of course, but the two portraits were not. If Mrs. Sinclair had not been so obviously *compos mentis*, Mason would have wanted witnesses, fearing the charge that he had bilked an elderly owner out of these priceless paintings and was suppressing the fact. He cherished the secret of the two Ford portraits. For whatever reason, his predecessor, since gone to God, had put the portrait of Bridget Doyle in the vault. Sometimes Mason had imagined that the man planned to spirit Bridget out of the museum. The painted eyes regarded him with amusement as he entertained this fantasy. Oh, it would have been possible, frighteningly so. Now, after years of cohabitation with the painting, parting with it would be far more traumatic than parting with Marjorie had been.

When Gearhart Glockner, the Ford expert closest to Fox River, had come from Indiana to see the landscapes, Mason permitted Gearhart to think the paintings were owned by the museum. The portrait of Bridget? Glockner squinted and shook his head.

"Close but no cigar. Not his kind of woman."

But a month ago, Glockner phoned to discuss possible unknown works of the great Ford.

18

"I keep hearing rumors of other portraits."

"Tell me about them."

"Oh, it's all nonsense, of course. A student of mine from your area thought Ford had done her great-grandmother. Margaret Sinclair."

"The Fords in the museum came from the Sinclair family." He paused in preparation for the lie. "Gearhart, I can assure you that there is no Ford portrait of her."

"Students," Glockner sighed. "Didn't you have a bogus Ford in your office?"

"You spoke in the plural, Gearhart. Were there other Ford portraits rumored?"

"Humor me, George. I shouldn't have to explain to you that one would kill to get at an unknown Ford."

He had no intention of encouraging Gearhart Glockner to come poaching on territory reserved for George Frederick Mason. His effort to impress Glockner with the upcoming Willa Keeler exhibition was unsuccessful. The call caused him to consider approaching Margaret Sinclair about Ford's portrait of her. If Glockner should babble in the wrong circles, the most unsavory types would descend upon Fairview and try to pry the portrait from the aged woman.

Miss Knutsen came in and stood before his desk. He had hired her a month before, a Nordic goddess who had spent the previous dozen years as confidential secretary to the spoiled scion of a Chicago family. She had looked him straight in the eye as she said this.

"What did you do?"

"We traveled a lot."

Miss Knutsen was not in her first youth. Her thick hair was still ash-blond but her body had arrived at a moment of truth when only discipline and diet could keep its abundance under control.

"There's no travel involved in this job."

"I want to settle down."

Again her gaze was direct. She stood there as if to be inspected. Mason's eyes dropped to her résumé but his eyes were as if blinded by the sun. How fortuitous that she should show up before he had even advertised the position abandoned without warning by the woman who had been here when Mason himself arrived.

She said, "I'm afraid I don't know anything about art."

"Who's Art?"

He laughed. She laughed. They laughed together. Hiring her, Mason felt that he was laying up something for the future.

"Do you know a Margaret Sinclair?" Miss Knutsen asked now.

"Why do you ask?"

"It was just on the radio. She died."

4

Cy Horvath was sent to Fairview by Captain Keegan largely out of deference to the prominence of the Sinclair family.

"We'll give them something for their taxes."

Cy nodded. Phil would not want to be told by Robertson to check out the house, make sure there was an autopsy, cover your rear end. The pain induced by the chief in Phil Keegan's rear end had no remedy.

News of Margaret Sinclair's death was on the radio as he drove to Fairview. Cy remembered what an adventure it had been when he was a kid to boat across the river and land on the Sinclair estate to explore. The river island was a favorite, but there were hundreds of acres of open land no longer farmed and woods. Cy had thought of it as a sovereign country, not really part of Illinois or the United States. There was a painting in the Fox River Museum that reminded him of that boyish trespassing.

A patrol car was parked in front of the house as well as the wagon from the medical examiner's. Nothing in Horvath's expression suggested the excitement he felt at the thought that Dr. Pippen might be on the scene.

Cy did not approve of professional women, by which he meant women who made a career out of their gender. He was undecided about Monique Pippen. A while ago she'd been right that Earl Waffle's death was murder, not suicide, and that had gained her points with Cy, if not with Phil Keegan.

"Lucky," Phil commented and drew on his cigar.

Well, Monique *had* made a guess. The medical facts were consistent with suicide, but they certainly didn't prove it.

"Call it a woman's intuition," Pippen suggested.

"So you can complain about sexism?"

"What's sexism?" Her eyes looked dreamily into his, but then she smiled.

"I'll look it up," he said.

"Let me know."

Whoa! Cy rubbed his mouth, in case she hadn't noticed his ring, and immediately felt ridiculous. Dr. Pippen had reddish-gold hair, a fashion magazine face, and was a medical whiz, even Jolson the coroner admitted that. She was shy of thirty, led a busy social life—Cy hadn't run a check, the information just came his way— and she certainly could have no designs on a married Hungarian detective lieutenant who had over a hundred pounds on her and was two heads taller. As he knew better than to tell his wife, Cy came to think of Pippen as his little sister.

In the room where old Mrs. Sinclair had died, Monique was busy with the body. Father Dowling had already left. Cy identified himself to a uniformed woman with funny eyebrows. Honora Brady, Mrs. Sinclair's nurse.

"Were you with her when she died?"

"I'd just stepped out of the room. Lieutenant, she was in her nineties. Her death was expected at any time. Why are the police here?"

"Did you call the doctor?"

"First I called Father Dowling, then I called Emergency. But I knew she was dead."

"Who else was in the house?"

"Dolly, the housekeeper. This is the chef's day off."

Dolly was locked in her room. "Booze," Honora whispered to Horvath. She banged on the door until she got an answer.

Cy talked to Dolly alone. She stared past him, repeating that she could not believe Margaret Sinclair was dead.

"How much longer did you expect her to live?"

She looked at him. "With care, who knows?"

"Wasn't the nurse always with her?"

"Always? Ask her that."

Honora had said she had been out of the room when the old lady died. "Where else would she be?"

"The kitchen. Usually. Except this was Regis's day off. Today she had a visitor. A bearded man."

"A stranger?"

"To me."

In the corner of the room a muted television brought its daytime dramas to Dolly's lonely room. Horvath's wife had told him about steamy stories on the soaps. Maybe Dolly thought she was in one.

When he went to the kitchen he found that Regis had returned and been told that Mrs. Sinclair was dead. The chef's reaction was to don his working clothes. Like Honora he was all in white, enveloped in the lingering aromas of his domain. He was a huge man with a tragic face.

"Was Honora here with you when Mrs. Sinclair died?"

"Ha!"

"You mean no?"

"I just returned to the house." He inhaled deeply through his nostrils. "Have you met her, Lieutenant?"

"Yes."

"Can we speak as men?"

Cy nodded, unsure what the question would lead to. It led to Regis's confession of a doomed love for the nurse. His voice trembled as he spoke. Honora was the only reason he had stayed on.

"I cook for myself! No one in this house eats. The old woman?" He threw up his hands. "Dolly? Her idea of a delicacy is soda crackers in a bowl of milk." His eyes closed in pain.

"Does Honora eat?"

"Like a sparrow." He spoke with sudden tenderness.

With the death of Mrs. Sinclair, Honora would leave the house. There was nothing to keep Regis here.

"I should have left long ago."

"Did you see a bearded man here today?"

He sat back. "A bearded man!"

"Dolly says she saw a bearded man."

"It's a wonder she doesn't see snakes."

Regis offered him coffee and he accepted. "Cheesecake, Lieutenant?" It was delicious. Regis watched him eat with envy in his eyes.

"Why aren't you having any?"

He patted his distended stomach and sighed. "I eat the way Dolly drinks."

"Where will you go if you leave here?"

"God only knows." He sliced himself a piece of the cheesecake and ate it with his fingers.

When he went back upstairs, Cy was disappointed to find that the body had been removed and Pippen was gone. He realized that he had been prolonging these pointless interviews to prove to himself that he wasn't fascinated by her. It served him right.

That afternoon Pippen sat down across from him in the cafeteria where he was trying to make sense of a Gleason column about the Cubs. She wore street clothes and placed a paper napkin on her lap before sipping her coffee.

"What's the verdict on Margaret Sinclair, Monique?"

"Well, she died."

"The undertaker will be relieved to hear that."

"The verdict is natural causes," she said. "Asphyxiation. My doubts were not shared."

Cy's fear that her lucky guess about Waffle had gone to Pippen's head and that she was working on a parlay seemed justified.

"Asphyxiation means she stopped breathing, doesn't it? What was she, ninety-five?"

"The heart attack was probably brought on by her panic when she couldn't breathe."

"Things pretty slow at the morgue?"

"Her death was odd, Cy."

He folded the paper, drank some coffee, wished he had stayed in his office. What Monique Pippen found odd was that Margaret

24

Sinclair had died from lack of oxygen when a supply was always beside her and she was attended by a nurse twenty-four hours a day.

"The nurse said the old lady sent her outside to bring in some lilacs."

"Were there lilacs in the room? The answer is no. The nurse is lying. The tank of oxygen beside the chair was chock full."

"Maybe the old lady knew how to use it on her own."

"She *preferred* to do it herself. I quote the nurse more or less on duty at the time. But she didn't use it when she needed it."

Cy had examined the apparatus. There was a plastic mask that was put over the nose and mouth to supply the needed oxygen. As far as Cy could see, a kid could do it. Or a very old lady.

"Maybe she just died, Monique."

"She couldn't breathe and panicked."

"And died of a heart attack. If the oxygen had been used . . ."

"The mask was hung up. If she had been taking oxygen it would have been in her hand or hanging loose."

"Not if the heart attack came first."

When Pippen wrinkled her nose, Cy had difficulty imagining that she was his daughter. He wasn't old enough to be her father anyway.

"Cy, I keep thinking of all those relatives waiting for her to go so they could divide the spoils."

"This could get to be a bad habit, you know, imagining crimes. The verdict is natural causes. Period. There is no mystery to solve."

"Terence Sinclair visited her that day."

"I just read about that." It was in the early edition. Terence Sinclair was a disgruntled heir who expressed concern about his grandmother's will. His beard reminded Cy of an old brand of cough drops.

"Where you going?" Pippen asked when he pushed away from the table.

"To see if we have a fresh body to keep you busy."

"I don't need another body," she said.

Cy kept his mouth shut. He kept his eyes locked with hers. He would not permit his glance to drop to the very adequate body filling her tailored suit.

"You know what I mean," she said weakly.

*　*　*

The next morning Cy went to the museum to look at the painting that reminded him of Fairview and was surprised by Pudge Hanrahan, a retired cop. Hanrahan looked the way Cy felt, being discovered in a museum.

"I'm on a special assignment," Hanrahan said. "What's your excuse?"

"I came to see this picture."

"Yeah?"

"They worried about theft?"

Hanrahan bragged that the security system was foolproof. "Anyway, these Fords are the only part of the permanent collection worth anything." He leaned toward Cy. "I quote Mason, the director."

"I like this one."

The painting was big as a blanket and could have been a snapshot from Cy's memory. He was certain it was Fairview.

"Ford's no local artist," Pudge said.

"That's a local scene."

"The brochure says he lived in Europe. Look."

The hell with it. Cy had no need to win an argument with Pudge Hanrahan. Hanrahan wandered off but later he stopped Cy when he was leaving to tell him Ford had spent time in Fox River, painting for the Sinclairs. "I asked," Pudge said. A fussy man of indeterminate age skated up to them.

"Is this the friend who asked about Clayton Ford?"

It was George Frederick Mason, director. Cy nodded. What the hell. If news of this got downtown, he'd never hear the end of it.

"You're with the police?"

"He's a detective lieutenant," Pudge said.

"Well." Mason brought his hands together, and raised his brows. Was he queer? "And why are the police interested in Clayton Ford?"

Cy told Mason of the painting he liked and why and wished he'd kept his goddamn mouth shut. Pudge stood there, nodding, smiling. Mason followed Cy's story with narrowed eyes.

"Have you seen the Willa Keeler exhibit?"

Cy got out of there. He would kill Pudge if anyone downtown asked what he was doing hanging around museums. On the other hand, Monique Pippen might be impressed.

26

The circled chapter number:

5

Peggy accepted an umbrella from the undertaker and started toward the gravesite with the rest of the family, picking her way among the irregular rows. What a racket the rain made on the ribbed dome of the umbrella. Her parents, close as lovers, foul weather intimates, shared a huge striped golf umbrella. Uncles and aunts and cousins first and second distributed themselves around the grave. Under a canopy that protected it from the weather, the casket had been rolled onto a device that would lower it into the ground. Father Dowling had said the requiem mass and now stood at graveside with the collar of his raincoat turned up.

Peggy thought of the old woman's tragic wedding trip to Italy which stood at the origin of them all, a family Garden of Eden. The image of her great-grandmother, at the age Peggy now was, widowed, pregnant, alone, filled her with a sadness she could not control. Suddenly she began to weep. She tried to stop, but the effort to master her grief caused her to sob aloud.

Her mother turned, startled, and Peggy attempted a smile, tipping her umbrella in order to hide. Geez. Maybe she should jump into the grave and do a soliloquy too. She had only been to two funerals in her life, an uncle's and that of a high school classmate who had driven into a bridge abutment while drunk. Whenever she spoke to Margaret she had known it might be the last time. The old woman's death was neither a surprise nor a tragedy—what must it be like to go on living when everyone else was dead?—but now, in the dripping graveyard, she thought of Margaret as young, a bride, reunited with her husband at last. Heaven as honeymoon.

Her mother, a knockout in black, a lace mantilla on her head, stepped under the umbrella with her and then her father joined them, his umbrella adding to the rain rattling off hers.

"I'm okay," she assured her mother.

A gloved hand enclosed Peggy's. "It's nearly over."

It turned out she was right. Father Dowling lifted his hand over the coffin in a final blessing and that was it. Free to go, the family prolonged it a bit, but then Aunt Maud strode swiftly toward the road and the exodus was on. Peggy took a final look at the coffin containing her great-grandmother's body, and then went with her parents among the gravestones to their car.

After Margaret's burial, sitting in the backseat of her parents' car, Peggy felt for the first time the finality of the fact that her great-grandmother was dead. It wasn't grief she felt. There was no further urge to cry, only an oppressive sense of the passage of time.

Her father stopped at the house on the way from the cemetery and Peggy went upstairs to her room to have a cigarette. The wrist of the hand that held her cigarette was turned toward her. Peggy looked at the veins and sinews visible just beneath the skin. In her blood and marrow Margaret Sinclair still went on. She was the only Margaret Sinclair left now. Then she remembered something.

She put out her cigarette and swung her legs off the bed. Still sitting, she closed her eyes. "May she rest in peace," she prayed. "God bless Margaret Sinclair."

The reception at Fairview was more like a wedding than a funeral, an almost festive family reunion, and, as always when surrounded by these related generations of semi-strangers, Peggy felt somehow diminished by the thought that, in the larger scheme of things, she was simply one of the Sinclairs, an easily overlookable item. That was Phase One. It gave way to the sense of how different they all were, as if the personality of Margaret Sinclair had been divided up among them. They were less like one another than like different aspects of her.

Gradually Peggy realized the significance of this gathering. Where the body is, there are the eagles gathered together. No wonder the family was here in force. With Margaret Sinclair dead, there could finally be a dividing of the spoils. The rain had stopped falling and the sun was at the windows when Uncle Terry announced that Mr. Cadbury would read the will.

Her father's older brother, Terry was her resentful relative, the one who had frittered away the money he insisted Margaret Sinclair give him, trying scheme after scheme meant to double the amount overnight and succeeding in losing it all. The fact that he was not given a second amount—he spoke of it as a loan—had embittered him. Now at last he would get a new stake. His frizzy hair was brushed up to obscure the avenue of baldness that ran over his head and he had a beard to match. His belly literally hung over the top of his trousers. He sipped a glass of juice and looked around at his brothers and nephews and nieces as if, at least for purposes of the will, he wished they were all dead.

Mr. Cadbury tapped on a goblet to call them to order and began to read. Joel Cleary, a good-looking junior member of Cadbury's firm, sat in a corner, observing. Peggy's sense that there was something venal in hurrying to find how the old woman had disposed of her wealth was not widely shared. The others might not be as needy as Terry, but they saw no reason to postpone the cheerful news.

The opening section in which Margaret bequeathed to each of them some particular item—a samovar, the large mirror in the upstairs hallway, the small red chair in a west wing bedroom, old Henry's binoculars for Terry—was extensive, but each recipient smiled in private recognition of the significance of the gift. Maud received some pearls, Peggy's father was given a Cord automobile that had been on blocks in the carriage house for forty years. That Margaret's diary as well as her portrait were going to Peggy brought murmurs.

Aunt Maud whispered, "I'd love to read it."

Peggy smiled, making no promises. The diary was said to cover the year of her great-grandmother's marriage.

Mr. Cadbury, having read the amounts left to the staff of Fairview—Dolly, the chef, a little to the nurse—sipped some of the water Joel Cleary had poured for him, then looked out at his audience over glasses halfway down his narrow nose. "That takes care of the more sentimental aspects of the will."

There was a stirring in the room that made Peggy want to get out of there. Joel Cleary was looking at her and she made a face. This was ghoulish, but what was the alternative? Sell all that they had and distribute it to the poor? To the shocked surprise of the family, it was something very much like that Margaret Sinclair had in mind.

"A few years ago, Mrs. Sinclair conceived the idea of a foundation to which the bulk of the estate would go, this house and grounds, her investments—"

"A foundation!" Terry cried. "What kind of a foundation?"

Mr. Cadbury took the sheaf of papers Joel Cleary brought from his briefcase. "I have the papers of incorporation here. It is a tax-free nonprofit foundation to be administered by a board."

"Who's chairman?"

Amos Cadbury cleared his throat. "I am." Members of the board included family members: Peggy's aunt, Maud Sinclair, Peggy, and Father Roger Dowling. The idea of the foundation was to ensure a continued contribution by the Sinclair family to the Roman Catholic Church, locally, nationally, beyond.

"Exactly how much money is going into this foundation?" Terry demanded. He was having trouble controlling his voice.

"This property has recently been appraised at three million dollars, more or less. The investments are currently valued at thirty-one million dollars."

"But what's left?"

"Something like a million dollars."

Terry stared wild-eyed around the room, as if he were dividing that paltry sum among so many and subtracting taxes as well. He raked his beard with a clawed hand. He was no longer alone in being appalled by what the old woman had done.

"It won't stand up," Terry cried. "I'll fight it."

Mr. Cadbury nodded. "She expected opposition. But I must tell you I gave her my solemn promise to defend this will."

"What are you getting?"

A murmured objection to Terry's question went around the room, but Cadbury held up his hand. "Because of the nature of the foundation, I have agreed to serve pro bono."

Calmer questions followed, seeking information about the precise nature and purpose of the foundation, and Peggy left the room. She went past the arboretum and up the wide staircase to the suite in the east wing in which her great-grandmother had lived. Her breath caught when she stood before the portrait as if for the first time. The woman in the picture was young and Margaret Sinclair had always been an old woman to Peggy, but the eyes and mouth, the angle of the chin were so powerfully reminiscent of the old woman that Peggy half expected to see her sitting in her chair when she turned. The oxygen contraption that had sustained her life was still there, but Margaret Sinclair was no more. There was only this portrait. Peggy closed her eyes and breathed thanks to her great-grandmother for giving it to her.

"You look like her."

She turned. It was Joel Cleary.

"Right now I feel like her too. Dead."

"This is for you." He handed her a package. "It's the diary she left you."

"Oh. Thanks." But it was all she could do not to tear open the package. She took out a cigarette and Joel Cleary lit it for her. It seemed a little pact, them against the old ones.

"You're lucky. Some of the things she bequeathed can't be found. Bunny Salazar was supposed to get jewelry that isn't where it's supposed to be."

"Maybe it's in the bank."

"I hope it will be that easy. I've been given the job of tracking the stuff down."

"Anything I can do to help."

6

In laying the remains of Margaret Sinclair to rest, Roger Dowling hoped he was laying to rest as well the thoughts that had been nagging at the edge of his mind since he had been called to Fairview to give the last sacraments to the old woman. Margaret's age alone made it ridiculous to think such thoughts. Anyone who wanted the old woman dead needed only a little patience. And of course that included Margaret herself. At ninety-five her days had been numbered, and no one understood that better than Margaret.

"Would it be a terrible sin if I just stopped relying on this silly thing, Father Dowling?"

She had just taken the plastic mask from her face. Margaret's need for oxygen often interrupted their conversations. He did not take her question seriously. She had asked versions of it before. But there was never hesitation on her part to take oxygen if she needed it.

When he arrived at Fairview and found her dead in her chair he had administered the sacrament conditionally. Precisely when death occurs had always been doubtful but now it was more of a puzzle than it had ever been. As he read the prayers over her he was distracted by memories of that question. Would it have been sinful not to reach for the oxygen when she needed it? He finished and stood for a moment, looking down at Margaret. Had she decided to let nature take its course? The tank was beside her chair; the plastic mask hung where it always had.

"Have you left her just as she was, Honora?"

"Yes, Father." Honora acted as if she shouldn't have to answer such questions. "Oh, the poor thing."

"You administered oxygen?"

"There was no point in it, Father, not when I found her." Honora's eyes widened with the admission that she had not been in the room. But it was not whether Margaret had been assisted that bothered Father Dowling. Had the old lady deliberately refused to reach out for what would have prolonged her life? It could be said that she had no moral obligation to do so, but Roger Dowling did not like the thought of Margaret preferring death to life.

He said to Honora, "Of course she could have helped herself."

"She always did, Father. She preferred to. And that's a full tank, Father." Honora indicated a guage.

Refusing the help of the nurse when she needed oxygen might have been a first step toward weaning herself from that essential condition of life. Her lungs could no longer of themselves provide the necessary air. The priest stood a moment longer before the dead woman. She had become a friend, no longer just a parishioner to whom he brought the sacraments. He said another, more personal prayer for her and got out of the way so the medical examiner could do his work. Or her work, as it turned out. Monique Pippen had arrived on the scene and begun the routine tasks of her grim profession.

Roger Dowling's eye was drawn to the portrait of Margaret. The painted eyes of the long-ago girl now looked down at her own lifeless body. It occurred to the priest that the old woman's death would alter the lives of many, most obviously her relatives. Knowing what he did of her will, he wondered what controversies lay ahead. The fragile old woman linked to life by that apparatus beside her chair must have seemed a vast obstacle to many.

"Is Regis here?" Roger Dowling asked Honora outside the room.

"Regis! No, he isn't. This is his day off."

Honora searched his face for a moment. "Father, if Mrs. Sinclair said anything . . ." She looked away. "She liked to make jokes."

Looking into the flat, featureless face, Father Dowling wondered if it hadn't been mean of Margaret to suggest that her all-too-plain nurse was up to romantic adventure with the cook. Even so, before he left the house, he went by the kitchen to see if Regis was there. He wasn't.

That night, to Father Dowling's surprise, Regis came to the rectory door.

"He says he's the cook at Fairview," Marie whispered, her tone heavy with disapproval. One of her pet peeves was a man on television who demonstrated cooking techniques. Marie seemed to see this as an assault on her sex and a threat to her kitchen.

The rectory did not provide adequate dimensions for the massive figure of Regis Factor. He seemed to squeeze through the door of the study and hesitated before taking the chair that even Phil Keegan found more than adequate. Regis looked questioningly at Marie until the housekeeper pulled the door shut with unnecessary vigor.

"I was not there when Mrs. Sinclair died. This was my day off."

"So Honora told me." Why did Regis feel it necessary to tell him this?

"Honora." Regis sighed the name. He worked his mouth, then pressed his lips, as if to stop them from quivering. Good Lord. Apparently Margaret had not been joking.

"It was my day off, but I was on the grounds." He looked abjectly at the priest. "I spied on her!" He seemed to have trouble believing this himself.

Regis went on. Father Dowling busied himself with his pipe. Regis was indeed smitten by Honora, but the reverse was apparently not true. It was the stuff of literature, of tragic as well as comic stories, but Regis was deadly serious and the pastor of St. Hilary's hoped that a sympathetic ear was all the chef needed.

"There is another," Regis said solemnly. He had gained control of himself and now seemed to wallow in the hopelessness of his position. He described taking up a position in a building below the house, a barn, where with binoculars he had watched his rival come and go. He knew the exact amount of time the man had spent in the house.

"Fifteen minutes."

"I see."

"Fifteen minutes less five seconds."

Had he used a stopwatch? A quarter of an hour did not seem a prolonged assignation. But Regis saved the most humiliating detail for last.

"He wears a beard. He is a little fat man with a beard."

"Have you gone to the police?"

"The police!"

"Aren't you suggesting that Honora deserted her post, that Mrs. Sinclair's death . . ."

Regis was on his feet, waving his hands, shaking his head. "No, no. Good God, I tell you all this in confidence. No one else must know. I had to tell someone and I thought, a priest . . ." He glanced at the door, as if to make certain it was shut. "Father Dowling, it is the bearded man the police must be told of."

"Why?"

"Because they suspect something, I don't know what. They were at the house, they even questioned me. They must not bother Honora. It was that man!"

"How well do you know the Sinclair family, Regis?"

"I don't understand."

"Have you met Terence Sinclair?"

The chef's expression made it clear that he had not. But he had heard of Terence's visit to Fairview the day his grandmother died.

"Terence wears a beard, Regis."

An expression of amazement formed on his face and he began to smile with relief. But then his tragic expression returned.

"It doesn't matter, Father. There is someone else. I know it."

"Have you told Honora how you feel?"

For half and hour he listened to the scarcely coherent romantic ramblings of Regis Factor. Dr. Johnson said that marriage has its pains but celibacy has no pleasures. An exaggeration, like the great man's jokes about the Irish. Had he said anything of the unwanted suitor's pain?

Regis's visit exorcised the uneasiness Roger Dowling had been feeling about Margaret's death. If Honora had had a visitor and left her post, it was not for long. And, as Roger Dowling had seen for himself, there was a supply of oxygen at her side which she was more than capable of administering to herself.

The funeral mass and then the ceremony at graveside, assisted by what seemed to be an army of Sinclairs, put Margaret's death in perspective. A woman of extremely advanced age had died. Far from being unexpected, her death had been awaited for years, not least by Margaret herself. But the family's long patience had not prepared them for the terms of Margaret's will.

7

Peggy ran through the rain to her car, tossed her bag into the backseat, and got behind the wheel. When she pulled the door shut the racket of the falling rain increased. She started the car and in moments before turning on the lights looked through the watery window at her father silhouetted in the doorway. She felt an impulse to run back and take him in her arms. Why was it only at moments like this that she loved her father with an aching love? They really didn't get along, they seemed to have so little in common, yet that man in the doorway was her link to the old woman they had buried today. She put the car in gear, turned on the wipers, gave a little toot of the horn, and shot out the driveway. Peggy had felt closer to her great-grandmother than she did to her own parents. Heading for the interstate, she told herself that she would never again come home to visit Margaret Sinclair. The rain running in rivulets down the windows of her car seemed to complement the tears that welled up in her eyes.

Later the rain stopped, but her little car was engulfed in water whenever a semi passed her. Bad weather seemed to provide a holiday from traffic laws. She pulled into the last oasis before the Indiana border, tense from driving in these conditions. She almost wished she had stayed the night at home and started back early the next morning. Almost. She loved her parents, but she no longer enjoyed being with either of them for any length of time and both together were too much. They sensed her feeling and each assumed it was the other's fault so they started bickering, adding to her desire to head for the hills.

Last year, during an intensely religious period in late winter, the gospel admonition that one must leave father and mother seemed a bonus rather than a burden. She had been reading a book on the Little Flower, full of photographs of the Carmelite convent in Lisieux. The beautiful Thérèse looked serenely into the camera lens with her almond eyes and Peggy imagined that the young and saintly nun was miraculously looking out of the nineteenth century into her very soul.

When she went to the occasional morning mass at Assumption, a parish church near campus, Peggy tried not to notice the three forlorn women in a front pew wearing dark blue polyester jumpers, white blouses, skirts that made their rumps look like what Aunt Maud called rumble seats, and silly little veils on their awful hair. It wasn't simply that none of them was attractive. It was their attire: Who could look attractive in those outfits? They were dumpy and pathetic. They had nothing to do with Peggy's daydreams about the convent.

"Vatican II," Leon, the pastor, said, lighting up. "The council." He might have been spelling it with exhaled smoke. "The orders updated and modernized their habits."

"Modernized?"

"They're supposed to look like other women."

"That's an insult."

He didn't understand. It didn't matter. By then she knew it had been a mistake to come to Leon to talk about the thoughts that had been stirred up in her by reading about the Little Flower. The pastor of Assumption, who looked so timeless and impressive when vested at the altar, in the rectory wore corduroy slacks, tennis shoes, and a bulky cable-knit sweater. His wild wiry hair was shot through with gray, but at fifty he behaved as if he too were a college kid. He took her to Mr. Donut the first time she came by the sacristy and it became a kind of habit. She went back because he was the only priest in town. But all he talked about was how terrible things had been before the council.

"You wouldn't remember that." He surveyed the chocolate-covered doughnut he held as if looking for a vulnerable spot, then sank his teeth into it. He could eat four of those at one sitting.

"No," she said.

He talked with his mouth full, which was all right, since this distracted her from what he took to be the horror stories of the pre-counciliar past. But it was in those supposedly Dark Ages of the Church that the Little Flower had lived.

"Jansenist," Leon said. His eyebrows needed trimming and so did his mustache, which was now full of crumbs and chocolate. Jansenist? It sounded like a swimsuit. Peggy had learned not to ask Leon for explanations. Of course she never told him that she herself was, well, maybe like thinking about the convent, you know. She didn't tell anyone, not even her great-grandmother.

It was an eerie and inaccurate thought that Margaret Sinclair had been almost a contemporary of Thérèse of Lisieux. If she had returned widowed to the States ten years or so earlier, Margaret might have stopped in Brittany and, in the convent parlor, chatted through a grille with the future saint. Last summer, during two weeks in France thanks to her father's frequent flyer plan, Peggy broke away from the kids she'd fallen in with after the soccer star from Loyola-Something crawled into her bed and began pawing her. He was too big to throw out and screaming would have been an hysterical reaction so she spent an hour squirming out of the dangerous position until he began to mewl and moan, so aroused he didn't need her any more. Then he spooned up behind her and fell asleep. She spent the rest of the night curled up on a cast-iron chair on the little balcony, wrapped in a blanket, feeling soiled and angry and hungry for God and innocence. With dawn Paris became a painting by Buffet, the art department at Sears. She took her things with her to the shower down the hall and left from there, never returning to her room. At the Gare St-Lazare she boarded the train for Lisieux.

She stopped in a *librairie* before going to the convent and was amazed at the number of books on the Little Flower. The town itself was, well, real, *there,* just a small town, and the convent, being an actual building in an actual setting, seemed almost an impostor of her dreams. The chapel was clean and bright but so like the First Methodist church in Sarasota that Peggy was in it for ten minutes before it entered her mind to pray. Then she prayed very fervently that she did not have a religious vocation.

She sat in a caned chair just inside the main door and looked blankly ahead. It wasn't that she thought the sort of business the soccer star had in mind last night was so impossibly necessary to her that she couldn't face the prospect of a narrow convent cot for the rest of her life. At the moment, chastity had an almost sensuous attraction. Nor was it that she had any competing notion of how she would spend her life. In the end, if her great-grandmother was any indication, there wasn't a lot of difference between nuns and non-nuns. It even sounded like a double negative.

Now, at an interstate oasis, sipping coffee from a plastic cone that fitted into a plastic multi-use base, she had her inheritance and was glad it wasn't money. The picture would be a precious reminder of their visits together. As for the diary, which was in the shoulder purse whose strap crossed her torso, it promised an intimacy with the old woman far beyond anything their conversations had provided.

"What kind of point should life have?" Margaret Sinclair had asked when Peggy tried to tell her of the thoughts she'd had sitting in the Carmelite chapel in Lisieux.

"Don't you think life should have a point?"

"I think it does."

"I mean here. People just do these basically unimportant things, over and over, and what's the point of that?"

"They end up old and decrepit, sitting alone in a big house, a nuisance to everyone."

Whenever Peggy embraced the old woman she was afraid to hold her too tightly, as if she might snap and break under the slightest pressure. Skin and bones, that was how she described herself. And behind her on the wall was the lovely Ford portrait showing her in the bloom of youth, her expression almost as enigmatic as that of the Little Flower.

A mass had started while Peggy sat in the chapel in Lisieux— other civilians, most of them women, having come and arranged themselves around the public part—and suddenly Peggy became aware of other voices, a bodiless choir that might have been coming in from heaven. After a time, she realized she was hearing the cloistered nuns. There was a grille to the right of the altar through which the nuns could follow the mass, as if they were the kibitzers and Peggy and the others at home. The voices seemed unnaturally high, falsetto, and so timid, as if they hesitated to disturb the air even in praise of God. It had been bone-chilling in its eeriness, beautiful, strange, unreal yet more real than everything else. But it proved to be no siren song for Peggy. When she left the chapel, after spending nearly two hours there, she had it fixed in her mind that a religious vocation meant getting a visa for France and living out her life in Brittany. In a way, the visit exorcised her vague desire to be a nun.

"Nuns are dead," Leon assured her.

"How so?"

"All these orders? Most of them are less than a century old. Think of them as the WACs."

It sounded like "wax" and Peggy thought it was some kind of scriptural allusion. But later, almost too late, Leon explained. Eventually Leon explained everything, the Wizard of Mr. Donut.

"When the war's over, that's it. Our school system is shot to hell, give it another five, ten years. We can't afford it. The nuns made it possible."

"They sound more needed than ever."

"They're dead."

Trying to follow the convolutions of one of Leon's explanations was a waste. He thought impressionistically, never quite making the connections he seemed sure existed among his wild thoughts.

"I went to Lisieux."

He stopped chewing. "Say it again." She did. "You make it sound foreign."

"It is."

He himself pronounced it Lissooo, holding the final note, his concession to the fruity French. "Tell me about it."

He was visibly impatient while she did, so she cut it short. "Anyway, I decided not to join."

He laughed. She laughed. A big laugh over their chocolate doughnuts. But Peggy felt sad, almost disillusioned.

"You should become a priest instead."

"Could I?"

"The whole thing'll go bust if we don't do something different. One other guy and myself are the only ones left from my class. We have to start ordaining lay people."

"That sounds logically necessary."

He nodded as if she were simply agreeing with him. In the rectory study was a shelf of textbooks he had used in the seminary, a logic book in Latin, smudged, much writing in the margins.

"Simple apprehension," he had translated the first chapter title. It sounded ominous. At any rate, it hadn't cramped Leon's style.

"I was on the flake myself for nearly two years."

He had been given leave of absence. Everyone was applying for laicization, before or after, usually after, they "lit out for the territory"—Leon loved Mark Twain—and he followed suit. After a clerical poker game, he was driving home and he just took the wrong turn and kept going. He went to Las Vegas and that seemed right; he felt he was entering hell. He won. He drove in with one hundred and sixty-three dollars and he drove out with more than enough to continue to California and keep himself until he found a job.

"I managed one of these." A Mr. Donut. "Coming here is like being there. They stamp them out like cookies."

"The doughnuts?"

"The buildings. I gained about forty pounds in the first three months."

"Did you get married?"

"Not quite."

"Why did you come back?"

He pushed up his chin with the heel of his hand. Looked at her, looked away. "I got tired of chocolate doughnuts."

"It looks like it."

It turned out to be a metaphor. Men left the priesthood to escape its routine, the repetition of tasks, the dullness of life. Mr. Donut was far duller than anything Leon had ever known before, and what was the point of it? The woman who found him attractive had two kids and a squalid apartment and spoke in a holler.

"If I'm going to die of boredom I'd rather do it here."

Her great-grandmother laughed when Peggy told her about Leon. "He sounds like an honest man."

"It's not much of a reason to be a priest."

"People usually have more than one reason for what they do."

Or don't do. The image of the future Peggy constructed was

42

multifaceted, a combination of activities and involvements, a dream husband, three perfect children, no worry about money or anything like that, there would be a continuation of the cultural interests stirred up despite the pompous teaching of Glockner, art chiefly. There would be travel, of course, and her spiritual life, as Leon called it.

" 'There is only one tragedy, not to be a saint,' " Leon assured her solemnly. Then he looked embarrassed.

"Who said that?"

The way he pronounced it she thought he was commenting on her need to ask. "Blwah." Leon Bloy. At the moment, Peggy had had her fill of the French.

She was also fed up with the oasis on Interstate 294. People ran, stopping inside the door and shaking off the rain, looking around. Bad weather makes people friendly. Peggy felt they were invading her reverie. She paid and ran out to her car, getting drenched while she unlocked the door, and inside, shivering, feeling suddenly very much alone, she started to cry. She sat there crying for God knows how long. Why, she didn't know. For her great-grandmother, for her parents, mainly for herself and for the way things turned out, never what you expected, like Lisieux. She started the engine and drove on to a motel across the Indiana border. It was stupid to drive in that kind of weather. She took the unit with the vague idea that she wanted someplace warm and dry to continue her crying.

In bed, warm and dry and wide awake, she thought of Joel Cleary and smiled. Forget it. He was in his late twenties. She should have checked his ring finger. Michele would never forgive her. It was in that motel in Michigan City, Indiana, that she first read the diary of Margaret Sinclair and, unexpectedly, began again to think of becoming a nun.

8

Sipping oolong in his shaded office with Wilbert Plunkett, George Frederick Mason found consolation in the fact that his visitor did not notice that the Ford portrait no longer hung on his wall. He had returned it to the vault where his predecessor had kept it and now waited in dread to learn what the Sinclair family would do. The other shoe had dropped but had not yet brought evil with it.

"Has the will been probated already?" Wilbert popped a Fig Newton whole into his mouth.

"Only read to the family."

"The old girl bequeathed us what we already have?"

As a member of the museum's board, Wilbert perhaps had a right to this possessive attitude, but Mason was put off by it. The paintings had not been mentioned at all, but it was a point he decided not to underscore, for his guest, the professor emeritus, was soon to depart for what had become an annual stay in Sardinia.

"More tea?"

Wilbert began smacking his mouth. "These things are as bad as caramels. How do you manage them?"

44

Working at the roof of his mouth with a hooked index finger, Wilbert looked at Mason through half-closed eyes.

"Did he always do women?"

"Every chance he got." Mason laughed. Wilbert made a face. "Joke. All but one of the subjects of his portraits are women."

"All but one?"

"One of the Harrimans. The Sinclair family is his connection with Fox River."

"I thought he was a native."

"Good God, no. He was commissioned to do a prenuptial portrait of Matthew Sinclair's bride. Later, when he became famous, Margaret began to collect Fords. It adds zest, doesn't it, knowing the artist?"

Wilbert looked at him sharply, as if he had been accused of something. "There was even a notice of her death in the *Herald Tribune*." Wilbert looked sheepish. "Reading that paper is a way of readying myself for Sardinia."

The thought of widespread, even global, publicity filled Mason with unease. It was bad enough that the local police seemed to be taking an interest in the museum's Fords. Mason had tried to learn from Hanrahan what their interest was.

"Cy Horvath likes that painting. That's it."

It would have been unwise to press it. Hanrahan looked stupid but one never knew. Mason wondered if Hanrahan really was retired. Was this an assignment? Suddenly Hanrahan made a gurgling sound. Miss Knutsen was approaching. It was all Mason could do not to tell Hanrahan he was not being paid to ogle his secretary.

"I want to hear all about Sardinia," he said now to Wilbert.

"Only if you take me to lunch."

"We can eat in the museum restaurant."

"God forbid. I'd rather treat you."

They agreed on the Athletic Club, where Plunkett was a member. The improbability of this was diminished when Wilbert pointed out its proximity to his apartment. That he should have chosen to live in the black glass box that had arisen on the banks of the Fox River a year or two ago—ultramodern, overpriced, far from the campus and his old haunts—surprised only if one did not understand Wilbert's resolve to make a decisive break with his working life. The surprise was that he had chosen to remain in Fox River at all.

"Just for the address." But Wilbert put a large, veined and mottled hand on Mason's sleeve. "And for the sake of a few old friends. I do of course retain a certain pathological interest in LaSallette." Wilbert pronounced the name of the Catholic college at which he had taught for decades in an excessively lingual way.

"When I retire—" Mason began, but stopped when Wilbert squeezed his arm.

"I hate that word. It makes me feel vulcanized. Everywhere in the world people go through the stages of life without the need to think of themselves as worn-out machines, useless." From angry, his tone became arch but ended plaintive. By fighting the inexorability of age, Wilbert, ironically, managed to look older than he was. He could not be much over seventy, but the green sport coat, open black silk shirt with paisley ascot to conceal his stringy throat, gray slacks puffy at the waist and tapering to the ankle, leather audible heels on his loafers, drew attention to him precisely as an old man trying desperately to look young. Worst of all was the strawlike hair, brushed forward and worried into a shape meant to suggest that there was more of it than there was. Mason wished Wilbert wouldn't paw at him as they walked the three blocks to the Athletic Club.

The trip to Sardinia would be his third, and Wilbert lamented that he had not discovered the island earlier. "When I was younger."

"Sea and Sardinia," Mason sighed.

"Precisely why I didn't go before. I hate Lawrence." A woman turned from a store window to stare at Wilbert. "Were you ever there?"

"A day in Cagliari."

"Avoid the cities. There are only two or three, of course. I cling to the coast. I adore Bosa."

The feeling that he had been indiscreet in talking to Wilbert Plunkett about the museum's Fords returned when he saw the trio in a corner of the dining room, huddled over their table. Once he noticed them, he could not keep his eyes from them and Wilbert became annoyed with his inattention.

"Whom are you ogling, George?"

"Isn't that Bunny Salazar at the far table?"

Wilbert tilted his chin and narrowed his eyes but of course he couldn't see to the tip of his nose. Finally he put on the massive heavy-framed glasses that dilated his eyes and admitted the outer world.

"Who is Bunny Salazar?"

At any other time Mason would simply have said a pain in the ass. Self-appointed patron saint of the annual Powderhorn Art Show, champion of the amateur and second-rate, herself the producer of hundreds of horrible watercolors, she had become Mason's implacable foe when he said no, sorry, definitely not, to Bunny's suggestion that he hang some of her *oeuvre* in the gallery. "To brighten up the place."

He had bristled at that, of course. Bunny had then urged Mason to exhibit the work of a girl who with rags and drift wood and papier-mâché made hideous objects that assaulted the senses and outraged any vestigial aesthetic sense. By the time he refused her watercolors things were already testy between them. Afterwards, a state of war existed.

"Bunny is a Sinclair."

"Surely not? Either the blood has thinned or the flesh has thickened. She doesn't look at all like the portrait in your office."

"Who is that odd fellow they're with?"

"A creature named Tuttle, unless my eyes deceive. I thought he'd been disbarred."

Wilbert's remark seemed to corroborate Mason's sense that Bunny and her husband Octavio were consulting with someone about their grandmother's will. This was conjecture and, even if accurate, there were a million other things than the Fords to discuss with a lawyer. It had crossed Mason's own mind that, if he were a relative, he would be furious about the Sinclair Foundation. To Wilbert's querulous question, he suggested that it was the foundation that explained the conspiratorial aura hanging over that far table.

"Tell me about it," Wilbert sighed, grasping his Manhattan. "We can always talk about Sardinia."

Mason told him what he knew, feeling again that it was unwise to turn Wilbert Plunkett's insatiable curiosity onto anything having to do with the Sinclairs.

"With priests on the board they ought to go back to the original spelling."

"I don't understand."

"Sinclair must be a corruption of St. Clair. I mean corruption in the linguistic sense."

"Roger Dowling is the only priest on the board."

The threesome across the room effectively spoiled Mason's lunch. Remembering his dream that the Sinclairs would forget all about the Fords on loan made him ill and Wilbert's chatter about the west coast of Sardinia did little to distract him. On another occasion he might have been fascinated by the Phoenician and Carthaginian lore Wilbert had picked up. He felt a powerful impulse to hurry back to his office. Had he really taken Bridget from the wall and returned her to the vault? He would have taken the picture home if the indictment of a Utah curator for doing something similar had not been fresh in his mind. In the space of a few hours his mood had changed from one of elation at the museum's good fortune to fear of a rapacious family's resistance to Margaret Sinclair's distribution of her worldly goods.

"What is that beeping?" Wilbert asked.

"It's me!" He opened his jacket and quelled the almost inaudible buzzing. "Excuse me, I must call the office."

Miss Knutsen, speaking like the voice of conscience before which one is ever in the wrong, wondered if he remembered his appointment with Maud Sinclair. Mason had not. He was certain he had never heard of any such appointment and he was prepared to argue about it.

"I left a note on your desk."

"When?"

"It's dated. I think 11:45."

"But I'd already gone to lunch!"

"Oh."

"With a member of the board!" What an annoying woman she would be if her beauty did not overwhelm him so. "When is Miss Sinclair coming?"

"In five minutes."

48

"My God!"

He slammed down the phone, went back to the table, made hurried apologies to Wilbert, and rushed out of the club. He actually ran up the street, something which attracted far less attention than he feared. Perhaps he was thought to be jogging. He would arrive sweating and bedraggled and at a severe disadvantage when he confronted Maud Sinclair.

9

If anyone had suggested to Marie Murkin that St. Hilary's rectory gave a hoot about social or economic status, paying more attention to the affluent or the prominent, the housekeeper would have been shocked. Nonetheless, the passing of Margaret Sinclair was unlike that of any other parishioner. As long as Marie had been in the rectory, which was a good deal longer than Father Dowling, the almost mythical presence of the aging dowager at Fairview had been felt. Father Dowling's immediate predecessor, a friar, had been delinquent in taking communion to the housebound and Marie had feared the old woman and her hefty annual donation would be lured away by some enterprising cleric. Father Dowling did not, of course, take orders from her but none were necessary in the matter of sick calls. He took to pastoral tasks with an enthusiasm unusual in a man ordained a quarter of a century ago and seemed to look forward to the day devoted to visiting the ill and elderly, at the county home and various rest homes as well as Fairview. The still mobile senior citizens of the parish spent a good deal of their day at the school, which had been transformed into a social center under the direction of Edna Hospers.

The news that Father Dowling had been named to the board of the newly created Sinclair Foundation and actually intended to spend time at Fairview getting the procedures established gave Marie Murkin misgivings. Not that she herself would ever think that Father Dowling had in any way whatsoever ingratiated himself with the old woman during those pastoral visits, but she dreaded the interpretation of others. When the creation of the foundation was announced along with Father Dowling's appointment to the board, Marie made a point to drift through the parish center to pick up any hint of wonderment at the pastor's new role. Talking with Edna Hospers had been a mistake.

"It's not a full-time job, is it, Marie?"

"Of course not!" But the truth was that Marie didn't know what Father Dowling's membership on the board might involve. The visit of the gigantic chef had been disturbing. It wasn't her fault the man had been audible through a closed door. For a moment Marie had thought the man would start crying, all that talk about spying on the nurse and a bearded man visiting the house. Honestly. What a commentary on things, hanky-panky among the help at Fairview while the old lady was breathing her last.

"I hate to think of him ever being reassigned," Edna said.

"Reassigned!" Marie stepped back as if she had been struck. "Where did you get such an idea?"

"Isn't that what you're getting at?"

Marie hurried back to the rectory and was almost relieved to find the pastor still in his study, filling the room with pipe smoke, frowning over a book.

"How did it go this morning, Father? At Fairview?"

He lifted his brows and removed his pipe. "The house is far larger than this one, you know."

Marie harrumphed. Had she ever doubted it?

"I suppose you'll need two or three assistants there. Perhaps we can persuade the cook to stay on."

"What on earth are you talking about?"

"Don't you think the parish needs a new rectory?"

"Fairview! The place is a mansion."

"'In my father's house,' Marie. You know the passage."

Oh, he was a terrible tease and she shouldn't give him these opportunities, but after Edna's remark Marie couldn't just laugh it off. She stomped off to the kitchen, but in a minute was back. She gathered up ashtrays and took them away for emptying. She brought them back. She straightened this and that around the study.

"Leave things alone, Marie. You know this room is off limits."

"How many days a week will you have to be at Fairview?"

"Marie, I'll go there for a few hours several times a week."

"I don't want people wondering."

"Wondering what?"

"Over at the parish center there's talk of your being reassigned."

That got a rise out of him. He leaned toward her and assured her solemnly that, God and the cardinal being willing, he intended to stay at St. Hilary's until he was carried out in a box.

"So don't spread any rumors, Marie. I know you have designs on my job, but the cardinal's hands are tied."

That quickly she lost the advantage. In the kitchen she poured herself a cup of tea and tried to regain her composure. Unsuccessfully. She decided to run over for a visit to the Blessed Sacrament.

On the way to the church, she saw the parked car and detoured by it, thinking it must be Captain Keegan, come early for the noon mass and whiling away the time, but it was Lieutenant Horvath. He got out, a huge muscle-bound man, whose gentleness made up for his menacing bulk.

"I hoped to see Father Dowling."

"Is it about Fairview?"

"Why do you ask that?"

It all fit somehow: what Edna said, the pastor's teasing, the male cook who'd come to tell what a fool he was.

"Father's in his study, but there isn't much time. He says mass in twenty minutes."

"Should I just go in?"

Marie considered ushering him in to the pastor, but it seemed a way of punishing Father Dowling to tell Lieutenant Horvath to just go right on in. She waited until he disappeared through the kitchen door and then went on to the church. During the noon mass she would be preparing the pastor's lunch, but she liked to pop over first to check on attendance. She had been doubtful when Father Dowling decided to say his daily mass at noon but she had been proved wrong

52

and she was glad to admit it. Maud Sinclair knelt in a back pew. Maud was not an unusual sight in the church, but Marie was made uneasy by the feeling that suddenly the Sinclair family seemed to confront her wherever she turned. She would love to ask Maud what the family thought of the way Margaret Sinclair had disposed of the family wealth, but of course she could never do that.

"Some of them will fight the will," Father Dowling had said blandly.

"I hope you don't get embroiled in a court fight."

"It wouldn't be a murder trial, Marie."

In a back pew of St. Hilary's Maud rattled off a *Memorare* before
taking an appointment book from her massive purse. Her afternoon
and evening were busy ones, but this was usually the case. She
scheduled herself carefully, as if determined to leave very few such
moments as that she was now enjoying. It might be said that
lunchtime was for lunch, but Maud ate lunch only in the line of duty
which, alas, was often. *Noblesse oblige.* But the truth was she did not
have enough to do.

Her life had cracked in two at the age of thirty-three. Up until that
time she followed a predestined track: eight years in the St. Hilary
parish school, Our Lady's Academy for high school, after which she
had wanted to study with Mesdames of the Sacred Heart. But
Hathaway Hall was already a Sinclair tradition. Raymond proposed
marriage on their third date, after a dance, when she was a junior.
She had not wanted to answer him immediately, but he held her
close and her head spun and she said yes, yes, yes. The buttons on
his uniform pressed against her daring décolletage. She felt enveloped in his masculine strength. Later, in the car, he kissed her and

54

she wished he would never stop. But he did. Nothing happened. He was a gentleman. And an officer. But her family was uneasy at the news.

Who was Raymond Renard? Where was he from? What was his family like? Where had he gone to school? She could answer the last question. He had attended Seton Hall, although what he had taken other than NROTC was unclear. Now he was in the Navy, stationed at Great Lakes; but there was no war on, his military career would be brief, a return for his education.

But then Vietnam heated up, so Ray would be gone at least a year. She was urged to wait until he returned, but Maud was certain that she and Ray had been thrown together by Providence and that was good enough for her. She flew to him in San Diego, where they were married in a lovely white Spanish-style church with a red tile roof, attended by strangers in a strange city, strangers to one another. They honeymooned in La Jolla, a week during which Maud discovered in herself a wild sensuality she had never suspected. They did silly things together which years later could bring a blush to her cheek. He tried to put on her panties and held her bra to his hairy chest. She let him come into the shower with her, where they soaped one another with increasing fervor and ended up on the floor, panting and laughing like greased pigs. The first time they went downstairs, holding hands in the elevator, pressed close together, the car doors opened but they did not get out. The doors closed and they went wordlessly up to their room where they flung off the clothes they had so carefully put on. He carried her naked to the bed, teasingly lifting his lips out of reach when she tried to kiss him, but they coupled before she was sandwiched between the bed and the great masterful body of her husband.

A week later, she stood with other women watching the line of ships head out to sea, in a panic that she would not recognize the one that took Raymond from her. She had the odd feeling that she was interchangeable with any of these other women, that Raymond could be any lieutenant j. g. It was a strange thought to have about the man she had married and with whom she had known a week of such wild intimacy.

His family lived in Hackensack and Ray wrote as if they might settle there, although San Diego had its attractions. He did not respond to her suggestion that they might even live in Illinois. She returned home after the honeymoon, and she soon realized she was pregnant. The news made her feel holy. She had never felt so exalted as when she wrote Raymond to tell him they would be parents. Carrying her baby, looking forward to his birth, gave point to her life and made the waiting tolerable. She wrote Raymond a little bit every day and his letters arrived regularly, full of unintelligible naval lore and anecdotes about men she had never met. But then, she wrote him about in-laws who were complete strangers to him. She propped Raymond's photograph up beside her when she sat crocheting with Grandmother Sinclair. On the wall was the portrait she was said to resemble.

"I hope he'll want to live here in Fox River, Grandma."

"What do his people do in Hackensack?"

"His father's in business."

"What kind of business?"

"Wholesale groceries."

All plans were vague plans in those days, and of course there was the gnawing fear that something might happen to Raymond. He was at war, after all. The newspaper accounts of the fighting were unintelligible, at once optimistic and pessimistic. Raymond was in the thick of it, plying the Mekong River in a small craft. Maud was waiting in San Diego with little Stephen when Raymond came home from war.

He was thin and weather-beaten and there was an old look in his eye, but his smile when he saw her, the awe with which he took their child in his arms, made her fall in love with him all over again. The hotel in La Jolla was booked until Doomsday and they had to settle for a cottage in a motor camp out past the Marine base. Even apart from the presence of the baby, it was not a place where they could behave as they had on their honeymoon. There wasn't a crib so they put the baby between them, but during the night Maud moved him to her side lest Raymond roll over and crush his son and heir.

"Son and heir." He liked the phrase. At the moment he was rich with money dealt out to him in cash when he was discharged. He still wore his uniform; he was still wearing it when they arrived in Fox River. Was it only a visit or something more? That had been unclear at the time, but the visit was prolonged and then William suggested that Raymond might want to look in on him at the office. William was the entrepreneur among her brothers, and he particularly liked

Raymond. "He talked me into it," was the way Raymond told her that he was going to work at Sinclair Printing, a business William had developed into a major factor in Fox River.

Raymond had worked on the student paper in Seton Hall, but William said he wouldn't hold that against him. He wanted Ray to develop a shoppers' guide he had bought.

"How?"

"If he knew, he wouldn't need me."

They didn't notice anything odd about the baby until they realized he was slow to walk. Grandma Sinclair listened when Maud first expressed her fears and urged her to bring Stephen to see her. She held him on her lap, she did the things adults always do with babies, she held the child to her breast and looked over his tousled head at Maud.

"Dr. Kunert," she said. "Take Stephen to him."

"Do you think . . ."

"Why don't we wait to see what the doctor says."

That is how it began, first Dr. Kunert, then a succession of others, as they resisted the diagnosis. Raymond wouldn't even talk about it. There was none of that in his family. They had been told it was not hereditary, but it was difficult to be rational when you faced the prospect of a child who would never become an adult however long he lived. Maud would have lost her mind if she hadn't been able to tell everything to Grandma Sinclair, everything, even about her quarrels with Raymond. Maud accepted the finality of Stephen's condition long before Ray could. Perhaps he never really did.

"Have more children," Grandma Sinclair advised.

Stephen was the only child she ever had. Tears now stood in her large eyes, making it impossible for her to see the open page of her appointment book. If her life were a book, the most significant page would be when she was thirty-three, a good year to be given a cross. That was when Raymond left her.

Two weeks before their tenth anniversary, he told her it was over.

"We tried, Maud. No one can say we didn't try."

She didn't understand him. Marriage wasn't an effort, it was a way of life. They had given themselves to one another forever, until death parted them. She did not understand, but neither was she surprised. Raymond had been unable to accept the fact that he had a retarded son. He was ashamed of Stephen. Even at home, he avoided him, and when on the rare occasion Maud found them together, Raymond looked sheepish, as if he had been caught pretending his son was normal.

Have more children, Grandma Sinclair had said, but the thoughtless sensuality of the week that had produced Stephen was no more. When he told her he was leaving, they had not slept together for over a year. That was dangerous to a marriage, she knew that, and if she found it difficult, how much more trying it must be for him. But the choice was his. She could not believe that he was living like a monk.

He wasn't. That is not the excuse he gave. He talked very fast and not quite coherently when he told her. He seemed to have rehearsed answers to her protests. Her pride prevented her from begging. Hers was the first divorce that had ever occurred in the Sinclair family. Maud was deeply ashamed, no matter that the fault was not hers. Except that in the awful days after Raymond left it was herself she blamed, sure there was something she might have done to prevent this. Holding Stephen, all she had left, she would rock him and try not to upset him with her tears and tell herself that she had given Ray Stephen and that was why he was gone.

"Nothing can be done?" Grandma Sinclair asked.

"No."

"Then we must accept it. The idea was entirely his?"

"Yes!"

She gathered Maud into her arms. How had she put it? Maud never remembered the words, only the thought behind them. It was no shame to suffer injustice; she had done nothing wrong. She must not blame herself. God is good. Grandma said that several times, repeating it because she must have known how hard it was to believe in the circumstances. God is good.

At thirty-three, with a retarded child, but with no financial worries, Maud was on her own. Within two years, Stephen had sickened and died. He was buried in the mausoleum chapel on the island at Fairview and she was completely alone. Without child or husband, she decided to call herself Maud Sinclair again. That was when she began to be active in the town, hyperactive, embracing what Father Dowling called the heresy of good works, and soon she was sure she had weathered the worst of it. Would life be possible if we could read the future? God is good.

It angered Maud that the family was getting involved in a public

58

squabble over Margaret's will. They were proving Margaret's implicit point. They were spoiled. They already had more money than was good for them. Except for Terry, of course. She glanced toward the altar, feeling the pharisee. The pearls Margaret had left her were nowhere to be found at Fairview and Maud was not a little peeved. She had actually looked around Dolly's room when she visited her, wondering if the housekeeper might have . . . Might have what? For heaven's sake. Amos Cadbury assured her he would find out what had happened. He was more upset than the members of the family whose special mementos from Margaret turned out not to exist. But Maud had seen the pearls she had been bequeathed.

She closed her appointment book and returned it to her purse. She would hear Father Dowling's mass and then go on to the museum. She would be precisely on time for her appointment with George Frederick Mason.

11

Marie Murkin's story that the old people in the parish center were talking about his possible transfer from St. Hilary's only meant that the housekeeper wondered what effect his connection with the Sinclair Foundation would have. Father Dowling had had some uneasy thoughts of his own after the newspapers made so much of the amount of money at the disposal of the foundation. Those around the cardinal would not be human if they had not thought all this money earmarked for promoting things Catholic was a bright prospect indeed for the archdiocese, particularly when one of their priests was on the board. It was not inconceivable that his presence on the board, given the stakes, might seem assignment enough for him. Why waste a man with access to the income from millions in a backwater like St. Hilary's? Roger Dowling stopped himself from rehearsing his response to a phone call from the chancery.

"Every member of the board will have other responsibilities," Margaret had said when he objected that his post as pastor of St. Hilary's would not give him time for foundation work.

"Even to call it part-time is more than I could accept."

60

"Father Dowling, it is a matter of a few hours a month. Would you like me to consult with the cardinal?"

"Oh, no. No need to bother him." He kept panic from his voice. He dreaded ever emerging from the obscurity in which he dwelt.

Amos Cadbury corroborated Margaret's estimate of the amount of time the foundation would require of him. "She very much wants you on the board, Father. Maud also holds you in high regard and she will be pivotal as we get under way."

"I have achieved a kind of anonymity with the chancery since coming here, Amos."

No need to explain to the canny lawyer. He wrote into the appointment the requirement that Father Dowling remain as pastor of St. Hilary's. Almost too much of a solution. Roger Dowling had no wish to suggest to the chancery that their hands were tied so far as his appointment was concerned.

His train of thought was broken by the appearance of Cy Horvath in the doorway of the study.

"Got a minute, Father?"

"I've got fifteen."

Subtlety was not Cy's long suit, and he went directly to the point. There was some question in the Medical Examiner's office about the death of Margaret Sinclair. No evidence or anything like that, just a question.

"Monique Pippen?"

"You remember her?"

"Phil Keegan won't let me forget. But I knew she did the examination at Fairview."

"Death was due to asphyxiation, meaning the old woman didn't get oxygen when she suffered an emphysema attack." Cy paused. "My words, I don't know how the M.E. would put it. She suffered a heart attack too but they think that was brought on by panic at the lack of oxygen."

"They?"

"Pippen."

"What do you think?"

What bothered Horvath was that there was only the report of the officers who had answered the nurse's 911 call and arrived before the paramedics and the M.E. Father Dowling looked at Cy, wondering if the lieutenant suspected what he himself had feared.

"Dr. Pippen doesn't think Margaret Sinclair brought on her own death, does she?"

The question surprised the detective, and Father Dowling took comfort from that.

"Pippen says the oxygen was right there by her chair. I saw it myself. There was a nurse on duty, yet the old lady got none. She wonders how come. I've got no answer I like."

"Cy, she was ninety-five years old."

Of course Cy knew that. What kind of an answer was it? Roger Dowling had met Monique Pippen since her unease about Earl Waffle's death had proved well founded, and he had been impressed. Minnesota Medical School, intern at Cook County, a residency in pathology at the Mayo Clinic, she had taken the Fox River job as a stepping stone to a return to Chicago. She had been a little embarrassed telling him that reconstructing how a person died required more imagination than people thought. People being Jolson and Keegan and their ilk, no doubt. What was her imaginative reconstruction of the circumstances of Margaret's death?

"You saw her yourself that day, didn't you, Father?"

"Twice. I brought her communion in the morning."

"The nurse there then?"

"She usually left me alone with Margaret." Monique Pippen's inquiry had apparently prodded Cy into a kind of investigation. "Have you spoken with Honora?"

Poor Honora, how would she react to questions about her service? Margaret had been reconciled to the nurse's incompetence, even amused by it, professing to be reassured by Honora's noble brow. A reference to the arches penciled over the large hazel eyes? In any case, Honora was the day nurse, on duty when others could come to Margaret's assistance.

"Not that I need any. A child could operate this." And Margaret demonstrated the ease with which she could clamp the plastic mask over her nose and mouth and flick on the flow of oxygen. After Margaret received Holy Communion that last day of her life, Father Dowling left her alone for a few minutes, to make her thanksgiving. He found Honora lolling in an easy chair, babbling away on the phone, a picture of indolence. Had she been on the phone to the bearded lover Regis claimed visited her later that day? Nonsense.

Cy's account of Margaret's last day made it seem busy. Father

Dowling had been there, but so had Terry Sinclair. Dolly too. And Honora.

"The chef was off that day," Cy concluded.

He might have let it go, but Father Dowling decided to correct Cy. Regis had spoken in confidence, but if surprises started showing up in Cy's inquiry it might seem Monique Pippen's speculation had some ground. After all, he himself had felt uneasy when he gave Margaret the last sacraments. He gave Cy an abbreviated version of Regis's remarks.

"Why would he spy on her?"

"Men infatuated with women do odd things."

Cy shifted as if embarrassed by this banality.

"He thinks a man visited her, Cy. A bearded man. In his state, it could be imagination. I hope you won't have to talk to Regis. He has sense enough to be embarrassed by what he did and he certainly would not want to cause Honora trouble."

It was time for Father Dowling to go say the noon mass. He invited Cy to have lunch with him afterward, but the lieutenant declined.

"Doesn't Terence Sinclair have a beard?"

Father Dowling smiled at Cy. "That's my guess too."

Good old Cy. Leave it to a Hungarian to keep his feet on the ground. They parted on the walk outside and Father Dowling went on to the church.

12

At lunch with the Salazars in the Athletic Club Tuttle had steak, spinach, and iced tea. Octavio's salad was liberally sprinkled with bacon bits and for dessert he had a chocolate sundae, lapping it up like a kid. No wonder he looked like Fernando Valenzuela. Bunny beamed at her spouse's indulgence but was not distracted by it. Tuttle said little, still unable to believe that he was lunching with members of the Sinclair family. He did not dare ask how they settled on him. It might have been blind choice. On the other hand, he had learned that his reputation sometimes oddly recommended him to unlikely clients.

"Mr. Cadbury has been our lawyer, whenever we've needed one, which thank God is not often, no offense, but he is determined to defend Grandma's will . . ."

"He hardly has a choice," Tuttle said, stirring his coffee. All he needed was a blindfold and a scales. He was a credit to the profession.

". . . and I am determined to fight it. It's ridiculous putting all that money into the hands of people whose idea of philanthropy is probably sending pittances to South Korean nuns."

Octavio, with whipped cream in the corners of his mouth, nodded in agreement. "Or holy cards to Nigeria." Obviously they both thought money sunk into Octavio's efforts would be money well spent.

"How many heirs are there?"

"This concerns the whole family," Bunny said.

"That's my point. Are you alone in wishing to contest the will?"

"Does it matter?"

"No. But it would look more disinterested if all the heirs were involved."

"Disinterested! I'm *not* disinterested."

Octavio said, "Won't you represent us otherwise?"

Tuttle addressed his answer to Bunny. "If you are determined to do this, I will represent you."

She thrust her hand at him and he had little choice but to shake it. Not that he hesitated. Octavio wanted to shake too. Tuttle would have liked to stand for this ritual so that everyone in the dining room could see. Of course it was doubtful that any of the diners would recognize him. Tuttle had never before in his whole life set foot inside the Athletic Club. It was not that he had tried and been rebuffed. The image he had formed of himself under the vicissitudes of life had not permitted him even to imagine himself lunching here. Was his hitherto pathetic practice to experience a quantum leap forward? He had expressed this hope to Peanuts Pianone when he put down his office phone after accepting the Salazars' invitation to lunch.

"What's a quantum?"

"The measure of a leap."

Tuttle did not know the meaning of the phrase. It was one of the ragtag collection of locutions and ideas he had picked up by osmosis over the years, part of his arsenal of verbiage to impress or at least confuse the court. Whatever "quantum leap" meant, it would have fit his presence here among the snow-white tablecloths and clinking china and silverware.

"I'll have to get a copy of the will."

Bunny opened her purse and brought out a small machine. "I taped Mr. Cadbury's reading, if that would help."

Taped it? Tuttle felt suddenly close to his clients. Bunny had obviously expected a far different distribution of her grandmother's wealth. There had been, she claimed, an earlier will that contained no mention of a Sinclair Foundation. The advanced age of Mrs. Sinclair when the will was changed plus the existence of the previous will provided some basis for a case. Tuttle did not imagine that the idea for the foundation could be set aside, but the amount devoted to it might be reduced and the difference distributed to members of the family. And to their legal representatives. One thing was certain, he would be happier discussing these matters with Amos Cadbury than with any of the Sinclairs. If he could get in to see him.

It took days to arrange the visit. Cadbury first verified that Tuttle was indeed representing Bunny and Octavio Salazar. He agreed to a meeting in the rotunda of the courthouse.

"If it's about the jewelry Margaret left her, I am doing everything to ascertain what happened to it."

"Their complaint is the foundation and all the money going into it."

"Contesting that will would be a waste of time," Cadbury said.

"How old was Mrs. Sinclair when she changed her will?"

Cadbury was visibly pained to be going into such matters with the likes of Tuttle. "It was only a few years ago."

"She would have been over ninety?"

"She was ninety-three at the time. And her mind was sound as a dollar."

"Any independent reason to think that?"

"Ask any of the family."

Tuttle looked beyond Cadbury at the bronze statue of an Indian warrior that commanded the echoing area in which they stood. "They're gerontologists, are they?"

Cadbury smiled as if with indigestion. "Not that I know of."

"When is probate?"

"Have you a copy of the will?"

He didn't mention that Bunny had taped Cadbury's reading of it to the family on the day of the funeral, though he was sorely tempted by any prospect of further annoying the patrician lawyer.

"Tell me about the Sinclair Foundation."

Tuttle listened as to a crash course in the setting up of a tax-free

66

nonprofit foundation. Who was he to wonder if there were any legal flaws lurking within the entity Amos Cadbury had fashioned? One did not require knowledge of the law to see that Margaret Sinclair had decided that her grandchildren and their children would be better off without any further distribution of wealth among them. Cadbury was not certain where Mrs. Sinclair had gotten the idea of a foundation, but it had appealed to her because she could define how the money would be used and thus extend into the indefinite future her desire to foster and support efforts which, if they were not formal activities of the Roman Catholic Church, were closely allied to the Church's mission. And she had been careful to make clear that she did not mean just any random notion of what that mission was. The point of reference was to be the official Magisterium of the Church as exercised by the Pope and the bishops in communion with him. That seemed to explain Father Dowling's presence on the board. Tuttle was impressed. Any lawyer could tell horror stories of the way in which the wishes of donors have been ignored by later dispensers of funds. A foundation was not proof positive against that, of course, but it provided some control.

"You were wise to remind her of that," Tuttle said.

"It had already occurred to her," Amos Cadbury said, head thrown back, eyes closed. This too will pass. "Of course I agreed when she mentioned it, but she had no need of me to bring up the matter."

"That's interesting."

"I told you, Mr. Tuttle. Her mind was clear as a bell."

Did Cadbury know what Peanuts had told Tuttle? The police were unhappy with the public account of how Margaret Sinclair had died. At least, Horvath was making inquiries. Tuttle wondered how this would affect his clients' interest. For he had also become the lawyer of Terence Sinclair, who had a bad habit of shooting off his mouth. On the other hand, he was even more determined than the Salazars to get money he was convinced was his.

"Blood is thicker than water, Tuttle." He rubbed his naked face, recently shorn of its beard. Was he preparing to look less seedy when affluence struck? If he was put off by the modesty of Tuttle's office he gave no sign of it.

"Was your grandmother senile?"

"Ha."

"Meaning no?"

"She thought we would be better off with less money. Strengthen our spines."

Well, it seemed to have worked. The prospect of poverty, or what would seem like poverty to them, had mobilized the Sinclairs and, improbably, put Tuttle into the center of things.

13

The level of the sea rises and falls in the round porthole and a similar sea rises and falls in me as I sit here blessedly alone. Groaning and straining, rolling, rising and falling. The ship inches forward night and day. Last night when they were all at meal I went out on deck and watched the ship's wake boil back to where we came from. It was very cold there and my hair and clothing were tossed violently by the wind. Water and wind, and above, so close, a sky strangely serene. It is a sin to wish that I might slip over and down into the water and be borne back even dead to home. . . .

Rain at sea, a watery world. Matthew imagines that I am well because I write in this diary. Poor man. This has been a terrible trip for him. I am no sailor. He reads but does not enjoy it, a novel from the ship's library. Yet he is content to be here in this cabin. The sea does not seem to affect him at all.

Peggy read the diary a page at a time, resisting the impulse to skip around in it, to see where and how it ended. Margaret had written in pencil, the letters and words precisely formed. Opposite the page she now read was a drawing of a porthole, careful, exact, and beneath it to the right the suggestion of the top of a head. A man's. Probably Matthew's. Peggy stared at the porthole as she might at something brought up from the wreck of the *Titanic*. The sketch increased her sense of being there with her great-grandmother, of *being* her, as indeed in some sense she was, a continuation at least, the blood mixed with how many other streams, seven, ten? Her parents each had four grandparents and she had the two of them, make it ten. She was at best a watered-down version of Margaret Sinclair. But having the same name should count as well.

Peggy had never kept a diary. Oh, she had begun one several times, made an entry or two. . . . She fanned the pages of Margaret's diary and was relieved to see that the entries continued. The book seemed full and she could see that the sketch of the porthole was only the first of many drawings. She shut the book and held it tightly against her, closing her eyes.

The moment being written about had to be important, or why take the bother to write of it at all? But Peggy lived either looking ahead, beyond the moment in which she was, or remembering. Could you keep a postdated diary, or whatever it would be called? She imagined writing now of her visits to her great-grandmother. That was far more appealing than writing about these final days before graduation.

Michele came out of the bathroom, wrapping in a towel, swaying and twirling, her long wet hair whipping about. She was like a dog fresh from a dip in the lake.

"Hey, you're getting water everywhere."

"I am a mermaid looking for a mere man," Michele sang. On the far side of the room, facing away, she took both ends of the towel and, moving her rear as much as the towel, did a shimmy. She looked like a car wash.

"You through in the bathroom?"

"It's all yours."

Michele was toweling her hair now, more humming than singing, having run out of words for her original song. Michele was manic with the thought that soon she could shake the dust of Hathaway Hall from her feet forever. It was Tuesday. Commencement was Sunday. On Thursday or Friday, Peggy was certain, Michele would turn

70

sentimental and react quite differently to the realization that their college years were nearly over.

There had been a note from Professor Gearhart Glockner asking Peggy to come see him. She remembered that when she stepped under the shower; perhaps it was the initial unwelcome pelting of water, the temperature not yet right, that reminded her of the art history professor.

"Did he say what he wanted?"

"You flunked and have to put in another year or two in order to graduate."

"Come on."

"That's the whole message, Peggy. He did suggest that you remember to take your pill."

Peggy stuck out her tongue. It was *de rigueur* to pretend they lived like girls in a brothel. Michele had had a boyfriend in junior year, her promiscuous year, as she referred to it, a big lanky deadhead Peggy had been shocked to find in bed with Michele one afternoon when she skipped class. Peggy was out of the room in half a second, stayed away until hours after supper, was herself safely in bed when Michele returned.

"Sorry," Michele said the next day.

Peggy shrugged. She felt more jealous than indignant. Until she met Gordon formally. He was good-looking and stupid, majoring in economics at Ball State.

"Ball State," Peggy repeated.

Michele had met him the previous summer, when they had told lies to one another about their respective schools. Maybe there had been something then; Michele was very vague about late-night beach dates at Lake Delton in Wisconsin where their families had rented cottages. In any case, here he was, ostensibly staying at a motel in town, sharing Michele's bed.

That had been last year. There was no mention of Gordon now except for coded references. As far as Peggy could tell, Michele's main complaint was that she would have liked to be the one to call it off. Her one trip to Muncie had been bad since his roommates continued to sleep in the room with them and seemed on the verge of treating her as a common possession.

Senior year Michele called her nun year, though she wouldn't have lasted a minute in a convent, the way she pranced around after a shower. Peggy regretted telling Michele of her reveries in Lisieux. Now she was pulled between eagerness to leave Hathaway Hall and the sad realization that this was a major turning point in her life. What was she going to do?

When Peggy came out of the bathroom, one towel around her head, another around her body, Michele was sitting on the edge of her bed with the diary open in her hands.

"Michele! That's private."

Michele looked up in goofy incredulity. "What is it?"

Peggy took the diary, trying not to snatch it away, and put it in her purse.

"I told you. My great-grandmother left it to me."

"Was it hers?"

"Of course." Now that she had rescued the diary, Peggy's anger disappeared.

"I thought she gave you a painting."

Peggy hooked her bra and pulled a sweater over her head. She turned to Michele.

"Did you tell Glockner about that painting?"

No need to answer. Michele's mouth fell open, the look of a woman belatedly realizing she had done the wrong thing. But Peggy didn't really care about Glockner. She could ignore the message. She would ignore it.

"Let's go eat."

"I'll just have some fruit."

This was Michele's morning fiction, that she could go to the dining hall and settle for a banana, or an apple, while all around her others were eating like crazy.

"I'm sorry about the diary," Michele said when they were headed across campus. The place looked as beautiful as it had in the photographs they had seen of it before enrolling. The dogwoods were glorious and peonies were beginning to blossom.

"It's just that I want to be the first to read it."

Michele nodded. She herself kept a diary/notebook/journal, she was never sure what to call it. In sophomore year it was a ledger she had brought from home with red horizontal lines and a green vertical line marking the margin, the page numbers printed. In it were her notes for *the* novel. Michele planned to write the definitive story of life in such a school as Hathaway Hall.

"This sort of thing is already as quaint as governesses. I have an obligation to get it down as accurately as I can so it won't be lost."

That sounded more like history than fiction to Peggy, but Michele's models were John O'Hara and Sinclair Lewis.

"You should like him, Peg, with a name like that."

Peggy had tried unsuccessfully to read Lewis after watching *Elmer Gantry* on TV. Michele wouldn't let her read the chapters of the novel she had written, but her diary/journal/notebook was always on her desk and Peggy had peeked into it from time to time. There were whole pages of names, there were entries several sentences long in which Michele reminded herself of an earlier entry in which she had jotted down some wonderful idea. The extended pages of writing seemed to be reports on things that had happened here in the room or in class. Michele eventually switched to a computer, but Peggy's curiosity had waned by then.

At the dining hall, they each took an apple and a carton of milk and went down to the lake and along the path to an empty bench. Ducks wandered from bench to bench to be fed.

"We should have grabbed some bread," Michele said, but coming to the lake had been a spur-of-the-moment decision, one made by a good number of their classmates as well.

"It's the diary she kept on her honeymoon," Peggy said.

"Wow."

"Oh, I don't look for any big revelations. But it's such an experience reading it now that she's dead."

"It says a lot that she wanted you to have it."

For the first time Peggy was fully struck by the significance of that. How self-centered she was! That she should have the portrait and the diary had seemed wholly unsurprising when Mr. Cadbury read the will. At the time none of her aunts or uncles or cousins seemed to care, let alone resent it. Now, according to her mother, grumbling had begun about the money. From one point of view a painting and an old diary were nothing, but from another they were the nicest things her great-grandmother could have given her.

While they were sitting there, Miss Whelan, the secretary of the art department, came up to them.

"Margaret, did you get Professor Glockner's note?"

"Yes."

"He's very anxious to see you." Miss Whelan was in her fifties.

She had worked here since she was a girl, and she was respectful to students but adoring of the faculty. That anyone would even hesitate when summoned by a member of the faculty was unimaginable to her.

"Do you know what he wants?"

Miss Whelan was shocked at the suggestion that she would say if she knew.

"I'll call him."

"He's in his office now."

"Thank you."

Miss Whelan hesitated as if she expected Peggy to come along immediately. Her pace quickened as she went on her way.

"Well," Michele said. "Anything I should know?"

"I told him this was the end. It's been great fun but it's just one of those things."

"Men!" Michele threw her apple core but failed to tempt any duck with it.

"If I thought it was something other than my body he was after . . ."

"I must tell you. He made advances to me in your absence."

They needed fans and crinoline gowns for this scene, but improvisation was the spice of life. What fun Michele was. And what a pain in the you-know-what was Professor Glockner.

Michele said, "I wish I was leaving for Europe right away."

Her parents had reluctantly agreed to what Michele called her *wanderjahr*, which she portrayed for parental consumption as a year of further study not confined to one university. It was to begin in Pamplona, but between now and then was the prospect of a summer working for a construction company. In the office.

"Something hardhat, okay, I could use that, but flat on my prat before a computer terminal eight hours a day, yuk."

Peggy herself had resolutely refused to sign up for interviews when representatives of various companies, corporations, and conglomerates came to campus. This seemed to number her among those who were headed for graduate school, but that wasn't it. The immediate future had been the great unknown until Aunt Maud proposed that she work for the Sinclair Foundation.

"Procedures for processing applications for grants will have to be worked out."

74

It was the fact that the foundation would be housed at Fairview that persuaded Peggy to put off her graduation trip until fall.

"I'll walk with you," Michele offered when Peggy rose, sighing, and turned in the direction of Spanner Hall.

"That's all right."

"I'm going to stop by the library."

It was Michele's practice to stand in the stacks of contemporary American fiction and commune with her eventual peers.

"If you dillydally long enough we can go to Europe together," Michele said as they set off toward Spanner.

Professor Gearhart Glockner was a stubby man whose body did not exhibit the classic canon which requires that overall height be eight times that of the head. His torso was too long, his legs too short, and his arms hung gibbonlike at his sides. His wild wiry beard was more a disguise than an adornment and his eyes rolled behind tinted glasses as if seeking the direction from which the next insult would come. He was not a prepossessing man. His current status was unmarried but it had been otherwise twice in the past and, despite the oaths and resolutions with which he reacted to desertion by his second wife, he longed to marry again. Not to have a wife seemed a public declaration that he could not find one. A withdrawn, inarticulate man, Glockner lived as if his every move was center stage and every hostile eye in the house was on him.

Whence this insecurity? He had been an only child, doted on by mother and father alike. He had never known want. He had done well in school. His passage through undergraduate and graduate studies to the MFA had been smooth. An analyst suggested that he had been permanently marked by being left behind unnoticed on a school trip to Philadelphia. Unmissed, he had stayed where he was, in the restored Continental Congress building, a stranger, an alien in his native land. A marriage counselor suggested he had suppressed memories of his parents making love behind the closed door of their room.

"They never closed their door," he corrected, a major mistake.

"Aha."

"They had nothing to hide. As far as I know they never made love."

"You mean you hoped they didn't."

What dirty minds these people had. This one was a woman and his only defense had been to play the game.

"They were always at it," he moaned, slandering his gentle parents. "Upstairs, downstairs, wherever he caught up to her."

The counselor quivered with prurient interest, feigning disgust at such animal behavior. Gearhart put forth his hand and she gripped it. She became his second wife. Her interest in sex was almost exclusively theoretical. She recommended unnatural practices to Gearhart to keep him from her bed. When they did make love it was less a conquest than a concession.

What he wanted was love, someone to look benevolently on Gearhart Glockner, to accept him for what he was, to admire him, to want him. This he had never found. His parents' support for his ambitions seemed to suggest he was going to need every advantage he could get. Not even they thought anyone could love him unadorned by degrees and position.

Art history is the fate awaiting those who realize they will never be artists. Glockner had imitative skills. His delight had been in copying acknowledged masterpieces; he might have made a good, if precarious, living as a fraud. But he would have felt more fraudulent producing the kind of painting that drew praise from his instructors. To be good at that sort of thing would have been worse than failure. The history of art provided an excuse for an unabashed admiration for beauty. He had spent a year in Florence, much of it in two rooms of the Uffizi to which he would march daily without so much as a glance at the pictures he passed. The gallery presented the perpetual possibility of overdosing. It was too much, far too much. Pictures were not painted to hang in clusters on walls facing other walls covered with pictures. Such abundance was self-defeating. The trick was to develop blinders, to look at each painting as if it were alone in the world.

Even so, Florence had not been the country of his heart. In part, the religious themes seemed to push him away, to make him feel an intruder. The memory of Berensen was still fresh but Glockner saw him as a warning rather than a model. He had a Rembrandt period. He thought seriously of doing his dissertation on Rembrandt, seeking racial and artistic affinity there, but a trip across the channel in the forlorn hope of sleeping with his traveling companion turned out to be a trip into Constable country. Landscapes. Constable, Turner, lesser lights, turned out to be what he had been seeking. He loved paintings that gave little clue as to the century in which they were made, pictures devoid of people. Out of this had come his devotion to the American painter Clayton Ford, whose landscapes, seen from a slight distance through narrowed eyes, might have been produced at any time during the past three hundred years.

It is sometimes thought that a scholar is moved by the urge to make something known to as wide an audience as possible. Not so. The true scholar is a jealous, covetous soul, consumed by the desire to possess something for himself alone, to know what others do not know, to have what others do not have, to see or read what others cannot. It is this that confers authority on him. Scholarship is a continuation of the schoolyard effort to be one up on threatening companions. Gearhart Glockner was a natural scholar.

At conventions and conferences he sat in on every paper that touched on his own interests, readying as he listened a question that would undermine any favorable impression the talk might be making, or helping to sink further a flawed presentation. King of the Hill is what it was; one stood tall on the bodies of fallen foes. The only person in the country Glockner truly feared in the matter of Ford was the ineffable George Frederick Mason in his dreadfully provincial museum where nonetheless authentic Ford landscapes hung. Four! There were only sixteen in all. More unsettling still was Mason's pretense that there were hitherto unknown Ford portraits. Glockner had phoned Gabbiano to corroborate his own belief that there were no unknown portraits by Ford. Of course he told Gabbiano why he asked. Let that whole New York crowd know. It seemed a way to deflate George Frederick Mason's stock, not that George's old mentor retained much respect for a man who had left New York for Fox River, Illinois.

That commercial and critical interest had shifted from Ford landscapes to his few portraits was an abomination to Glockner, though scarcely surprising. The currents and eddies of fashion in the art world rivaled those in women's clothing. The trick, he had assured himself, was to remain calm, remain focused, rest assured that the wheel would turn back again. But his nights were disturbed by the thought of Mason at work on a monograph which would further inflate the estimate of Ford's portraits, thereby devaluing Glockner's authority in the painter's landscapes. Peggy Sinclair's offhand remark earlier in the semester that Ford had painted her great-grandmother had hit hard, and it was not easy to pretend that the possibility meant little to him. Indeed, apart from the call to Gabbiano, a plan grew in him to encroach on Mason's territory, to seize the role of discoverer, write the article that would electrify the art world.

It was to his advantage that Peggy Sinclair was on campus, where he could corner her. He had called the *Fox River Tribune* and had their recent Sinclair stories faxed to him. That the old woman's portrait had gone to her great-granddaughter was buried in the story. Peggy had returned to campus yesterday. She must have received his message. It was imperative that he not overwhelm her with eagerness. Cool. He must be cool. But he was reluctant to go down the hall to the lavatory for fear she would show up in his absence. He had arrived at his office just after six and it seemed midday when Miss Whelan finally arrived. He sent her off to tell the Sinclair girl in person that Professor Glockner wished to see her.

It was 9:45 when Margaret finally came. Glockner waved her to a chair as if in distraction.

"I've finished the paper," she said.

"What?"

"The term paper. It's in my computer, I just have to print it out."

He had no idea what she was talking about. Hanging his glasses from one ear, he rubbed his eyes. It appeared that she still owed him a term paper.

"Aren't you graduating?"

She seemed to take his question as a threat. Of course. She would think that the missing paper could keep her from receiving her degree. But for him to do that would be to incur the wrath of the registrar and run the risk of being sued by her parents.

"What mark did you get?"

"A-. But you said I should consider it an Incomplete."

"Get the paper to me as soon as you can."

She started to rise and he held up his hand. "Wait. There's something else."

She sat. How to begin? But it was too late for artifice even if in his eagerness he had been capable of it.

"You must be quite excited about your inheritance."

"How did you hear of it?"

"I've visited Fox River several times. Mason, the director of the museum, is by way of being a friend."

"I haven't been there since I was a kid."

"I must have mentioned the Ford landscapes there in the class you took."

"Yes."

"Mason, like many others, is wild about Ford portraits. I should warn you. He probably has designs on your grandmother's gift."

"My great-grandmother."

"I can't blame him, of course. Not that I accept his conjecture that the painting is a Ford."

"It's a portrait of my great-grandmother. I really don't care who did it."

He winced at such heresy. "I don't mean he would try to buy it. But he quite understandably will want you to let him hang it . . ."

She was shaking her head. Glockner was delighted to see her stubborn expression. Mason would find it difficult to persuade this girl to do anything she did not choose to do.

"Of course you will want it for yourself for a time, but later . . ."

Her head continued shaking. Good girl.

"My great-grandmother had it in her room. Visitors could see it, but it was not a public thing. That is how I mean to keep it."

"How large is it?"

Despite having taken his course, she held up her hands like the fisherman in the joke. The size seemed right for a Ford portrait. He asked her to describe it, and it was painful to sit through her inarticulate and uninformative remarks, but he smiled encouragement as if her words were worthy of a catalogue.

"I'll get the paper to you today." She was standing. He let her go. It had been a dissatisfying interview; his anxiety was not really lessened. Whatever the girl's attitude, George Frederick Mason seemed on the verge of an art historical coup.

"Just give it to Miss Whelan."

Alone, he sat brooding behind his desk. It had been right not to tell her he had actually seen the portrait. She did not know, he was sure of it. The only one who could have told her was the old woman, and she was dead. Glockner did not know what to make of the fact that he had visited the old woman on the very day she died. Finding Fairview had been easy enough. He had parked and gawked a bit, just an interested tourist. The main entrance was open except for a screen door. He let himself in. He wandered through the rooms as if the house were a museum. Voices drew him toward the kitchen. A man and woman.

"I have to get back to her," the woman said, her voice playful.

A man's voice. "You want me to carry you up?"

Up. The massive staircase invited him. Since entering the house, he had passed beyond all ordinary restraints. He went up.

She sat alone, a shrunken figure in her chair, some medical contraption at her side. She turned as he entered the room and Glockner smiled and bowed.

"Who are you?"

But he had seen the portrait now. He went to it and stood studying it. No doubt was possible. It was a Ford. The sound of the old woman's breathing distracted him.

"Thank you," he said.

He left the room, went down the stairs and out to his car, meeting no one. It occurred to him now that he could have walked off with the portrait. But that kind of possession did not interest him. He would own it by becoming identified with its discovery. He would write of it. He would deprive Mason of the coup. Gearhart Glockner would introduce it to the art world. He was confident that he could gain the cooperation of his student, Peggy Sinclair. Imagine a kid that age owning a painting worth millions.

15

Phil Keegan's wife had been in her forties when she died, leaving him and the girls bewildered and alone. His daughters were married now and living a thousand miles away in two directions. Phil's life had found a groove that depended on at least ten hours of work a day and his friendship with Roger Dowling. Phil was not given to self-pity, but he couldn't help mentioning that Margaret Sinclair had outlived his wife by half a century.

"Margaret was a widow at twenty, Phil."

"Yeah."

Dead in her extreme old age, yet Cy Horvath was for conducting an investigation because Monica Pippen in the Medical Examiner's office had a gift for fictional reconstruction of events, he complained.

"Monique," Roger Dowling corrected. "Phil, the most that could be shown would be that the nurse was negligent, and even that is doubtful. She was as helpful as the old woman let her be."

"Did Cy talk with you?"

"Yes. And I told him I visited Margaret the morning of the day she

82

died. I brought her communion. I was also called to give her the last sacraments."

"Was she alive?"

"Probably not. I administered them conditionally."

"So where's the negligence?" Phil flourished his cigar. The Cubs were on the tube but they had cut the sound when the home team fell behind by eight runs in the first inning. "Just kidding."

"Phil, the reason Dr. Pippen or anyone else might ask about Margaret's death is that she died of asphyxiation. Lack of oxygen. But oxygen was always kept next to her chair and she was under twenty-four-hour nurse's care."

"Why the hell didn't someone say something at the time?"

"Because of her age."

"You think someone killed her?"

"Let me tell you how it was at Fairview."

Roger told him of poor dough-faced Honora Brady with her penciled brows and puzzled expression. The woman was lazy, no doubt of that, and looking after Margaret had been a dull and routine assignment, day after day after day, with nothing happening, no change in the patient except that she grew steadily older. Her emphysema was controlled by oxygen, Margaret could administer it to herself, and if Honora had often left the old lady alone, something easily imaginable, there surely had been no malice in it. She may have been sent for lilacs as she said.

"So what are you talking negligence for?"

"I'm not suggesting a crime occurred, Phil. But Monique Pippen could perhaps make a case for negligence."

"The prosecutor would love that."

"Phil, neither of us wants any fuss made of this. That's why it's important to know what did happen. I think Margaret's nurse went AWOL for ten or fifteen minutes, during which time the attack came. She wouldn't have been there to help, but even if she had been, the chances are Margaret would have fended for herself. I've seen her do it: wave off the nurse, put the mask to her mouth, and turn on the flow of oxygen. The nurse knew all this. She wouldn't have thought her absence endangered her patient's life."

"How do you know she was playing hooky?"

"Something she said."

"That she was out gathering lilacs?"

"The chef who is infatuated with her thinks a man came to see her. A bearded man. Of course Cy thought at once of Terence Sinclair. He was at the house that day and wears a beard."

Phil groaned. "The family complaining?"

"No."

On the TV there was a shot of the bleacher crowd going nuts, so they turned up the sound and for the next several hours enjoyed one of the most dramatic comebacks in Cubs history. The excitement drove out the annoyance Phil had felt listening to Roger talk about Margaret Sinclair's death and it didn't come up again before he left, but on the way home he decided to stop by his office.

Strange how a familiar place looked different at different times of the day. In the daytime, his apartment did not seem quite home since he was so seldom there before dark; and, if night work was not rare, still the halls and offices were not what they were during the day. Not that he was going to his office. He went to Records and checked out the names of the officers who answered the 911 from Fairview the day Margaret Sinclair died. The first thing he noticed was the name of the woman who had placed the call: Honora Brady. The nurse. The report was routine. Elderly woman found dead in chair. The nurse told them this had been expected daily. Age of deceased, ninety-five. It was hard to fault the officers. Plus, they might have been a little intimidated roaring up to the Sinclair mansion. If they had started asking a lot of accusing questions, chances are they would have been taken to task for that.

Keegan did go to his office then, got comfortable behind the desk, and lit a cigar, which made three over his quota for the day. Pippen was just woolgathering, going to Cy with a what-if account of Margaret Sinclair's death. Had she even known what Roger Dowling had told Phil, that old Mrs. Sinclair had a goof-off nurse who was in the habit of leaving the old lady to her own devices? The nurse said she was gone for a few minutes to cut some lilacs for her patient. If Monique ever learned what the chef had told Roger Dowling, Keegan feared he would never hear the end of the death of Margaret Sinclair. Why had Roger told him all these things? Phil decided that the pastor of St. Hilary's only wanted to alert his old friend so he and the department wouldn't be subject to criticism.

The worrisome thing was that some Sinclair would get it into his or her head that the Fox River police had failed to act competently when they showed up at Fairview and decide to raise hell about it. Phil did not like to think what Robertson would do with a weapon like that.

Roger Dowling's superiors left him alone to run his parish, but Phil Keegan was under the command of Chief Robertson, a political hack who had been wished on the department by a mayor who had beat the grand jury out of town when his term was up and was now living the good life in San Miguel de Allende. Robertson had been reappointed by two successors and Phil had given up hoping he was merely a temporary phenomenon. Besides, an alternative might be worse. Might be. He found that difficult to believe.

He smoked half his cigar before snuffing it out. He had made up his mind. It went against the grain in several ways. It seemed a concession to that cloudhead Pippen; it seemed to call into question the conduct of the officers who had gone to Fairview; it was the worst kind of speculative inquiry. He would tell Cy to halt his unofficial investigation. Keegan simply did not see how the department ran any risk of a charge of incompetence.

He was still at his desk when the news about Regis Factor came in. Margaret Sinclair's chef had been found dead in his room at Fairview.

"It looks like suicide, Captain."

"How did he do it?"

"An overdose." The officer cleared his throat. "An overdose of oxygen."

16

The leaden light of dawn lifted Fox River into silhouette but there was the promise of pink on the teeth of the sierra of downtown buildings when Cy Horvath sped through the city toward Fairview, his eyes sticky with sleep.

"I'll be there when you get there," Keegan had said.

"Where are you now?"

"In the office."

It was not yet five o'clock. Lilian had moaned when the phone rang and she moaned again when Cy got out from under the covers and sat in momentary stupor on the edge of the bed. Either Keegan had gotten up very early or he had never been to bed. Cy dressed in the semi-dark and used an electric shaver as soon as his hands were free. Regis. When someone you've just met dies you think he only lived a week. Cy patted Lilian as he left the room and she moaned in response.

At Fairview an officer stood guard at the front door, which meant that his partner was inside with Keegan.

"Where's the body?"

"I better show you." But he hesitated, as if he would be deserting his post. Cy looked at the three cars parked in the drive. The east was aglow now and the air was filled with the sound of birds.

"Let's go."

The nurse, wrapped in an orange robe and wearing large puffy slippers, sat in a straight-backed chair in the upstairs hallway. Her open mouth and tangled hair didn't help. She looked the way she would look when she was an old woman. Cy sent the officer back to the door and said to Honora Brady, "What happened?"

"He's dead! Regis. In there." Horror shone in her eyes as they darted down the hall. Keegan and the other officer were in the room.

"Tell me about it."

"He did it with Mrs. Sinclair's oxygen. Taped it to his face and turned it on."

"You found him?"

"No! I woke up when the police came."

"You called the police?"

She looked at him as if he were retarded. She hadn't called the police.

"The housekeeper?"

Honora snorted. "She's so drunk she doesn't know what happened."

"The police came and woke you up and then what?"

"I took them up here and showed them where Regis's room was and . . ."

Cy went into the room where Keegan was leaning forward, examining the body. Regis, fully dressed, lay on a huge bed beside which stood the contraption that had supplied Mrs. Sinclair with oxygen. But it was the color of the face and the bulging eyes that hit Cy. Keegan looked back over his shoulder.

"Adhesive tape, Cy. Wrapped right around his head."

"You call the medical examiner?"

"Heidl did." Heidl was the officer with Keegan. He looked as if he wanted to get away from the gruesome scene and Cy told him to go down with his partner.

"You going to want us any more, Captain?"

"Make your report."

That meant go, and Heidl went.

"You figure he taped himself up like this, Cy?"

"You see who's out in the hall?"

"The nurse?"

"Regis was in love with her."

"With the nurse?"

It was incredible, particularly when one had seen Honora in her present condition. When Dolly came to an hour later, under the ministrations of Agnes Lamb, who was summoned to the scene by Keegan, she looked better than Honora had.

"I am going to leave the house today," Honora said. "Today is the day I was to move out and now this has to happen."

"When did you last talk to Regis?" Cy asked her.

"What do you mean, talk to him?"

"Come on, Honora, cut it out. The man's dead."

"Well, I didn't do it!"

"He loved you."

"Who told you that?"

"Didn't he?"

"I don't know if he did or not. It didn't matter."

"You got someone else?"

"You have no right to ask me that."

Did that mean yes or no? Cy wished Agnes was in on this, but she was with Dolly. She had given the housekeeper an ounce of bourbon and that seemed to restore her.

"Sober her up and she'd be useless," Agnes said.

Honora was disgusted with Dolly and as disgusted with Regis as respect for the dead permitted.

"Who called the police, Honora?"

She didn't know. Keegan had joined them.

"Maybe he did."

"Regis?"

Phil nodded. "She can help us out on times."

"She" was Monique Pippen who had come running up the staircase, her open coat billowing, two assistants at her sides, and sailed into the room Keegan indicated.

"You think Regis called the police to tell them they would find his dead body here?"

Honora seemed to be appraising the idea as she expressed it. She fell silent.

"It was a man who called 911?"

88

"We'll check."

When Pippen eventually emerged from the room, following her assistants, who carried the body bag, she joined them.

"That's a weird one," she said.

"Try this," Keegan said. "He calls 911, tapes that thing on his face, turns it on full blast and is dead as a mackerel when the police arrive."

Cy said, "They had to roust the house first, and that meant waking up Honora Brady. That took time."

"I'll get an answer to that," Pippen said. "If it is suicide, it's a new way. Drowning in oxygen."

"Fish do it all the time." Cy and Pippen looked at Keegan, who stared back at them defiantly. "And find out where all the Sinclairs were when this happened."

Cy thought of Terence, the bearded Sinclair, but said nothing. Phil would expect him to make the connection. Terence had been at the house on the day old Margaret Sinclair died.

17

Honora Brady was a graduate of the nursing school of St. Nicholas Hospital. From the day she entered the program she had hated it. She was not a good student, and the smells and hurry and people of the hospital made her want to go hide in her room. Nursing became like singing: She had to be near someone who could carry the tune so her own unsteady voice had something to key on. As a student nurse in the wards, she never took the initiative, and always called in someone else if anything serious came up. Others were flattered rather than irked by this and she became well-liked, a distinctly new experience for her.

Why had she wanted to be a nurse? She had fancied herself a beautiful angel of mercy in starched white dress, winged cap, and dark blue cape, an object of admiration, even of love. What did bedpans and thermometers and whining patients have to do with that? She was particularly put off by the comatose or aged hooked up to machines and bottles and other monitors. Honora would have quit if she had had any alternative to nursing.

She didn't. She had pestered her parents for years with her

ambition, they had sent her to nursing school at some sacrifice, it was a dignified and profitable occupation for a woman.

"One you can practice throughout your life."

Meaning, after she married. Honora had sometimes been pawed by male patients, and in the elevator once an intern pressed himself against her backside and blew in her ear, but he got out on maternity and she never saw him again except from a distance. Forbidding memories of the pressure of his body against hers became a spiritual struggle she seldom won.

When she became an RN, Honora switched to General and it was another world. The nurses all talked like trollops, the interns and bachelor doctors took liberties. Honora listened and watched aghast, but she remained an outsider. It was a bloody stint in surgery that drove her to special nursing. This paid at least as well as hospital work, she could do as little or as much as she wanted, and when things were slow, she could always work at Riverside, a retirement home filled with ancient men and women who were docile and required only routine watching. It was there, at age thirty-eight, that she met Lester Pincus.

Honora had heard that God created a man for every woman, but it is up to us to find our providentially intended soul mate. It never entered her mind that Lester might be the man for her. She hadn't even noticed his interest in her until Joyce kidded her about it.

"I don't know what you're talking about."

"Come on. When you're out special nursing he hardly ever visits."

Lester had an aged grandmother in Riverside and Honora preferred male patients, so it wasn't by accident that he kept showing up wherever she was at Riverside. Finally, in the recreation room, she confronted him.

"My name is Honora Brady."

He nodded. She watched his eyes. She knew what she looked like. The only thing worse than the artificial brows she penciled on were the unadorned and hairless fatty folds above her eyes.

"Coffee?"

He meant the weak brew that was available in paper cups from a machine. She took him down the hall to the nurses' lounge and poured him a mug of real coffee.

He was a good listener. She found that out right away, because once she started talking it was as if she couldn't stop. You'd think she'd been in solitary confinement for years and just had to babble now that she had the chance, and she told him so.

"The Prisoner of Zenda."

He explained what he meant, the message scratched in the metal plate. He became pretty chatty himself. They got along.

But when she took a special nursing job he made no effort to look her up. Honora called Joyce, just to keep in touch, and had to ask if Lester had been around.

"When you're not here? You're kidding."

Of course she had looked him up in the phone book and he had said where he worked, so finally she stopped by the Fox River Historical Society. It was like a library, sort of, but with glass display cases scattered around, full of medals and silverware and weapons of the past. There were life-size models clothed in period dress, and even a replica of an early settler's cabin with a mannequin mother cooking at the open hearth, her husband and children watching from a board-plank table.

"Here's some coffee."

She turned to Lester and took the cup, looking him straight in the eyes. That seemed to be the best way to get his attention. She had deliberately come here to see him and she wanted to know what he made of that. It was there in the Historical Society, back in his office, that he pressed against her the way the intern in the elevator had, only front to front. She closed her eyes. She knew what was going on, she was a nurse, and afterward he was a mess but he kissed her face all over, then hugged her again, keeping his lower body arched away.

It was because of Lester that she took the job at Fairview. He got almost excited when he told her of the opportunity, but Honora had come to prefer Riverside. At least she saw him when she worked at the rest home.

"You're just trying to get rid of me."

"You take the job at Fairview and I'll visit you there."

And he did, just showing up; she didn't know how he got into the house. "I'll be your secret," he said. It seemed an odd kind of courting, probably because it wasn't courting. He apparently had no thoughts beyond their being together. Of course he wanted to hold her tight and all that and she held him off until his pleas melted her heart. If she had had any spunk at all she would have delivered an ultimatum. The truth was, she wasn't that sure she wanted things any different.

Sometimes, when everyone was asleep, they would explore the great mansion at Fairview. During the day, he did a bit of that himself, when she was busy with Margaret. "All that fuss over her," he said, and Honora knew he was contrasting Margaret Sinclair's situation with his grandmother's at Riverside. It was very strange, but exciting. Honora had never known anyone like Lester, but how many men had she known?

They never talked of what they did together and she certainly mentioned it to no one but the priest. In confession she called it "an impure act with another person" and, if asked if she meant fornication, was indignant in her denial. Were contraceptives involved? "Certainly not, Father." She always got off with a light penance. That's what Lester Pincus was, a light penance. There seemed no reason to mention him when Lieutenant Horvath asked her questions about the day old Margaret Sinclair died.

"Is something the matter?"

There was no expression on his face to speak of. "We're just trying to get clear on precisely what happened that day."

"The woman had a stroke. The medical examiner was here minutes after it happened."

"You called her?"

"I called 911 as soon as I saw what had happened."

He nodded in approval, but Honora did not like this questioning. God knows she had taken advantage of old Margaret's independence. It was such a bore to sit in the room with a silent old woman, listening to her rasping breathing, ready to jump up and help her with the oxygen, only to be waved off. Ninety-whatever and she was still as independent as you please. How differently people aged.

"You were right here when the attack occurred?"

"She'd sent me on an errand. When I came back . . . ."

"An errand?"

"She wanted her tea."

That easily she was past it. Lieutenant Horvath registered what she said without reaction, but it was nice to hear it aloud. It sounded so matter-of-fact. She certainly was not going to mention that she had been fending off Lester when the attack occurred. She hadn't been away from Margaret all that long and, besides, Lester had gone to check on her once. But there was no need for anyone to know any of that.

She hadn't known what terror was until the night Regis Factor committed suicide.

Ambrose Ravel, one of the auxiliary bishops, stopped by and asked Roger Dowling to give him a tour of Fairview. The cardinal himself telephoned to congratulate Roger on his appointment to the board of the Sinclair Foundation.

"It won't involve much time or effort, Your Eminence. I accepted only at the insistence of Margaret Sinclair."

"I'm told there's a great deal of money involved."

The foundation set up temporary quarters at Fairview. Two days after Regis Factor's death Father Dowling and Amos Cadbury met with Maud there for what turned out to be a first convening of the board. "We are the executive committee," Amos said, spreading a patina of legality over their discussions. It was agreed that Peggy would come on as administrator, at least through the summer, and be named to the board as well.

"My grandmother thought a good deal more of her than she did of the rest of us."

"I'm afraid Joel Cleary has had no luck locating the pearls and the other jewelry, Maud. These are the notes Margaret gave me." He passed some handwritten sheets to Maud. "I should have checked to make sure these things were in the house. I simply assumed that Margaret had done that. You see she says they're in her bedroom."

"Her hopes were chiefly pinned on you," Father Dowling said to Maud.

"I am not immortal." Maud said this as if she were the one who might need convincing.

Father Dowling agreed to stop by for an hour or two on several weekday mornings to help process the requests that already were coming in, to establish guidelines for ranking and selecting among them, and to draft form letters of receipt, regret, and of happy outcome. Eventually, they would have to hire an executive director, but it seemed wise first to get the thing underway themselves, to insure that it incorporated Margaret Sinclair's desires. Roger Dowling waited for a lull before telling the others what he felt they should know.

"The medical examiner's office is expressing some puzzlement over the circumstances of the cook's death."

"Nonsense," Maud said.

"Is that the extent of it, Father Dowling? Only puzzlement?"

Phil Keegan had told him of the ambiguity of the answer Monique Pippen had given him. Phil seemed angry that the medical examiner couldn't pinpoint the moment of death. But she would not give a definite answer as to whether poor Regis could have reported his own death before taking his life.

"I was a nut to give her an opening, Roger," Phil growled.

"You'd need a murderer."

"Oh, she's got one. The nurse. Not only that, she also likes the idea of the nurse killing Margaret Sinclair by withholding oxygen and then doing in the cook by pumping him full of it. After he just lay there while she taped the thing to his face."

"No signs of a struggle?"

"None."

"This must stop," Maud cried. "I will not have them engaging in speculation about my grandmother's death."

Amos was frowning. "Surely they don't really think someone killed Margaret, Father?"

"Maud, you know Honora Brady?"

"The nurse? Of course I know her. She was devoted to my

96

grandmother, always hovering over her, always at her side, despite somewhat high-handed treatment by Margaret. That nurse kept my grandmother alive. As for Regis, the man was twice her size."

Amos said with great deliberation, "I shall advise Chief Robertson to stop this inquiry immediately. There was nothing odd about Margaret Sinclair's death. I share your outrage, Maud."

"That might be more of a spur than a deterrence, Amos. Phil Keegan is handling it with great care."

Maud's eulogy of Honora Brady was overdone, of course, but it was ridiculous to think that the nurse had killed Margaret. If she had played any role it would have been because of negligence. She had told two different stories about her absence from the room when Margaret died. She had gone to get some lilacs for the room, she had gone for Margaret's tea. She could have been disporting with Regis, except that his love was clearly unreciprocated. The bearded man? But that must have been Terence Sinclair. The one possibility that could still disturb Roger Dowling was that Margaret had deliberately failed to avail herself of oxygen when she needed it. Was oxygen an extraordinary means of prolonging life? If so, she had no obligation to take it.

"That's why Pippen thinks Honora Brady . . ." He stopped when Roger Dowling put up his hand.

"It makes no sense, Cy. What had she to gain? Nothing. Margaret's death ended a very undemanding job."

Too bad such matters had to mar the first meeting of what Amos called the executive council of the foundation, but soon they went on to other matters. Maud made a motion that they seek historical landmark status for Fairview. She imagined conducted tours of the house and grounds. Was she seeking to protect the estate from her unhappy relatives? Terence Sinclair had now joined with Bunny and Octavio Salazar in the challenge to the will, and several other heirs were associated with the suit. But no other Sinclair could match the intensity of Terry's interest in overturning the will. For years he had lived in the desperate expectation that wealth awaited him when his grandmother died, pestering the old woman to advance him sums in the expectation of the eventual windfall. What would he have said if he had learned what the fragile old lady had done in her will? Now he was unlikely to stop short of reversing her final wishes. Amos Cadbury dismissed this threat.

"For two reasons. First, I wrote a will I know to be unbreakable. Second, they are represented by Tuttle."

"Tuttle!"

"Precisely."

Maud too was surprised. "They could so easily have discovered the man's reputation."

"Maybe they want someone a little sleazy."

Roger found himself almost wishing that the family could break the will. Most of the things that needed doing in the Church did not require money, only courage and a response to grace. He half regretted not making this argument to Margaret. Meanwhile, Amos returned to Maud's proposal.

"Maud, I can't agree with you that we should seek to have Fairview declared an historic landmark. On the contrary. I think we should put the estate on the market."

"Sell Fairview!" Maud was shocked.

"We scarcely need more money, Amos."

"No, Father, we don't, but it would be a peace offering to the family. The proceeds could be divided among them."

"Who could afford such a purchase?"

As it happened, Amos had several buyers in mind. Birch Coulee, the country club, was eager to annex the property as a site for a new tournament-class course. Various corporations, not all of them Japanese, could imagine their headquarters there.

"Did you ever discuss selling Fairview with Margaret?" Roger Dowling asked.

"No. But then I seldom made suggestions."

"And she never brought it up?"

"Neither one way nor the other."

Maud kept her counsel, but Roger suspected that she would be a formidable obstacle to Amos's plan.

"Come for a walk, Father," Maud said, when the meeting was over.

"I don't want the two of you conspiring," Amos called after them. His laugh seemed genuine enough.

They walked in silence to the river, where Maud looked out at the water. An island just offshore was reached by an arched wooden bridge over a narrow channel. On the high point of the island stood a chapel. Margaret had told Father Dowling that years ago, during May, the whole household would go in procession along the road and over to the island where the rosary was recited in front of the chapel.

"Is your husband buried there?" Roger Dowling had asked the old woman.

The question startled her. "Oh, no. No. He died in Italy. I thought you knew the story."

The island was clearly the goal of this walk with Maud. Halfway across the bridge, they paused. There was the sound of crickets, the croak of frogs, and from afar the sound of an outboard motor as a fisher headed out into the river.

Maud pointed out the chapel, then shaded her eyes and studied his face as if his reaction was important to her.

"Have you ever seen it, Father?"

"Your grandmother told me about it."

"That's where she should have been buried."

It had not occurred to Father Dowling to wonder why the body had been taken to the cemetery. If he had thought of it, perhaps he would have supposed this small mausoleum chapel was full.

"It wasn't in the will, was it?" The bridge was in the shade and he had a chance to catch his breath.

"She should be buried there. And Matthew too."

Maud seemed pained that her grandmother lay miles away in a cemetery while her husband, dead so many years ago, moldered in an Italian grave.

"It is a peaceful place," he conceded.

"It's where they belong."

"You must ask Amos Cadbury why the arrangements were made as they were. I'm sure he followed your grandmother's will."

"First I want to make sure you're on my side."

The island was the property of the Sinclairs and seemed to confer on them ownership of this stretch of the river as well. While other Sinclairs talked of contesting the will, Maud's interest was to retain the estate and get her grandparents together at last in the mausoleum chapel on the island at Fairview. Of course she would resist Amos's notion that they sell the estate.

They went on to the chapel, along an island path lined with flowers gone wild from lack of care, roses, peonies, forsythia. The general aspect of the island was somewhat unkempt but the approach to the chapel and the area immediately around it had once been carefully tended. On the final approach to the chapel, the path was terraced and Roger Dowling found the going easier. Maud's eyes shone as she looked up at the Gothic facade with the Blessed Virgin in her niche above the entrance. She pointed to the legend over the door. *In memoriam Elizabethae Sanctae Clarae 1944.* Maud pronounced the words unsurely.

"Elizabeth Sinclair," she said. "My little sister."

Her grandparents' reburial here was important to Maud, but Roger Dowling felt that he was being told the major reason why she would never agree to the sale of this property. She leaned forward as if drawn by some force, reached out her hand, and laid it on the surface of the door.

"Little Beth," she said softly.

"Is it just a mausoleum?"

"Oh, it's a chapel. Beth's grave is located beneath the center aisle."

"I'd like to see the inside."

"That's why I brought you here."

Maud unlocked the chapel door. Inside was an altar; several prie-dieux flanked the gravestone sunk into the floor. The stained-glass windows were glorious with the sun shining through them. There were other markers. One bore the name Stephen Renard.

"My son," Maud said quietly. She turned to Roger Dowling and her eyes were full of tears.

Son? Maud Sinclair? How could an old maid have a baby?

"Will you help me, Father? If you make the point to Mr. Cadbury, he'll listen."

Support her view that the foundation must keep the estate? For Maud this was far more than retaining her memories. Fairview and this island chapel were sacred places for her. No wonder she wanted both her grandparents here. Was there room for them? Bringing the body of Matthew Sinclair from Italy might pose insuperable problems.

"Bring it up at the board meeting, Maud." Did she realize that control over such matters had passed to the foundation?

"I'll have Peggy's support."

They walked back in silence. Her niece made four Sinclair votes on the board: Maud, William, Philip, a farmer in Auckland who had

100

not returned for the funeral, and Peggy. It would be Sinclair against Sinclair if the threat to contest the will went forward. Amos's plan to sell the estate to provide new funds to distribute to the family ran athwart Maud's obvious determination to keep Fairview and rebury her grandparents in the island chapel.

Like many sentimental people Maud prided herself on being hard-headed, but her emotions were undeniably engaged by Fairview, especially the island and its chapel. Father Dowling had not known how to react to her mention of Stephen. Maud imagined that her grandmother had told him everything about the family, including her marriage and divorce and retarded son who had died before he was a teenager. The house would be sold over her dead body, Amos Cadbury had best make up his mind to that. Indeed, she intended that her own dead body would end up in the island chapel with her son's. This was not sentiment, it was family loyalty.

She had not felt sentimental at Hathaway Hall for Peggy's graduation. Of course she had fond memories and had been aware of how long ago it all had been, but what alumna would not? The current administration could prattle all they wished about improvements and advances; the brochures they mailed certainly sought to suggest that the old school had been transformed, but Maud was struck by how unchanged it was.

Brooding over one's age and the passage of time was self-indulgent. In any case, it was not something to which she felt particularly tempted. But in that setting it was impossible to avoid the realization that the years that had taken their toll on her had left the campus and familiar buildings uncannily as they were when, as young as Peggy, she had received her diploma and gone down that long drive in her grandmother's great sedan into the wide world.

Meaning Fox River, Illinois. Maud had returned for her fifth reunion but never again. The spectacle of grown women giggling again like undergraduates and trading false memories of their glorious girlhood decided her. Maud had loved Hathaway Hall but she had never felt a desire to sentimentalize her stay there.

But at Peggy's graduation, Maud had broken away from Peggy's parents, Dennis and Vivian, when they left the refectory. She wandered down to the lake; the power of the place to evoke painfully sweet memories caused her almost to collapse on a bench from which she looked in a dazed way at the ducks gliding on the water. They might have been the same ducks of her days here. Of course that was absurd. But it was equally absurd that this place and its buildings should seem utterly unscathed by the years.

"Miss Sinclair?" Maud sat up with a start. The short bearded man bared his teeth as if for brushing. "I'm sorry to startle you. I'm Professor Glockner. Peggy took my course."

"And what do you teach?"

"Art history."

"I had no idea that was one of Peggy's interests."

"It is one of yours, though, isn't it?"

What a curious little man. Professor? In her day all the professors had been female. Maud wasn't sure she approved of letting this sort of person loose among the students.

"George Frederick Mason is a friend of mine. We share an interest in Clayton Ford."

"For heaven's sake."

He sat beside her on the bench, but barely. "Perhaps Mason has mentioned me."

"Did you say Laughlin?"

"No, Glockner." He laughed nervously. "I've become a synonym for Ford landscapes."

"We have several in Fox River."

"I know them well. They belong to your family, I understand."

103

Maud was surprised to hear this but she said nothing. How could this man know more about the affairs of her family than she did? Surely Margaret would have said something if those landscapes still belonged to the family. Maud had always assumed that Margaret had given them to the museum. God knows they had been hanging there long enough. Even as Maud imagined herself discussing the matter with Mason, she was certain that the curator was already uneasily aware of the status of those paintings. Did he live in dread of their repossession? Imagine the Fox River Museum without its famous Ford landscapes. It would contain nothing of importance. Of course, even if the paintings had only been loaned, it would be a selfish thing to claim them, hang them in one's home, keep them from the public. Maud had been raised to accept the responsibilities of wealth and possessions.

"Where would the art world be without the generosity of families like yours," Glockner said unctuously, as if following her thoughts. "All the other Fords are owned by museums."

"How many are there?"

"Landscapes? Eleven besides those in Fox River."

"And how many portraits?"

Glockner frowned and pulled at his beard. "The number is disputed. As you may know, he did not sign his portraits."

"Why not?"

"Because he considered them lesser work. I tend to agree with him. Your niece caused a stir in my class when she mentioned that one of her relatives had been painted by Ford."

"My grandmother."

"It was not a portrait known to exist." The teeth appeared and disappeared. "I made a special trip to Fox River to examine it."

"Grandma showed it to you?"

"You must have noticed the portrait hanging in Mason's office."

Maud had sat on the bench because she had been affected by memories of her school days. Now this preposterous little man was saying things that made her everyday surroundings suddenly strange. She had a vague memory of a portrait hanging on Mason's wall but was nonetheless certain it had not been there the last time she was in the director's office. The subject of that portrait was certainly no Sinclair, but the style of the painting, now that she thought of it, was not unlike that of the portrait of Margaret hanging at Fairview.

"How much are Fords worth, I wonder?"

"I shudder to think what an auction might bring. But no museum would let a Ford go."

Glockner went on to talk of Sotheby's, of what Cassatts and O'Keefes and even the work of lesser American artists had brought recently.

"Twenty-nine million dollars?"

"The world has gone mad. But how do you price the priceless?"

"Are you suggesting that a Ford painting would bring so much?"

"Easily." He spoke without hesitation. "No wonder Mason is so grateful to the Sinclair family."

Of one thing Maud was certain: There had been no provision for any painting other than Margaret's portrait in the will. If those paintings, the landscapes and the portrait in Mason's office, did still belong to the family and if they would command the kind of price Professor Glockner suggested, they represented an alternative to Amos Cadbury's alarming suggestion that Fairview be put up for sale. Discontent with the will would evaporate in a minute at the prospect of the sums those Ford paintings could bring. Nonetheless, Maud realized that she would rather not have learned this. Glockner was poised on the edge of the bench, as if awaiting her reaction. Had he told her these things to stir up trouble? If he was at all like Mason, that would be perfectly imaginable.

"What attracts a person to art history, Professor Glockner?"

It was not the response he expected, Maud was glad to see. He got a less precarious purchase on the bench, but continued to face toward her.

"Many things."

"I suppose all education and scholarship is a matter of looking backward."

His smile was forced and it raised his glasses and narrowed his eyes. "It must seem that way."

Maud crossed her legs, lay an arm along the back of the bench, and looked toward the buildings of the college. "Mediocre students, teachers with the limited gifts they have, mulling over books and art and music produced by people they would be very uncomfortable with." She turned toward him. "Do you suppose Clayton Ford had any premonition that he would fall into the hands of someone like George Frederick Mason?"

"That question is often asked about the great patrons and private collectors."

"But the patrons knew the artist and commissioned the paintings. He knew he was dealing with them. I'm thinking of later, the buying and selling, the intrigue, the outright thefts."

"Theft!"

"Napoleon filled the Louvre with stolen art, didn't he? The Elgin Marbles. Goering."

"You're numbering Mason with them?"

It was tempting to go on, but it would have been grossly unkind to do so. Still, it was a forceful realization. Imagine this fawning little fellow claiming to be a synonym for Ford landscapes! The argument for museums was that art is transferred from owners who enjoy it in selfish solitude to public places where all can come, but the curators and experts were far more snobbish and possessive than any private collectors Maud knew. After all, her family, notably her grandmother, was numbered among the latter.

Margaret had been a very selective collector, and how shrewd she had proved to be. When she began collecting Fords he was not exactly a nobody, but how many would have ranked him as high as he now was? It would be interesting to discover what Grandma had paid for her Fords.

Maud rose from the bench and the little professor scrambled to his feet. "I've not yet said what I came to say. It is my ambition to write a monograph on the Clayton Fords in the possession of the Sinclair family. They have been insufficiently studied. The portraits are completely unknown."

Maud was filled with distaste at his obsequious manner. And there was something else. He gave the distinct impression that such a commission would be repayment for what he had told her.

"I could not speak for the family."

"Will you speak to them?"

She said neither yes nor no. She let him think she would consider the matter. She had no intention in the world of becoming involved with this dreadful little man. Had Peggy profited from his course? It was difficult to believe.

106

"Say hello to George Mason," Professor Glockner called after her. "He will be interested to know we have finally met."

And now, weeks later, driving away from Fairview after parting from Father Dowling, the thought came to Maud as an inspiration. Amos Cadbury had not casually mentioned the desirability of selling Fairview in order to raise money to placate the Sinclairs who were dissatisfied with the provisions of Margaret's will. From the moment he proposed his alternative plan for Fairview, Maud had been steeling herself for a fight. She had taken Father Dowling to the island so that the priest would understand what was involved in Amos's suggestion. And now she had a *tertium quid* which would be acceptable all around. If the Ford landscapes in the museum were indeed still the property of the family, they could be reclaimed and sold and the considerable proceeds, if Professor Glockner's hints were true, more than gladden the hearts of all her relatives.

Peggy had begun working for the Sinclair Foundation a week after graduation. Her parents accepted the postponement of her European trip when she explained that she was putting it off until she and Michele could go together in the fall. She did not tell them that she intended to retrace her great-grandparents' honeymoon route. Michele was all for it. In the meantime, she would help with the setting up of the Sinclair Foundation and ponder what she would do with her life after the European trip.

Urged by her father, bread upon the waters, she dropped in on Octavio Salazar to be shown around his operation. She was glad she did. The remodeled firehouse in which Project Justice and Peace was located stood on a triangular island of land formed by the errant alignment of blocks in the original residential section of Fox River. No planner's grid had determined these streets. A plaque on the patch of lawn behind the building indicated that it was here that troops had mustered during the Civil War. The brick looked new, all the paintable surfaces had been freshly painted, the little parking lot was jammed with cars. Peggy parked up the street and looked at what her father called Project JAP. She saw no people. Meaning poor people. This neighborhood was once again an affluent one, the big old houses coveted by those who did not want to live in the suburbs. Like the firehouse, those houses looked redecorated and pampered. But where were the objects of the concern for justice and peace?

Bunny and Octavio were not interested in the direct action of relieving the sufferings of the underclass, important as that was. Far more important was the work of altering the structures that produced such suffering. What was the point of helping this person or that if the system of which they were victims was left unchanged? Octavio spoke with persuasive conviction, sitting in shirtsleeves behind his desk.

"We've got the Rescue Mission, Salvation Army, and thank God for them. And we support those efforts, morally, financially. It's the *political* task we concentrate on."

Octavio came from a wealthy Puerto Rican family, which ironically made him a member of an ethnic minority, thus able to gain easy access to state legislators, the local congressman, and the state's senators. He also worked with private industry, urging them to relocate in distressed areas so that the poor could be lifted permanently from their condition. Finding such economic ghettos in Fox River had never been easy, but Octavio's zeal was a flexible one. Besides, society had to be remade.

"Sinful structures," he said, his heavy eyebrows dipping in disapproval. "The Pope has said it all."

Peggy didn't know what to make of all this. She imagined Leon at her side and could almost hear his comments.

"This is why Bunny and I are outraged by the will, Peggy. Think of how we could put Sinclair money to work here."

"Did Margaret help you?"

"She was our original backer, and she continued to help. That's why we find it hard to believe she ignored the Project completely in her will."

It dawned on Peggy that Octavio thought she had come in response to the discontent already expressed by Bunny and Terry and other Sinclairs. Had that been her father's intention?

"We're going to fight it, Peggy. We've talked with a lawyer."

"Amos Cadbury?"

"He's the enemy. Who talked the old lady into changing her will? That's the question. An old lady in her nineties."

"Any news about the jewelry Margaret left to Bunny?"

He rolled his dark eyes. "Don't get her started on that. Cadbury was going to take care of everything but nothing has happened."

The foundation would dispense several million dollars a year and the first applications that Peggy read made Bunny and Octavio look typical. Amos Cadbury was relying on Father Dowling to separate the wheat from the chaff. It looked as if they would give an enormous number of small grants, sending money where it was really needed.

"We will support Bunny too," Amos said.

"A peace offering?"

"Your great-grandmother gave them money. I think we should follow her guidance."

Peggy wondered if Mr. Cadbury was more worried about the contesting of the will than he let on. Joel Cleary, the young lawyer who had been deputized by Amos Cadbury to help her work out a statement of purpose and conditions for receiving money from the foundation, dismissed this. But then he showed her his crossed fingers.

"I doubt that Amos is anxious to have it become a matter of dispute. Selling Fairview was meant to raise money to placate the heirs." He smiled. "The other heirs."

Joel had been present at the reading of the will the day Margaret was buried. There was no wedding band on his finger. He was bright and fun and very efficient. Peggy came to enjoy her work more than she would have thought possible. The first time Joel asked her out they played tennis.

"So we both went to school in Indiana," Peggy said.

"Is Hathaway Hall in Indiana?" Joel Cleary seemed unwilling to accord her school parity with Notre Dame.

"Were you an undergraduate there too?"

"Just law school."

There was something sheepish in the admission, as if he weren't a real Damer after all. Peggy had been to South Bend several times for football games, once while she was a student at HH. She still thought of Notre Dame as a boys' school, as where she would have wanted to go if she were a boy, and it had been a bit of shock to see the coeds.

Joel had been out three years, passing the bar the summer after

110

graduation, then joining Amos Cadbury's firm. Peggy almost envied him the clear path he had staked out for himself.

He was bouncing the side of his racket off the toe of his sneaker as they rested between sets. Behind them on the river road were intermittent sounds of traffic and from the river the insistent protest of an outboard motor as some boat beat on against the current. The clay courts on which they played were public and in at least as good repair as those at the club. It was Joel's suggestion they play here.

"For one thing, it's less crowded."

"Why?"

He shrugged. "Who knows? Who cares? Without a reservation there's no way we'd get on at the club."

"My game won't be affected."

It turned out she was as good as he was, unless he was underplaying, which she doubted. He did not look like a man who would lose on purpose, if at all. He had won both sets but she had taken a game in each of them. As far as Peggy was concerned, that was more than enough tennis for a June evening. She said so when he asked if they should play another game.

The difficulty with playing at Horton Park was that there was no place to change. They had come in tennis clothes and it looked as if they were stuck with them for the rest of the evening. Peggy presumed there would be a rest of the evening.

From the tennis courts they drove to Joel's apartment which, she noticed, had its own tennis courts.

"Yuppies," he said when she mentioned this.

Which is what she would have thought he was. He had prepared himself for a career in law, his foot was on the bottom rung of a ladder he was sure to climb steadily and quickly, he would end up with a great deal of money. But like herself he would start with a great deal too, if not exactly in the pocket, then in a trust fund. Maybe that's why he wasn't a yuppie.

The apartment was very bright and uncluttered, planes of plaster and glass, light-colored furniture, what looked to be a lime-colored carpet.

"It's patterned after one of the waiting rooms at the office."

Here she was, alone with a man in his apartment, but it seemed the most natural thing in the world. Not because she didn't find Joel attractive. She did. He was. And he seemed to like her. After all, he'd phoned her. She was already imagining how she would describe this to Michele, when he flicked on the television.

"We can catch the end of the White Sox game. How about popcorn?"

He made it in the microwave and they sat on the floor, the bowl between them, drinking beer, eating popcorn, and watching the Sox play baseball. Peggy hated baseball. She did not understand the game, because she had never wanted to learn. Surprisingly, she found the game interesting, and Joel enjoyed explaining it to her, though he couldn't explain the gestures a coach was making when a player was at bat.

"He's telling him what to do."

"Isn't he supposed to hit?"

"There's a man on first."

"Does it have to be empty?"

"Are you kidding me?"

"Joel, I really don't know."

He left the set on when the game was over, turning down the volume.

"Have you read old Mrs. Sinclair's diary yet?" It was Joel who had brought it to her when Amos Cadbury read that portion of the will.

"A bit."

"Not very interesting?"

"When I was a kid I always ate an ice-cream cone as slowly as I could so it would last."

"What does she have to say?"

"She kept it on her honeymoon trip to Europe. Her husband died on that trip, in Italy. It's eerie reading the first entries, knowing what will happen, knowing she didn't know. I wouldn't want to be God."

"If you were God you could change the future."

"It would still be the future."

He looked at her. "You remind me of Margaret. I went with Mr. Cadbury several times when he had an appointment with her. I was there when she wrote the will some of your relatives don't like."

"How am I like her?"

"Things she said. Surprising things."

"Like what?"

"Once Amos Cadbury called her a matriarch, with all those generations of Sinclairs who would never have been without her.

'They still aren't,' she said. I guess she meant without her. It was that kind of remark. Ambiguous."

"And that's the way I talk?"

"You will in your nineties, anyway. Want more popcorn?"

"Do you?"

"We'll split one."

She agreed. From the kitchenette he said they'd have to attend a Notre Dame game in the fall.

"I won't be here."

His face appeared. "Why not?"

"Dad gave me a European trip for a graduation present. The idea was that I would go this summer."

"It's probably good for a year, isn't it?"

"I suppose it is. Anyway, I like what I'm doing." Right now, being in Fox River was pretty nice.

"Where will you go?"

"To the Amalfi coast where my great-grandfather died. He's buried there. Father Dowling has been on that coast but never at Maiori."

"Your great-grandmother liked Dowling."

"She certainly trusted him."

113

21

Putting through the call to Parker was one of the most significant deeds George Frederick Mason had performed as director of the Fox River gallery. The question was whether the deed was befitting the director. In any case, it was a turning point.

Getting the number had been an accomplishment in itself, since he didn't want to leave a trail that later could be followed. "Mason? Ah yes, I remember when he was sniffing around everywhere trying to get in touch with Parker." The imagined, haughty voice did not match Glockner's, but it was of Gearhart Glockner he thought. To deliver himself over to the tender mercies of the Glockners of the art world was a definition of professional suicide. On the other hand was the instant dizzying fortune represented by the Ford portrait.

Maud had told him of Glockner's importunate request and, if her disdainful account had been reassuring, Mason waited in trepidation for her to mention the portrait missing from his office wall. She did not. When she left, in his outer office with Hazel Knutsen as witness, he brought Maud's hand to his lips. He felt like groveling at

114

her feet, kissing her shoe. Hazel's eyes followed him as he drifted back into his office.

He did not doubt that the painting that had hung in his private office for years was an authentic Ford. Prints and microfilms of the extant portraits were inconclusive, of course, but he had spent a total of forty-eight hours with three undoubted Ford portraits and had satisfied himself that the portrait of a subject known only by name at which he had gazed for years was indeed the work of Clayton Ford. The brush strokes alone did not prove it, nor did the liberal use of cadmium white, picked up probably from Sargent's *Fountain in the Villa Torloni*, nor even the use of charcoal in conjunction with oil, though all these together constituted a powerful argument. The matter went beyond argument when he noticed what had never been noticed before. On the back of the canvas, in the upper left-hand corner, *cf*, followed by a date. A curator's identification? That had been his first thought, with the date a date of purchase. But all three of the portraits had what he took to be initials and the only link between the paintings was the painter; they had never in their subsequent history been in the care of a single person, the putative author of those initials. Moreover, two of the dates definitely matched the times when the paintings were done. Mason flew back to Fox River with a conclusive criterion of the authenticity of the portrait.

His portrait, as he thought of it. The only one who seemed to notice its absence from his wall was Hazel Knutsen.

"Where is she?"

"Normally she's kept in the vault."

"I prefer it here. I've always thought she's keeping an eye on you."

When he returned from the inspection of other Ford portraits, he remained calm. A lesser man would have raced from the airport to the gallery, rushed to the vault, pulled out the portrait, turned it around, and studied the upper left-hand corner. Either the initials would be there or they would not. If they were . . .

But he chose to prolong the agony, not least because of the implications for his future deeds if he authenticated the portrait as a Ford. He introduced another step. He went from the airport to his apartment, had a good night's sleep, and in the morning telephoned young Peggy Sinclair.

"She's not here," her mother said in the guarded tone of one who

115

hadn't recognized his voice. No reason why she should, of course, although he liked to think of himself as practically a member of the family.

"George Frederick Mason," he said, as if owning up to something. "I was hoping to get a look at the portrait of Margaret Sinclair."

"Always on the prowl, aren't you?"

He tittered, although he did not quite like the implications of the remark. Still, Vivian was being playful and that restored his sense of closeness. "I hope she hasn't given it away."

"The portrait? Oh, no. It's here. Come now if you want to see it. I'll be here until lunchtime."

"I'd hoped to give you lunch."

"That's what I had in mind."

Well, well. The flirtatiousness of the middle-aged matron was a subject on which George Frederick Mason was an unwilling author- ity. His volunteer tour guides all signed up in the hope of adventure although God knows what most of them would do if a real chance for dalliance presented itself. He had learned the unseriousness of the arch remark, the coquetry, the lidded look. He told Vivian Sinclair he would be there before she could say Clayton Ford.

"I spent ten minutes trying to remember who Clayton Ford was," she said when she opened the door to him.

A study in yellow and white, she stepped aside and in he went. Following her instructions he went right on up the stairs and down the hall. He stopped in the doorway and Vivian walked right into him. He turned and she looked up, flustered, wary, as if she expected him to lunge at her.

"We're all alone," she said in a thin voice.

"Is the portrait in this room?"

"Yes."

They stood immobile, as in a morality play, but in the end habit, fear, and a disinclination to rock the moral boat won out.

The portrait was propped against the wall as if it were a bulletin board. Mason sat on the unmade bed and looked at it. The lighting was bad, he was looking from the wrong angle, but nonetheless the power of the portrait was undeniable.

Vivian sat next to him on the bed, but that was all right. The danger was past and they both knew it. She stretched her legs straight out before her so that her shoes almost touched the portrait.

116

"Be careful," he said reflexively and then, "Sorry."

"No, you're right." She pulled her feet toward her. "She was beautiful when she was young."

"Yes." And Ford would have brought out all the beauty that was there, by suggestion rather than by realist excess.

He got up from the bed, knelt, and turned the picture around, pretending to search all over the back of it but bringing his eyes finally to the upper left-hand corner. *cf. 7.iv.12.* It said something for his maturity that he did not shout. He put the picture back the way it had been.

"It should be hung, shouldn't it?"

Against all his training and instincts, he said, "It's all right there, as long as no one stumbles over it."

"Is it worth much?"

He laughed. "That would be difficult to say."

"Not that it matters. Peggy wouldn't let it go for the world."

"That's the real value of any painting. To be owned and appreciated by the right person."

"Or in the right gallery?"

He laughed. "Preferably that, of course. Then many more people can admire it. Not that I'm suggesting Peggy do anything but hang onto this. It can only increase in value."

"What do you suppose it would bring?"

That was twice. He looked thoughtful. They left the room and went down the hall to the stairway. She must have thought he was trying to come up with an accurate guess; he was looking for some way not to alert her to the real value of the painting. But if he misled her, that could haunt him later.

"Three million?"

"My God, are you serious?" She had stopped, laying her hand on his arm. She looked as if she wanted to run back and take another look at the portrait. Mason was beginning to regret having answered her question.

"At least that."

"But Grandma Sinclair couldn't have meant to give such a valuable thing to Peggy." Her eyes darted about as she thought. "George," she said, taking his arm and starting them down the stairs. "Please don't mention this to anyone. I hate to think of the dissension it would sow in the family if it were known Peggy had been given such a valuable painting."

He locked his lips and threw away the key.

"Now, what are we going to do until lunchtime?"

They drove along the river road toward downtown and the museum. Not that he meant to stop there. He wanted to be alone when he checked the portrait in the vault. For now he did not even want to think of it. The three million figure he had mentioned was low. That was what he might get through someone like Parker. There wasn't time for thinking anyway, since Vivian decided to make him her confidante and unload on him all her vague discontents. Poor little rich girl. Pampered, jaded, bored, it was a wonder she didn't drink, but at lunch she confined herself to two glasses of Chablis. He could have kissed her when she offered to take a cab from the restaurant, saving him the bother of driving her home. He did kiss her when the cab came, on the cheek, just a business lunch.

He parked in the basement garage, glanced in the direction of the vault, but took the elevator to his office. He read his mail, returned a few phone calls, then wandered from the office without telling Miss Knutsen where he was going.

To get to the vault he went through two steel doors with coded locks and then let himself into the vault itself. His pace quickened unwillingly on the way to where the portrait was stored among things that would hang on the walls upstairs again only over his dead body. Was the portrait a jewel among zircons? He put his hand on its frame. What if he was wrong? What if this canvas was no more valuable than those among which he had concealed it?

He eased it free and leaned over. He could not see, the vault was too dark. Turn on the lights? No. He pulled the painting completely free, carried it across the open space beneath the night light. Holding the painting in both hands, he turned it slowly. There was nothing in the upper left-hand corner.

His head drooped in despair. He thought he was going to cry. If he had, if his eyes had blurred with tears, he might not have seen the writing in the lower right-hand corner. Upside-down! He was holding the picture wrong.

He turned it slowly counterclockwise until the writing was in the upper left-hand corner: *cf. 7.iv.12.* He did weep now, tears of relieved happiness. He was holding in his hands an authentic

118

Clayton Ford portrait, one not previously known to exist. His mind filled with the mad thoughts he had had for weeks.

He carried the portrait from the vault and through the two steel doors, propped it against his car, opened the trunk, and put it inside. When he returned to his office he had not been gone fifteen minutes.

He sat at his desk for the rest of the day, grinning foolishly, in a euphoric daze. For now it was sufficient to know that the painting was authentic and that it was in his possession. He had hung museum paintings in his home before, there was a precedent for that, however risky a thing it was. That he was taking the Ford portrait home did not in itself mean anything yet.

Cf. 7.iv.12. He felt a chill when he realized that was the same date as the portrait of Margaret Sinclair. Doubt swept through him. Someone who had learned what he had, of the initialing and dating on the backs of the portrait canvases, had imitated Ford's style and then written the date of one of the authentic portraits on the back of the imitation.

That made no sense. But neither did it make sense that Ford should sign two paintings the same day. An artist might do that if he finished two paintings at the same time. Or remembered to sign one when he was signing another. The fact that both portraits were in the possession of the Sinclair family was not conclusive. The old lady might have decided to buy a good imitation of a painter she was collecting. Art forgeries exert a strange fascination, as do imitations. Mason had a vivid memory of a Japanese artist at his easel in Versailles making an exact copy of a painting hanging there. Photographically, painstakingly exact. The new bright colors made the copy seem more beautiful than the original. But then once Charlie Chaplin had entered a Charlie Chaplin look-alike contest and come in third.

He worked until the normal time, drove home, took the painting inside, no longer with any doubt at all that this was an authentic Ford portrait. If the portrait of Margaret Sinclair was genuine, so was this.

Later that night he managed to get Parker's number. When he had worked in New York, he had heard Parker cursed daily by Gabbiano. The man had no ethics, critics would not be surprised if he knowingly dealt in stolen property. When an Ambrosiana manuscript showed up in his catalog, setting off an imbroglio in Milan that lasted for months, Parker had escaped any charge of deliberate wrongdoing. Of course the manuscript had been stolen, an inside job, and of course Parker had done business with the Ambrosiana, but the suspicion of many that he had somehow blackmailed the guard and arranged for the transfer of the manuscript from Milan to his New York gallery had remained only a suspicion. George Frederick Mason could appreciate now that a reputation like Parker's had its plus side. After all, for all his bitching, Gabbiano had dealt with Parker. Now he himself was eager to contact the man.

He reached him from his office the following day, letting Hazel Knutsen put through the call, and arranged to meet him in New York. He would be there for an art history meeting and could slip away unnoticed. Parker expressed no surprise at the insistence on secretiveness.

"Give me a clue," Parker said before hanging up.

"Ford."

He formed the word but his throat was so dry it did not emerge. He tried again.

"Ford."

A pause. "See you next Tuesday."

Her mother had hung the portrait downstairs in the living room and Peggy agreed that it looked better on display than just leaning against a wall in her room, but nonetheless she was a little miffed to have the picture treated as if it belonged to the family. Peggy locked the diary in a drawer of the desk in her room.

Memories of her great-grandmother were kept fresh by the diary, yet altered as she read in it. For example, the entries she had read the night before. She continued to ration them, keeping an eye on the proportion of unread to already read pages, wishing she could hold herself to one entry a day, but that was impossible. Each page was divided so that when she opened the book she was faced with four entries. She could not keep her eye from sliding across and down the page.

The set space for an entry had made Margaret an expert in compact conciseness and she developed a kind of shorthand to save space. Brgt stood for Bridget, the maid who had accompanied her and Matthew on this extended journey meant to be a point of reference for the rest of their lives. The assumption was that they would never visit Europe again and so must fully absorb what they saw now. Peggy felt herself to be a flighty tourist by comparison. How many cities had she flown into, half looked at, gone on from, always on the unspoken assumption that she would one day be back? The camera took the place of memory, even of the contemporary look. Why waste time on a place once one had captured it on film?

Thus far Peggy had read about the train journey east, boarding the ship, the careful recording of the layout of the steamer, their cabins.

Brgt unable to function as maid with all the servants on board. It maddens her to be waited on by others and have nothing to do. She will not read and the pitch of the ship makes sewing difficult.

Thus far Peggy had two abiding impressions. There was no love lost between Margaret and Bridget her maid. And Matthew did not emerge clearly from her descriptions of him. More often than not he was a male pronoun, so much always there he became invisible. Or was it modesty that led to such reticence?

Joel Cleary had been deputized to help Peggy set up the computer at the foundation offices at Fairview. Peggy had been out with him twice since they played tennis, once to an unsavory Rodney Danger-field movie and once to dinner and a summer stock production of *Hello, Dolly.* Suddenly at his place afterward he had grown passionate. They had opened the glass doors of the balcony and sat half-in, half-out of the living room, propped on pillows, eating popcorn, their feet through the open doors and onto the balcony. What they were doing was lying on the floor and she was yielding altogether too much. She struggled free and got to her feet. His hand closed around her ankle, and this seemed to be the most intimate thing he had yet done.

"This is how the Whatchies express affection," he said, looking up at her. She dipped back to bring her skirt against her legs.

"On the floor?"

"He grips her ankle like this." He held her now by thumb and forefinger, his other fingers tattooing gently on her naked ankle. Her leg, concealed by the full skirt, seemed bare to his hand. All he need do was slide it upward. Which is what he did, accepting her invitation. She stood looking through the open balcony doors as if unaware of his hand but her mouth was open, the better to breathe,

122

and she was trying to figure out when she should stop him from doing what he was doing. In his arms on the floor she had technically been more vulnerable but now she was a slave girl on the block and the half-disdainful sultan was amusing himself by kicking her tires.

She stepped free of his hand and turned, her skirt swirling nicely, and padded to his refrigerator.

"What, no milk?"

"There's juice."

She had tomato juice, walking around the apartment as she drank it, slipping into her shoes. He was propped on his elbow, watching her. She was trying not to think that she wasn't the first girl he had lain on that floor with. It was ridiculous to think that he had been living his life in expectation of meeting her and taking her out. She really didn't know him. She had no idea what made him tick. She told him so.

"Oh, can you hear it? I'll have to get it fixed. Peggy, I'm a lawyer who works in a law office. I do what lawyers do."

What was wrong with that? Did she want him to say that he lived for the day he could run white rapids in the Colorado River, spend a week in a Trappist monastery, devote a year of his life to the poor of Delhi? He was just a good-looking, bright young lawyer, luring prospects to his apartment. Is that all he had seen in her, a tumble on the floor? An ankle to caress?

"You need something on that wall." She pointed to the bare expanse opposite the balcony.

"'My last duchess'?"

She turned in delight to find that he was now serious. She knelt next to him and offered him her juice. He shook his head.

"What would you suggest?"

"Well, you can't have Margaret Sinclair's portrait."

"The security isn't good enough in this building anyway."

She was puzzled by the remark until he explained that it was the value of the painting he meant.

"My parents have hung it on our living room wall."

He tipped his head. "I suppose it seems dumb to lock up everything worth stealing."

"It was painted by a man named Ford."

"Who went on to invent the automobile."

"And a method for crossing rivers. A most ingenious fellow. The

123

Norwegian form of the name is Fjord. He thought of changing his initials to A. F., but he couldn't afford it."

She had risen as she spoke and now danced out of reach of his hand.

"You're the first ankle man I've met."

And she blushed. It was the kind of thing she might say to Michele, but to Joel Cleary?

She telephoned Michele to tell her all about it.

"Marry him," Michele advised.

"I thought I'd wait till he asked before deciding."

Michele, speaking from the standpoint of pure or impure theory, advised a seduction scene.

"We've had that."

"Oh?"

"I escaped unscathed."

"Escaped? Peggy, you've got it all wrong. What is the proper response to obscene phone calls? Comply. Arguing from analogy, the point of a seduction scene is to be seduced."

"How's your summer going?"

"That's mean."

"I meant your writing?"

"Writing as therapy. I think some pharaoh collects boys as they approach puberty and ships them out of this town. I feel as if I'm living in a girls' camp. Remember camp?"

Michele went on about it, making Peggy half-wish she were ten years old again and looking forward to Camp Tonnadoonah. It was clear to her now that there was no point in trying to convey the sensuousness of a man's grip on one's bare ankle. Given the turn in the conversation, she would have felt that she was corrupting the innocent if she explained it to Michele. She thought of herself thinking of the convent and a sweet, sad smile formed on her face.

They drove to Cleveland for an Indians game and stayed on for a concert but the main point of it was to go to Akron and show Joel to Michele. Michele's eyes widened at the sight of him and then rolled toward Peggy.

124

"No wonder you've given up thoughts of the convent!"

Good old Miss Subtlety. "Joel is thinking of the Trappists himself."

"I love their cheese."

They got along fine, a real ménage à trois, as Michele said, digging Joel in the ribs. Peggy was beginning to wonder if this visit had been a good idea. It struck her that she gained by the contrast with Michele. By comparison, she must seem mature. Prettier too, although Michele had her charms. Joel made the mistake of expressing interest in her novel.

"How much have you written?"

"It's still in the planning stage."

"How long does that usually take?"

The question suggested that Michele had written a shelf of novels before this one. She avoided Peggy's eyes. "It varies."

"What exactly does planning consist of?"

Michele told him how Sinclair Lewis had gone about writing his novels and Willa Cather hers. She was very good on the notebooks of Dostoyevsky. Michele devoured literary biography, looking for every crumb of information on how a writer wrote, where, how much, with what, when, and how often.

"Trollope is very frank, but unreliable."

"How do you proceed?"

"I belong to the school that favors lengthy portraits of the characters before beginning the draft."

"So you've done a lot of writing on it?"

She rolled her eyes, turning to Peggy. "I want to hear all about life at the foundation."

"That's why we came. We're taking you out to dinner."

Peggy stayed with Michele and Joel went to a nearby motel. "Very impressive," Michele commented. "Very moral. Marry him."

"He still hasn't asked."

"Tell me you're kidding. He could eat you alive! The way he looks at you."

Peggy smiled, not wanting to discourage this. She had no idea how she and Joel looked from the outside, to the objective observer, or whatever Michele could be called. Of course Michele had never been guilty of understatement in her life, anything she said had to be taken with a grain of salt, still it was music to Peggy's ears to hear how Joel hovered protectively over her, hung on her every word, was a perfect doll.

"I disapprove of the separate bedrooms idea is all. How long has this been going on?"

"For years."

"Then you've never?" Michele's eyebrows danced.

"Would you believe me if I said no?"

"Ha!"

"Then yes."

Michele squeezed her arm. "Tell me everything."

"I'm lying, there's nothing to tell. You're not supposed to believe me."

"You're saying no?"

"That's right."

"I don't believe you. No, wait. The way he looks at you, sweetheart. The way you look at him. Those are not virginal exchanges."

"Could we talk about your sex life for a change?"

Michele pinched her lips between her fingers, then let go. "There."

"There what?"

"We have just covered my sex life."

"Are you really working on the novel?"

Michele looked abject. "Peggy, here I am, a mindless job to keep body and soul together, this great apartment, all the time in the world, I sit down every morning and just cannot get started. I've tried all the tricks I know."

She had tried writing the final chapter first. She had tried to get going by copying a page of someone else's stuff. "Flannery O'Connor. I was so depressed by how good she was I couldn't do a thing of my own. The idea is, you steal a page and then go on with it so what develops is your own, and then you lop off the stolen page."

"Why not just sit down, write 'Once upon a time,' and continue."

"Send me your first novel when you finish it."

"I don't write novels."

"That's obvious."

"I'm just trying to help."

"I need love," Michele moaned. "If I had a man like yours . . ."

"You'd write a novel."

"I'd live a novel. That's what I need, experience."

126

"How are your savings?"

"There I can report success."

"We have to make reservations."

"By the time September comes you and Tarzan will be on your honeymoon."

Margaret's diary came up and Peggy told her how things had gone thus far.

"Haven't you finished yet?"

"I try to hold myself to one page a day."

"How long a stretch does the diary cover?"

"Oh, months. More. Not nearly enough. Bridget is such a character!"

"Bridget?"

"Margaret's maid. Younger but a really sassy Irish lass. Matthew is more amused by her than Margaret, although she seems to love to write down funny things the girl says and does."

"For instance?"

Peggy told Michele the story of the German steward aboard ship who had designs on Bridget. All this was conveyed with a good deal of indirection and Peggy had trouble imagining Margaret so reticent and oblique. Finally Matthew was asked to speak to the persistent steward, something he did with dispatch, warning the German that if he did not stop his harassment of Mrs. Sinclair's maid, he would speak to the captain. When the steward did in fact desist, Bridget was unhappy, and unhappier still when Margaret teased her about it. Finally Margaret summoned the steward to do a number of pointless tasks about the cabin. He sensed the changed attitude in Bridget and soon all was well. Until Matthew came upon Bridget in the steward's arms, threatened again to go to the captain, and found himself scolded by both his wife and her maid. Peggy did not tell Michele the sentence with which the account closed. "Still I trust that B and I have not voyaged in the same condition."

Nor did she tell Michele about taking Monday off. When she and Joel left on Sunday, Michele assumed they would be driving through to Fox River. But Joel had made reservations at a plush motel near the Indiana border and it was there, slightly drunk on champagne and feeling thoroughly seduced, that Peggy gave herself to Joel Cleary.

23

New York was hot and muggy and dirtier than Mason remembered it. Gripping the cardboard tube in both hands, he took a cab from the airport, but was spared the usual chatter since this driver apparently knew no English. His name on the license looked Arabic, perhaps Iranian. It was conceivable that the next installment of the Mideast war would break out on the streets of New York. The sleazy look of the city fitted in with his reason for being here. He would be glad when he had met with Parker and his cards were on the table. Then one of two things must happen. He would become a rich man, or he would end in prison. Perhaps both. He had hardened himself with such cynical thoughts, but he was quivering with fear. The yellowing plastic divider between the driver and himself might be the grill through which visitors would speak to him at the penitentiary.

MUSEUM DIRECTOR STEALS PRICELESS PAINTING. Ever since making this appointment he had been experiencing an agony of remorse which periodically gave way to euphoric visions of a future beyond the dreams of avarice. He would take the money, invest it in gradual amounts over a period of years, creating an excuse for such an

128

increase in income. The IRS was only part of it, of course. He did not want Marjorie coming at him with grasping hands. Eventually, he could break free and . . .

How weak imagination was when it came to picturing an existence without care, means more than sufficient to satisfy any whim, the ability to go wherever and whenever he wanted. His mind offered him only the airbrushed lies of travel agencies. The nightly news gave a truer picture. Latin America? Forget it. Europe? Dingy or glitzy, overrun with migrant workers and tourists. The Far East? A cheap suit was not worth the risk of figuring in a bloody uprising. Japan was too expensive. The only possibility that did not threaten was Alaska, but he was not the type. Still, watching a film about homesteading, the camera crew crossing the great untamed expanse by train, he felt vestigial twinges of Huckleberry Finnism, one of the standard childhood diseases when he was young. A boy on a raft on a river sliding into the unknown.

But that had nothing to do with wealth. Before he boarded the plane for New York Mason had run the gamut of emotions toward his potential bonanza. He hurried through LaGuardia, a jaded jet-setter already nostalgic for the days when he had to scrape and save. But when the cab arrived at his hotel in the Fifties he found he did not have enough cash. The driver came in with him while he cashed a check. This had the effect of making him feel like a poor boy again.

There was a message from Parker awaiting him. An address on Twenty-first. Twenty-first! What the hell was down there? The note was signed Wolf, a precaution, so maybe the address was a precaution too. He went up to his room, rinsed his face, changed his shirt, and picked up the tube containing the Ford portrait. Removing the painting from its frame had been a delicate business, the first step in his act of theft. No, the second. The first had been spiriting it out of the museum. Where did such deeds begin? Mason had the sense that he had been fated to do what he was doing since he had been a mere zygote in his mother's womb, that he was no longer in control of his life. The thought relieved some of the pressure on his conscience. He could believe now that from the very beginning his interest in art had been mercenary. His often-expressed distaste for Gabbiano, the sorcerer whose apprentice he had been, could be seen now as simply resisting his own destiny. Marjorie and her ineffable daughter Ginger had deflected him for a time, but from the moment he hung the

Ford portrait of Bridget on the wall of his office he had, however unconsciously, begun to steal it. So that was step one. Hanging the portrait in his office.

He emerged from the elevator and as he crossed the lobby heard his name called. "George! George Frederick Mason."

Dear God. He turned. It was Ginger! Mason had the desperate thought that his careful plans were going to become unglued, and how fitting that his former stepdaughter should be the instrument of his undoing. It ran in the goddamn family. She seemed to have wings as she came toward him, her yellow cloth coat flying behind, her now red hair looking like a bird's nest, her eyes glinting with contacts. She was beautiful and in a split second Mason remembered the lust that had undone him with her mother.

"I don't believe it," she cried, moving in a circle around him. Others in the lobby looked on, wondering if they should recognize him. He had meant to slink in and out of town and here he was on display in the lobby of the Kuipper Hotel. "Does Mommy know you're here?"

"It was a spur-of-the-moment thing." He tried to release his hands from her grip. They seemed to be doing the Virginia Reel.

"She'll be furious."

"She's in town?"

"No! That's my point. But you're on your way?"

"That's right, that's right."

"Come." She tugged him across the lobby to the door. "I have a cab waiting. I'll drop you where you're going."

Short of devastating and public insult there was nothing he could do. Oh, later he thought of alternatives, but at the moment being dragged out to her cab seemed part of the destiny he had come to New York to fulfill. Ginger scampered into the cab ahead of him and he saw in retrospect how easily he could have shouted some feeble excuse, slammed the door on her, and disappeared down the street. But he got docilely in behind, even letting her take the cardboard tube to facilitate his entry.

"Where to?"

He read the address on Twenty-first Street. Her mouth fell open. The driver shook his head. He hadn't heard, but then Mason was addressing Ginger.

"What in the name of God is there?" she asked.

130

"An art dealer."

"I don't believe it."

"Parker."

"Parker is just around the corner. You could walk."

"He wants me to meet him there."

Ginger's expression sought exoneration from the universe. She took the paper and read the address to her driver. She seemed to adopt another language to do this.

"You look beautiful," he said, when the driver spun away from the curb. The words came involuntarily from his lips. She lay an impossibly long pale hand on his.

"You've become so distinguished. I wish we had kept you as my father."

Perhaps in French that was a compliment; in English it was only ambiguous. Who was Ginger's father now? He found he resented being thought of as a parent. Ginger was beyond the age when she needed a father. What she needed was a husband. The pale hand that covered his was full of rings, but none of them connoted marriage or even engagement.

"How is your mother?"

"Impossible. But you already know that."

"Where is she?"

"The Virgin Islands!" Ginger laughed and squeezed his hand. He found this oddly exciting.

The cab was marooned in traffic. He could have walked faster. In his youth he would have. And in those days one could ride from one end of Manhattan to the other for a few dollars.

"But what are you up to, Ginger?"

The question set off a recitation reminiscent of a patter song in Gilbert and Sullivan, charming even if one did not catch all the words. Her voice was musical, she looked lovely with red hair, her pale skin was rendered somehow translucent by it. The yellow broadcloth coat covered a white linen dress with an extremely full skirt that Ginger gathered about her legs in a provocative way. She stopped.

"You're not listening to a word I say."

"I'm having thoughts I suppose would have to be called incestuous."

The cab began to move. When she smiled a bubble formed in the

131

corner of her mouth and when it burst it seemed the most sensuous thing he had ever seen.

"How long are you in town, George?"

"Could we get together?"

"I'm not sure. What does incestuous mean?" But she dug her nails playfully into the flesh of his hand.

"We could find out together."

Mason could not believe he was saying this and the sense of having stepped into a role that had been awaiting him for all eternity increased. It was Manhattan, of course. He had always been incredibly horny in Manhattan. That's why he got tangled up with Marjorie. There had been other, briefer, sadder liaisons as well. Forays into the Village where coeds came for adventure, the hotel bars where out-of-town matrons were not loath to have a drink with a man about town. These fugitive affairs did not satisfy and Marjorie, of all people, had seemed the promise of stability, continuity, the acquisition of a personal history rather than a jumble of episodes. What did Ginger represent?

She leaned toward him and kissed his cheek. He realized the cab had stopped. He opened the door, then turned to her. She smiled.

"I know your hotel."

And then he was on the walk watching the cab move back into traffic. He had been deposited before a rather unsavory doorway. The address seemed right but he had not taken the slip back from Ginger. A powerful odor emanated from the door. No wonder. BAUER'S GYMNASIUM. Of course. Parker had always been a boxing fan. Mason stepped into the doorway and in three steps came to a window covered with cyclone fencing.

"It's a buck to go in," a voice said.

Mason got out a dollar and managed to make out a man in a cap whose profile looked like Play-Doh. There was a door to Mason's left. When his dollar disappeared a buzzer sounded and he opened the door and stepped into the all but overwhelming aroma of the gymnasium.

There were two raised rings, in one of which a sparring match was going on. In the other, a fighter threw punches at a leather shield held up by a trainer. Along the walls of the room, bags were being tattooed by fighters with taped hands. The fighters were easily recognized by their diffident arrogance, the sly glance seeking

132

acclaim. There was a great deal of sweating and spitting going on, but the distinctive thing about this monument to physical fitness was the haze of cigar smoke that hung over the room. Three-quarters of the way into the gym Parker stood, dark suit, snow-white shirt, subdued tie, only the gold tooth revealed by his smile suggesting affinity with this level of society. The art dealer was following the sparring match as if an international crown hung on the outcome of the lethargic exchange of blows. The fighters wore protective head-gear as well as leather groin protectors. Suddenly one of them threw a great, looping haymaker that caught the other on the side of his helmet, staggering him and making a parenthesis of his legs. Another blow to the midsection, delivered with firmly planted feet and a turn of the whole body, sent the reeling opponent to the canvas. The smile was gone from Parker's face. He looked around angrily and saw Mason. That was when Mason realized he did not have the cardboard tube containing Clayton Ford's portrait of Bridget.

Parker cast a disgusted look at the fallen fighter and came to Mason and shook his hand.

"You found it?"

"Here I am."

"Come by cab?"

"Yes."

Parker searched his face as he asked these questions. Mason was trying not to cry at the thought of the valuable painting in the custody of Ginger. What if she left it in the cab? She might forget taking it from him, think it had been there all along. Parker stepped back to get a full view of him.

"You bring it?"

"Yes, of course."

"But you don't have it with you."

Parker seemed almost cheered by this and Mason realized that it had been stupid to bring the Ford to the gym.

"We can talk here. Who would think we're talking business in a dump like this? Cigar?"

Mason took it, accepted a light, inhaled. The painting had to be safe with Ginger. She would realize he had left it, take it with her, phone him at the hotel later. Oh, dear God, let it be so. He was almost ready to promise God he would return the portrait to the Fox River Museum, its rightful owner; that is, unless the Sinclairs decided to

133

repossess their paintings and someone remembered the Bridget that had hung in his office. Of course someone would remember. Maud Sinclair for one had seen it a dozen times at least. So had his secretary. Miss Knutsen. What a damned fool he was to think he could get away with this!

"You think it's a genuine Ford?"

"I know it is." He blew cigar smoke toward the invisible ceiling.

"You're the Ford expert," Parker said. His brows met and merged over his meaty nose.

"I will tell you an infallible way to identify a genuine Ford."

"When can I see it?"

"You think it can be sold?"

Parker's mouth dimpled at either end and his lower lip rolled over. He nodded. "There are ways. It's discovered, much hullabaloo, I represent the discoverer, sell it, you and I are instant millionaires."

Mason inhaled deeply and nearly passed out. A millionaire!

"That's if there's no chance I get my ass in a sling. Tell me how you got it."

Parker asked no embarrassing questions as Mason told him of the Sinclair family, the landscapes, the portrait of Margaret not in the museum, the portrait of Bridget.

"So you're representing the owner, who wishes to be kept out of this?"

It was like being asked a question by someone preparing his income tax. "That's right."

"Who knows you got the portrait?"

This was the crucial question. A truthful answer would have stopped the deal cold. "Nobody."

"The Sinclairs?"

"No."

"None of them? It sounds like quite a tribe."

"None of them."

"That's hard to believe. There must have been a record of the gift or loan or whatever it was."

"Only a number is given, not a description of the paintings. The number is hard to read." He waited. Parker understood. "Even if it were thought a painting was missing, no one would know what it was."

134

He kept blocking the image of Maud from his eye as he said these things.

"Okay. When can I see it?"

"You know my hotel."

"I'll call you. Best we not meet there." Parker looked around the gym, but even he seemed to find it wanting. "I'll pick another spot. Anyone know you're here to see me?"

"No." Ginger's remembered laughter rang in his head. But Ginger didn't count.

"Good. We'll keep it that way. I'll call you."

They shook hands again. In the street outside, Mason felt at once elated and depressed. A scream would have done service for either. He ran to the corner coffee shop where, after negotiations, he was permitted to look at the Manhattan directory. When he had it he realized he did not know what Ginger's last name might be at the moment. Nor Marjorie's either. It seemed a negative comment on what we are pleased to call Western civilization. He had no choice but to return to the hotel and wait for Ginger to call. Maybe she already had. Maybe there was a message from her awaiting him.

He ran into the street, risked his life flagging down a cab, and as they started off uptown realized he might have telephoned the hotel to see if there were any messages for him. Stupid. Stupid. But there was no message. When he got to his room he would lie down and cry.

He had his meals sent up. He sat in the room for three days, but Ginger did not call. Parker did and Mason lied shamelessly to him. The most incredible thing. He had packed the wrong painting. He would have to return to Fox River to get the Ford portrait.

"You talked with someone else," Parker said.

"No! Honest to God, no."

"I don't believe you about bringing the wrong picture."

"All right, all right. This is what happened."

In his story, Ginger was the daughter of an old friend, not his stepdaughter. They had shared a cab; incredibly, he had left the tube; she was on her way to the Virgin Islands. He could not ask her to make a special trip to bring it back.

"Go get it."

"I thought of that."

"So?"

135

"She's cruising. I'm not sure of the itinerary. They'll stop at lots of places."

After a long silence, Parker said, "Call me when you get your head screwed on straight."

On the third day, Ginger called. He cried out with relief when she said, yes, he had left the tube; yes, she had taken it when she got out of the cab; yes, it was with her.

"I'll come get it."

Her laughter made him want to crawl through the wire and into her throat. "That might be hard. I joined Mommy in the Virgin Islands."

She promised to mail the tube to him as soon as she returned.

"Is it valuable, George?"

"It is to the owner. Let me give you my home address."

She repeated it back to him. After he hung up, he fell back on the bed and a moment later was in a deep sleep, making up for the restless, hellish nights he had spent waiting for Ginger to call.

From his motel room on the outskirts of Fox River, Glockner phoned Mason, to find that the director of the Fox River Museum was out of town. Out of town? In New York, came the prim reply, and the way the woman said it made it clear that Mason almost never went to New York. Professor Gearhart Glockner hung up the phone and flicked on the television, listened for a moment to the grunting on the HBO soft-porn movie. Geez.

As a graduate student Glockner had done research on the pornographic graffiti at Pompeii and written a paper whose thesis was that the data suggested a period when decadent hedonism had been within reach of the common man. Briefly. The golden moment had been ended by a flow of lava. Now Glockner had the sudden realization that he lived in a time when titillation that would have been beyond the means of an oriental satrap was only a videotape away from anyone. To say nothing of pornographic phone calls. Glockner had placed one once, in the interests of science, and had been more embarrassed than aroused. In *After Many a Summer Dies the Swan*, Aldous Huxley portrayed pornography as a sophisticated

137

pursuit, the indulgence of an elite who doubtless would have fought to keep it out of the hands of the many. Only a Vesuvius could put an end to the kind of garbage at his beck and call in the privacy of his motel unit on the outskirts of Fox River.

He pressed the remote control and ecstasy dwindled to a point of light and disappeared. If he had kept Mason's secretary on the line, he was certain he could have learned from her what he had come all this way in the outside hope of worming out of Mason. Glockner had been haunted by the thought that Mason or the Sinclair family or both would talk Peggy into putting her Ford portrait in the Fox River Museum and his old enemy would get first crack at studying it and publishing what he learned. Maud refused his calls. Mason wrote a letter.

It was too philosophical by half. The Ford collection of the Fox River Museum would not, alas, be enlarged, as he had so confidently hoped. Margaret Sinclair had disposed of her portrait in her will, and the museum had not figured in her plans. Mason went on to say that this setback made the Fords hanging in his care all the more precious, even if they were there only on loan. He was happily reverting to the received opinion that it was Ford landscapes that would stand the test of time, while his portraits would retain what interest they had because of the independent interest of their subjects, not because of the artist's rendering of them.

What nagged at Glockner's mind was Mason's mention of "portrait" in the singular. But surely he had mentioned two before? A telephone call might have settled the matter, but Glockner wanted to see Mason's face when he put the question to him. A fantasy suggested itself, thoughts of Mason stashing away a Ford portrait and surreptitiously putting it on the art market. If as stolen goods it brought him only half its likely market value, he would have a fortune. Of course it was absurd to imagine Mason having either the guts or the brains to do any such thing. Not that Mason was honest. A lifetime in art history, buying and selling, preserving and caring for works of art, eroded the moral fiber of the best of men. And remember that Mason had been connected, however briefly, with the notorious Gabbiano.

Who has not dreamed of coming into possession of an art treasure? There were out-and-out pirates, of course, thieves who broke in and stole. At a slightly higher level, there were the Parkers. But

138

even at the lofty levels there were the lately revealed shenanigans of the sainted Bernard Berenson. The art world was a world of hype: of hype alone in the case of contemporary art, of hype allied with genius in the case of earlier works, works like those of Clayton Ford.

After a week of concentration, of trying to dredge up from memory exactly what Mason had previously said, Glockner was positive his old friend had mentioned two unknown Ford portraits. The letter might simply have been ambiguous.

"Did I only mention one? My dear fellow, there are two. I thought I'd made that clear to you."

Thus might Glockner's suspicion, and hope, be puffed away by a single remark. He found himself hoping Mason was crooked. He grew certain that he was. He resolved to go to Fox River, face Mason down, destroy his reputation with the Sinclairs, and receive permission to do the monograph on their Fords.

He had come, he had called, he had found that Mason was out of town. In New York. Disappointment gave way to a quickening of hope. Parker was in New York.

Having come this far, he did not intend to drive back to Indiana and face a summer of wondering whether Mason was on the verge of a bonanza. He showered, changed shirts, and drove to the museum, took the elevator to Mason's office, walked in, sat in the chair next to the secretary's desk, emitted a great sigh.

"Professor Glockner. You remember me."

The woman moved her head in a birdlike way, a smile coming and going on her generous lips.

"You called earlier."

He ignored this. "The last time I visited my dear friend Mason was . . ." He threw back his head, ran his fingers through his beard, and studied the ceiling. So far so good. "Last spring," he said, dropping his chin, leaning forward, and glaring at her as if daring her to contradict him. His eyes dropped to the nameplate on her desk.

"Miss Janeway," he began.

She laughed and turned the nameplate around to reveal another name. HAZEL KNUTSEN.

"You've changed your name."

"Janeway's the name of the girl who worked here before. Why buy a new holder?"

She was new; he could tell her anything.

"Our main common interest is, of course, the work of Clayton Ford." No reaction from her. "Ford. The painter. Mason was so proud of his portraits. May I?"

He was on his feet and through the door of Mason's office before she answered. The wall was bare. He turned to the startled Miss Knutsen, who had run in after him.

"Where is it?"

"What?"

He pointed. "The portrait that hung on that wall. A Ford portrait."

"I don't know." She seemed more amused than disturbed by his accusative tone. Was she in on it? Glockner could see the portrait as if it still hung there. Now he was absolutely sure. Mason had claimed it was a Ford. He had ridiculed the idea, convincing, as he had thought at the time, Mason himself. Then Mason mentioned yet another alleged Ford, a portrait of . . .

"Margaret Sinclair," he said to Miss Knutsen.

Miss Knutsen showed relief. "Mrs. Sinclair was a good friend of the museum."

"Not friendly enough to leave her portrait, though, was she?"

"I know nothing of that."

"Have you coffee made?"

She didn't, but she was willing to humor him with a cup. Instant! Dear God. Glockner looked around. If he were in charge of an operation like this, instant coffee would be banished forever. He was seated next to her desk when Miss Knutsen took the call from New York.

"Mr. Mason," she said caressingly.

Glockner held up his hand, pantomimed his desire not to be mentioned. Miss Knutsen nodded elaborately. She was taking notes. After a full minute she read them back to Mason.

His instructions were for her to telephone Mr. Parker at the number given and inform him that Mr. Mason had been unexpectedly called back to Fox River. He would get in touch with him at the earliest opportunity.

"Yes, Mr. Mason," she said, her head rising and dipping, rising and dipping.

Glockner turned away when she began to read back what she had written, but only to direct his good ear toward Miss Knutsen. He felt almost solemn at this miraculous confirmation of his hunch.

Miss Knutsen hung up and Glockner turned and looked at her with complicity, waiting.

"That was Mr. Mason."

"I gathered."

The lines above the bridge of her nose deepened. "I hope everything is all right with him."

"He was always a mysterious person," Glockner said. "When we were boys." Boys! They had been graduate students of long standing when they met.

"I didn't tell him you were here."

"Just as well. This visit was supposed to be a surprise. Guess who got surprised." He shrugged and laughed. "Did Margaret Sinclair leave more paintings to the museum when she died?"

"It went to her great-granddaughter!"

It! Glockner shook his head, picking up her sense of indignation. "What a disappointment."

"Just a girl, too, of the same name as the old woman. Mr. Mason talked to the parents . . ."

"Peggy Sinclair?"

Miss Knutsen nodded. "Mr. Mason gave them some idea of the value of the painting."

Glockner closed his eyes for a moment. He rose. "I've taken up altogether too much of your time. I know there's no point in asking a loyal secretary to keep a secret from her boss . . ."

"Your visit?" She slapped at flies. "I won't say a thing."

He doubted that. He shook her hand. Odd how well they got along. Women as a rule did not like him. The beard, his stubby body, the glasses whose tinted lenses never completely cleared, even indoors. He held her hand longer than necessary. She had the kind of beauty he dared not aspire too. Armfuls of blond hair, ice-blue eyes, a bosom ample and plush. Lay thy sleeping head, my love. . . . She freed her hand.

"Do you eat lunch?"

"I was just going to run over to the Taco Bell."

They ran over together. She ate with a gusto in keeping with her Amazonian dimensions. Glockner toyed with a taco half full of crumbly hamburger and shredded lettuce. Miss Knutsen looked him in the eye while she chewed and he was reminded of the movie *Tom Jones*. A pink little tip of tongue emerged now at one corner of her

141

mouth, now the other. Her knee was definitely pressing against his. But when he pressed back she moved hers.

"Where are you staying in town?"

He told her.

"Water beds."

"How did you know?"

A silence. "It's what they advertise."

"Where does the great-granddaughter live?"

A call to the relevant Sinclair number brought the information that Peggy was at work, who was calling?

"Professor Glockner. She was in my art history class at Hathaway. Didn't we meet at graduation? I understand Peggy has come into possession of a portrait of her great-grandmother."

"Yes! I hope you don't have designs on it. The local museum is dying to get hold of it."

"If it's a Ford, I don't blame them. Is there the slightest chance in the world I might see it?"

There was. He came out of the booth and Miss Knutsen smiled when he formed a circle with thumb and forefinger. They walked slowly back to the museum.

He watched her go rapidly to the door of the museum, a classic figure hurrying toward the reflection of itself. The glass doors were an imperfect mirror of the passing parade, suggestive of the semi-unreality of the deeds of men. She paused in the opened door and looked back at him. Fingers waggled and she was gone.

25

Tuesday after the trip to Cleveland, at mass in St. Hilary's, Peggy stood to go to communion and then, remembering, sat down. She did not feel in a state of mortal sin, but she was. She had to go to confession before she could approach the altar. The prospect did not trouble her.

"I made love with the man I love."

That is what she would confess. It didn't even sound like a sin. That had been the odd thing about talking to Leon, realizing what a strong sense of sin he had. It dawned on her that the first step in being religious had to be the sense that one was in deep trouble and incapable of getting out of it on one's own. It needed grace and forgiveness.

"I don't have a sense of sin," she told Leon.

"Of course you don't. You've been robbed of it. I'm okay, you're okay. Do you really believe that?"

"That you're okay?"

He didn't even smile. "Are you happy?"

"Happy?" Of course she wasn't happy. Was anyone, outside of

143

television commercials, Dad bringing home the new car, Mom and the kids in ecstasy, the next-door neighbor rushing in with the new laundry soap . . . "Sometimes."

"I don't mean contented, feeling no pain, that sort of thing. Do you feel that you are what you are meant to be?"

You had to get used to Leon, but better him than other priests she'd met. Leon described the common human predicament; others looked down from somewhere else, giving instructions to the poor souls below. Still, it would be easier confessing what she and Joel had done to another priest—Father Dowling, say—than to Leon. Leon would be genuinely saddened and disappointed, even though he spoke to her as if she were living the life of a houri. She had never quite corrected him. He saw her both as herself and as the representative of her generation, of the spoiled young women of Hathaway Hall. Student Health Service was dedicated to the proposition that students will be promiscuous and gave counsel about, equipped for, and arranged for the rectification of the consequences of the sexual activity of the female scholars. Not to be sexually active was almost deviant—or so, at least despite Phonsie, went the official health service line.

Was it really true? Michele and Peggy had discussed it endlessly, speculating about classmates. The lesbians were the most doubtful of all, full of theory and borrowed rage, as if they were an oppressed group. But they had their subsidy, their offices in student affairs, their hotline. Michele had dialed it one night, to find out where the meetings were, but a husky voice urged her to stop by the student center, then switched her to a tape that assured her that her yearnings were perfectly natural and that she mustn't feel guilt. Michele vacillated between obvious eagerness to become part of the presumed swim of things and the attitude that she was saving herself for serious misbehavior when she got out of Hathaway. She had gone to student health and been fitted with a diaphragm, confiding to the nurse that she was having an affair with a professor.

"You didn't!"

"I did and she said, Hirkus? Hirkus!" Hirkus, sweatered, loafered, rumpled, taught math and rushed from blackboard to students, peering lasciviously at them through off-center glasses, rubbing the chalk with the ball of his thumb, specks of foam in the corners of his wide mouth.

The nurse's question turned Hirkus into a man of mystery for a week or two. Michele kept an eye on him—"I won't say I'm tailing him."—to see if she could surprise him in a liaison, but nothing manifested itself.

How childish all that seemed now. How childish her conversations with Michele over the past weekend seemed after what had happened on Monday. At mass, not going forward to receive communion, Peggy assured God that she was serious about Joel. There was something almost holy about their love and God, who had made them male and female, surely understood how it was. Peggy felt that the Cleveland trip and its outcome sealed their relationship. One of the most beautiful moments had been when he held her in his arms, their spent nude bodies clinging together, and whispered that she was his wife.

So how was she supposed to feel like Mary Magdalene, for crying out loud?

"How was your friend?" Father Dowling asked, and Peggy did not at first remember that she had told him she was going to Ohio to see Michele.

"She can't wait until we leave for Europe in September."

Joel did not come by Fairview that first day back as he had promised, which was just as well, with Father Dowling there. She had mixed feelings about being alone with Joel. She had given him rights over her and she did not know how he would behave.

Father Dowling frowned over applications for grants, putting them in different piles. "How did so many hear of the foundation so quickly?"

"This computer program is nearly ready. I'll be able to process them easily once I have the basis on which to rank them."

"That's the real difficulty," Father Dowling said.

He was right and the remark diminished the work she and Joel had done.

"Joel took yesterday off too."

He meant yesterday as well as today. Peggy wondered what he made of her reaction.

"I suppose he was visiting his family."

*　*　*

She would have liked to sit in front of Margaret's portrait and see if she could tell her of what had happened with Joel. The diary made her seem so near.

She wished she had kept the painting upstairs in her own room. Enjoying it downstairs was more difficult. She did not like to be surprised gazing on that remote and beautiful face. She knew she resembled the portrait. Her mother remarked on it, so did her father. If she were a New Age freak, she would develop a theory that Margaret had been a previous incarnation of herself. The only trouble with that was that their lives had overlapped.

The fact that the painting was valuable, very valuable, extremely valuable, had gotten to her father.

"It makes me nervous to have it just hanging there."

"It always hung at Fairview."

Her father sipped a gin and tonic and squinted at the painting. "I like it, but I find it hard to believe someone would pay a fortune for it."

"A museum," her mother corrected.

"The Fox River Museum is chock-full of Fords now," Peggy said.

"Who was Ford?"

"No relation," Peggy said.

"You don't know?"

She gave a sketch based on what she remembered of Glockner's class. Ford, Clayton, born Prairie du Chien, Wisconsin, 1880, early education local, Jesuit prep school, apprenticed to Howard Pyle, the man N. C. Wyeth learned from, with the intent of becoming an illustrator, his landscapes a record of where he lived, Illinois, Pennsylvania, Ohio, then upstate New York before he left for England. He ended up in Italy. If the landscapes were weekend work at first, the portraits were a means of fast money, but Ford could do nothing slapdash. The landscapes were in the opinion of some overdone, too worked, but the portraits had a latent tragic tone, eliciting the fragility and mortality of the most self-satisfied burgher. Or, as in the majority of them, the burgher's wife.

"And old Margaret had herself painted?"

"It was done just before she was married. At the Sinclair place. Ford painted in a kind of barn, and a maid named Bridget was painted at the same time. Her presence made it all right for Margaret to sit for an artist."

146

"How much did Mason say it was worth, Viv?" her father asked, and Peggy tuned out the conversation.

She felt more affinity with Margaret then ever before, now that she had fallen in love with Joel Cleary. The portrait had been painted just months before the wedding. In the diary the sitting was referred to several times, Margaret alternating with Bridget as Ford worked.

> Low crowned hat with a wide brim that shades his face even when his head is tipped back, open white shirt, breeches tucked into his boots, always talking, always laughing, the smell of paint mingling with the sweet smell of the meadow. The chair we sat in was placed so that we looked out over the fields. I stared at a distant windmill thinking oddly sad thoughts, it seemed so futile there, drawing water up and out of the earth in order to sprinkle it on the ground again, and he liked that. Brgt didn't like him at all, or perhaps she liked him too much. After seeing the ocean and England that he talked about we'd like to tell him what we think of them. Our pictures wait for us at home. Odd.

The passage was written as they passed Gibraltar, entering the Mediterranean, nearing Naples and the fateful stay at Maiori.

Peggy looked for premonitions in the entries of what lay ahead, but the diary was as much about Illinois as about the strange sights Margaret was then seeing. They had a tone not unlike the sadness she felt looking at a distant windmill when Ford was painting her. Peggy, ignoring her parents' jabber, felt a bit the way Margaret looked. The futility of things? Had Margaret, as she sat looking out over the meadow, thinking of her coming marriage, of a life together with the man she loved, been bothered by how little that was?

It wasn't simply that, after all the giggling and whispering and anticipation, sleeping with Joel hadn't been the end of the world. It had been nice, very nice, wonderful really, but the act itself, doing that with him, couldn't be the meaning of life. Peggy couldn't imagine sleeping with someone she didn't love, doing that just for the fun of it. Taken by itself, the fun just wasn't enough. It had to be with someone you loved, it had to mean something beyond the moment. She could see now that the point of it was to make babies. Not that they had tried to make one, he had come as prepared as she had so that was covered, but the point was you had to think of it. What they were doing was making sure it didn't have its natural consequence. But when you loved someone, that was the consequence you wanted. Otherwise, she might just as well go to bed with Michele. I mean, if a little fast fun under the sheets were the only point of it all.

In her wedding trip diary, Margaret made allusions to the chance of pregnancy. Odd, because some of the entries suggested that, with the rough crossing and the excitement of England and now on board ship again, they were postponing the big event.

26

Roger Dowling did not begrudge his work with the Sinclair Foundation but he was determined not to let it interfere with his regular pastoral life, one of whose duties was to visit the sick of the parish, something he did once a week. It was that practice which had brought him to Fairview and Margaret Sinclair. Now when he came to Fairview it was to look after foundation business rather than to bring Margaret Holy Communion. The only one who complained that he was not as available as before was Phil Keegan.

"Once the procedures are set, it won't take more than a few hours a month, Phil."

"You get paid?"

"A stipend."

He took it only because it enabled him to help Edna Hospers, whose oldest would be starting college in the fall. She could not afford to send him on the salary he paid her for running the parish center.

"I'll only take it as a loan, Father."

"Of course."

"With interest."

"Oh, I draw the line there. Usury is against my religion."

Peggy Sinclair was a bright if somewhat mystifying young lady. Father Dowling found himself wondering what view of life lay behind the face so reminiscent of the portrait of her great-grandmother. Her Catholicism seemed to have been formed largely by conversations with a flaky priest named Leon and a fitful devotion to the Little Flower. Peggy's obvious interest in Joel Cleary made Father Dowling wonder if she knew the young man's history. Marie Murkin would have just told her, but Father Dowling could think of no justification for letting Peggy know of Joel's wife in South Bend. Divorced wife, true, but insufficient grounds for annulment. And there was a child too.

Knowing this and watching Peggy respond to Joel's charms gave Roger Dowling a sense of how painful omniscience would be unless accompanied by omnipotence.

He came to Fairview as he had during Margaret's lifetime, after his round of sick calls. Now the last person on his route was Pinkie at the Riverside Home for the Elderly.

"Pinkie what?" he asked her when they first met.

"Little Pinkie." She crooked her little finger and gave him an undentured smile.

The nickname was developed from her family name, but he called her what everyone else did.

"Are you a Catholic?"

"That I am, Father. From my mother's knee."

"And what is your parish?"

She shook her head. "No you don't. They'll come with a box of envelopes and I just can't afford it."

Is that what being Catholic meant to her, money in the collection box? When he asked if she'd like him to bring her communion, she worked her lips and dropped her chin to her chest.

"It's been years, Father."

"Why's that?"

"I stopped going to confession."

"I'll hear your confession."

She threw up her hands. "That's why I stopped. They wanted me to go face to face, the way they do in Italy, just chatting away with the priest, if you please."

150

"Are you sorry for your sins?"

"What sins?"

"The ones you wouldn't confess face to face."

"Oh, aren't you the sly one!"

"Pinkie, feel contrition for your sins and I'll give you absolution."

Her eyes sparked. "Just like that?"

"Are you sorry for all your offenses against God?"

What did the phrase call up in her old mind? Her expression became sad but then she looked up at him and nodded. He made the sign of the cross over her and recited the formula for absolution.

"You didn't give me a penance."

"Do you have a rosary?"

She pulled a rosary with large black beads from under her pillow and held it up. He told her to say the Sorrowful Mysteries.

"I don't know the mysteries."

"Just say the Hail Marys then."

"All of them?"

"Yes. And the next time I come I'll bring you Our Lord in Holy Communion."

After that, they were good friends, and he stopped by whenever he could. She was a Cubs fan, poor thing, and he brought her a pennant for her wall and a cap to wear while she listened to the games. On radio. Television was for soaps. How she could simultaneously follow the game and one of the turgid dramas on the screen, Roger Dowling did not profess to understand. Perhaps it made the ball game tolerable. Phil Keegan shook his head when he told him about Pinkie and the Cubs.

"That's where we all belong, drooling in an old folks' home. You have to be senile to support that team."

The pre-season had been one of phenomenal success for the Cubs, always a bad omen. They proceeded to lose ten straight when the season opened, seven of them in Wrigley. Summer stretched before them like an infinite waterless waste.

A story in the Fox River paper about the challenge to Margaret Sinclair's will put the foundation in a bad light. The things that Bunny and Octavio Salazar could do for the poor if all that money had not been diverted into churchy projects of dubious value to society were stressed. Tuttle appeared on television in his tweed hat, speaking with uncustomary confidence about his clients' prospects.

He mentioned the name of Amos Cadbury at least a dozen times during the sound bite, conveying the impression that he and the premier lawyer of Fox River were working closely together in order to resolve the unfortunate differences within the Sinclair family. It was out of the question for Amos to respond. The quarrel, insofar as it was one, belonged in a courtroom. Courtrooms, unfortunately, were not what they had been. Amos could not discount the effect of such slanted publicity on a judge.

"We must placate your relatives," he said to Maud.

"None of them needs money, Amos. But Margaret did treat them badly."

"The proceeds from the sale of Fairview . . ."

"No. Never. Not Fairview."

Amos had no desire to add another Sinclair to those arrayed against him. And then Maud mentioned her family's paintings on loan to the Fox River Museum.

"You're sure they're on loan and not gifts."

"There must be a way of finding out."

Not only did a search fail to turn up any deed of gift, what Amos did find suggested that the paintings were indeed on loan.

"Are they valuable, Maud?"

"Amos, if they are on loan, I think our family bickering is over."

"Father Dowling," Peggy called, catching up with him after he had left the house. He stopped and waited. She stood in front of him and tried out various expressions, then gave up. "Remember what you said the day when I came back from seeing my friend in Ohio?"

"No."

"About Joel. You said he must have been visiting his family too. What did you mean?"

"What I said."

"But his family lives here in Fox River."

"His parents do, yes."

And so he told her, wishing the task had fallen to someone else, but doing it because it was obvious that Joel had said nothing to Peggy. But why should he unless there was something serious on the horizon? Perhaps only Peggy thought so. All the more reason why she should know about Joel's wife and child in South Bend.

She took it well, nodding through the tale, her expression much the same as when they discussed a grant application. Thank God it did not register more strongly with her than it did.

But when they parted and he got to his car he looked back. Peggy had gone onto the veranda and sat in a white wrought-iron chair looking out toward the river. She might have been her great-grandmother, carrying the burden of almost a century's knowledge.

Roger Dowling decided he would speak to Joel too.

27

Tuttle tried to accustom himself to the thought that his efforts on behalf of the Salazars were going to be successful, and in a way no one had even dreamed of. The Ford paintings in the Fox River Museum could be reclaimed by the family, and it was the suggestion of the officers of the Sinclair Foundation that they be sold and the considerable proceeds distributed among those members of the family who had been disappointed by Margaret's will. There was little doubt that Amos Cadbury was behind the decision of the board.

"I had no idea he would agree so easily," Tuttle told a beaming Terence Sinclair.

"Agree?"

Tuttle held his tweed hat behind him and spun its rim through his fingers like Arab worry beads. What he was saying was not entirely bullshit; even so, he was relieved at Terry's lack of skepticism. Of all the Sinclairs, he was most at ease with Terry. He could even imagine asking him to share Chinese food with Peanuts. Another with whom the world had hitherto dealt harshly. But now the sun was breaking through. Tuttle had been startled to learn of the kind of money the portrait of Margaret Sinclair could bring on the open market.

"Millions?"

Glockner nodded, reminding Tuttle of one of the innumerable coaches who had gotten him through law school and then the bar exams. Tuttle had trouble figuring out what the Indiana art professor's angle was. Glockner described himself as an expert on Ford paintings. "Landscapes, chiefly, but I know the portraits too."

This was a new world to Tuttle. The market for art made as much sense to him as the Illinois lottery. The way Glockner described it, it sounded like a con game. The professor spoke of art dealers as little better than common crooks. And he didn't think a whole lot better of Mason, the director of the Fox River Museum. He would have wasted Tuttle's time telling him what a bastard Mason was, but the sum of money Margaret Sinclair's portrait was allegedly worth was a more interesting topic.

"When you say millions, can you be more specific?"

Glockner waved an impatient hand. "It doesn't matter, it's all academic. That girl will never let go of her great-grandmother's portrait. She made that perfectly clear."

Glockner seemed pleased with this, but Tuttle was toying with what could be represented as yet another manifest injustice in old Margaret Sinclair's will. She had given a portrait worth millions to a great-granddaughter hardly out of college. It had been Tuttle's intention to lodge this grievance squarely in the minds of his clients, but then the Sinclair Foundation announced its decision to reclaim and sell the Ford landscapes and distribute the money to the members of the family. So it didn't seem untrue to suggest to the Salazars that the decision about the landscapes had been made at his prompting. He had been about to put into effect Plan A, the effort to gain control of Margaret's portrait. He did not even dare to think what he could charge his clients now that things were turning out so well. Would Amos Cadbury give him a hint?

To think the question was enough to know the answer. Tuttle shrugged the thought away. His purpose in life was not to gain the approval of Amos Cadbury. If Amos had his way, Tuttle would have been disbarred years ago.

Telling Peanuts his good news turned up an unexpected and

155

puzzling bit of information. The mozzarella in the corners of his mouth made Peanuts look like a mad dog.

"Looking into what? For God's sake, the old lady had to be a hundred! All anyone who wanted her dead needed was patience."

Peanuts chewed with concentration. He had told Tuttle all he knew. Horvath was engaged in some kind of investigation into the circumstances surrounding the death of Margaret Sinclair. Tuttle, half accustomed now to the prospect of good fortune, asked himself if he had been about to urge his clients to settle for half a loaf. If there was something funny about the old lady's death, maybe the will in its entirety could be thrown out. The thought of splitting thirty-five million as well as the proceeds from the sale of the Ford landscapes made Tuttle's head spin. In the open box on his desk, a wedge of pizza cooled, its topping congealed. Tuttle was reminded of a reproduction in an art book he had flipped through after talking with Glockner. That morning, before he rinsed off his breakfast plate, the smeared yolk and toast crumbs seemed a composition at least as interesting as those he had seen in the art book. The thought of food followed the thought of money. But it seemed an odd idea of good luck to think of having junk food with Peanuts every day.

He devoted the afternoon to reflection, putting on his thinking cap. Tilted over his face, his tweed hat filtered the air he breathed, but the reduced intake of oxygen seemed to stimulate his brain. He switched the upper and lower of his crossed feet on the desk; his joined hands were splayed over his stomach. The thought that occurred was that Amos Cadbury, alerted to the police investigation and worried that the will might be successfully contested, had decided to neutralize the unhappy Sinclairs by throwing them the bone of the Ford paintings in the museum.

Bone? As close as Tuttle could guess, those paintings could bring in a minimum gross of twenty million. That meant at least a million to every Sinclair into the third generation. But what if that, as well as the rest, could be had? Amos Cadbury's apparent generosity made sense in this imagined scenario. Give a little, save a lot. That was not a truth Tuttle had learned in law school, but from his sainted father, memorialized in the legend on the office door: Tuttle & Tuttle.

While he was waiting for Peanuts to pull the file on whatever Cy Horvath had come up with and pass it on to Tuttle, the man who had cooked at Fairview killed himself.

156

"Maybe," Peanuts said.

"Maybe? Can't they make up their minds?"

Peanuts's curiosity was limited and this had the effect of limiting what Tuttle could learn from him. Regis had been left a nice little sum by the old lady, ten thousand dollars, which did not strike Tuttle as a motive for suicide. Until Peanuts mentioned there was a broad involved.

"I know you must be sick and tired of this," Tuttle said when Honora Brady answered her door, "but I have a few more questions."

Parked conspicuously at the curb was a patrol car with Peanuts behind the wheel. See no evil, hear no evil, speak no evil. Peanuts was a fourth monkey: Find out no evil. If Tuttle wanted to bother the nurse who had looked after Margaret Sinclair, he could count Peanuts out.

"I've said all I know about Regis Factor."

Tuttle smiled. "Repeating prods the memory."

"I'm sorry he did what he did. I know nothing about him."

What was that they said about Luther? Ye protest too much? The pasty-faced nurse seemed too anxious to get rid of him.

"Oh come on, Nurse Brady."

"What's that supposed to mean?"

He tipped his head to one side, and looked knowingly at her.

"I never went out with him!"

"I suppose other people could be lying."

"What other people?" And then anger replaced worry. She glanced at Tuttle. "You're trying to trick me." She stepped back and slammed the door.

While Peanuts drove, Tuttle thought, but he was not inclined to try out loud what he was thinking. Even if Honora Brady was worried, it probably didn't mean anything. Nonetheless, when Peanuts dropped him off, Tuttle got into his Toyota and drove back to where Honora Brady lived. He parked down the street, adjusted his tweed hat, and got comfortable. He could think, or sleep, as easily here as in his office.

But he was awake when the guy showed up. He went up the walk, knocked on the door, and was practically pulled inside by Honora Brady. Tuttle smiled as if acknowledging inaudible applause. Call it instinct, call it a second sense. Sometimes he almost frightened himself.

Half an hour later, Honora and the man came out. Tuttle followed the car to a McDonald's, where they went inside to eat. He went through the carry-out and parked where he could both eat and keep an eye on the couple. Honora was talking a mile a minute. They hung around as if they were dining in a gourmet restaurant, then went to a movie in the mall. Tuttle had already seen it. He settled down in his parked car, a row away from theirs. When he woke up, the car was gone, the mall parking lot all but empty. Tuttle's only consolation was that he had taken down the tag number of the car.

28

Honora had decided to lay down the law and she didn't care what the consequences were. She had been through hell during the past couple weeks and Lester had been no help at all. If anything, he made things worse, and right from the start.

"No," he said, when she suggested she tell the police they'd been together at Fairview at the time Margaret Sinclair died, when she should have been with the old lady. Just no.

"Lester, I can't stand all these questions. And I've mixed up my stories. I told one person I'd gone to get her tea and another she wanted lilacs in the room and I went for some, and I don't remember who I told which story."

"I checked on her and she was all right. What did you do wrong?"

"Nothing!" Only she had, they had, though maybe not what the police were talking about. His visits to Fairview were irregular; he just showed up, without warning, silent as a cat. She would look up from her paperback and there he was, looking into the room but not so Margaret could see him. Once or twice, when Margaret had nodded off, he came silently into the room, curious, curious . . . That day he just nodded from the doorway and disappeared and that was it. Honora tried to stay in her chair, force him to come into the room so she could introduce him to Margaret. Maybe then the old lady would stop teasing her about Regis Factor. But she couldn't wait him out. She would think of his being discovered in the house by Dolly or by Regis, and how would she explain a secret visitor? "Oh, I know him, this is Lester Pincus." She could just hear herself saying that to Regis and Dolly when they thought a thief was in the house.

He was waiting for her in her room, the sun soft upon the drawn shade. It was all foreordained, fated. This was what he had come for and by meeting him in her room she permitted the inevitable to happen. Afterward, while he used the bathroom, she raised the shade and with a great effort kept her mind a total blank. He came squinting into the sun-filled room and her breath caught. He was so good-looking! The beard, the dark blue knit tie against the lighter blue of his shirt, the navy blue blazer. Honora was almost overcome with love for Lester and no longer felt the least bit of shame.

He was right. There was no need to let others know of what they had done. But after her reaction to Lester with the sun upon him, the familiar question rose to her lips.

"What is all this leading to, Lester?"

He sat beside her on the bed. "We have to wait until my ship comes in."

"I don't understand."

He patted her hand. "It won't be long. I promise you."

He meant until they married—what else could he mean?—but she could not bring herself to extract the explicit promise from him. It would be fatal to seem too anxious; she understood that. Couldn't he guess that she had never attracted a man like Lester Pincus in her whole life, and now that she had she would die if she lost him?

She would have left it at that, she would have, but when the police asked her about the bearded man who visited the house the day Margaret Sinclair died, Honora almost fainted, but she managed to ask where they had heard such a thing. Dolly? Honora just looked at Lieutenant Horvath. If he didn't know a helpless alcoholic when he saw one he should seek another line of work.

"You mean she was seeing things?"

"Isn't that part of it?"

"Regis says he saw a bearded man, too."

160

"Just repeating what Dolly said, I suppose. It was his day off. The two of them are trying to cause trouble."

"Why?"

She hesitated. What would Lieutenant Horvath's reaction be if she said the chef was crazy about her, pestered her all the time, baked things for her that she refused to eat because accepting offerings from him would just be the start and she didn't want anything to start. Dear God, before Lester there had been no one, and now she had two men, but what could she do with two?

"I'd rather not say."

"Has Regis got something against you?"

"Ask him."

The first chance she got, she told Lester of this new development. "They saw you, Lester! I knew this would happen, the way you just pop in and out as if you lived here."

"No one saw me."

"Lester, both Dolly and Regis told the police there was a man with a beard at the house that day. No one would pay any attention to Dolly, but Regis is another matter entirely."

Lester counseled silence. Volunteering information now would only get her into trouble. She listened and eventually agreed. It all came down to Dolly, after all. Regis wasn't even in the house. The decisive thing was that her being with Lester in her room had nothing to do with the death of Margaret Sinclair. Except for the oxygen.

She left him in her room—he liked to leave at a time of his own choosing—and went back to Margaret, to find the old woman dead. The oxygen apparatus had been moved, causing a wrinkle in the rug, and the plastic mask hung loose. It might have fallen from Margaret's hand. When Honora put it back on its hook she noticed the gauge. The tank was empty. No wonder. The cock was turned wide open. Dear God, it would look as if Margaret had tried to ward off an attack and found there was no oxygen.

Honora took the empty tank down the hallway, where she called 911 before returning with a full one. She had scarcely gotten it into place when the police car with siren wailing came up the driveway and she hurried downstairs to let them in.

She told no one about the empty oxygen tank. It was her duty to check Margaret's supply, but to leave her alone without making sure that everything was at hand for her patient in case something happened in her absence—well, Honora did not want to explain that to anyone, not even to Lester. Of course Lester would not have understood about the oxygen when he checked on Margaret. During all the fussing over the body, Honora had been on pins and needles, fearful someone would notice that the oxygen was not connected. When Father Dowling gave Margaret a final blessing, he stood there, frowning, and Honora was certain he had noticed the oxygen and would ask her why it wasn't hooked up. But he didn't notice. No one did before she got a chance to fix it.

So Lester had been right about Margaret. Everything went smoothly enough. On her last day, figuring she had nothing to lose and owed herself the satisfaction, Honora told Regis Factor just what she thought of him for lying to the police about her.

"I never lied to anyone!" He threw back his shoulders and seemed to inflate. Honora half expected him to lift from the floor, like a blimp.

"Oh, didn't you?"

"No."

Honora believed now that the bearded man must have been Terence Sinclair, who had visited his aunt that morning. She had heard Father Dowling say as much. But Dolly and Regis had not known that when they blabbed to the police.

"Then they must have lied to me about your telling them I had some man visiting me the day Margaret died."

He seemed to collapse then, deflating as if she had stuck a pin in him and all the air was going out of him. Air. Oxygen. It was as though he thought the same thing. That night he killed himself in that awful way, using Margaret Sinclair's oxygen, the supply that had been too late to save Margaret killing him.

In the days since his return from New York, George Frederick Mason felt that he had experienced more of hell than Dante ever dreamed of. Lying sleepless in his bed at night, he tried to imagine how he could have been so stupid as to leave the portrait in the cab with Ginger. The whole point of his being in New York was rolled up in that tube, yet he had left it behind as if it were an old newspaper. How easily Ginger might not even have noticed it when she got out of the cab! Sometimes he thought it would have been better if she had ignored it. He would have called the cab company—but which one?—and asked if anyone had turned in a tube, they would say yes, he could have gone to pick it up, and today he would not be haggard from lack of sleep, his bowels a mess.

While he went through the agony of the damned, Ginger and her goddamn mother were sunning themselves in the Virgin Islands! It sounded like a nostalgia trip. Oh, how he hated women! He hated Parker too. He hated all the uncultivated gawkers moving through the museum, standing bewildered before a picture, then moving on to another equally bewildering one. They oohed and ahed at the Ford landscapes, as the catalog instructed them to do, stood open-mouthed, marveling at the realism. What an unworthy fate for works of art, to be displayed to the great unwashed masses for their lack of comprehension. As a curator he was supposed to rejoice that the day of the private collector was past, when great works of art had been enjoyed only by the owner and the owner's chosen friends. Margaret Sinclair. Better that, far better that, than this. "This" at the moment being an extended family of apparently retarded rustics who were arguing among themselves as to whether or not a barn in a Ford rural landscape was one they knew in the flesh, so to speak. What in the world difference did it make? If they wanted a reproduction of the barn, let them take their Kodaks to it.

Mason paced up and down an aisle at right angles to that in which the Fords hung, waiting for the area to clear. He made many a valedictory visit to these jewels of the collection, trying to reconcile himself to their loss. Of course they would end up on other museum walls. And he wanted to admire the handiwork of an artist whose portrait of Bridget Doyle might prove the making or the undoing of George Frederick Mason. When these bumpkins left he would cordon off the area in order to study in peace the most priceless items in the whole museum, whose days here were numbered.

While Ginger browned herself on the beach, time sifting slowly through the bottleneck of the present, grain of sand by grain of sand, Gearhart Glockner appeared in Mason's office. The dumpy figure of his old foe might have been cause for amusement at another time, but now Gearhart loomed before him like the personification of conscience. Gripping the arms of his chair, staring at his visitor, Mason sought to hypnotize Gearhart. Do not look at the wall. Do not look at the wall.

"I went round to see my old student Peggy Sinclair and the painting that has come into her hands. George, they have a portrait worth millions hanging on the wall of a living room whose style could roughly be described as Midwestern Rococo. The girl was offended when I told her what it would bring at auction. 'It's my great-grandmother,' she said." Glockner was mimicking, with surprising success, Peggy Sinclair's voice. Well, he spent his life among nubile young women; it was only natural that he should become like them.

"Gearhart, are you sure it's a Ford?"

Glockner lowered his head and looked at Mason through the thatch of his brow. The expert in ambush. "It's a Ford."

"How do you tell?"

"How do you know a person belongs to a given family?"

"Family resemblance?"

"Exactly. And what is that? No one thing. A subtle combination of things."

"Too bad he didn't sign them."

"Oh, he signed them, all right."

Mason's heart felt as if it were being squeezed by a fist. "His portraits aren't signed!"

"Not in the usual sense, no. But there is no doubt when you're in the presence of a Ford. His style, the use of the palette knife, the colors—those are his John Hancock."

Mason realized that he had been holding his breath. He sighed with audible relief. Glockner had not discovered the initialing on the back of the canvas.

"I was also shown a copy of the will, George. I wanted to see the statement of the gift. Have you seen it?"

"The will? No."

"It's not as long as I would have thought."

"Who else got paintings?" He released the question as Noah released a dove from the Ark, half dreading what it would bring.

"No one."

Glockner was always apodictic but he obviously took special pleasure from providing Mason news of his own backyard. Of course there was no legal need to mention the Fords here in Mason's museum. No more had Fairview been left to anyone in particular. Such things belonged to the family and were at the family's disposal. Gearhart had all this from a lawyer involved in the affairs of the family.

"Amos Cadbury?"

"No. A man named Tuttle."

Mason said nothing, but his inner man was splitting his sides laughing. Tuttle. Wilbert Plunkett had been right about Tuttle. The man was the laughingstock of Fox River. It was just when he felt safest that the blow fell.

"Where's your Ford?" Glockner asked offhandedly.

"Fords, my dear fellow. Fords."

"I mean the portrait that hung there." Glockner twisted in his chair and pointed.

"A portrait? Now what would that have been? When were you last here?"

"It was hanging there every time I came. You asked me if I thought it was a Ford."

"I did?"

"It wasn't, of course."

"No family resemblance?" His soul seemed to have fled his body and to be hovering over the scene, aghast at his ability to go on chatting as if maximum danger did not threaten.

"I'd like to see it again."

"So would I."

"What happened to it?"

"It was only on loan. It's gone to the Virgin Islands, poor thing. God knows what the climate will do to it. I miss her."

Did Glockner believe him? It was maddening not to know, but Glockner, with his beard and dark glasses, would be formidable at a poker table. There was no way of telling what he might be concealing. Doubt would have been preferable to being called a liar if the conversation did not suggest that others too might recall the portrait's hanging on his office wall.

"I told Peggy Sinclair to have a good copy made of the portrait, hang that on her wall, and put the original in a safe place, preferably Hathaway Hall."

On any other occasion, Mason would have been outraged by such poaching on his territory, but he had deeper worries today.

"The parents at least were interested in the possibility of having a good copy made. Not, however, interested in donating the portrait to Hathaway Hall."

"I'll urge them to take your advice."

Gearhart seemed more annoyed than pleased by such magnanimity. "The girl will never permit it. She reminded her mother of the silver and jewelry she keeps in a bank vault. Admittedly, that does seem to be a way of *not* owning something."

"Jewelry too can be copied."

He knew nothing of that, whereas they both knew how uncannily like the original painting a copy could be; and now, with computer-ized methods, it was more cloning than copying.

When Glockner left, off to Italy for the summer, the son of a bitch, Mason accompanied him to his car and stood watching him drive off, the apparent courtesy a desire to make certain Gearhart was indeed on his way. He turned and trudged back inside, dragging his heavy, invisible chain. "That man is a pest," he cried, as he was passing through Miss Knutsen's office.

"I know."

He stopped and looked back at her.

"Last week he wasted hours just sitting here talking."

"Last week!"

"When you were in New York."

Mason looked wildly about at this surprising revelation. Why hadn't Glockner mentioned visiting when the director wasn't in? Why hadn't Miss Knutsen told him this earlier? Did Glockner perhaps imagine that Miss Knutsen would automatically tell him of his visitor? He did not trust himself to ask these questions. Thank God the man was leaving the country. He toted this added burden into his office and slumped into the chair behind his desk. He was still half-sitting, half-lying in his chair when the phone rang. He stared at it as if he might never answer another phone in his life. And then he thought of Ginger and snatched up the instrument.

"It's Maud Sinclair," Miss Knutsen said.

"Maud Sinclair," he repeated.

A click and then the distinctive voice of Maud. "George, you're in. I am two blocks away. I would like to come see you if I may."

"Of course, of course."

Why not? Let everybody come. Maybe Maud too would look at his wall and ask where the portrait was. My God! He could not lie to her as he had to Glockner. He went into his private washroom, put his hands on the basin, and leaned forward, looking himself in the eye. He could slash his wrists, let life trickle away down the drain, be found, bloodless and dead, a tragic figure, by Maud . . .

When he emerged, refreshed, face scrubbed into life, he heard Maud in the outer office, and a moment later she marched in. He always felt about to be mugged when she approached swiftly to within four feet, stopped, thrust out her hand, and then they were shaking as if some momentous bet were being recorded.

"I know how devastating it must be for you to face the prospect of my family removing all its Fords from the museum. Nor do I overlook the fact that you did not, as you must have been urged, engage counsel to contest this decision. Your reaction has been a tribute to your calling. It shall not go unrewarded. I do not intend to leave the museum empty of the work of Clayton Ford. If the family does not agree to leave one of your choosing, I personally will buy it and give it to you."

"That is very generous of you, Maud."

When he was informed by Amos Cadbury that the lawyer had researched the terms of Margaret Sinclair's gift and was satisfied that the Fords were only on loan to the museum, Mason had surprised himself by the aplomb of his reaction. From that moment he felt he could receive the news that he had terminal cancer with perfect equanimity. Now he nodded calmly as if Maud had told him the rain had stopped, the sun was out, and the voice of the turtle is heard in the land.

"Those paintings will bring a fortune, Maud. Millions."

"Maybe you'd prefer a Ford portrait." She looked around. "Where is the painting that always hung there?"

"Being cleaned." How easily the words came.

"I love that portrait. It seems the twin of Margaret's own."

They went into the museum to visit the Fords hanging there, the traffic having slowed considerably. Maud shook her head. "If you say millions, you know what you're talking about, but it doesn't make much sense, does it? Poor Clayton Ford might have used some fraction of that in his lifetime."

Poor Clayton Ford! Poor George Frederick Mason would be more like it. After Glockner's visit he had kicked himself for not having had a copy of the portrait made before he went to New York. But he would have had to send it to New York to have that done. In any case, he could have had his cake and eaten it too, so far as anyone would know. Maybe he would do that yet, before relinquishing it to the auctioneer. Maybe the Sinclairs would permit copies of all the Fords now hanging in the museum to be made. The bumpkins wouldn't know the difference. But, oh, what a fall he faced in the profession! Being director of the Fox River Museum was going to be on the level of watching over a student art show.

Later that day, in his apartment, he opened the closet in which he

168

had put the frame of the Bridget portrait. The squared emptiness made his stomach pulse with pain. He had to get the portrait back before an audit of the Ford holdings of the museum was made.

What a fool he had been to imagine no one had noticed or would remember that portrait hanging on his wall. Forget a Ford! It was absurd. He prowled his apartment, talking aloud to himself as he did not dare to do at the office. Once Miss Knutsen had whispered that his radio could be heard even with the door closed. He actually did have a radio in his office, so she might have been playing it straight. But at home he could rant and rave to his heart's content, and it was of Ginger and Marjorie, her mother, that he raved.

What a fateful thing to run into Ginger in the hotel lobby, to share a cab with her, to forget the painting, and then Ginger, having taken it to her apartment, not realizing what it was, flew off to the Caribbean! He should have asked if she would arrange for him to be admitted to her apartment immediately so that he could retrieve the tube and painting, but at first it had seemed important not to let her know what it was he'd left in the cab. That seemed foolish now. What difference did it make what she thought? But the thought of Ginger thinking was difficult to form and he let it go.

He got out an aging album and studied decade-old photographs of Ginger. This entailed seeing Marjorie too, unfortunately, but it was as if the pictures brought him closer to Ginger and thus to the portrait he had been about to purloin.

God can bring good out of evil, he thought suddenly. No, God had prevented evil. Imagine that he had actually put the portrait in Parker's hands. That alone would have counted as theft, seeking to dispose of a painting that was only in his care. God had prevented that by causing him to forget the painting in the cab and then by sending Ginger improbably to the Virgin Islands. He stopped pacing, welcoming this interpretation, relieved by the thought that George Frederick Mason figured prominently in the providential plans of the Almighty. By delaying his perfidy, God had given him a second chance. Ginger would return to New York, mail the painting, he would restore it to its frame, hang it on his office wall, and everything would be as it had been. To escape professional ruin would compensate for the loss of the Fords.

Tears of relief sprang to his eyes and Mason sank to his knees, his arms outstretched. If he had a whip he would flog himself.

"Peggy?"

"Yes."

"Joel."

He paused but she said nothing, letting time pulse by. What did she have to say to him that he would want to hear?

"I've been a shit."

"Joel, listen. I don't need to hear you say things like that about yourself."

"You've every right to hate me."

Was it hatred that she felt? After talking with Father Dowling, all she could think was that Joel had let her learn that way what he should have been man enough to tell her. Maybe he *was* a shit.

"You never said you weren't married."

"Oh, come on. I'm not married. That's all over with. It was a kid thing, long ago, in law school . . ."

He was still talking when she put the receiver back where it belonged.

The phone began to ring again almost immediately. After a dozen rings, her mother called from downstairs, "Peggy, is that your phone?"

She eased the receiver from the hook, depressed the buttons, then left the receiver lying on her bed and went downstairs.

"Who called?"

"It was a wrong number."

Her mother was reading a glitzy novel, a chubby paperback whose cover looked as if it would glow in the dark. Romance. How could a grown woman get anything out of reading such improbable junk? Vivian turned a page, her eyes still focused on the book. Peggy wondered if she had even heard the answer to her question.

She drove out along the river road, heading for Fairview, as if she were on her way to talk to Margaret. She hadn't been there for two days, not wanting to face Father Dowling until she had talked with Joel.

High school, college, she had never really loved anyone before Joel. She should have known something would go wrong. She was no gung-ho Catholic; in fact, she was ashamed at how bland she was about her religion, talking with Leon had at least that Socratic effect on her. I believe that I do not believe enough. But life had to be more than one thing after another, and religion, the belief that we've been created to go on forever and ever in a place that makes more sense than this world, was an answer to that question, or fear, or doubt. What if life at bottom really made no sense and was only an idiot's tale? She couldn't stand that, and the fact that she couldn't counted against its being true. If nothing made sense, why should that rub her the wrong way? It should make sense that nothing made sense if she was part of an absurd world.

She hadn't had thoughts like that since after a session with Leon, when she would go down by the lake and look out at the ducks and imagine that she was having very deep and profound thoughts. A few tries at expressing them to Michele had convinced her that they were best divulged only to the ducks.

Joel left messages for her at home, and twice, before leaving the house, she noticed his car parked up the street and left by the back door. She didn't want to see him; she didn't want to talk about it. Nothing he said could change the one unalterable fact. And she had no wish to rail at him, jump all over him, make him feel worse than he did. Because she did not believe she'd been only a casual lay for him. Maybe the first time he took her to his apartment and made a move, if something had happened then, it would have been trivial and she would have been a fool afterward to think she was anything more than a diversion. But that was not how it had happened. They had come to know one another. She had come to love him. The night in the motel had not been a quick roll in the grass, but writing a check on the capital of their mutual love, one that morally had to be postdated, but would eventually be part of the life they shared. Their married life. That was what they had had before them. Maybe he was dumb enough to think he could have that a second time. She wished she could be as dumb.

It would have been easier if he had simply seduced her under false pretenses, retreating later behind the convenient tragedy of his marriage. But if it had meant that little to him, he wouldn't be trying to get in touch with her now. And that made it all the more important that she avoid him.

At Fairview, she took the road around the house and drove down past the barns and outbuildings toward the river. She left her car and went down the path to the bridge that led to the island. The air was full of the sound of birds, the rustle of leaves, the drone and whine of insects. A squirrel, its tail curled over its back, dug importantly in the ground beneath a magnolia tree that Peggy suddenly realized was full of cardinals.

She crossed the bridge and went up the path to the chapel. Maud stood there and she might have been waiting for her. Somehow, Peggy managed not to seem surprised to find her aunt there either.

"Have you ever been inside, Peggy?"

"No."

"This is where I want Margaret and Matthew reburied."

The key Maud fitted into the chapel door looked like a prop from a fairy story. The door squeaked nicely on its hinges as she pulled it open. A musty mixture of incense and the smell of candles greeted them. Sun came through a stained-glass window above the altar and a dancing palette of light lay on the marble floor. It deepened the letters carved in the gravestone set in the middle aisle.

"That is your aunt's grave."

Peggy went closer to the altar and turned to read the legend

172

engraved in the marble slab. ELIZABETH SINCLAIR, FEBRUARY 24, 1944. The chapel was like a miniature church with kneelers on either side of the aisle. The windows on the river side were dark and mysterious-looking. What were they like when the setting sun shone through them?

"This place could give death a good name, Maud."

"Father Dowling has agreed to say a mass here for your aunt."

An aunt she had never known. "Could I come?"

"Of course. As long as you tell no one else. You can see that not many people can fit in here."

Did Maud really think there would be a stampede of Sinclairs to attend a memorial mass in the island chapel? Credulity seemed to run in the family.

(31)

The Sinclair family's decision to reclaim paintings long on loan to the Fox River Museum was big news, both locally and nationally. Amos Cadbury, whose role it was to speak for the family, discussed the transfer in tones so matter-of-fact one would have thought the topic of the interview was the reproductions sold in the museum store. The Channel 9 interviewer, her tone shrill with accusation, sought to liken what was going on to the rape of the Sabine women. The analogy was Amos's. It was a major lapse, failing to take into account the illiteracy of the arrogant journalist as well as the odd resonance "rape" has in a nation of sexually active morons.

Maud was finding it difficult to remain calm as she described the interview for Father Dowling.

"I thought Amos did rather well, Maud."

"Then you haven't been listening to the local talk shows. Neither have I, but Peggy tells me we are being talked of as if we were robbing the public treasury."

"It is the nature of news to be transient."

"I know," Maud sighed. "And all the shock and indignation are rhetorical devices to sell the news. Still, it's painful."

With the names Sinclair and Ford filling newspaper columns and airwaves, Father Dowling found Phil Keegan's mystification when he came to watch the Cubs on television forced. Phil brought with him a phone message taken down by a police operator.

"You know anyone named Ford, Roger?"

"Henry. Tennessee. Mary. Edsel."

"I mean local. I guess." He handed the note to Roger Dowling.

The message was printed in pencil on a form. The line for the name of the caller was left blank. The time was earlier that morning, more like last night. "Ford portrait unsafe."

"Is that all?"

Phil nodded, but his eyes were pulled toward the television where Harry Caray and Steve Stone were discussing the game that was about to begin. "Three little words. He repeated them twice, then hung up."

"He."

Phil nodded. "Cranks." He held out his hand and Roger Dowling returned the telephone message. Phil crumpled it and arced it toward the wastepaper basket and missed. Roger retrieved it, banked it off the wall, and canned it.

"Luck," grumbled Phil.

"Practice."

Surely Phil must connect the cryptic message and the portrait of Margaret Sinclair that had been given to Peggy. The artist was Clayton Ford. Margaret had mentioned the name several times with obvious pride. She collected Fords in what she described as a minor way. It was that collection she had loaned to the Fox River Museum, but all of them were landscapes. The only portrait was that of Margaret. But then Phil Keegan had written Margaret Sinclair off his books. Cy's checking out of Monique Pippen's fantasies had turned up things which had no explanation but did not seem to matter.

The situation invited suspicion if one's profession were to suspect, so Father Dowling felt he understood Cy's continuing curiosity. There was now no way to verify Monique Pippen's claim that the oxygen beside Margaret's chair should have prevented the emphysema attack and related stroke. There had been a full supply available. Pippen thought the absence of the nurse warranted at least some kind of admonition, but Keegan was willing to leave that to the Fox River medical society. The priest's thoughts focused on Margaret. Had Margaret chosen not to take oxygen that was readily available?

He stopped himself with an inner shout. The cases they had wrangled over in moral theology came back to him, but even more vividly the actual cases of the marriage tribunal, where niceties of distinction in deciding what a person had or had not intended to do were crucial. Thank God for baseball. He concentrated on the set and in moments was swept up in the fortunes of the game. But during a commercial those three words Phil had brought formed themselves in his mind. *Ford portrait unsafe.*

The clamor over the Sinclairs and their paintings made it unlikely in the extreme that Phil did not recognize the significance of the warning. However nonchalantly, he had thought enough of the call about a Ford portrait to pass it on to Roger Dowling. Of course the police were far more occupied with the death of Regis Factor.

"It's the damndest suicide I ever saw."

Phil described the way the mask—Margaret's mask—had been taped to the chef's face.

"He did that himself?"

"There were no signs of a struggle. He looked laid out by McDivett. But it's the phone call that has Cy going. If it's suicide, Regis first calls nine-one-one to report it, then goes through with it."

"What was his motive?"

"He's about to lose a cushy job? He's despondent because the nurse doesn't love him?" Phil smiled, then turned to Roger. "Or overcome with guilt because he killed the old lady and the way he kills himself is meant to tell us that."

"Cy thinks that?"

"No. But I imagine the thought would occur to you. It occurred to me."

"And?"

"He was nowhere near the house the day the old lady died. Died. We have no reason to think it was anything other than a natural death." And Phil turned back to the television.

The next morning, at Fairview, Roger Dowling went to the room where Regis Factor had died. Of course there was no indication of what had happened there, any more than a pall hung over the room

176

in which Margaret had died. He opened the closet and found the oxygen apparatus standing there. It seemed another actor in the dramatic events of the house in recent days. What would Phil say if he knew that Regis had been at Fairview the day Margaret died, spying on Honora, mistaking Terence for her lover? Terence was more likely than Regis to have deprived Margaret of oxygen.

Peggy was at work when he went to the rooms they had turned into offices of the Sinclair Foundation. Mindful of what Phil had said, he asked her about the portrait of Margaret.

"I have it in my room at home."

"So you saw it this morning."

"I see it every morning. My mother had it hanging downstairs, but I'm selfish. I took it upstairs again."

"Someone called the police to warn of danger to a Ford portrait."

"The police?"

"They've dismissed it as a crank call."

"I never knew there were so many cranks."

Peggy had been down ever since learning that Joel Cleary had been married before, and the hullabaloo over the removal of the Ford landscapes from the museum was an added weight. Apparently her main consolation now was reading Margaret's diary.

"She wrote of the time her portrait was being painted. Ford painted her maid Bridget at the same time."

"The Sinclairs commissioned a portrait of a maid?"

"Ford did it on his own, as a gift."

"So your portrait is not the only one."

"Oh, he painted quite a few."

"I mean locally."

"Well, it was painted locally. Who knows where it is? There's no record of it."

"How do you know that?"

She made a face. "Art history at Hathaway Hall. Professor Gearhart Glockner."

Fairview, for all its elegance, was not centrally air-conditioned. Margaret had dismissed suggestions that a central system be installed and resisted having single units hanging from the windows, although she did make an exception for the servants' quarters. The windows were open in the room where they worked and the curtains moved in the slight breeze. Peggy seemed mesmerized by them.

"Reading Margaret's diary is so strange," she said. "Now whenever I come here I seem to awaken events recorded in the diary. Ford had a studio in a barn out there toward the river. It's still there. Once I drove Margaret around the grounds and we stopped there and she told me of those months before her wedding, having her portrait painted, her maid playing chaperone and having her portrait done too. It's all there in the diary."

Peggy was reading the diary at a very deliberate pace. Roger Dowling asked if he might look at it and was surprised that she had it with her. Not that it was valuable, like the portrait; just precious. Peggy handled it as if it were a breviary.

"Bridget Doyle," he murmured, turning the pages.

"Don't tell me about anything past my marker." She put her hands to her ears as if he might begin reading aloud.

He mentioned these things to Maud, who spoke with authority on the matter.

"Of course there's a portrait of Bridget. It hangs in Mr. Mason's office at the museum. At least, that's its usual place. George tells me it is presently out being cleaned."

"Then it's missing?"

Maud tucked in her chin and raised her brows. "That's a dramatic way to put it."

Several days later, on his way back to the rectory from Fairview, Roger Dowling took a detour and turned in at the museum parking lot. As he got out of his car, the St. Hilary's parish center bus drove in, horn tooting. Father Dowling waited while Edna Hospers helped a dozen old folks out of the bus.

"They're going on a tour," Edna explained. There was an understandable note of relief in her voice. She would return for them in exactly two hours.

"Are you going back to St. Hilary's, Father?"

"I just this moment parked my car. It's been years since I looked at the collection here."

"You can join the tour."

But Roger Dowling had no wish to be herded about the museum and hear canned descriptions. He remained in the parking lot talking with Edna until the contingent from the parish center had been greeted by a museum guide and ushered through the main entrance.

The director's secretary was made nervous by the sight of Roger Dowling's Roman collar and scooted into the adjoining office from which, seconds later, George Frederick Mason appeared, a quizzical expression on his florid face, arms open in greeting.

"Father Dowling. Maud Sinclair said you might drop by."

"Did she?"

"Of course, I thought she'd tell you to wait until Bridget returns."

"The portrait?"

"Exactly. But come in anyway, Father."

The director's office had an antiseptic air about it, very modern, planes interrupted by simple solids, cubes, spheres, pyramids. Roger Dowling would have thought it an uncomfortable room until he took the chair Mason indicated and felt supported as if in the hand of a giant.

"That is her place," Mason said, indicating the wall next to Father Dowling.

"I have a friend who is a policeman and he told me they received a crank call that a Ford portrait was in danger."

Mason's hands lifted helplessly and he shook his head. "The police too. I have been receiving similar calls ever since Bridget went off for a cleaning."

"Here in town?"

Mason turned his head sideways, but his eyes remained on his guest. "It is a rare skill, the cleaning and restoration of artworks. One possessing it would not have enough business in Fox River to make a go of it. No, I had to ship Bridget off to New York. How I miss her." Mason sighed. Anyone might think he was speaking of a flesh-and-blood woman rather than a painting.

"You've been getting crank calls?"

"An occupational hazard, Father. I am asked in sinister tones what I have done with the painting that hung there."

"But who would know?"

Mason laughed. "I will not permit myself such questions, Father. Where would it end? Why should it begin?"

"I envy your philosophical nature, Mr. Mason. This on top of losing the Ford landscapes."

"Father, I just thank God we had them as long as we did."

Of course the sight of a Roman collar turned many people into lay preachers, but Mason seemed genuinely resigned. Father Dowling had the odd thought that Mason and Honora Brady possessed a similar resilience. The nurse laughed off Regis's story of a secret lover. Mason smiled through the loss of the central attraction of his museum. The pastor of St. Hilary's felt chastened before such virtue and quelled the accompanying skepticism. But he drove to his rectory in the confidence that both Ford portraits were accounted for.

Nonetheless, he felt a vague unease he did not understand. That night he dreamed of Margaret's diary, and it seemed a menacing volume. But before breakfast was over he had put such thoughts from his head.

"Mr. Tuttle is here to see you. Are you in?"

"Of course."

"Tuttle, the lawyer." She handed him a card, her brows raised, eyes wide.

"Publicans and sinners, lawyers, housekeepers, it's all one to me, Marie."

She hesitated, in search of repartee that did not come, then bustled from the room to tell the little lawyer that the pastor would be happy to see him.

Tuttle felt more at ease with the pastor than he had with the housekeeper. What a woman. Tuttle's profession, or at least his standing in it, had acquainted him with condenscension; he knew the vulnerability of the salesman appearing unwanted on the doorstep. But his luck had changed—knock on wood—and he was more put off than he would normally have been by the hostility with which Mrs. Murkin answered the door.

"This is a very busy time of day," she said icily.

Tuttle felt that he had failed to give some password that would have gained him easy entry. Priests don't lock themselves away from people, do they? He took out one of the cards he'd had printed since fortune in the form of the Sinclair family had smiled upon him.

"Show him this."

It worked. A moment later, Mrs. Murkin reluctantly led him down the hall to the smoke-filled study of Father Dowling.

When he was settled in a chair, Tuttle put his hat on his knee, leaned back, and, with closed eyes, inhaled deeply.

"Doesn't this bring it back, Father? How many rooms filled with tobacco smoke are there any more?"

The priest laughed. Tuttle was fully at ease now. He wished Peanuts Pianone were here to observe the new Tuttle. The truth was that Tuttle had not been seeing as much of his old friend on the Fox River police force of late. The other day, Peanuts had looked in, obviously put off by the sight of Miss Tuchman at her desk in the outer office, hands poised over the keyboard of the word processor she had insisted he rent.

"Wanna go out for some Chinese?" Peanuts asked.

"God, I wish I could."

"Or send out for a pizza?" He glanced at Miss Tuchman.

"Give me a rain check, Peanuts, okay? How long you on duty?"

Peanuts looked betrayed and Tuttle did not blame him. They were comrades, the two of them, often whiling away hours in his office, feasting on franchise food. Peanuts was an invaluable source of information, not that Tuttle thought he was exploiting their friendship. Peanuts just told him things. And it never did a lawyer any harm to know what the police were up to. Guilt led him to seek Peanuts out and Tuttle would have sworn that Tuttle Senior was looking out for him from upstairs because it was then that Peanuts told him about the telephoned warning about Ford paintings being in danger. Once this Sinclair matter was wrapped up, he would take Peanuts to the Great Wall of China and buy him the Singapore Special. This nugget about the paintings was more obviously to the point than Peanuts's info about Honora Brady's boyfriend. Tailing the nurse had paid off, just in case.

His name was Lester Pincus and he was director of the Fox River Historical Society. Tuttle sauntered through the main exhibit, feigning interest. It all looked like a bunch of junk to him. He had never understood how people could get excited about something just because it was old. Paintings now were something else, they represented money, but the stuff in the cases at the Historical Society looked like anyone's attic when Tuttle was a kid.

"Looking for anything in particular?" Pincus asked, his manner lukewarm.

"You know, I've never been here before. Quite a place."

"Look around as much as you'd like."

"Thanks. I will. Fascinating."

Pincus went back to his desk behind a counter and Tuttle tipped the brim of his hat over his eyes so he could get a fix on the guy while he pretended to check out the display cases. Pincus was presentable enough, even good-looking, and Tuttle couldn't figure him hanging out with a woman with the looks of Nurse Brady. It was the beard that interested Tuttle, but he didn't know what to do with it. Unless Lester was the guy Dolly and the cook had seen at Fairview the day old lady Sinclair died. Tuttle would bet Lester had visited the nurse there more than once. When he had tailed them it was pretty clear they were an established couple. There was a phrase used of women, they're all alike in the dark, that suggested an explanation of Lester Pincus and Honora Brady, but these were murky areas for Tuttle.

Now, talking with Father Dowling, it occurred to him that they were a pair of celibates.

"I'm representing members of the Sinclair family, Father Dowling. I guess that puts us in the same boat."

"Oh, my position isn't that exalted."

"I'll tell you one thing, Father Dowling. I'll be glad when those paintings have been auctioned off. Things that valuable, well, you can never have enough security."

"Where will the Fords go?"

"A Chicago warehouse. Temperature control, good security, insured. They'll be as safe as they are now in the museum. I'm not worried about that."

Except he was. He didn't need to tell a priest that nothing was safe on this earth, where rusty moths consume and all that. There wasn't a warehouse built that couldn't be knocked over if someone made up their mind to do it. Still and all, he didn't think anyone would call the police to warn them about the paintings in the museum.

"It's the unaccounted-for paintings I'm thinking of."

"Unaccounted for?"

"Well, let's not go into that. Peggy Sinclair has a painting worth millions. The police have received warnings that a Ford portrait is in danger. I thought you ought to know. For whatever it's worth."

Father Dowling thanked him but didn't pursue the matter. Still, Tuttle felt his mission had been accomplished. A mission on behalf of his clients. For all he knew, the family would go after the painting Peggy Sinclair had, and Tuttle didn't want to be dealt out of his take on several millions more.

Back at the office, he told Miss Tuchman to call Officer Pianone. Peanuts was free.

"I'll have my secretary make reservations at the Great Wall," Tuttle said grandly.

"Reservations? You mean take-out?"

"I just want to make sure we get a good table."

He put down the phone, got his feet up on the desk, and settled his hat over his eyes. Somewhere above him Tuttle Senior looked benevolently down. Tuttle felt like a boy scout, one good deed after another.

33

Monique loaned him the audio tape of the Regis Factor autopsy and Cy listened to it in his car, wanting the distraction of traffic and the sights of the living while Jolson's monotone went into grisly detail as to what he was doing to the body of the dead chef. It was one of the mysteries of Monique Pippen that this sort of thing was the stuff of her day, yet she professed to wonder how Cy could have chosen a life where violence was a constant threat.

"No one's threatening me."

"You know what I mean."

She patted his suit jacket. He had shown her his revolver, feeling like a schoolkid. No need to tell her how seldom he had fired the thing. Outside of practice at the police range, that is.

Cadavers were no threat, they were already dead, and her job was to ascertain how they'd got that way. She was willing to explain how Regis had suffocated from a relentless flow of oxygen, his nose and mouth covered by a plastic mask that had been taped to his head in such a way he would have had trouble getting it off even if he had tried.

"You think he tried?" he asked Pippen.

"I think he didn't. His arms were at his side."

"Maybe they were held there."

"Why do you say that?"

To make her eyes sparkle the way they did, maybe. Playing to her tendency to look for farfetched explanations did not make Cy proud of himself. And it was farfetched to think that the presence of the oxygen apparatus at both of the recent deaths at Fairview was significant. Or, if significant, not in the way Monique would have liked. Regis Factor had been a romantic, no doubt of that, and his eyes must not have been too good either. Falling in love with Honora Brady defied reason. Monique, characteristically, took the opposite view.

"Because *he* was such a Don Juan? The man weighed three hundred pounds, he was bald as my knee. Maybe he could cook, but what else? The mystery would be if a professional woman with Honora Brady's prospects responded to his attention."

"Yeah."

"You disagree?"

"They made a matched set, okay? Let's just leave it at that."

But Monique never left anything at that. Despite her insistence that there had been foul play at Fairview, it took her a while before she settled on the truly mystifying fact, the 911 call that the body of Regis Factor would be found at Fairview.

"A man's voice," she reminded him.

"You think it was Regis?"

"Was there any other man in the house?"

"Who said the call came from the house?"

"How would anyone not there know about the body?"

But finally she was intrigued by the thought of Regis, in despair over his love for Honora Brady, deciding to commit suicide, getting everything ready, then making the 911 call before he went through with it.

"Why?"

"Suicide is a statement, Cyril." No one called him Cyril, but he did not object. "The whole point of it is to say farewell to the world. If no one ever knew . . . Well, that's unlikely. But Regis wanted a hullabaloo afterward so Honora would know. Remember, that was Honora's last night at the house."

186

"Too bad."

She looked at him quizzically. When she frowned a little wrinkled horseshoe formed on her forehead. Every morning now, driving downtown, Cy made a resolution to keep away from Monique. He was convinced that if he got through a whole day, then two, without seeing her, the spell would be broken. Telling himself it was a harmless fascination no longer seemed to exonerate him. He felt like a damned fool. He was too young to be going through a phase. He had a wife, he was happy. If Lilian could see him mooning around Monique, her razzing would be a cure, but he couldn't risk desperate remedies.

"Too bad?"

"If he killed himself, there's no one to blame it on."

"Oh? How do you think Honora feels?"

Cy gave up. He was damned if he would be cast in the role of Honora Brady's defender. He did drop in on Terence Sinclair.

"You shaved your beard."

A pair of marbles looked at him. "You a barber? I thought you were from the police."

Terence had an office at his brother William's building, a messy place. He sat at a computer that conveyed to him the fluctuation of stocks.

"We're investigating the death of your grandmother's chef."

Terence's hands were poised over the keyboard as if he were a pianist. He waited.

"You heard of it?"

"I heard of it."

"Did you know Regis Factor at all?"

Terence had the petulant edginess of a loser. "Are you asking me if we were friends?"

"When did you last see him?"

"I don't know."

"Mr. Sinclair, I know these questions may seem pointless. But this is the second death at Fairview in a very short time and it's our job to make sure that no crime has been committed."

"Isn't suicide a crime?"

"Do you think your grandmother committed suicide?"

"I meant Regis!"

"Have you been to Fairview since she died?"

"Of course."

"When was that?"

"The day of the funeral. What did you say your name is?"

"Horvath. Lieutenant Horvath."

Cy braced himself to hear the speech about Terence Sinclair being a taxpayer and therefore Cy's employer and why was he wasting the time of both of them. But Terence pushed away from his computer and rubbed his face.

"It's strange not having her out there at Fairview. Old as she was, I guess I thought she'd live forever. Thank God I went out there that day."

"The day she died?"

Terence nodded.

"What time was that?"

They were back on familiar ground. Agnes had talked with Terence and they had the time of his arrival and departure from Fairview. Cy couldn't figure Terence out. He was now a mourning grandson rather than one of the heirs most noisy about fighting Margaret Sinclair's will.

Ginger phoned to say the tube was in the mail and George Frederick
Mason surprised himself by the calmness of his reaction. Maybe, as
Father Dowling had said, he was becoming a philosopher.

"Oh, yes. Thank you, dear, I've been wondering about that."

"I have a confession to make, George. I took a peek."

"I don't blame you."

"Who is she?"

"Someone named Bridget Doyle."

"Why did you bring it to New York?"

"By mistake, if you can believe it. Some idiot here packed the
wrong painting."

He had tipped back in his chair and addressed the ceiling as
much as the telephone. The lie was for the record, in case it ever
came to light that he had flown off to New York with the Ford
portrait. Not that he was worried now. Not any more. He felt that he
was floating midway between the floor and ceiling of his office. A
wave of gratitude swept over him and he said what might be inter-
preted broadly as a prayer. That feeling persisted after he hung up.

In the panic he had felt at mislaying the painting, he was certain a malevolent power was in charge of the universe with a particular interest in making George Frederick Mason miserable. Now, with relief just a UPS delivery away, that cosmic power was revealed as basically benign, reassuringly determined that his life should have a happy ending. He must not forget how he had gotten into this predicament that had been aging him these past weeks. He had— say it in whispers—fully intended to steal Ford's portrait of Bridget, sell it to Parker, and become an instant multimillionaire. Not only would that have been grand larceny, it would have been a betrayal of the trust placed in him by the citizens of Fox River in general and the Sinclair family in particular. To think he had imagined no one would notice the picture was missing! Platoons of people had descended on the museum, asking about the portrait of Bridget. How mad he had been to imagine that the Sinclairs, a covetous clan, with the notable exception of Maud, would overlook a fortune in Ford paintings. Doubtless the envious Glockner was making anonymous calls to the police, a pitiable troublemaker. When Father Dowling showed up in his office, Mason steeled himself for an accusation from the priest. But none had come. Thank God he'd been spared the consequences of his own intended perfidy.

Now that relief was in sight he could permit himself to dwell on the fate he had narrowly avoided. To steal a priceless painting and not even profit from the theft. Dear God. His calmness left him as he thought of it.

He got out of his chair and crossed to his washroom, where he rinsed his face with cool water and scrubbed it briskly. There was a springiness in his step as he went into the outer office, where he stopped and grinned at Miss Knutsen while rubbing his hands.

"Good news?"

It took an heroic effort not to confide in her. There was an odd office-time intimacy between them, but a reticence as well, largely due to the fact that her beauty intimidated him. Still, he told Miss Knutsen things he told no one else, if only because there was no else to tell. Marjorie, for all her faults, had been an ear into which to pour his grievances and joys, a sounding board, however generally out of sympathy with his desires. Talking with Miss Knutsen was a far cry from that, but it was preferable to talking to himself. One spoke to communicate one's thoughts to others, that was the point of it. To talk to oneself was redundant, neurotic, however necessary. Not to hear objectified in sound one's otherwise inchoate and shapeless cogitations was not really to think at all. Better talking to oneself than not talking at all. But better yet to address his receptive receptionist.

"That was my wife's daughter Ginger."

"Oh." Miss Knutsen looked unsure of Ginger's status, given that description.

"I never adopted her."

"It must have been nice to hear from her." A pink tongue moistened her ruby lips.

"Yes."

What an idiotic exchange, but he could hardly blame Miss Knutsen. "I'll be in the gallery."

He mingled with some schoolchildren who were being shown through by one of the volunteer museum guides, Sandy Sonnebohn of the Junior League. It seemed unfair of God to confront him with Sandy when he had just fled Miss Knutsen. The jacket of Sandy's white linen suit strained with the burden of her ample bosom, which had been buttoned into subjection but threatened to throw off its chains. The golden-brown flesh glowed like fruit in a basket against the white material of her suit. She turned, saw him, for a moment reacted in the manner of a student teacher being monitored by her superior, then responded to the frankness of his gaze, female to male. Mason bowed to her, smiled, stayed with the group. Weeks of fear were gone and other emotions, freed from suppression, emotions that had lain latent for longer than weeks, emerged. He had forgotten for too long the attractiveness of a mature young woman.

"We come now to landscapes by the renowned painter Clayton Ford," Mrs. Sonnebohn lisped prettily. "Perhaps you would like to take over, Dr. Mason? This is Dr. George Frederick Mason, director of the museum."

"Not at all, Sandy. Carry on."

But he continued to hover at the edge of the group, a mixed bag of teenagers, boys and girls, unattractive in their pimply awkwardness, making Sandy Sonnebohn seem by contrast the quintessential object of concupiscence. Mason was at once surprised and delighted by the horniness he felt. It was with the sense of a satyr keeping his hooves hidden that he moved along with the group.

When Sandy started discussing the final Ford, he broke away, got

191

into the elevator, and went down into the vault. Tomorrow he would return the portrait of Bridget here. The frame was in the closet of his bedroom. He had meant to mount some other picture in it after a decent lapse. Thank God he had kept it and kept it at home. Once Bridget was back in the vault he would, with some fanfare, take her out, perhaps with Glockner there, and Maud. That would bring the whole silly episode to an end.

After half an hour's enjoyment of the prospect of redemption, dark thoughts began again. He remembered his belated realization that he could have had a copy of the portrait made, hung it on his wall, and then slipped away to New York and Parker with the original. Having escaped exposure, having tasted the sweet wine of relief, he began to flirt with the possibility of achieving his original aims. That would have been entirely out of the question only a week ago, when the Sinclairs announced that they intended to repossess the paintings and auction them. Mason had vetoed the formation of a citizens committee to fight this denuding of the gallery. He had ignored Wilbert Plunkett's garbled cable from Sassari. He had acted out of remorse and a resolve to avoid all temptation in the future. Now he told himself that a copy of Bridget could provide a second chance at a fast fortune. He must discreetly look into a way of having such a copy made.

And, of course, he thought of Parker. The dealer would know how to get such a copy made without the risk of its becoming public knowledge. He could even suggest to Parker that getting such a copy had been the point of his earlier visit.

One of the curious aspects of these awful weeks had been the absence of any pressure from Parker. The dealer had agreed to meet with him in the expectation of some advantage, yet Mason had shown up empty-handed, offered a silly excuse, and fled, and Parker had not followed up on it. Strange. Of course Parker was up to his neck in deals all the time. One painting more or less would mean little to him. But he would have been more than justified in expressing anger at Mason, scoffing at his excuse, and demanding to know what the hell had really happened.

If George Frederick Mason had permitted himself to imagine, before that ill-fated trip to New York, that it would turn out as it had, what he would have feared most was putting himself into the hands of Parker. Whatever the outcome, Parker would know his larcenous intent, and that made him vulnerable to any future moves the shady dealer might care to make. From which it followed that even now, with the painting on its way back to Fox River, Parker could conceivably exploit his knowledge of Mason's intention.

When he got into the elevator to go back to his office, some of the mood with which he had left it half an hour before was gone. The pure redemptive joy of his original reaction had given way to shameless ogling of Miss Knutsen and then Mrs. Sonnebohn. Then he had actually begun to connive again to defraud the museum in his care of one of its most precious paintings. Alone in the elevator, he spoke sternly to himself.

"You don't deserve to be let off the hook, you silly ass. It would have served you right if the painting had been lost and Parker got word out that you wanted to sell it to him. Your career would have been over. The Glockners of this world would have roared with laughter. You silly, silly ass."

The doors slid open and there stood Sandy Sonnebohn.

"George! Where did you sneak off to?"

"I've been down in the vault," he said, taking her arm and leading her through Miss Knutsen's office and into his own. "I want to congratulate you on the way you lead a tour."

He closed the door after them."

"Your reward is a glass of sherry."

"At two-thirty in the afternoon?"

"I have a bottle of two-thirty sherry right here." He threw open a cabinet to reveal the cache of liquor with which he entertained when such entertainment was called for. It was most definitely called for now.

"As I came upon you lecturing your little group, I suddenly saw you as the subject of a Sargent painting." He turned and gave her a knowledgeable look. "I am thinking of his use of white."

She was suitably pleased to figure in such romantic fantasies. She tucked in her chin and gave him a lidded look.

"White is my favorite color."

"As it was Sargent's. Do you know his *The Fountain in the Villa Torlonia*? No. I'll show you a reproduction. Art has become largely a matter of reproduction," he said throatily, handing her a sherry.

"If I drink this, I won't be responsible."

"That is promised on the label."

He had put her on the divan which with two matching chairs made a semicircle around a round glass table. Kneeling beside the table, he opened the album of Sargent prints and showed her the picture of the woman painting in the Villa Torlonia.

"Why is it named after the fountains?" She sat forward and her knees touched her rib cage.

"Wonderful!" he cried. "That is precisely what I have always objected to. It should be called . . ." He hesitated, turned to her, looked toward the ceiling for a moment, and then lowered his eyes. "Portrait of a lovely lady."

Sandy had no doubt that he was addressing her. Her smile dimpled her cheeks nicely. "Show me some other things."

They had two glasses of sherry together and might have had a third if Miss Knutsen had not decided to appoint herself representative of the moral law. The first time she buzzed, he ignored it. He was seated next to Sandy on the couch now, his arm flung carelessly behind her head. It was so much like a first adolescent date that he loved it all the more.

"Your buzzer is buzzing."

"That's not the buzz that has to be answered. She's just letting me know someone called."

Her lips were shiny with sherry and her eyes slightly unfocused, perhaps because of his proximity. The buzzer sounded insistently again.

"I don't think she'll take no for an answer."

"Neither will I."

She pushed playfully at his chest. "Better answer it."

Before rising he leaned toward her, wanting the kiss all this had been leading to, but she turned at the last moment and his lips pressed her cheek. It was with a sense of having been toyed with that he crossed the room to his buzzing phone.

"Your super called to say a UPS delivery came to your apartment."

"Thank you, Miss Knutsen."

"I thought you'd want to know." Was she jealous? Perhaps the afternoon had not been wasted. How could he be angry with her for telling him the good news he had been anticipating?

"Important?" Sandy asked.

He wagged his head. "More or less. I'm going to have to go home."

"Can I drop you off?"

It might have been the promise of a continuation of what they had begun, but the way Sandy had turned away from his kiss suggested that she was just a tease. But what a sumptuous tease she was.

"I have my car," he said, his voice sad, face twisted into feigned regret.

Gordon, the building factotum, did not answer when Mason knocked on his door. After several minutes, Mason rattled the knob and was surprised to find that the door was unlocked.

"Gordon," he called musically, pushing the door open and peeking inside, a big phony smile on his face. "Gor-don?"

What a nice little place Gordon had. It was a truncated version of the apartments above, a lower ceiling, the windows flush with the ground, but cozy. The blinds were half drawn, creating a chiaroscuro effect, and in a corner the eye of a television glowed, though there was no sound. Keeping his hand on the knob, Mason stepped further inside. Was Gordon perhaps enjoying a nap? But Gordon was not there. And then from a window he spied him out on the walk.

He dashed outside and hurried toward Gordon who, when he noticed Mason, began frantically waving for him to stay back. Mason stopped. The contraption Gordon held had begun to move antically while he waved, but now with both hands he brought it under control. It looked like a metal detector and for a moment Mason thought he had surprised Gordon in an effort to augment his income by looking for lost treasure—coins or pieces of jewelry—but the annoying roar of the gadget suggested otherwise. Of course. Gordon was trimming the little ribbon of grass between the walk and the building, doubtless too narrow for him to reach with his tractor mower. With the air of one giving a performance, Gordon continued his work.

In saner times the man would have been flogged for keeping his master waiting. Gordon was in his twenties, wore faded jeans low on his hips, a ring of keys clipped to a belt loop bounced off his butt as he made sweeping movements with the trimmer, one sleeve of his T-shirt was rolled up to hold a pack of cigarettes and reveal the tattooed Marine Corps emblem. The slack-mouthed concentration with which he trimmed the grass suggested mop-up operations on a

Pacific atoll. Still smiling, not showing his mounting impatience, Mason consigned the insolent bastard to the lower reaches of hell.

"Hi," Gordon said when he turned with an expectant smile after shutting off the roar of the trimmer. Did he expect applause?

"A UPS delivery came for me."

Gordon looked dumb, shuffling mentally through the myriad details that crowded his life.

"You called my office."

"Oh, yeah! Come on."

They went inside, where Gordon handed over the tube as if it were the baton in a relay race. Mason acknowledged delivery with a nod and headed immediately for the stairs.

"It was prepaid," Gordon called after him. "There was no charge."

Good try, you son of a bitch. But as Mason mounted to the lobby and the elevator that would take him up to his floor, his annoyance with Gordon fell from him like a used skin. He rose through the shaft, eyes closed, holding the tube with both hands, not voicing the gratitude that filled him. He let himself into his apartment, closed the door, hurried into the living room, and let out a great roar of triumph. His ordeal was over at last.

In that moment he understood why primitive peoples worship inanimate objects. To burn incense before the tube containing the portrait, to sacrifice Gordon, say, in a humane but definitive way, did not seem farfetched. For that brief moment Mason felt that there was a perfect mesh between the moments of his individual life and the cosmos. He was synchronized with ultimate reality.

The masking tape at one end of the tube would be what Ginger used to close it up again after taking a peek. He removed it carefully as if the tape, like the tube's contents, was worth millions. And then he was easing the rolled-up canvas free. He spread it on the dining room table, weighted its corners with bric-a-brac from the sideboard, and again felt an urge to worship. The portrait had never looked better. Bridget's eyes, about to narrow skeptically, even as her lips were about to form what one was sure would be a sardonic smile, looked into his, an old friend. He leaned forward and gave her a kiss.

A thought occurred. He removed the weights and turned the canvas over. His expression grew concerned. He again bowed low, but now he was frantically searching the back of the canvas. There was nothing in the upper left corner! Was he holding it upside down?

But he searched the diagonally opposite corner, then all the corners, then the whole extent of the back of the portrait. There was no doubt of it. The authenticating mark was not there. The *cf* signature he had seen there earlier was gone.

He grabbed the painting by a corner and went into his den where he put it under a stronger light. He used a magnifying glass. He employed touch and smell and even taste. It was an amazing job.

But there was no doubt about it. Ginger had sent him an all-but-perfect copy of Clayton Ford's portrait of Bridget Doyle.

Peggy had taken the portrait of Margaret back to her room and propped it up where she could see it easily when sitting on her bed. She wanted to be able to look at it when she read the diary, but she also saw the danger in letting the portrait be treated as a family possession. It would be like the Fords in the museum. Those landscapes had been there forever; no wonder people thought they were a permanent gift. The longer Margaret hung on the living room wall, the more her parents were going to think of it as theirs as much as hers. But if Margaret Sinclair had wanted Vivian and Dennis to have it, she would have given it to them. It was the only painting mentioned in the will.

Her mother appeared round-eyed in the doorway and when she saw the painting slumped in relief.

"I thought we'd been robbed."

Peggy made a face. Even Father Dowling had warned her that someone might steal her portrait of Margaret. "I like it here."

Her mother studied the portrait in a preoccupied way. "Isn't this a little selfish?"

"How so?"

"Who can enjoy it if you have it up here?"

"The living room isn't exactly a public place. Besides, the painting is mine."

Her mother sat on the bed. "Peggy, I know you don't like to talk about it, but remember what that painting is worth. You heard the estimates. Dr. Mason as well as your professor agreed. That is a very valuable painting."

"I didn't need them to tell me that."

"Not just sentimental value. At auction that painting would bring in several million dollars." She turned to look at it, as if to overcome her own incredulity. "That gives you a tremendous responsibility, Peggy."

"You think I ought to sell it?"

"I think you ought to give serious thought to its security."

Her father, on the other hand, approved of moving the painting back upstairs.

"If the family sees that, they might want it too. Here you are, the youngest Sinclair, given a fortune while the rest of the money, pffft!"

"Wait till they sell the paintings from the museum."

He nodded. "They're your main protection against being sued."

By her relatives? The Ford paintings in the Fox River Museum had indeed cheered up her aunts and uncle and cousins. And her parents too; she couldn't exempt them from what seemed to her a mindless greed. Why should people who had more than enough be so eager for more?

Because it was there, no doubt. Because it had to go somewhere, and the Sinclair Foundation was not in the family's control and would be dispensing money that might have been theirs to who knew what crazy causes?

"Where does Octavio stand on Liberation Theology?" William asked. "I don't think Grandma would want to support the Sandinistas."

But Bunny and Octavio had fears of an opposite sort. "He's more likely to bankroll Opus Dei."

SINCLAIRS: BENEFACTORS OR INDIAN GIVERS? That was the title of the story in a Chicago paper. Fortunately the headline caused a boomerang reaction and the paper came under fire from Native Americans.

Her father said, "We'll have to have it officially appraised for tax purposes."

"I have to pay taxes?"

"Honey, you may not be able to afford to keep that painting."

All her life Peggy had heard people complaining about taxes: income taxes, property taxes, taxes on investments, a background buzz of discontent, but it had never before had anything to do with her. Like many people who had everything, Peggy wanted to think that she could easily get along with very little. A stripped-down life with few possessions almost seemed a natural right she had been deprived of by the accident of birth.

"We don't own things," her uncle William was fond of saying. "The government lets us use them for a fee—the federal government, the state government, local governments. They are the real holders of property; we are borrowers. What we pay for is the privilege of watching the damned market behave like a roller coaster, taking with one hand what it gives with the other. We get to pay large sums to insurance companies against loss, theft, or fire, not to mention the cost of maintaining real property. And all the while, the hyenas in Congress are dreaming up new ways to make it more costly for us to use what they believe really belongs to the public."

That was just the beginning. He was capable of going on and on, the weirdest little smile on his face, as if he enjoyed talking about how tough it was to be rich. Uncle William's argument that wealth was created by entrepreneurs carried weight; he was a businessman, not just a drone playing the market with inherited money.

When Maud mentioned reburying Margaret and Matthew, Peggy suggested it might be more practical to take Margaret's ashes to Maiori.

"Glory be to God," Maud cried, but she gave Peggy a hug. "If anyone is going to be moved, it's him."

They thought of Matthew Sinclair as a stranger, almost an alien, yet it was into his family that Margaret had married, it was his name that she and all of them bore. Why hadn't Margaret brought the body of her husband home? It was understandable in the horror and sadness of his death and the need to make immediate decisions with no one but strangers to advise her—except, of course, Bridget—that Margaret had had her husband laid to rest in the local cemetery in Maiori. But later, at home, with the passage of years, why hadn't she

200

thought to bring Matthew's remains to the island mausoleum where his forebears lay? If only that question had occurred to her while Margaret was still alive!

Peggy did not want to think of Joel while staring at her great-grandmother's portrait, despite the relief she felt now knowing she wasn't pregnant. That was odd; she hadn't been consciously worried. What a dreadful prospect, though, to be pregnant with the child of a deceitful man. She would not have wanted to put her disapproval of abortion to that kind of a test. The truth was she prayed to her departed great-grandmother that nothing would come of it, feeling embarrassed at bringing such a matter to the attention of the old woman. But of course the painted eyes expressed no shock.

However wise and experienced in the ways of the human animal Margaret Sinclair might have become over her long life, at Peggy's age she would have been astounded to think of supposedly respectable young people falling into bed with the ease they had. Her one lapse made Peggy feel truly part of a generation which, allegedly, was free and easy in sexual matters.

"Did Margaret ever speak to you of Bridget Doyle?" Peggy asked Father Dowling.

When they were at Fairview together, he often asked to see Margaret's diary. He had read it all by now, but promised not to give Peggy any clues as to what lay ahead in unread entries.

"The maid? No."

"She was there when Matthew died."

That was what fascinated Peggy about Bridget. What had happened to her? Aunt Maud, the reluctant historian archivist of the family ("Doesn't anyone else care?"), was able to tell Peggy that the maid had left the family employ a year after Margaret's sad return to Fairview as a widow.

"Why did she leave?"

"To marry." Maud had a way of whistling through her teeth as she read. She turned the pages of an old ledger, one that recorded household expenses. "It's not here. But I know the man she married was named Pincus."

"Pincus? Is that Irish?"

"I've no idea." Maud seemed to find the question odd, but then she was unacquainted with Bridget as she entered into her mistress's diary. Father Dowling asked for the ledger and was soon poring over it.

"I wonder where they went?" Peggy mused.

"Went? Pincus lived right here in Fox River."

This time he surprised Ginger, arriving in New York unannounced and going immediately to her apartment. What could she do but open the door to her former stepfather?

"George!" she cried, but she seemed to be addressing someone behind her. Well, it was just too damned bad if he'd surprised her in an embarrassing situation, although how any daughter of Marjorie's could be embarrassed by anything in the romance department was beyond him. She stepped aside only when it was clear he would have bowled her over if she blocked his way. George Frederick Mason was in no mood to be a gentleman.

"I received the painting," he said, dropping his bag on the way to the couch. He was exhausted but at the same time full of nervous energy. He had flown to New York to save his life and by God he meant to do it.

"Oh, good."

"It is a very good copy. I've come for the original."

Ginger was a lovely thing, no doubt of that. The cornucopia of her bosom emerged from the sheer black robe she had pulled over her black nightie when she came to open the door. He was surprised she had bothered. Thank God she had. Mason could not figure out which side God was on in all this, but he didn't mean to rile the deity if he was still at least neutral.

"The original." Ginger sank onto an ottoman, one hand going automatically to her hair in which a black satin ribbon sat awry.

"The painting you took from the cab was a Clayton Ford original of inestimable value. What you mailed to me was an excellent copy worth a comparative pittance. Where is the original?"

"George, I honestly don't know what you're talking about."

This was a possibility he had pondered during the past agonizing hours. Even if Ginger too had been victimized, she could be of help. But was she as innocent as she claimed?

"You do realize I am going to sit here until you tell me all about it?"

"Well, you can sit here as long as you like. This is all mumbo-jumbo to me." She rose and went into her kitchen. Out of sight, she called, "Coffee?"

"Black."

"Good, I'm out of cream. Sweet and Low?"

"Plain."

"Good," she said for no stated reason.

Fetching coffee was just a delaying tactic, he told himself; she knew what had happened to the original. She brought in coffee on a tray and when she bent to put the tray on the table her mammalian status was established beyond dispute. She is trying to divert me, he thought with satisfaction. She was her mother's daughter after all. An unbidden memory of Marjorie holding him to her bared bosom in her Rose O' Sharon mood roared through his blood like a freight train. His ears were ringing from exhaustion and lack of sleep. He took the cup she handed him, forcing himself to look into her eyes. He surprised there an expression of concern.

"You look awful, George."

"I feel awful. How would you feel if someone had bilked you out of a picture worth millions?"

"Millions!"

"Conservatively speaking, three or four. Who knows what might happen at an auction?"

"Was it going to be auctioned?"

He looked at her warily. "Not by me," he croaked.

"Why did you bring it to New York?"

His bladder was killing him. One sip of coffee made him aware of his discomfort. He put down the cup and stood. Ginger was on her feet at the same time, looking expectant. Did she think he might go away?

"Where's the bathroom?"

She came fluttering along with him, to show the way. The closed bedroom door seemed to explain her antsiness. He almost envied her. If the most she had to worry about was concealing a lover in her bedroom until she got rid of an unwelcome guest, she was a fortunate creature indeed.

When he washed his hands, he got a good look at himself. Bloodshot eyes, imperfectly shaven, manifestly a man ready to go over the edge. He splashed water on his face and rubbed it briskly with a towel, trying to bring back the look of life.

"I brought it to New York to have a copy made," he announced on his way into the living room. Like Ginger at the door, he wanted to be heard by the occupant of the bedroom too. A witness at the trial? Dear God! Panic came rushing back.

"You must have mixed up the copy and the original," Ginger suggested.

"There was no copy! Not yet. I came to consult with an expert to get advice on artists who make copies."

"Oh."

"I was on my way to meet him when we shared the cab. Parker."

She jumped at the word and then jumped again when Parker himself emerged from the bedroom. He had had ample time to dress, of course; he might just have come in off the street.

"You're full of shit, Mason," he said matter-of-factly. "Pour me a cup of that coffee, Ginger."

It surprised Mason that he was not surprised when Parker came into the room. His original idea had been that Ginger was Parker's accomplice. He had sent her to intercept him at the hotel, knowing where Mason would be; she had insisted on his sharing her cab, her task to take possession of the painting. How easy he had made it for her. He recited all this to an impatient Parker.

"Yeah, yeah. So what?"

"So Ginger was lying to me."

205

"Was she? So what again? You're a thief, Mason, you're in no position to get on your high horse."

He was right, of course. Mason could have wept because Parker was so right. No wonder Ginger was unperturbed at the revelation of her role. Can a thief be robbed?

"Parker, I have to have that picture back. I'll be ruined!"

"You've got a good copy."

"I need the original. The owners are reclaiming all the Ford paintings from the museum."

"It doesn't belong to the museum?"

"It was on long-term loan from a family named Sinclair. There has been a death and now they want the pictures back."

"You some kind of nut, Mason? You stole a picture on loan that they're asking back?"

"I thought no one remembered the portrait."

Parker looked at him with contempt. "Just overlooked the fact you had a Ford portrait they owned?"

"It's no good to you, Parker. It can't be sold."

"Who says I got it?"

"You admitted it!"

He turned to Ginger. "You hear me admit that?"

"Leave me out of this," she cried.

Parker walked to the window and looked out over midtown Manhattan. "I'll tell you a story, Georgie. A Ford portrait is going to be discovered down near Morristown where the artist spent a certain period of his life. This portrait is not listed in any account of Ford's production. The discovery will be a sensation. After considerable and appropriate hoopla, it will be auctioned for a very large number." He turned from the window. "You do know that, don't you? The portrait isn't listed among Ford's works."

"It's his."

"I believe you. Mason, I'm going to be generous. You're in for ten percent. I could leave you out in the cold. I didn't even have to provide you with a copy. But what the hell, I can see the fix you're in. Ten percent of what an authentic but unknown Ford portrait will bring is not pickled herring. Okay?"

Once larceny has entered the soul it eats away what little moral character was there. Mason avidly followed what Parker said. Ten percent was better than zero. Was it possible to conceal the exist-

206

ence of the portrait from the Sinclairs? Could he fool them with a copy?

Parker sat next to Mason on the couch. Ginger refilled their cups, a distracting interlude.

"You're gonna need a story, of course. What you have there is a copy and where did you get a copy of a painting no one knew existed? No problem. The copyist, let's say, did his work however many years ago you need. He had come upon the painting in Morristown. He mentioned it to me just a week ago. He took me down there and by God if it wasn't an authentic Clayton Ford he'd copied. The copy came into your possession while you were still married to Marjorie. It never occurred to you that it was a copy of a Ford, or maybe it did, that doesn't matter, you kept it, you still have it."

Listening, George Frederick Mason felt a terrible weight begin to lift from him. Parker's story sounded plausible. Why would anyone doubt the word of George Frederick Mason? The story had the added advantage of covering his rear from Glockner. As soon as that portrait was "discovered" by Parker, Glockner would recognize it as a picture he had seen on Mason's office wall. By God, the scheme could work. What was ten percent of several million?

"We got a deal, George?"

Ginger looked on expectantly, Parker extended his hand. Mason took it and shook it. He really had no choice.

"Don't forget this," Ginger said an hour later when he got up to go. She held out the tube in which he had brought the copy of Ford's portrait of Bridget Doyle.

"Guard it with your life," Parker advised.

It had been his intention to get a hotel room and sleep until he woke up and then roll over again and sleep some more, but instead he directed the cab to LaGuardia. He would do his sleeping in Fox River, after he had framed the copy and hung it up on his office wall.

He realized he was smiling. He felt relaxed. God was on his side after all.

37

Roger Dowling found the wedding of Bridget Doyle and Timothy Pincus in the parish records, the entry made by one Father A. O'Neil, his remote predecessor as pastor of St. Hilary's. The research, once embarked upon, recalled his days at the archdiocesan marriage tribunal, but he went on despite that.

At the Fox River Historical Society, to which old city and county records had been removed, Father Dowling was given somewhat grudging help. The attendant seemed to think this was not an appropriate way for a priest to show interest in the departed. Maybe he was right. The first Pincus showed up in a Fox River city directory at the turn of the century, but the listing grew until at the time Bridget married there were nine. Timothy Pincus, the name linked with Bridget's in the parish records, was not listed in the city directory, but perhaps his father was. There had never been a Pincus in the parish. He had already checked on that. The director cleared his throat. He had suggested that Father Dowling check records on microfilm, but the priest wanted to see the thing itself, even if this meant having the disapproving director brooding over him. The young man looked like pictures of the last Czar of Russia so it was hard to hate him, but he certainly was a fussbudget.

"How would you go about finding a person who married in 1914?"

He looked at Father Dowling but said nothing. Was he deaf? He repeated the question, speaking loudly and forming the words with care.

"I'd have to know a lot more than that."

"I know her name."

"Good."

"I know her husband's name. I know the year they were married."

"Month?"

He tried to recall the page in the parish record. "I'm not sure. Except that it was during the summer."

The man's arms remained at his sides when he walked, giving him the appearance of floating. At the computer, his fingers flew over the keys and lists began to form on the screen. He hit a button, typed Pincus, and a smaller list formed.

"There it is. July 24, 1913."

"Would they have signed anything when they got the license?" Names and, he hoped, addresses too, someplace to start.

The Czar looked at him, round brown eyes staring through round glasses. "All the data we have is there."

Father Dowling would not have wanted to explain to anyone why he was doing this, to Marie Murkin, say, or Phil Keegan. Margaret's diary along with memories of odd things she'd said seemed to converge on a point he would not have dared express. Peggy's fascination with her great-grandmother was understandable enough, as would be any Sinclair's. Maud, of course, drew the line of her curiosity at the maid. She was interested in the family, the Sinclairs. What heresy she would have thought it if anyone suggested to her that not being a Sinclair was a cross even a Sinclair might be able to bear.

His persistence won the grudging respect of the attendant. Besides, it was a slow day. What would a fast day at the archives look like? The city directories seemed a favorite of his. "Lester," he said when Father Dowling asked his name.

"What do they call you?"

"Lester."

"Lester what?" The man was now checking the index of the *Fox River Tribune.*

"Pincus," he said, and Father Dowling assumed he was reading from the screen.

"I meant *your* last name."

"Pincus," he repeated, frowning at the screen and making a column of names slide by. "Lester Pincus."

"Why didn't you say so?"

"I thought you could read."

"Read what?"

"The nameplate on my desk. I thought you were pulling my leg. Some people find archivists funny, they find the work funny, saving, storing, cataloging. I suppose it does seem strange. Maybe ninety percent of what is here will never be looked at. I think of that sometimes. Maybe ninety-five percent. The thing is, you don't know in advance what will be important."

"Do you know the Bridget I'm looking for?"

He nodded. "I think you mean my grandmother." How old was Lester? The atmosphere of his workplace might slow the aging process, but Roger Dowling supposed he was forty.

"As a girl she worked for Margaret Sinclair."

Lester raised and lowered his head. "The Margaret Sinclair who died recently. I know. My grandmother wanted to attend the funeral, but that was out of the question, in her condition."

"Bridget Doyle's still alive!"

Lester nodded. "Alive but not very well. She resents the nursing home, of course. Most old people do, those who aren't senile. My grandmother is far from senile. A very sharp mind. I enjoy talking with her when she'll talk about the past, but she dislikes that. Maybe she pretends to dislike it, in order to annoy me. She is very contrary. Why were you interested in her?"

Father Dowling backed away from Lester and sat down. Bridget Doyle. Rest home. Pincus. Pinkie?

"Are you all right?"

"I just realized I know your grandmother. I take Holy Communion to her once a week."

Lester offered him coffee, by which he meant instant, which tasted awful. Marie would never approve. It made his mouth sticky and dry. But he drank it all, in appreciation of the sentiment.

Lester invited Father Dowling behind the counter to his desk and, sure enough, there was his name big as life: Lester Pincus. Lester, unsurprisingly, given his work, had developed a very elaborate tree of the Pincus family.

"It's become a popular hobby, genealogy. I get letters, phone calls, people come in. I thought that was your interest until you said you were trying to find out about Bridget Pincus."

"Maybe I'll take it up."

"If you are all Irish, it should be easy. Contact Dublin Castle. The Irish are almost as good as the Mormons in keeping records."

His father had warned him against delving into the family's past, wryly suggesting there would be horse thieves and smugglers among their forebears. There was Adam, in any case, and that was bad, or good, enough.

"The Pincuses posed a problem," Lester said pedantically. "I didn't know my grandmother had ever had anything to do with the Sinclairs until she said she wanted to go to that funeral."

"She went on Margaret Sinclair's wedding trip, as her maid. Margaret kept a diary and of course there are many mentions of Bridget."

"Bridget kept a diary too. She still does."

Father Dowling let it go. He felt he had already intruded too much into Peggy's interest. Let her seek out her great-grandmother's maid.

Riverside Residence was not accurately named, being located on a street perpendicular to the Fox, any view of the river blocked by an intervening high rise as well as by large old trees which, in this rainy summer, did not seem, in the errant golfer's hopeful phrase, ninety percent air. None of this mattered to most of the residents, of course. The retirement home could have been on the moon, deep in the country, downtown, it wouldn't have mattered, and as for golf, if the patients had ever played, they would play no more. The landscape had ceased being either favorable or unfavorable to a shot to the green.

Peggy parked on the river road and walked up past the high rise and under the great hovering oaks to what had the look of a motel: one story, an asphalt turnaround circling past the entrance, overhanging eaves with the small windows tucked up under them like sleepy eyes. She went right inside to an empty waiting room. A counter window with closed louvered doors suggested naptime. Peggy cleared her throat, tapped on the counter, finally sat on the edge of a chair, waiting. In a minute, she got up and walked to the

212

closed double doors and pushed them slightly open. A low, narrow corridor seemed to extend for miles, an exercise in perspective. The matching closed doors on the opposite side of the waiting room gave a similar view, except for the sight of a woman standing at a doorway a third of the way down the corridor. Peggy pushed through.

The woman wore a white dress and a thick cardigan sweater. No wonder. When the doors swung shut behind her Peggy felt she had entered a refrigerator. But it was the smells of age rather than the temperature that characterized the corridor, which seemed narrower and lower now that she was in it. The woman was looking into a room and turned incuriously at Peggy's approach.

"Mrs. Pincus."

The woman nodded. When Peggy did not go on, she said, "Who you here to see?"

"Mrs. Pincus."

A delayed and exaggerated look of comprehension. "I thought you was Mrs. Pincus." She dipped forward in feigned and silent laughter. "What's her first name, dear?"

"Bridget."

The merriment disappeared. A sweatered arm pointed. "At the end, on the right."

Peggy caught a glimpse of a toothless old woman behind the nurse, bright-eyed at all this excitement and, as she continued down the hall, she could not resist looking into other open doors. In some rooms thin hairless heads with large earphones clamped on watched televised antics; in others a spectral figure was fragilely arranged in a wheelchair and stared vacant-eyed at nothing. Some lay flat on their backs in bed, sunken faces and bony noses pointed ceiling-ward. Peggy's spirit dropped as she went. She had come in much the same mood she had gone to talk with Margaret, but these sad wrecks gave a truer sense of old age than Margaret Sinclair ever had.

Peggy slowed as she neared the end of the corridor, then peeked around the door of the last room on the right. A figure in an Indian blanket robe sat hunched at a desk, still thick salt-and-pepper hair brushed and clean and arranged with artful indifference on the bowed head. She seemed to be writing. Peggy tapped.

"It isn't four yet," a firm voice said. She did not turn.

"Mrs. Pincus?"

What Peggy would come to realize was unheard-of formality

213

caused the old head to turn. For the first time Peggy felt those bright malevolent eyes upon her. "Mis-sus Pin-cus? Who in the world are you?" Peggy stood in the doorway so the old woman could see. "Not one of the guards. Obviously. You mustn't treat us like adults. That's the first rule here."

BRIDGET PINCUS was typed neatly on the card slipped into the permanent holder on the door.

"I'm Margaret Sinclair."

"God in heaven!"

Bridget had turned her wheelchair from the desk, but now she put her hands on the wheels and gave Peggy a frightened look. She began to roll warily away. She was studying Peggy's face as she did this, and her fright increased.

"Margaret Sinclair was my great-grandmother."

The chair came to a stop but the sound of the old woman's shallow, rapid breathing continued. A full minute went by before the sardonic expression with which she had greeted Peggy returned.

"You could be her as she was, you know. You're very like."

"Are you busy?"

A barking laugh that would become familiar. "I have a very heavy schedule. At four I receive my insulin shot, after which I am taken to the rest room. Dinner follows but, as for the evening, my plans are fluid."

She laughed again. As with Margaret, Peggy did not have the sense of being with an extremely old lady. Gestures, the flow of talk, negated the appearance.

"I wanted to go the funeral, but of course they wouldn't let me."

"Then you know she's dead."

"What brings you here?"

She decided not to mention Father Dowling. "Your grandson Lester at the county archives."

"Lester!" She shook her head. "If I'd drowned my children, the world would have lost nothing. Oh, maybe one or two were keepers. But *their* children!"

"How many children did you have?"

"Nine. Nine that lived."

"My great-grandmother had only one."

A sideways look as she worked her mouth. Bridget seemed to

214

swing between being an ancient woman and an ageless conversationalist.

"Whose daughter are you?"

"Dennis's."

"He's a son of Henry's, of course?"

"Henry's dead." Peggy had vague memories of her portly grandfather, Margaret's only child.

"I know. How many cousins do you have?"

Peggy had to think. Bridget said, "Imagine how many you'd have if they'd all had families the size of mine."

"How many grandchildren do you have?"

"Too many." That laugh. "There's a photograph in the dresser, taken on July Fourth. It's just a group of strangers to me. Some of them I've never met. That's not a complaint. I wouldn't want children brought here with all these corpses. It's a depressing place."

Bridget exempted herself from the common ailment. If Peggy expected an excited reaction when she offered to take Bridget outside, she was disappointed. Just a nod of assent. Peggy felt they were escaping when she pushed her down the corridor. The nurse in the cardigan sweater was framed in the reception window in the waiting room, the louvered doors folded open.

"You should be resting, Pinkie."

Bridget ignored her, pointing at the matching swinging doors. Peggy looked at the nurse, expecting to be forbidden, but the large woman had apparently said all she intended to. Through these doors a large recreation room in which three old men sat opened off the corridor, and sliding glass doors led to a patio. One old man sat a little straighter and looked with glinting eyes at the two females. Peggy slid open the door and Bridget wheeled herself through.

"Do you want to come outside?" Peggy asked the old man with a glint in his eye. His expression did not change.

"He can't hear you," Bridget called back to her. "Most of them are stone deaf."

"What were you writing?" Peggy asked outside, pulling a lawn chair up beside Bridget. Whatever it was had disappeared into a drawer before Bridget had wheeled away in fright.

"My diary."

"A diary! Margaret kept a diary too, on her wedding trip. She gave it to me."

"I've been keeping a diary for over seventy years. Lester confiscated it and put it into that silly place where he works. My diary! Does it matter that I object? Of course not. First you lose your teeth, then your hearing, then your rights. They treat us like children here, but to be treated that way by relatives is cruel."

"I don't think my great-grandmother kept a diary after the wedding trip."

"I got the habit from Margaret. In the afternoons we both sat down and wrote a page or two, probably about one another. She was a terror to work for."

"She did write about you in her diary."

"Did she now? Well, I wrote about her as well. Keep hers private, child. Don't let Lester have it."

Peggy assured Bridget that she would never part with the diary.

"Maybe Lester would have felt the same if I'd only written one volume."

"It's the most precious thing I have of hers. That and her portrait."

Bridget fiddled with the wheels of her chair. "The one Clayton Ford painted?"

"Do you remember him?"

"Of course I remember that scoundrel! Didn't he have us both sit for him, down in the barn he'd turned into a studio? We didn't dare go alone, so he would paint one, then the other, back and forth."

"So long ago," Peggy said.

"It doesn't seem so to me." She thought. "Seventy-five years ago this very summer."

"His paintings have become very valuable."

"He's dead, I suppose."

"Oh yes."

Bridget looked at her for a moment, then turned away. A squirrel scampered across the lawn to a tree.

"At Fairview there were black squirrels."

"There still are."

"His father, Matthew's father, brought them in from somewhere in Indiana. Goshen?"

"When did you last see my great-grandmother?"

"After I left to marry? Twice. Three times at most. We had nothing in common."

A male nurse came looking for Bridget, a tray of needles and a medicine bottle crooked in his arm. Peggy marveled at the stoic way in which the old woman accepted her injection.

"Shall we pee now, Pinkie?" he asked merrily.

Bridget cast a look at Peggy.

"I'll be back, Bridget."

This too was greeted stoically. Bridget's hand when Peggy took it had the same dry smoothness as Margaret's.

Glockner read about it in Fiesole and nearly choked on his croissant. One or two heads at other tables turned but he ignored them, pushing his bearded face closer to the newspaper. The reproduction of the painting, imperfect, out of focus, blurred, would nonetheless have been enough to convince him, Glockner was sure of it, but the accompanying story of Parker's discovery at a New Jersey auction removed all doubts. *Ritratto di una Misteriosa* was the legend under the picture. Clayton Ford's hitherto unknown portrait of a subject not a Sinclair. The gall!

Glockner licked the stickiness from the tips of his fingers in a nervous little rite he did not know he'd developed, one finger after another being attended to as he continued to read. The enormity of it was such that in Phase Two he began to doubt himself. Parker, for all the rumors about him, most of them floated by his bested competitors, was a successful and, as these things are measured, reputable art dealer. He could not afford to be associated with an out-and-out . . .

Out-and-out what? That the portrait being called the New Jersey

Ford had hung on the wall of George Frederick Mason's office in Fox River, Illinois, was beyond doubt. Glockner had difficulty recognizing students currently in his classes, he had no memory for their names because he did not want to remember their names, but he had never seen a picture he could not infallibly remember as to where, when, and for how long he had studied it. This was a picture he had seen several times. He would stake his life on it.

He was seated at an outdoor table which because of the pavement leaned to one side. The wedge of wood stuffed under one leg to steady it had been kicked free and Glockner, with folded arms, the newspaper set aside, slightly tilted, looked out over the valley. Here he felt as if he were vacationing in a Renaissance landscape. English was the dominant language at this *pensione*, British English, but good old American too. Because his table was atilt, the water level in his glass was perhaps ten degrees off. One adjusted for such things, preferring a world of parallels, circles, relative sizes established by perspective. Perhaps the inclination of others would be to believe that story of a discovery in New Jersey.

Glockner snatched the copy of the *Herald Tribune* a girl with a diminutive torso and ballooning bottom left on her table. In it was a picture of Parker shaking the hand of a somewhat bewildered fellow from whom he had bought the picture for one hundred thousand dollars. Not exactly the New Jersey lottery but, then again, who could say what a picture is worth? Of course, if Glockner was right, that happy recipient of one hundred thousand unexpected dollars was part of the scheme to provide a phony provenance for the portrait. The great mystery was not the subject of the painting but how George Frederick Mason fitted into the fraudulent scheme.

Half a cup of lukewarm tea remained in his pot. Glockner carefully poured it out, put a slice of lemon in the cup as well, loaded it up with two packets of sugar and, holding the cup at eye level, sighted out over the Tuscan hills, Diogenes on the lookout for an honest man. It was not the scenery he saw, these hills, these rocky valleys, middle palette colors paling in the pitiless sun, a landscape to which he had flown business class to avoid the tourists and was paying through the nose at high season to see, his soul needing nourishment, refueling, respite from the Indiana air. He saw only an inward drama, the gutsy machinations of Parker the wheeler dealer, the Iacocca of the art world, Mason who would have come to know

219

him when he worked for Gabbiano, and that wife of his, what was her name? But she had been the wife of so many. Marjorie! A plush, bosomy woman out of Peter Paul Rubens, who made the anorectic starvelings she moved among long for such ripeness. Poor Mason had been Lazarus to her Dives, or was it the other way around? But one cup of such water would be heaven enough for him. *Il naufragar m'é dolce in questo mare* . . . She knew more of art than Mason would ever know—than I will ever know, Glockner admitted—and could add to that her knowledge of human nature, meaning the endless folly of the male sex. Art dealing is a form of seduction, after all, and what's wrong with mixing up the literal with the symbolic, the primal thing as well as its intricate mimicry in gallery and auction? He who thinks the prominence of nudes in artworks is irrelevant to the turn toward culture on the part of the *nouveaux riches* should have a little chat with Marjorie. And her daughter! Cindy? Cinnamon? Ginger! Her name was Ginger. Glockner cried it aloud like a guess at charades and again heads turned.

He was making an ass of himself out here, but he had to think. His room was on the *primo piano* in back, its window giving him a view of a wall six feet away, another window, in which an ancient woman seemed always to be sitting until a narrow sun slanted between the buildings and she closed and battened down her window against it. She was in the window now. Glockner closed his, pulled curtains and drapes shut and in the darkness, his now bared feet flat on the cool marble, pursued the spoor of his suspicion.

Nine-thirty in Italy. They had hours to sleep yet in mid-America; in Manhattan it was another story, with night birds like Marjorie and Ginger just turning in. In his darkened room, he continued to reconstruct what had happened from the wire service story in the *Herald Tribune* and the more impressionistic account in *Il Messaggero*. He cracked his window open, to check his watch and assure himself he had an extended period before placing a call to the States would make sense, and also in order to see as he made a list of such facts as he knew:

1. That alleged Ford portrait had hung in Mason's office.
2. If he had seen it there, others had too.
3. Like the other Fords in the museum, it came from a local family, the Sinclairs.

220

4. Peggy Sinclair, one student he could remember, had quite literally in her possession as her very own a Ford portrait of her great-grandmother. (Maybe now she and her family would believe it was insane to hang it on their living room wall where moth and rust consume and thieves break in and steal—it was a sign of his excitement that he tended to think in imperfectly remembered scriptural passages.)

5. Mason's Ford portrait (forget the alleged, Parker was no fool), entrusted to him as museum director, probably on loan from the Sinclairs, had now allegedly been discovered in a New Jersey auction.

6. Either Mason was in on it or he wasn't.

Glockner turned the paper over and pushed his glasses up onto the bridge of his nose. He felt uneasy. No wonder! Two ebony eyes in pouches of leather stared at him from the window across the way, as if it were the intensity of her gaze rather than his need for a sliver of light that had opened his window. Gray hair, black dress, whatever beauty she once had now turned to wizened ugliness, the woman stared malevolently at him. Was she thought to have the evil eye? Glockner shivered, pushed the window shut, and went into his bathroom and turned on the light.

Two columns on the back of the paper, one to be filled with consequences of the assumption that Mason was in on it, the other on the assumption that he and his museum had been robbed without his help.

If he were an innocent victim:

a) he would already have reported the loss of the painting, though admittedly that could have been done discreetly;

b) but now he would have to raise a public ruckus—the so-called discovery had been stolen from his museum;

c) the family whose painting it was would also sound the alarm;

d) there would be a *cause célèbre* which very well might, he had to face this, redound to the glory and reputation of George Frederick Mason;

e) Mason's previous associations with Parker would suggest how he had been victimized.

Glockner wished he had gone to a café. He needed coffee, at least a Coke, a dose of caffeine. The tannic acid of tea left his mouth dehydrated and there was none of the satisfaction of feeding an addiction. He ordered *thé limone* at breakfast because he needed more liquid than an espresso could provide to accompany the consumption of his croissant, and the *caffe latte* here was simply dreadful, goat's milk, perhaps. He turned off the bathroom light, pushed open the door, and leaned out. She was still there, like one of the Fates. Could she see him despite the darkness of the room?

He slammed the bathroom door shut and turned on the light again.

If Mason himself were one of the thieves:

a) and had earlier reported that the painting was missing, he would not immediately be suspected;

b) but if he had not and it now became known that his early career had involved dealings with Parker . . .

Glockner crumpled the paper. No. If Mason was guilty things would proceed just as apparently they now were. Unless he announced that the painting supposedly discovered in New Jersey was a Ford that belonged in Fox River, Illinois, the discovery would be accepted as indeed a discovery. After appropriate fanfare and publicity, Parker would put it on the block and realize an unprecedented price and whatever fraction of that Mason got would put him on Easy Street forever.

There was a single test of Mason's guilt: his continued silence. If he did not protest, it could only be because he stood to gain from the scenario Parker had cooked up. Mason an art thief? Every art lover is a potential thief. There are fewer thieves than there might be only because of the probable consequences. Offered an undetectable opportunity to appropriate a work of art, who could resist? The ring of Gyges. Add to that the lure of venality, ease, comfort, a life of leisure . . . Of course Mason would succumb to the temptation. As he elaborated it in his imagination, Glockner committed the same sin in his heart. He envied Mason! And this was an intolerable attitude toward his old enemy. Contempt, hatred, at least amusement, yes; but envy, never!

Glockner spent the rest of the day in churches and the following day risked an overdose in the Uffizi, moving from room to room like a drunk on a binge. But he had decided to go home early and did not intend to waste entirely this expensive trip. Because he'd paid such an exorbitant sum for his ticket, he could fly home whenever there was room for him. And there was a seat on a TWA plane out of Malpensa in Milan two days after the first newspaper story appeared.

The follow-ups on the story were exercises in creative writing, something in which Italian journalists excelled. Their readers were theirs because of the ideological bent of the particular newspaper, the myth of objectivity not yet having ruined the Italian press, so Glockner got Marxist, Fascist, Socialist, and Christian Democratic accounts of the sociological significance of a priceless work of art emerging from obscurity in the way the Ford portrait had in New Jersey. On the left, the great collectors were written off as the robber barons of the art world, the capitalist continuators of the Medicis. *Il Tempo*, by contrast, stressed their philanthropy, pointing out how many public collections in America were named for the original donors. Getty, whose grandchild had been hounded about Italy and kidnapped by terrorists who sent his severed ear to the old billionaire in a fruitless effort to pry ransom out of him, was already more renowned for the California gallery bearing his name than for his oil wells and chain of service stations.

On and on and not a single new fact about the alleged discovery. The *Herald Tribune* was two-thirds quotations from the stock markets of the world, an unconscionable amount of cricket on its sports page, and one small story on page two. It did not tell of a voice of protest raised in Fox River, Illinois. It did quote Parker opining that his Ford would bring a record amount when Christie's auctioned it.

At Malpensa, Gearhart went upstairs and lied his way into the VIP lounge to put through a call to Mason and over ocean, via satellite, halfway around the great globe itself, the chirping voice of Hazel Knutsen, she of the massive tits, came to him.

"Is the great man in?" he asked, after identifying himself.

"I just got in myself!"

"What time is it there?"

"Aren't we in the same time zone?"

"My dear, I am calling from Milan."

"Oh sure. And how are things in Milan?" Her tone suggested he had to get up earlier than this to fool her.

"Well, it's mid-afternoon, for one thing. I'll be knocking on your

223

door this time tomorrow. Look, don't tell him I'm coming, understand? It's a little joke."

"Are you really calling from Italy?"

"Yes."

"You could be in the next room."

"Tomorrow I will be," he said. "You expect him to be in tomorrow morning?"

"Not before ten."

"I wouldn't want to fly all that way to find he'd gone to New York."

"Wouldn't that be terrible?"

"I'll be there before he is tomorrow."

After he hung up he sank into meditation, ignoring the matinee idol attendant who seemed about to ask if he were traveling first class. Such scrutiny made Glockner feel particularly scruffy, a dumpy, bearded figure whose glasses obligingly darkened to the light. He put out his hand as if to pick up the phone and place another call. An echoing announcement got his attention. The attendant was diverted by the entry of several authentic VIP's. Glockner slipped out into the great terminal. He had an hour before his plane could be boarded. More than time enough to check the newsstand to see if there was anything further on *il ritratto di una misteriosa.*

40

Bridget's handwriting was readable only with difficulty. She wrote with a soft lead pencil given to smudging as the heel of her hand followed the words across the page. And she obviously wrote pell-mell, paying little attention to punctuation. Each entry was a long, uninterrupted paragraph with thoughts and sentences flowing into one another. The backward slant of the script added to the difficulty. But none of this annoyed Peggy as she settled down to the first notebook, a school exercise tablet, in which Bridget began what would become a lifetime habit but was then simply an imitation of Margaret Sinclair, a way to stave off boredom when her mistress was busy penning her own account of her wedding trip.

> Terrible tossing about all night the boat rolling back and forth and the bath water hot as can be but rusty and it sloshes about so much I keep my eyes shut I don't want to get what She's got if she has anything I mean the poor man out on the deck all bundled up round and round all day she seems perky enough alone she doesn't deceive me my dread is that she will want to talk about it

she has to talk to someone or she'll bust but dear God don't let it be me since all she wants is to talk not listen and I'd like to tell her a thing or two all her life she's looked forward to such a voyage, her honeymoon and all, and it's a pity to let the sea spoil it all—if that's what it is!!!

The dash and exclamation point served Bridget well enough, she had no need for commas and periods. Periods. Was that the problem? But neither Margaret nor Bridget said anything that could be taken to mean that, and of course neither would come right out and say it. What circumlocution did they have for it anyway? Would the wedding date have been chosen without any thought of such things?

There was a slapdash air to Bridget's style that made Peggy expect more straight talk but the maid was in her way as reticent as her mistress. Margaret figured almost always as the feminine pronoun, capitalized—She or Her—but Matthew as the masculine only by and large. Bridget spelled out his name the first time it occurred in an entry and then he became M.

How fascinating it was to have another account of events that had for so long teased Peggy's imagination. Not that Bridget wrote only of Margaret. Peggy got a far better sense of the ship itself, the personnel, the other passengers, even a more vivid picture of Matthew Sinclair, in the maid's scribbled recollection of her day. Bridget had a birthday at sea and was embarrassed by the fuss made over it.

They came to the table the two of them one with a violin and the other doing the singing and I blushed so hard my face hurt and M just sat there smiling and Her not up for the occasion the singer called me Mrs and after happy birthday what request would I make and I couldn't think of anything but hymns until M said Londonderry Air meaning Danny Boy and like a fool I cried but it was wonderful and I took some cake back to give to Hans who teased me about how old I was—eighteen years old! and what is to become of me . . .

The contrast was with her mistress, only two years older but settled into marriage with a man Bridget obviously admired and with a comfortable future ahead. Bridget couldn't help being friendly with Hans the cabin attendant and the maids whose station was just down the passageway. One of the dramas when the Sinclairs boarded and found that Bridget had been assigned a cabin many decks below was to secure her transfer to their deck. The purser gave her a suite of her own—he had nothing else—so that her accommodations matched those of her employer. The maids and Hans took all this as great luck for one of their own and came to have tea or broth with her in her cabin. Hans delighted and frightened her by appearing at the porthole that looked out on the deck, turning the oval window into a picture of a grinning satyr. "What a picture Feet of Clay could make of him," was Bridget's final comment on that apparition. Feet of Clay, Peggy eventually realized, was Clayton Ford.

Lester couldn't let her take Bridget's diary from the archives and his suggestion that he have a microfilm made was silly. She'd have to buy or rent a reader as well. Besides, it was the notebook itself she wanted to read; she wanted to feel its pages and see for herself the scrawl of Bridget's hand. The little tablet itself was like a memento from a tomb, a relic of what was no more. Bridget described herself now as a first-class relic.

"Not the kind they keep on display in church." Her eye rolled to Peggy. "Do you go to church?"

"You sound like my great-grandmother."

"Margaret."

"That's my name too."

Bridget studied her. "You are very like her." She frowned. "So watch your step."

"What do you mean?"

"Oh, she was a devil, she was." But it was Bridget who had a devilish look as she said this.

"I'm reading your diary too, you know."

"You're not!"

"Oh yes I am. The beginning, the trip to Italy."

But Bridget looked more pleased than angry. "I haven't any recollection at all of what I said."

"You bring everything to life."

"Ha. It's called the Irish Bull. You may find things you don't want to know."

"You and Hans?"

Did Bridget recall the German boy with the long lashes? It seemed unfair to have access to Bridget's past when she no longer remembered those particular events.

"Of course I remember," the old woman said, tugging a pillow out from behind her back. Peggy took it, puffed it, and, while Bridget sat forward, tucked it behind her again.

"But not Hans?"

"I think you're making him up."

"I never tease a tease."

Peggy could see why the old woman had such a reputation with Lester. Her grandson was a silly person in Bridget's eyes and she could not disguise her feelings.

"A grown man puttering around in a place like that. He's no better than a librarian. It's woman's work, no matter what he says."

"The fact that women can do it too doesn't mean it's unimportant."

Bridget gave her the fish eye. "When men have babies and women grow beards I'll talk to you about all that."

Bridget had gotten it into her head that Peggy was an avid feminist, always about to turn a conversation in the direction of women's lib, an ideologue. Or was this just more of her teasing?

After the discovery of the Ford portrait in New Jersey Peggy tried to get Bridget to talk about the artist.

"Oh, what a rogue he was! Up to no good at all times, as I warned Margaret. Young ladies in those days had no idea at all about men, what makes them tick, what they want, and he was a romantic devil."

A smile played on her chapped lips and she nodded in agreement with her thoughts. "I had a talk with him about it. We went together when he painted his pictures but he was always surprising me alone and I knew he'd do the same with her."

"Surprising you?"

"Now I'm not going into all that. Good God, the man has been moldering in his grave for years." Then her smile came back. "But what a billy goat he was."

Michele had sent her a story about the Ford painting discovered in New Jersey and Peggy stared at the reproduction of the painting. How familiar it looked. Perhaps because of its similarity to the portrait of Margaret. She'd thought of bringing the portrait for Bridget to see, but the newspaper picture offered an easy alternative.

"They've found a painting by your old boyfriend," she teased, when she had pushed Bridget onto the patio.

"I always preferred plumbers to painters."

"I'm speaking of Clayton Ford."

228

"He was no boyfriend of mine, my dear, and not for want of trying."

"Do you have your glasses with you?"

They were slung around her neck but had slipped under her robe. She fished them out and put them on her nose.

"I hate these things. Bifocals. I never know where to look." She took the clipping and studied it for a silent minute, then looked up at Peggy. "That's me. You wouldn't think so now, but that's the girl I once was, the summer he painted Margaret and myself, going from one canvas to the other, commissioned to do her by Matthew, doing me for the fun of it. Well, he might as well have, because I was surely going to be there when he painted Margaret. How on earth did it end up in New Jersey?"

"Bridget, are you sure?"

"That that's me? Of course I'm sure. I was very pleased with it and he said I could have it, but Margaret wanted it to remember me by. She was always certain I wouldn't be in her service long, and she was right. It's strange, I forgot that painting, yet now I remember so clearly sitting there in the barn, Margaret and I taking turns being still, while he worked and talked, oh, how he talked. It was an experience for Margaret, she had never heard a man go on like that." Her voice drifted away.

"Neither of those paintings was known to exist, your picture or Margaret's."

But Bridget turned her chair to face Peggy. "Don't read my diary any more. I don't want you reading in it, do you understand? Promise me you won't."

"Reading it along with Margaret's makes me think I'm there."

"I'll speak to Lester about it if I have to. He pretends to make such a big thing of the Pincus family, and then to let you read that."

"Bridget, okay. I had no idea it was so important to you."

"Neither did I. But I do now. I should never have let Lester know about it. It's all pride, you know. He told me of all the nobody families represented in the county archives but where are the Pincuses? Once I understood what he meant, I mentioned the diary. The next thing I knew he'd taken it. He doesn't care about it. He just wanted some Pincus thing in the building."

Lester showed little interest in his grandmother's diary, she was right about that. He seemed to have looked into it only to the extent required to catalog it.

"Afraid to find a family skeleton?"

"Don't tell me if you find one."

Peggy did not consider her response to Bridget's request an agreement. That the old woman had grown uneasy at the thought of someone reading a diary she had kept as a girl was understandable enough. The wonder was that it had taken her so long to complain about it. Had she remembered something about those times she didn't want Peggy to know? It was a Jane Austen world, or the world of *Little Women*, that Peggy entered when she opened either one of the diaries. She half-expected, half-dreaded, encountering intimate revelations, but surely Margaret would not have given it to her if there was anything like that. The next time she went to the archives, she asked to see the very first volume of Bridget's diary.

"I really shouldn't let you use originals like that."

"I'll be careful."

Peggy told him she wanted to see what his grandmother had written at the time Clayton Ford was painting Margaret and Bridget had to chaperone the event, but he seemed disinterested in the contents of the things over which he exercised such conscientious vigil.

The tone of this very first attempt at a diary on Bridget's part was very different from the second volume Peggy had been reading. Imagine the young girl starting that first page. And she was still at it, even though her arthritis made moving the pencil over the page painful.

Unsurprisingly, Feet of Clay figured prominently in the entries. The diary was prompted by a girlish bet, Bridget warning her mistress that the painter was falling in love with her, Margaret indignantly denying it, Bridget offering to keep watch and record all telltale signs to overcome her mistress's skepticism. It seemed clear from the entries that Margaret, far from being angered by the suggestion that the man painting her picture was infatuated with her, wanted Bridget to prove it was so. Matthew was seldom mentioned by the two. The explanation for that, it emerged, was that he was spending the summer in a Chicago bank. Out of sight, out of mind. By then Margaret's coming marriage to Matthew had been more or less arranged, whereas the bearded painter in the barn was moved by the impulse of his heart.

Peggy began to share Bridget's fears that Margaret Sinclair was being careless about the occasion of sin. The letter K began to appear, then a string of them KKKKK. And then Peggy understood and her heart sank as if this were a contemporary drama. Margaret Sinclair had allowed the painter to kiss her!

Thank God for all these interesting revelations. They distracted her from the ache she still felt about how things had gone with Joel Cleary. Her mother urged her to take his call.

"One at least, Peggy. He sounds as if he'll keep on calling until you do."

"Mother, he's a married man."

"He said you'd say that."

"Have you talked with him?"

"Peggy, I almost feel I know him, answering the phone so often. He said to tell you he has applied for an annulment."

"Should I send a card?"

㊶

Mason rehearsed the exchange a hundred times, in his head, aloud, awake, asleep. He had lived since returning from New York in keyed-up anticipation of the topic being raised, the question asked. It did not seem possible that no one in what WFOX liked to call the Greater Fox River Metropolitan Area had read the story of the newly discovered Ford portrait. Of course the *Tribune* had not picked up the wire service story—that would have required some minimal literacy on the part of its staff—but surely even the most Philistine of his fellow citizens must from time to time cast an eye on a Chicago paper. There had been a mention of the discovery on cable news, even a microsecond appearance on the screen of the portrait. That night George Frederick Mason had not slept a wink, positive that the puzzled questioning would now begin.

Parker refused to take his calls and he was forced to communicate with his fellow thief through Marjorie, whose manner, softened doubtless by the prospect of millions, was reminiscent of the charm that had deceived him long ago.

232

"The brochure for the auction is a work of art in itself," she assured him. "A lovely essay on Ford's work."

"By whom?"

"Squall thought it unwise to involve you, George."

"Squall?"

"Pasquale. He got permission to use an article that first appeared in *Art Quarterly*."

"By Gearhart Glockner!"

"I think you're right."

If she heard his groan she ignored it, babbling on about how excited the auctioneer was at having a Ford to offer. It was the first product of this all-but-legendary artist to be publicly sold in over half a century. Some of his work was still in the hands of heirs of their subjects, but most had been donated to museums. Was she presuming to inform him about Clayton Ford?

He was physically ill after that call. That the ineffable Glockner should actually appear in the catalog seemed to tempt fate beyond permissible limits. Not that *Art Quarterly* would have needed Glockner's permission to grant reprint rights to his article. The prestige of the publication made art historians willing to waive the Emancipation Proclamation in order to appear in its pages and Glockner, like many a person getting established, had gladly signed over all rights in perpetuity for the modest stipend offered. It would be merely a courtesy were the editor to inform Glockner, and courtesy was not a virtue one associated with the editors of *Art Quarterly*. Nonetheless, Mason was certain it was only a matter of time before he heard from his old rival.

"Professor Glockner called," Miss Knutsen informed him when he came in, gaunt, exhausted, harried, at ten o'clock.

He managed not to clutch his heart. "Who!"

"He's in Italy!"

He could have kissed her.

"He'll be here tomorrow. He phoned from the airport."

"But tomorrow is Saturday!"

She waited for him to say more. It was insane to suggest that tomorrow's being Saturday could somehow save him. He went on into his office, closed the door and tried to pass the framed copy without looking at it, and failed. It was unnerving how indistinguishable the copy was from the painting that had hung there for so long.

Tomorrow Glockner would study that copy and the long dreaded yet eagerly anticipated conversation would begin.

When Miss Knutsen asked if he'd like coffee he told her to bring him a can of Diet Coke from the machine downstairs. Vodka in coffee lost its punch. The combination of Valium and vodka was probably unwise, but wisdom seemed an ideal so beyond his grasp it would have been a quibble to worry excessively about his physical health. His soul was sick unto death. He imagined his insides as a baroque allegorical painting, tormented figures writhing voluptuously as they were prodded into the flames by the forks of demons.

There was a look of disapproval on Miss Knutsen's face when she brought him the soft drink. She had read an article on NutraSweet which suggested that it was carcinogenic. Like breathing, like tap water, like mother's milk, no doubt. Alone, he poured a water glass half full of vodka, then colored it with Coke. There was a level of alcohol in his blood below which he dared not go until this punishing ordeal was over. It is no small thing to steal a painting worth millions of dollars.

Sometimes, after a bracing belt or two, he imagined himself a dashing Robin Hood, redistributing wealth in an imaginative way. And, after all, who was the poorer for what he had done? The Ford portrait itself continued to exist, unaffected by the machinations— Manhattan cab rides, kidnapping by the fulsome Ginger, being sent out to a copyist while Pasquale Parker prepared to stage the New Jersey discovery. In a short time, it would hang on a new wall, ready to be admired. That this would not be in the Fox River Museum seemed unimportant. What was more, the world was richer for this magnificent copy. Had he not sequestered the original for his own more or less private enjoyment? Only a handful had ever seen it.

But it was that handful that had made him a stranger to sleep and a friend of alcohol. Who were they? Glockner, of course. Maud Sinclair. Anyone else? He racked his brain. Dozens had been in his office, but with how many had he gone on about the Ford on his wall? The gallery was full of Fords. What was one more, except to the aficionado? He remembered with self-loathing his several attempts to overcome Glockner's skepticism and convince him the portrait was genuine. The argument had no doubt etched the portrait into the bastard's memory.

But it was young Margaret Sinclair who provided the occasion for a dry run through his rehearsed scenario.

He knew a moment of panic when Miss Knutsen said Margaret

Sinclair had come to see him. Had the old woman struggled free of her tomb and come in graveclothes to point a bony finger of accusation at him? He would not have wanted to see his own expression when the lovely young lady came into his office and went immediately to the framed copy.

"It *is* here!" she cried. "Aunt Maud was right." She turned to Mason and held out what looked to be a newspaper clipping. "A friend of mine sent me this from the Cleveland paper. There's been a terrible mistake."

He managed a theatrical laugh as he started around his desk. The laugh became a yelp of pain when his thigh was caught by the corner of the desk. He limped back to his chair and she approached him with concern.

"Are you all right?"

He nodded, biting his lip, and reached for his glass. He drank thirstily as she watched. "Would you like a Coke?"

She tipped her head in thought, then nodded. "Sure. Just give me a little of yours."

"I'll get more ice."

He took his own glass to the fridge too and put in two more cubes. There was Coke in his fridge! That Hazel had not remembered was one thing, but how could he have forgotten? God, he would be glad when this ordeal was over. Banging his leg seemed providential. It had drawn her away from the copy.

She took the glass he offered and waited for him to limp to his chair. They toasted one another. She closed her eyes and shook her head.

"That tastes funny."

"It's the NutraSweet."

She shrugged and drank again. It wasn't until he drank that Mason realized he had given her his glass. The girl was swilling almost straight vodka. Dear God. He laid the clipping on his desk and smoothed it out.

"Yes, yes," he said. "I've heard of this. It makes our copy both less and more interesting, doesn't it?

"Is that a copy?"

"Amazing, isn't it?"

"But why?"

"One can only speculate, of course. It's not unusual, as perhaps you know, to have good copies made of valuable paintings. Much as paste copies are made of jewelry. It's a kind of insurance."

"But how did the original get away?"

"Good question. As I said, one can only speculate."

With young Margaret, his speculation concentrated on a simple mix-up. The original had been given or sold or taken and the copy left.

"Of course I've always feared it wasn't a genuine Ford."

"But it looks so genuine."

"And now we know why. It is a very good copy of a genuine Ford portrait."

"Did you tell my great-grandmother it was a copy?"

"I blame myself now, but it would have seemed churlish to have expressed my suspicion of the non-authenticity of the one when she had provided the museum with so many genuine Fords. My solution was to hang it here, in my office."

Why had he agonized over this conversation? The plausibility of what he was saying was overwhelming. Who could doubt him? Not young Margaret Sinclair. She pushed her glass toward him.

"Could I have some more?"

He dragged himself to the fridge and brought back a can of Coke, which he opened and put before her. She drained what was left in her glass and smiled as she filled it again. His hand went to the drawer where he kept the vodka, but he stayed it. Confidence grew in him because of the girl's credulity and he embroidered the tale he had given her in skeleton form, dramatizing his *crise de conscience* when he realized that one of the paintings Margaret Sinclair had given to the museum was in fact only an exceedingly clever copy.

"If it had been authentic, I would have been able to create quite a stir in art circles. You can imagine. Announcing a hitherto unknown Ford portrait! I confess that I did draft an essay that would have argued that where there is a copy there must be an original. A kind of call for a global search for the lost Ford. But I abhor such sensationalism. Even more I abhor the drudgery of writing. Besides, Margaret Sinclair would not have permitted it. In any case, I didn't do it. I don't expect any criticism on that score."

The girl had grown strangely somber. "I wonder if mine is only a copy."

It was a moment of truth. Mason knew of a certainty that the girl's portrait of Margaret Sinclair was genuine. It bore on the back of the canvas the authenticating *cf* plus the date.

"That's the question I asked myself. It's why I asked to see the portrait."

"Professor Glockner said it was authentic."

"Did he?"

It was a dangerous moment. How corrupt had he become? He was tempted to contest Glockner's appraisal, to sow the seed of doubt in this girl's mind, tell her that, in his expert opinion, while it was not of course a copy, he rather doubted . . .

"Not that it matters," she said. "Not really. It's the painting my great-grandmother had hanging in her house and left to me in her will."

"Of course."

"Do you think it's a Ford?"

"I would stake my reputation on it," he said, and a balloon of righteousness began to inflate within him. How good it was to be good.

She pushed away her glass. "I must be allergic to— What did you call it?"

"NutraSweet. No need for you to diet in any case, my dear."

Careful, careful. The combination of fear and vodka made him randy, as if sinking into carnal forgetfulness was the present meaning of life. He stood. His thigh where he had struck it against the desk was throbbing with pain. It was an excuse to drink, and he wanted to get rid of this girl and take his medicine. He walked with her into the outer office, where Miss Knutsen displayed her teeth in a smile. God, she was beautiful! As if to get out of harm's way, Mason took Peggy's arm and steered her abruptly into the main area of the museum.

"Would you like to inspect your family's Fords?"

"Is the copy ours too?"

"It belonged to your great-grandmother." He felt that he could learn to speak while smiling and take up a career in television preaching. But it was a skill useful in his own trade as well. It was past time he mastered it.

"I've found the woman who sat for the original."

"Someone named Bridget, isn't it?"

When he went by Miss Knutsen he stared unabashedly at the tantalizing breasts on display because of her half-buttoned blouse. He felt reckless and horny. "Button up," he said, but he said it with a smile. She gasped and he pulled the door shut behind him, his inner man already across the room, tugging open the drawer that contained the vodka.

42

Tuttle pondered Octavio Salazar's question. "How can a painting be great without a great subject?" The question embodied a stern criterion to apply to Ford's languid landscapes with figures, a woman indolently holding a parasol in a boat being beached by a young man whose straw hat, held by a ribbon, was pushed back to reveal tousled locks damp upon his forehead, his eyes for the disdainful lady alone. Octavio asked aloud what the message of this picture was. The attraction of the unattainable? A young man's penchant to pursue the girl who least likes him? A home truth there, perhaps. Tuttle was trying to convert from the metric system the catalog's statement of the size of the paintings—five feet by seven? It must have been one hell of a job of work to cover that much area with paint, Octavio ought to grant the artist that much.

"Sweetheart," Bunny said. "You know nothing of art."

The couple kissed to show it wasn't a serious disagreement. Tuttle figured that before color photography people had to rely on paintings.

"A painter flatters his subject," Octavio said, addressing himself to Tuttle in an effort to get the last word.

"Do you know Goya's paintings of the Spanish royalty?" Bunny asked Tuttle.

He shook his head. The less he said in such conversations, the better, that was his rule.

They had come to the Fox River Museum to see what if any changes had been made in the paintings on exhibit, given the much-publicized announcement that the Sinclair family intended to remove everything they had loaned to the museum. Tuttle, over his head and loving it, was acting as legal adviser to the Sinclairs. Boxleitner, a North Shore sharpie, represented the citizens' group formed without the approval of George Frederick Mason to contest the "confiscation" of the paintings.

"Is there any chance the court will say these paintings belong to Fox River and not the family?"

Bunny was standing before a Ford landscape as she spoke and her voice was dreamy with appreciation. Octavio was unmoved by the relatively small, relatively bare picture. In the immediate foreground, a weatherbeaten wooden fence provided perspective for the distant barn, a building in good repair by contrast, framed by a stand of trees.

"Not while I represent you," Tuttle said.

"Do you recognize it, Octavio?"

He tucked in his chin and squinted. "No."

"It's Fairview. The house is just beyond those trees. I recognize that barn."

Octavio hummed in a neutral key.

"It's a crime to try to take this from the family."

"The other side says it would be a crime if the Fords were auctioned off."

Bunny made a face at him. Tuttle thought they would kiss again. They sat on a bench, waiting for Maud to show. The purpose of the visit had been for Maud to solve the mystery of the discovery in New Jersey. Tuttle had wanted to peel off after the meeting with Maud. Oh to be in his office, shooting the bull with Peanuts. He could not get rid of the fear that at any moment Bunny or Octavio would realize their mistake and fire him. Maud Sinclair made him even more uneasy.

"Maud, what do you make of the discovery of an unknown Ford portrait in New Jersey?" Bunny had asked.

"I hadn't heard of it."

"There was a piece in the paper. I believe there was something on television as well."

"I know nothing about it." Maud's tone suggested that what she did not know could not exist.

Octavio handed clippings to Maud. Tuttle wished his clients had told him of this.

"This is preposterous," Maud said, taking the clipping to a window to get more light on it. "That painting hangs in the Fox River Museum."

"Are you sure?"

Maud's glance was that of one unacquainted with doubt. Bunny, far from being put off by her manner, obviously envied and admired it. Octavio was not cowed as Tuttle would have been.

"Maybe he painted her twice."

"Two paintings of the same subject?"

"Why not?"

Bunny backed him up. "All it means is there are now two hitherto unknown Ford portraits of the same woman, grandmother's servant, Bridget Doyle, one in Fox River and the other in New Jersey. I suppose, if Bridget moved to New Jersey . . ."

"We will look into it immediately," Maud announced. She examined her watch. "I will meet you there in twenty-five minutes."

It was a minute shy of that when she arrived and they all marched in to see the director.

"She's still here in Fox River," George Frederick Mason said, leading them into his office. He pointed to his wall as he spoke and Maud and the Salazars obligingly followed the direction his hand indicated.

"There it is," Maud said, as if triumphing over Octavio's doubts.

"That is, however, a copy, Maud. As I explained to your niece."

"What niece?"

"Margaret. Peggy. She saw the same story, remembered this painting, and came to me about it. I had to tell her this is a copy. She in turn told me the subject of the portrait is still alive and here in Fox River."

240

"Well." Maud rose and floated to the painting and frowned at it, as if to show what she thought of a mere copy.

Bunny asked, "Are there copies of any other Ford paintings?"

Mason sighed and brought his hands together like a priest. "Pursuing a suggestion of Maud's, I've been looking into the cost of having good copies made of all the Fords hanging here. Before the great exodus."

Maud ignored the implication of flattery in this remark. "It is odd that a maid's portrait would be copied."

"It would have been copied as a Ford painting, not as the likeness of a particular servant."

"Would your grandmother have had it done?" Octavio asked. "The portrait was in her possession, wasn't it?" He turned to Mason. "When did that copy come into the possession of the museum?"

"At the same time as all the other Fords."

"Twelve years ago," Maud replied.

"Is it possible to learn how old a painting is, George?"

"I suppose you could determine that by consulting the still living subject."

"I meant how old the copy is," Octavio said.

Mason was lying, Tuttle was sure of it. The guy was half fruitcake and he sounded strangled when he talked. He reminded Tuttle of a guy who had sold him a used car that turned out to be a retired taxi. Tuttle's confidence began to build. If this was the big time, it looked just like the small time in which he had hitherto dwelt.

Later, when Tuttle arrived at his building, he found Peanuts parked outside. Peanuts motioned him over.

"There's some guy waiting to see you."

Tuttle smiled down at the one friend he had in the Fox River police force. Maybe in the world. How to explain to Peanuts that life was no longer what it had been, a scramble for clients, avoidance of creditors, a hand-to-mouth existence? Tuttle was seriously thinking of hiring Miss Tuchman full time. He wasn't responsible for her benefits as a Kelly Girl, part time, but this seemed the moment to accept the fact that his life had moved up at least a notch. Out of superstition or caution, he did not want to flaunt the fact that he was representing members of the Sinclair family. The Sinclairs brought

241

him into the public glare without effort on his part. If only his father were still alive. Tuttle senior had had an unwavering faith in his son, supporting him through the five years he had needed to finish law school. He had died a week after Tuttle passed the bar on the third try, but he had been granted immortality in the name on the door: TUTTLE & TUTTLE.

"Did he say who he was?"

"Some kind of professor."

"Gearhart Glockner," the man said when Tuttle came inside.

"Welcome back, professor. I thought you were going to spend the summer in Italy?"

The bearded expert on the work of Clayton Ford groaned audibly. "Do you still represent the Sinclair family?"

"I do. Come on up."

The baggy seersucker suit Glockner had obviously been wearing for more than twenty-four hours, the beard, the dark glasses, made Tuttle feel he was confronting a bail bondsman rather than a professor. Of course, his image of the professor had been formed in law school, but even so. The bearded Glockner held no fears for Tuttle.

"Miss Knutsen told me a group has formed to keep the Ford paintings in the local museum."

"They're wasting their time. Where did you say you teach?"

"Hathaway Hall."

"Where's that?"

"Indiana."

"Never heard of it."

"I'm not surprised. We do have a number of girls from this area enrolled, however. Margaret Sinclair, for one."

Tuttle nodded. He wished he'd stayed with Peanuts.

"I was told you represent the people trying to keep the Fords in the museum."

"That would be conflict of interest."

Glockner's glasses had slid down his nose, revealing his bloodshot eyes. "Miss Knutsen seemed very sure about it."

"The museum director's receptionist?"

"Yes. Yes."

"I am still advising the Sinclair family."

"Then you are indeed the man I want to see. What would you say if I told you a Ford portrait was stolen from the Fox River Museum, a painting worth millions?"

"I would hope you had a solid basis for so serious a charge. *Are* you telling me that?"

"Yes!" He rummaged in the pockets of his suit and extracted some newspaper clippings, which he piled on the desk. Tuttle turned them over with a letter opener. They were what he expected, what Octavio had had. "I know for a fact that painting was hanging in the office of George Frederick Mason, the director of the museum, only a month ago."

"I can understand why you would have thought so."

"What the hell does that mean?"

"I have already discussed the matter with Mr. Mason. The picture in his office is a copy of the original that was discovered in New Jersey."

Professor Glockner laughed. It was not a happy laugh; it was, in its way, an insulting laugh, seeming to mock Tuttle's intelligence. Tuttle mastered his impulse to overturn a wastebasket on this idiot's head, sitting in silence until the laughter dwindled and stopped. Glockner removed his glasses and dabbed at his eyes, chuckling, then shook his head.

"He told you it was a copy, did he?"

"That's right."

"Did he tell you when he discovered that it was a copy?"

"Please explain."

"Until there's an original, there's no copy, is there? A painting is simply a painting until you discover there's another exactly like it. Then you either have a repetitive artist or an original and a copy."

The answer to this was obvious. Mason's answer, that is. He called his painting a copy because its original had been discovered. Prior to that, he would not have called it a copy. Tuttle said as much to Professor Glockner.

"Meaning George Frederick Mason does not know an original Ford from a copy, no matter how well done."

"You think he should have?"

"It's an academic point. I have examined the painting that hung in his office. It was definitely not a copy. I speak as a recognized expert on the work of Clayton Ford, including his overrated portraits. I had no knowledge such a painting existed. Only a few months ago I had

243

no idea Ford had done the portrait of Margaret Sinclair. I also examined that. The one was as authentic as the other. If the painting now hanging in Mason's office is a copy, that can mean only one thing. He is a participant in the theft."

"Those are serious charges."

"I flew here from Italy as soon as I realized what was going on. The giveaway was that Mason made no protest, no claim that the supposedly discovered painting belonged here and indeed had been in his museum. I must congratulate him on having the copy made, although that was probably Pasquale Parker's idea. I suspect Mason was simply counting on the forgetfulness of visitors to his offices."

Tuttle was reluctantly giving up the idea that his visitor was nuts, a resentful academic bent for whatever reason on ruining the career of George Frederick Mason. But then, he had been sure that Mason had been lying to the Salazars and Maud.

"You're a recognized Ford expert?"

"Look me up in *Who's Who*."

"I will." At the library, of course.

"And I will gladly supply other proof of my credentials. The integrity of the art world is at stake here and I did not intend to sit sunning myself in Italy while a fraud like this was perpetrated."

"You know Mason?"

"We're old friends. But Parker is also a friend of his. Whoever ends up as the rightful owner of the Ford paintings in the Fox River Museum has an interest in this matter—the family, the city, whoever. You can't let him get away with this."

"I assure you, Professor Glockner, that if things are as you say, no one will get away with anything." Tuttle felt that he was a ventriloquist dummy and Amos Cadbury was speaking through him.

For the first time since arriving, Glockner relaxed. "Do you have a rest room?"

"You must be dead tired. Why don't we book you into a hotel while I map out a course of action? One thing. You said Mason's secretary spoke to you of these things. Why should she do a thing like that?"

Glockner shrugged. "Women trust me."

43

Now that the accusation was public, George Frederick Mason felt reborn. It was, he realized, the uncertainty and waiting, imagining what might be going on in the camp of the enemy, that had turned him into a trembling neurotic. Now the dreaded possibility had been realized, the worst conceivable case come true. He had been called a thief, a custodian who turned a public trust into private gain, a practitioner of fraud and deceit. It was almost refreshing to have all that out of his head and into the real world.

"Nonsense," he replied, a great serenity coming over him when he saw that Amos Cadbury himself was astounded by the bill of particulars he had just recited. The lawyer's eyes were fixed on Mason. Maud, the Salazars, Father Dowling, and Peggy Sinclair stared at the portrait on the wall. Tuttle, having positioned himself behind Cadbury, nodded as if to endorse the accusation. Glockner had not taken a chair but stood, legs apart, hands joined behind his back, balding head tipped back, studying the picture through his tinted glasses.

"This is a copy," Glockner announced.

"We already know that," Maud sniffed.

"How can you tell?" Bunny asked.

Glockner turned, tipped his head, and took an untinted look at her. "Tests will have to be made, of course."

"There is no need for tests," Mason said. "We all now know that is a copy. I examined it again as soon as I heard of the discovery of the original and verified that this is not an authentic Ford."

"Because it was recent?" Glockner stepped toward the desk. The lenses of his glasses darkened and lightened as he moved. There was something simian in his approach, as if he might spring upon the desk and begin to scratch himself.

"I came to no conclusion about that. It was quite an easy matter to determine it was not by Clayton Ford."

"An easy matter," Glockner repeated, turning to the others. "Then you should have noticed it before. Isn't Ford your speciality?"

"Yes, he is. And yours too, as you tirelessly remind us. You seem strangely unexcited to learn there is a Ford of which you had no knowledge."

"If you mean the portrait of Margaret Sinclair, I say and declare that I am overjoyed to know there is one more Ford portrait than was thought to be the case. As for this . . ."

"Have you seen the painting in New Jersey, Professor Glockner?" Maud asked.

"My dear lady, I have not had a decent rest in days. I flew directly from Italy when I sensed something quite wrong was going on here."

"You mean you're suffering from jet lag," Mason said helpfully.

"What did you look for when you examined this painting to see if it was a Ford?" Maud asked.

"Perhaps we should ask Professor Glockner what he looked for just now when he glanced at the painting."

And all turned to Glockner. Knowledge of one's guilt is power, Mason discovered. He alone of those in his office knew precisely what had happened. Glockner, motivated by malice, jealousy, and a smidgen of concern for the profession, had made a few inspired guesses. But Mason, aware that the real sequence of events was unknown to his rival, and that Gearhart was building on guesses, felt an almost unfair advantage.

"When I confront a painting I bring to it an expertise accumulated over a professional lifetime." Gearhart filled his lungs with air.

"There is an almost instant convergence of experience on the artwork before me. I know that is not a Ford in the way in which any of you knows that a desk is not a chair."

"Intuition?" Mason asked. He felt a traitor to the profession by thus inviting the skepticism of the unwashed on knowledge patiently acquired over years, but then he had already betrayed his profession for a pound and not a penny.

"I said that careful testing must be done."

"To substantiate your guess? But no tests are necessary. That is not a Ford original. I have made a simple test that puts the matter beyond all doubt."

"You yourself told me that was a Ford!" Glockner cried.

"Nonsense." Mason looked at the others one by one and felt that they were leaving Glockner and coming to him. When he got to Father Dowling, the priest's eyes made him uneasy, and he looked hastily away.

"What is the simple test?" Cadbury asked.

"Although he did not sign his portraits, Clayton Ford did mark them in a distinctive manner."

"And what is that?" Glockner cried. "I know of no such mark."

"So far as I have been able to learn, no one else does either. My article on the subject is nearly done. It will be a small but important contribution to our knowledge of Clayton Ford's work. Knowledge, not intuition."

Perhaps if Glockner had come in idealistic anger rather than out of spite and vanity he would have proved a worthier opponent. Mason could see doubt enter Cadbury's eyes. Tuttle's grip on his tweed hat tightened and Octavio Salazar looked with narrowed eyes from Mason to Glockner and back.

"That painting is one of those my grandmother loaned to the museum?" Maud asked.

"Yes."

Tuttle stirred. "Are you conceding the premise of the question? Margaret Sinclair loaned and did not give the paintings?"

"Do I get to decide?"

Young Peggy, bless her heart, laughed. Glockner glared at her.

Maud went on. "If it came to the museum at the same time as the other paintings, it must have been given when? At least twelve years ago?"

Leave it to Maud to stick to the point. Odd that her question should be more dangerous than anything Glockner or Cadbury had said.

"The dating of paintings is something we can do with great accuracy."

"So if it were made at the same time as the original, were of the same age, that could be learned?"

"That's right."

"There is no other such copy of a Ford in existence," Glockner said, his voice rising as he sat down. "This fake is the only one I have ever heard of."

"Fake?" Cadbury asked.

"Copy."

Mason pounced on the lawyer's point. "I thought for a moment you were suggesting that Margaret Sinclair sought to deceive . . ."

"Margaret Sinclair! You are the one who insisted that was a Ford."

"If I thought that was an authentic Ford, Gearheart, I would have announced such an exciting truth to the world. I said nothing. Doesn't that strike you as significant?"

"You were concealing it!"

"Concealing a copy?"

"You didn't know it was a copy."

Mason shook his head and looked to the others for help. "I'm afraid I'm not following this. Are you accusing me of being ignorant that this is a copy or of knowing it was? Are you suggesting that, given the enormous interest in Clayton Ford, I would have kept secret that Margaret Sinclair had in her possession two portraits by Ford of which no one had any knowledge?"

"Two?" Bunnie asked.

"There is the portrait of Margaret herself that she left to her niece here."

Peggy said, "This painting is of Bridget Pincus. She worked for my great-grandmother many years ago. Ford painted them at the same time."

"The portrait of Margaret is an authentic Ford," Mason said. "I have examined it. It has the distinctive mark I mentioned."

"What is this distinctive mark?"

"If we had the other painting here I could show you in a moment."

"Intuition?" Glockner asked.

248

"Quite the contrary. It is a mark anyone, expert or not, can see."

"Yet no one, no one who has devoted a lifetime to Clayton Ford, knows of it?" Glockner's voice broke.

"I know of it," Mason said quietly.

That had been Round One. It was agreed that they would reconvene the following morning with the portrait of Margaret on hand and Mason would demonstrate his point. Glockner's exhaustion, the conflicting schedules of others and, Mason hoped, waning interest, dictated a postponement.

After his antagonists were gone, Mason's hand went to the drawer in which he kept his vodka but stopped. No. It wasn't drink he wanted. What he wanted, and needed, was an extended rest. It was three in the afternoon, not too early to call it a day, go home, soak in the tub, crawl into bed, and sleep until he awoke. Glockner might be suffering from a little jet lag, but George Frederick Mason had been through weeks of agony. The confrontation in his office was comparable to a fever breaking. The worst was over. Now all he need do was go on lying and he was home free.

What he wanted more than sleep and the return of innocence was to talk with Parker in order to get late details on the planned auction. The dealer was in his quiet way stirring up excitement in the art world. Rumors were rife as to the price the portrait might bring, but the dealer had yet to settle on the minimum acceptable offer. Since Mason's treachery and lies made sense only because he was to profit from them, he needed reassurance that things were going smoothly.

He tried to tell himself that everything was much better this way, with Parker in on it and managing the New York side of matters. Pasquale was a knowledgeable old devil and was unlikely to be taken for a ride in the sale. Alone, Mason might have earned far less than he would as a participant. He might almost have planned it this way, although losing the original in the cab he shared with Ginger was hard to see as part of any plan of his. But of course Ginger's seemingly serendipitous appearance in the lobby of his hotel had been part of Parker's plan. How naive he had been, chatting in that gym about a painting as if Parker had not already decided how he could profit from the deal far more than Mason was suggesting.

I'm lucky he didn't simply hire someone to steal it from the museum, Mason thought, shivering as he did so. Mason could hear himself breathing as he imagined where he might now be if he had not transferred the portrait from his wall to the museum vault. What would he had done if the painting had simply disappeared, and from his apartment, not the museum? Could he even have sounded the alarm?

Such dark thoughts now only heightened his sense of relief that things had taken the turn they had. He was seated at his desk, smiling, when Miss Knutsen looked in.

"How did it go?"

He waved a hand weakly. "My old friend Glockner brought all those people here to accuse me of . . ." He looked at her. "He wasn't clear what his charge was. In any case, he meant to make me out some kind of scoundrel. He failed."

Miss Knutsen too looked at the painting rather than at him as he spoke. His annoyance was brief. Her fulsome figure, the way her hair hung down her back when she lifted her face to study the portrait, the unconscious moistening of her lips, fascinated him. Of course she was curious about it. And then inspiration struck.

"Why don't you telephone the *Tribune* and see if they'd like to do a story on that painting. Just get Henry Dillon on the line. I'll talk to her."

You want everyone to know this is a fake?"

He lifted a finger and waggled it. "Language, language. Glockner had to be corrected for calling that painting a fake. A copy is a fake only if it is claimed to be an original."

"He told me it was a fake."

"Glockner?"

"Mr. Mason, I feel I should tell you about his efforts to find out things from me."

"Glockner's efforts?"

"Yes." Her eyes were wide. "I thought he was a friend of yours so at first it didn't seem strange. But today, when he showed up with all those people . . ."

"Judas with the high priests," Mason said with some satisfaction.

"I've been trying to remember what I might have told him, things he might use to harm you."

Mason rather liked the way the toes of her shoes turned inward. She held her dictation tablet in both hands. She might have been a schoolgirl expecting a reprimand were it not for the ripe dimensions of her body. He remembered the scarcely admitted thoughts he had had when he hired her. Since, this magnificently mature woman had become a fixture of his workplace, someone he saw so often he no longer noticed her. Now, with the barred light from the blinds falling on her, values of light and shadow emphasizing nature's generosity in endowing her, he felt as he had in art school just before the model stepped out of her robe.

"I'd like to paint you," he murmured, holding up a letter opener with his thumb pressed against it, closing one eye. He moved his hand pruriently up and down. "I haven't painted anything for months but how I would like to now. Would you let me?"

"I didn't even know you painted." There was a flattered flutter in her voice.

"I haven't shown much. To be good is nice, but I know I'll never be great."

She looked as if she wanted to contest that. She glanced around his office as if expecting to see what was not there.

"Where do you paint?"

"My studio is at home." He rose. Seize the day. "Why don't we go there now?"

"You're the boss," she said after the slightest of pauses.

Roger Dowling sat through the meeting in the office of the director of the Fox River Museum with the sense that he and the Sinclairs were being drawn into an ancient quarrel between Professor Glockner and George Frederick Mason. How obvious are the foibles of professions other than one's own. Despite the fact that potential millions were allegedly involved, Roger Dowling felt that he had landed in the midst of a campus squabble between two prima donnas. Of course, two prima donnas was a contradiction in terms.

Glockner unwisely turned the meeting into a contest between his authority and Mason's. But Mason admitted the painting hanging on his wall was a copy. How he could have realized this prior to the discovery of a painting identical with it, which he was willing to concede was the original, would have been difficult to see had not Mason himself claimed that there was a telltale feature of any authentic Ford portrait. The one on his wall did not have it. The portrait of Margaret did. If the painting in New Jersey had it, then it was indeed authentic and the original of the director's copy. Tomorrow they would convene again so that Mason could point out the identifying characteristic on the portrait Clayton Ford had made of Margaret in the weeks prior to her marriage.

"It's a portrait of Bridget," Peggy said, when they were on their way to the parking lot. "Or a copy of a portrait."

Roger Dowling recalled what he had read in Margaret's diary about those days prior to her marriage when Clayton Ford had painted her and Bridget her maid. Pinkie. He had brought Pinkie communion a few days ago but left immediately afterward, to go to Fairview. Too much of his time was being taken up with matters concerning the Sinclair family.

"I think I'll stop by Riverside to visit her."

Peggy made a little face. "Half the time I don't know what to make of her."

"What do you mean?"

"Things she says about my great-grandmother. It's pretty clear from Bridget's diary that they both had a crush on Clayton Ford."

Peggy let it go and Roger Dowling was relieved. They got into their separate cars and he watched Peggy drive away. Bridget must surely have known what he had learned by comparing the entry in the St. Hilary records and those Lester Pincus had let him see. If Peggy knew she gave no sign of it. He put his car in gear and started out of the parking lot. What kind of answer would he get if he put the question directly to Bridget? Margaret's allusions to her wicked past might have had a basis in reality after all.

He found Pinkie running a rosary through her hand, even though she was watching television.

"Is it some new devotion?"

"The rosary? You're teasing."

"I meant along with the television."

"But I'm praying for them. The troubles they have, Father."

She meant the characters in the daytime drama she was watching. He offered to wheel her out onto the patio, as Peggy said she had done, but the old woman wouldn't hear of it. She turned off the television, rolled her chair to bedside, and buzzed for the nurse.

"Is there any coffee, Gloria? I have a guest."

This was the nurse he had met the first time he came to Riverside. Her white uniform was so heavy with starch it might have been a plaster cast. Whenever Roger Dowling arrived Gloria stared at his collar. Then it came.

"I've left the church, Father."

"I'm sorry to hear that."

"I go to Reverend Keener now. You probably know him."

"Isn't he on television?"

"Oh, he's much better live. I was driven to it, Father."

"How so?"

"My family was in St. Waldo's parish for three generations. I went to the school. It's awful what's happened. Mass there isn't mass, it's amateur night on Ed McMahon. Awful. No real prayer, no sense of sin, no crying out for salvation."

"You could come to mass at St. Hilary's."

"Reverend Keener's good enough for me."

"I think you should give St. Waldo's another chance."

"That'll be the day."

Now, asked by Bridget to bring coffee, she made a face. "There's a machine that squirts colored water into plastic cups. I'd have Coke, if I were you."

"Would that do, Father?"

"Why don't we split one?"

"Good."

"Peggy Sinclair enjoys her visits with you, Bridget."

"She's a good girl but she's too curious about what went on a million years ago. My father used to say, don't get too interested in your ancestors. She thinks Margaret was born a grand old lady."

"Has she told you about wanting to bring Matthew Sinclair's body back for reburial here, to lie beside Margaret?"

"No!"

"It won't be easy, given all the red tape."

Of course it was Maud's idea to bring Matthew's remains from Italy to the island chapel at Fairview, seemingly as added insurance against any attempt to sell the estate. Her son, her sister, were sufficient reason for her own determination, but the reburial of Margaret and Matthew would involve all the Sinclairs.

"You mean in Italy?" Maud said when he had mentioned red tape to her.

"Yes."

"But couldn't the embassy help? And the Vatican? Father Dowling, do you know someone in Rome who might help?"

That was when he mentioned Corbett. They had been students

together in Washington. Corbett, brilliant, suave, imposing, had been sent on to Rome for further study. He was still there, an archbishop whose career had been spent in one dicastery or another. Corbett had been on the Roman Rota when Roger Dowling was on the Chicago marriage court and their friendship had continued at long distance. Whenever Corbett was in the Midwest, they arranged for dinner in Chicago. In recent years, Corbett had been expressing the desire to visit Roger at St. Hilary's in Fox River. He promised Maud he would ask his friend about the prospects.

"I wouldn't count on success, Maud."

"I would never forgive myself if I didn't try."

Bridget clearly thought the whole idea was nonsense. But it was Peggy's curiosity she knew of.

"Oh, I'd give anything if I'd burned my diary and Margaret hadn't given Peggy hers. She shouldn't bother her head about all that."

"It was a terrible tragedy," Father Dowling said. "And a lifelong sad ordeal for her. The young married couple in a far land and him dying like that."

Bridget looked at him for a moment. "They never got along."

"Margaret and Matthew?"

"Fought like cats and dogs. Oh, not noisy, but the whole thing was a mistake, a terrible mistake, and she knew only after it was too late."

"She didn't love him?"

"Oh, she loved him well enough." Bridget looked at the television and seemed surprised there was no picture.

"I knew Margaret only in these past few years."

"When I knew her not at all."

"You never got together?"

"What did we have in common but a few years a long time ago? Our paths went in different directions. Of course it's impossible to live in Fox River and not keep up on the doings of the Sinclairs."

Gloria returned, holding up a can. "All that's left is Sprite. Is that all right?"

"Sprite is right," Bridget said, a bit sharply.

Gloria opened the can and poured two clear plastic cups full, waited for the foam to settle, then topped them off.

"Cheers," Roger Dowling said, lifting his to Bridget.

"Cheers," she repeated, but her tone was sardonic.

"What was Clayton Ford like, Bridget?"

"A devil. The sad thing is that she met him because the Sinclairs wanted her portrait painted before the wedding."

Sad? "And yours as well."

"So I could keep an eye on them."

He could not bring himself to ask her directly the question that had been nagging at his mind. But he thought he knew the answer. When he left her he was surprised to find a uniformed Honora at the nurses' station.

"Father Dowling," she cried, as surprised as he was.

"I've been visiting one of the residents. So you're working here now?"

She explained to him that she worked in the rest home between special nursing jobs. As they talked, they moved past the nurses' station and through the doors into the waiting room.

"Can I light my pipe here?"

"We better go outside." But first she left her tray at the nurses' station and made sure the drug safe was locked.

She led him out onto the patio, where they sat and he filled and lit his pipe.

"Is one of the patients here your parishioner?"

"Do you know Bridget?"

Honora gave him a look. "Of course."

"I bring her communion once a week. Not today. This visit was on the spur of the moment."

"She's one of our problem children." Honora's eyes widened but her penciled brows did not move.

"Was she here when you worked here before?"

"Oh yes."

"How well do you know her?"

Honora put one hand over the other. "How do you mean?"

"Since you took care of Margaret Sinclair, this will interest you."

And he told her that Bridget had been Margaret's maid, long ago, and had even accompanied her on her honeymoon to Italy. Honora listened in fascination to the story of the fateful honeymoon trip and of the young bridegroom's fall from the balcony.

"He got up to close the window because of the storm?"

"That's right. Honora, do you remember the portrait of Margaret that hung on the wall of her room?"

"Yes."

"The artist painted Bridget at the same time."

He began to tell her of the fuss at the museum but the nurse was so obviously preoccupied that he stopped. No doubt her mind had fastened on the tragic accident in Maiori so many years ago.

45

Talking with Father Dowling was a tonic for Honora, almost as good as going to confession, something she had not done for too long now. How many times had she permitted Lester to cling to her with the usual results? But she was more bothered by the fact that she had not seen him for a week. In their relationship he was the pursuer and she the pursued, and she was not used to any prolonged absence on his part. He had been almost a nuisance during the months she was at Fairview. Whenever she returned to her room she half expected to find him waiting for her there, and she had lived in dread of his being discovered by Dolly or Regis.

How terrified she had been when the two of them told the police of having seen a bearded man at the house on the day Margaret died. Honora felt guilty enough already without people learning about her and Lester. Good Lord, to return and find Margaret dead and see that the old woman had tried desperately to make use of her oxygen when the tank was empty! All the while the police and medical examiner were there in the house Honora regretted having replaced the empty tank with a full one, a tank she had not connected. Surely someone would notice and ask, and what in the name of God would she say then? Margaret would have no more use for it, of course, but Honora did not want anyone to realize that the old woman might not have died when she did if oxygen had been available. It was negligence on her part, negligence pure and simple. No one had to tell Honora that.

When Dolly and Regis reported seeing a bearded man around the place that day, of course she had thought they meant Lester. If she wasn't expecting someone to point accusingly at her, she might have remembered Terence Sinclair's visit, but her memory was clouded by her own guilt. She would have told the police everything too if Lester hadn't stopped her.

"But they saw you, Lester."

"I don't think so. They never did before."

"Lester, I know those two. They spy on me. I don't care how careful you were, they saw you."

If it had only been Dolly, she wouldn't have cared. Anyone could see the housekeeper was either gaga or drunk, but Regis was an imposing figure and difficult to disbelieve. Well, as far as that goes, Honora had certainly told Regis what she thought of him! Afterwards, in her room, thanking God it was her last night at Fairview, she couldn't sleep, the angry words she had addressed to Regis echoing in her mind. Finally she did drop off only to be wakened by what sounded like the last trump, a police siren wailing up the road. Minutes of chaos and then the horrible discovery of Regis Factor dead.

He had killed himself because of her. Honora found it difficult not to take a kind of perverse pride in that. It was another matter, remembering the last angry things she had said to him. She felt half responsible for his death. Guilty. Bless me, Father, for I have sinned. But how on earth could you confess such a thing? All she could say was that she spoke in anger to another person, but that didn't begin to cover the guilt she felt. When she learned later that the police had decided Terence Sinclair was the bearded man Dolly and Regis had seen, the cook's death seemed more tragic than ever.

"I was so mad at him because I was sure he'd seen you and all along it must have been Terence Sinclair."

Lester listened, looking thoughtful. Finally he shrugged. "I told you not to worry."

Sitting on the sunny patio with Father Dowling, enjoying the sweet smell of the tobacco he smoked, she would have liked to tell him everything about that last day of Margaret's life. In his presence, thinking of Lester, she felt soiled and used. She was flattered by Lester's love; it still made her dizzy to think that such a good-looking man was attracted to her. If there hadn't been Lester, she might have been interested in Regis. Might? Of course she would have been. Wasn't it just like life that as soon as she had one man another came along? When Father Dowling asked how well she knew Bridget, Honora wanted to tell him she knew the old woman's grandson quite well. But then he got on to the paintings and Honora just sat and listened.

"I wouldn't mind having that," Lester had said early on of the portrait of Margaret Sinclair. He was whispering. Margaret was in her chair, facing away from them, and Lester had come into the room as if he were deliberately courting discovery. If Margaret had turned around Honora might simply have introduced him and that would have been that, but Lester obviously relished these secret visits to Fairview. That portrait had fascinated him. It was the main reason that, from time to time, he would come softly into Margaret's room.

"She wouldn't part with it for anything. Isn't that vain, an old woman always looking at a picture of herself when she was young and beautiful."

"Is there another like it in the house?"

He meant another portrait, not of Margaret, just another portrait. How was Honora supposed to know?

"Look around, will you?"

And she did, feeling dumb, looking into every room, but she found nothing. Lester looked himself, moving quietly through the house in the middle of the night, Honora at his side, her heart in her throat. Anyone would think they were burglars.

"Ask her," Lester said.

"Ask her what?"

"If there's another portrait."

To Honora's surprise, Margaret was willing enough to answer the question. All the other paintings by Clayton Ford were in the Fox River Museum. Only one of them was a portrait.

"She gave it away?" Lester seemed angry about it.

"You can't have everything you want, Lester," she scolded. "The historical society is bursting with things already."

"It's my job," he said, managing a smile. "I want all the local artifacts I can lay my hands on."

"The painting in her room is the only one left."

"It'll do."

"I don't think Mrs. Sinclair would sell it."

"Maybe we should steal it."

"Lester!"

But it became a little game, planning the imaginary theft. Lying on her bed, snug in his arms, she listened to him develop elaborate schemes of pirating the painting out of the house. He could take it to the historical society for safekeeping. That was the wrinkle. Once he had stolen it he wouldn't be able to let anyone see it. Of course it had all been just silly talk.

After Father Dowling left, Honora still had two hours left on her shift, and they were busy hours, but she felt lighthearted. She would telephone Lester and tell him she had learned something very, very interesting. Of course she wouldn't tell him on the phone. So they would get together and then, when she felt good and ready, she would tell him that Bridget, his grandmother, had been painted by the same artist who had done the portrait of Margaret Sinclair he had admired so much.

"Honora, I can't. Not tonight."

"Well, I suppose it will keep."

"What?"

"Something I found out that you'll want to know."

"About what?"

Don't tell him. Let him stew. But the bland way he'd said he could not come see her bothered her. "Your grandmother."

"Is something wrong with her?"

"I wouldn't keep that a secret, would I?" Her teasing tone sounded wheedling in her own ears. She had the terrible feeling that things were altering between her and Lester. "I'll give you a hint. Think of Margaret Sinclair's portrait."

"Do you mean Clayton Ford's portrait of my grandmother?"

"You knew! How did you know?" She felt so deflated, but of course the explanation was so obvious. "Bridget told you."

"Honora, the papers have been full of it."

The way he said it made her feel more stupid than what he said.

"When will I see you, Lester?"

Half a minute went by before he said, "I'll be by to see my grandmother."

After he hung up, Honora felt as she had before she met him, dumpy, dull, and unattractive. It was because he came to see Bridget that it first started, and he seemed to be telling her that things were back to where they'd been when she was all alone.

He had been her secret as she had been his, they'd agreed to that from the beginning. This involved only themselves. That was why they almost never went places. His family? He made a face. "You'd never talk to me again if you met them." There wasn't anyone she wanted him to meet. It was enough, when they were out, for strangers to see them together.

Now her emptiness increased at the thought that no one else would even know if he never came to see her again.

Peggy had just got home from the museum when Professor Glockner telephoned and asked if he could come see her and Peggy wished she hadn't taken the cordless phone onto the porch. But she said sure, when would you like?

"Are you free now? Before our next meeting with Mason I'd like to examine the Ford portrait in your possession."

The visit to Mason's office had made her impatient with all this fuss over Ford paintings, but she couldn't think of a plausible excuse to put him off. Figure of fun though he was, he still was her old professor. Nonetheless, she was not in a hospitable mood when the rumpled Glockner rolled out of his car and shuffled up to the house. Peggy was having iced tea on the porch and writing a letter to Michele. She'd been sitting there when the phone rang and hadn't moved since.

"This is iced tea, would you like some?"

"I'd much rather look at the painting."

This fitted the impression he created among the girls at Hathaway

Hall, a man totally engrossed in his work. One day he would look up to find that his life was over and he hadn't really lived at all.

Peggy got up and led him inside. "Make yourself at home. I'll be on the porch. You won't be disturbing anyone."

She had settled down and picked up the tablet containing her unfinished letter to Michele when he spoke behind her.

"Where is it?"

She had given in to the silent treatment from her parents and brought the portrait downstairs again. "It's hanging in the living room."

"The living room."

"The large room with the fireplace. It's hanging over one of the couches."

"I don't see it."

Peggy put down her tablet and got up again. As she went inside she was thinking that she would include this in her letter to Michele. A visit from the mad Professor Glockner who can't find the living room.

The painting was not hanging over the couch in the living room. She turned a puzzled expression to Professor Glockner. "I'm sorry. I had it upstairs for a while. It must be there. Just a moment."

She ran upstairs and looked in her room, but the painting wasn't there. It wasn't in any of the upstairs rooms. Peggy came downstairs slowly, trying to remember if her father had said anything about moving the portrait. Before calling him, she looked through the whole downstairs without finding the portrait. Glockner followed her wordlessly through the rooms and stood to one side while she waited for her father to come on.

"Dad? Peggy. Where's the portrait of Margaret?"

"Where? It's in the living room."

"No it isn't."

"Is this a joke?"

"Dad, I'm perfectly serious. It isn't hanging where it's been. Would Mother have taken it somewhere?"

"Peggy, hang up. Don't touch anything. I'm going to call the police."

Peggy was almost surprised to find Professor Glockner still standing there.

"It's been stolen, hasn't it? I was afraid this would happen. I warned you. A painting that valuable just hanging on the wall in a house anyone could enter!"

"You told me so?"

"I'm sorry, Peggy, but I did indeed tell you so."

Two hours later it was generally agreed that the portrait had been stolen. Professor Glockner was abject that such a work of art had been taken away as easily as a stereo or TV set. Her father's reaction seemed gauged to what the painting could be sold for. Peggy herself felt that someone had stolen her great-grandmother from her.

"Maybe it will be discovered in New Jersey," Professor Glockner said with a snort.

Cy Horvath and Agnes Lamb checked out the theft of the painting. Phil Keegan was madder than hell at the way the Sinclair family seemed to dominate the work of the department lately and it didn't help that Robertson kept urging his captain of detectives to keep the prominent family placated.

"Placated." Keegan took his cigar from his mouth and looked at it. "I guess he means we should stop them from suing the hell out of one another and not remove the bodies of suicides from their family estate."

Professor Glockner latched on to Cy and took him out to the porch where the owner of the stolen painting, Peggy Sinclair, was sitting calmly.

"Tell him," Glockner said to Peggy.

"Why don't you, Professor?"

Cy had the feeling that Glockner would have taken over even if Peggy Sinclair had begun. The professor's account sounded like an indictment of Peggy and her family. "This is a painting worth millions of dollars. I do not exaggerate. It is worth that much because it was painted by a great, great artist. Of course his work attracts thieves and charlatans. We have already seen that." He looked at Cy and Agnes over the rims of his tinted glasses. "Have you heard of the famous discovery in New Jersey?"

"Why don't you tell us," Agnes said, sitting down.

It brought back vague memories of school, someone talking your arm off and not worrying at all that you might just get up and go. A captive audience. He and Agnes had to listen to this, Cy supposed, but it was not easy to make sense of Glockner's spiel. If he sounded accusing when he spoke of the way Peggy and her parents had kept the missing painting here in their home, with no security whatsoever, he sounded like a prosecutor when he got going on the director of the Fox River Museum. Mason. Cy remembered Mason. He wouldn't want to have to choose between Mason and this mad professor.

"Are you suggesting that the director of the museum stole the painting?" Agnes asked.

"Whoever stole the portrait allegedly discovered in New Jersey is behind this, depend upon it."

There was no evidence of a break-in, but there was no need to break in. Glockner was right, anyone could have walked into the house and walked out with the painting. But not just anyone knew it was there.

"Who did know?" Cy asked Peggy.

"My family. Father Dowling. Professor Glockner."

Glockner made a farting sound with his lips. "Anyone with an interest in Clayton Ford could have discovered the whereabouts of the painting. That it had been left to Peggy was a matter of public record. Where had she put it? One need only put two and two together."

"Is that what you did?"

Glockner's glasses altered from twilight to midnight and back again. "I did not have to. We were to convene here tomorrow."

"Why?"

Glockner displayed his hands, apparently to indicate the absurdity of what he was about to say. "George Frederick Mason was going to show us an infallible sign that the portrait was painted by Clayton Ford. Now, of course, he no longer faces the embarrassment of such a showdown."

Well, that gave Mason a motive of sorts, Cy supposed. After they had heard all Glockner and Peggy and her parents had to say, Cy and Agnes drove to the museum, where they found the director had gone for the day. The administrative offices were locked. No one knew where Mason was, not the woman who ran the gift shop, not the head security man at the front door.

"He don't check in and out with me," he said to Cy.

"Horvath, you back?"

Cy turned to see Pudge Hanrahan, the retired cop who was now a museum guard. Hanrahan stared at Agnes and Cy introduced her. They walked on a bit with Hanrahan.

"We hoped to have a talk with Mason."

"He left," Hanrahan said.

"You see him go?"

"They left a couple hours ago."

"They?"

"Mason and Miss America." His eyes darted to Agnes. "His secretary." Hanrahan crossed his eyes.

They resisted Hanrahan's invitation to view the Willa Keeler exhibit.

"I'll come outside with you," Hanrahan said. "I need a smoke."

That was how he had noticed Mason leaving. He was standing on the service ramp, smoking a cigarette, when Mason and Hazel Knutsen came out and got into the director's car. Hanrahan had got out of sight but saw them drive off together. He looked as if he would say more if Agnes weren't there.

"Something going on there, Pudge?"

"He's crazy if there isn't."

Cy let it go at that. Glockner had given them lots of leads as to where a stolen painting might have gone, but Cy wanted a less angry authority. Mason seemed the obvious choice.

"Are we going to his home?" Agnes asked in the car.

"Maybe they're at her place."

"I got both addresses."

"Where?"

"Security."

"Some security."

On the drive to Mason's apartment, Agnes wondered if letting himself be seen leaving the museum with his secretary was Mason's way of establishing an alibi.

268

"You think he stole the portrait?"

"The girlfriend will back up his story. Nice."

Gordon, the maintenance man, provided a third party and he listened slack-jawed while Cy put the question to him.

"They don't log in and out." Gordon grinned at Agnes.

"Meaning you don't know?"

"I didn't say that, so I couldn't mean it." His grin grew wider.

Agnes stepped closer to Gordon. "Did Mr. Mason return to his apartment this afternoon?"

"That's his car parked over there."

"Answer the goddam question."

Gordon's grin faded. "Yeah. He came back. They're still up there."

"When did he get home?"

"During the seventh inning stretch. I looked out and saw them coming in."

"Can you read a clock?"

Gordon tried ignoring Agnes. "About three-thirty," he said to Cy.

"With a woman?"

"With a woman," Gordon said.

"And they're still up there."

"Shall we look?"

"Your word is good enough for us," Agnes said.

Cy hesitated, then nodded. She was right. If they went up and Mason answered his door, they would still have to rely on Gordon for corroboration that he had been there for hours.

48

The theft of Margaret's portrait, indeed all the events of the past weeks, confused Maud, and she was not accustomed to confusion. Bickering in the family, public criticism of the Sinclairs, now the theft of Margaret's portrait! Maud had not imagined the death of Margaret Sinclair would have such an effect on her, on the family, on the community in which they lived, yet ever since they had buried her, following Amos Cadbury's advice and not using the mausoleum at Fairview, a series of things had happened, one emerging from the other, much as rings formed in the water below her when a fish leapt for a moment into the world of air and then disappeared.

She stood on the high arched wooden bridge that led to the island. What a work of craftsmen it was, its boards pegged rather than nailed, but their grain had deepened with time and weather and they were beginning to crack and splinter now. The bridge had grown more beautiful with age, Maud thought. She did not quite lean against the railing as she looked down at the dark water lapping at the supports of the bridge. The time she had set aside for the great confrontation between Professor Glockner and George Frederick

270

Mason was now her own. There was no longer a painting to provide Mason an opportunity to triumph over his accuser. The summer morning was warm, the air alive with insects. She felt melancholy in a melancholy setting.

Maud looked toward the island where the white facade of the chapel was just visible through the trees. But she turned away and retraced her steps to the house.

Peggy had been excited to learn that Bridget Doyle was still alive, but the woman held no interest for Maud. Once she had been connected with the family, but that was long ago. Odd that her portrait, too, should be creating such a fuss.

"Shouldn't it belong to her, Maud?"

Maud stared at Peggy. "The painting was in Margaret's possession. She gave it to the museum."

"Or a copy of it. I think Bridget's family should own the original."

"Apparently they got rid of it."

But Maud did not want to talk about Bridget. It disturbed her that all these events distracted from what Margaret had intended. The Sinclair Foundation was the heart of the will, although Margaret had sworn Maud to secrecy when she revealed her plan.

"Money has progressively weakened this family, Maud. From a moral point of view, I've come to think riches should not be inherited. It is a disadvantage to be advantaged and I don't intend to aggravate the problem by distributing yet more wealth among my children's children."

The link between Margaret and the third and fourth generations was the one son to whom she had given birth as a widow, the fruit of her honeymoon, the child without whom the Sinclair name would have died out in Fox River. Henry Sinclair. Henry VIII. Much of the wealth Margaret had to bequeath was due to the efforts of Maud's father. On Maud's dresser was a photograph of herself in Henry's arms on the day of her baptism. How uncomfortable he looked holding the blanket in which his daughter was wrapped. Maud herself, a bonnet pulled down over her just-christened head, peered out from his embrace. Familiar though it was, that photograph had not lost its power to make her want to cry.

Just when the commotion stirred up by that awful newspaper story because of the simple truth that the paintings Margaret had loaned to the museum still belonged to the Sinclair family—just when all that seemed to be dying down, a new squabble broke out concerning the portraits of Bridget and Margaret made by the painter Clayton Ford in the month prior to Margaret's marriage to Matthew Sinclair.

After the meeting in Mason's office, Maud had gone with the Salazars and Glockner to a nearby tearoom. Professor Glockner was an unlikely ally, but she had the feeling that something was not quite right in George Frederick Mason's reaction to the sensational charge made by the Hathaway Hall professor of art history. His occupation must be very much like that of a man of limited means working for a wealthy patron. All that wealth and none of it his. Mason had never disguised his faint contempt for the clientele of his museum.

"He mustn't be allowed to get away with it," Professor Glockner said over and over again. He seemed to be addressing Maud as an alumna of Hathaway Hall, invoking the high moral code stressed there, replete with Shalt and Shalt Nots but going far beyond the decalogue in detail. Glockner was suggesting a new prohibition. Thou shalt not steal Clayton Ford originals and replace them with copies, however well done.

Would preventing Mason from getting away with it be enough for Glockner? Maud doubted it. She realized that the bearded little man with the tinted glasses was engaged in a vendetta against the director. Theirs was an intense professional rivalry, a battle to the death, no prisoners taken.

"He should never have been put in charge of one Ford, let alone so many. Do you know what he did in New York before coming here?"

"What?" Bunny asked, though she probably knew Mason's vita as well as anyone.

"He was a dealer. More accurately, he was apprenticed to a dealer, a dealer whose reputation is no better than it should be. And do you know that dealer's name?"

Maud lifted her brows receptively.

"Gab-bi-a-no," Glockner said, rocking forward in his chair, pronouncing the name as if he were giving language instructions. "And he had dealings in those days with Pas-qua-le Par-ker."

"Parker! But isn't he the one . . ."

Glockner rocked back, nodding approvingly at Bunny. QED. It was his last opportunity to undermine his rival before the great revelation Mason had promised, the identifying mark of a Ford portrait, to be illustrated with one authentic portrait still available.

272

Now the portrait was stolen and Glockner forced himself into the center of events, as if he rather than the family had been outraged. Maud was not likely to forget that Glockner had taken his story to Tuttle, as if Tuttle and not Amos Cadbury represented the Sinclairs. Alas, it was a pardonable mistake. The Salazars had done the same. Her own family bothered Maud far more than Professor Glockner did.

"Oh, you were right, Grandma," Maud said aloud, as she climbed the veranda steps and continued on into the house. "You were right as rain about us."

She did not mean to exempt herself from the old woman's concern for what wealth had done to her progeny. Contesting the will might have offended Amos Cadbury's professional pride, but it struck Maud as impious. How dare they question the wisdom of what Margaret Sinclair had chosen to do! But her own efforts since had been to deflect that greed onto some object other than the will and the foundation. Maud held in memory the looks exchanged among her nephews and nieces and cousins. Even William's mustache twitched with satisfaction as he nodded agreement. The expressions were emphasized as in a Renaissance painting, each face illustrative of a different way in which the human spirit can go wrong, the lighting coming from a candle, the faces in the foreground of the painting, the background dark as pitch.

Peggy's reaction to the theft of Margaret's portrait was puzzling. Her stunned sadness had not expressed itself in the anger Dennis and Vivian poured out to reporters. And no one, needless to say, had surpassed Professor Glockner.

"It's a pattern," he cried. "It's all of a piece. An imbecile can see what's going on. First the one, an inside job. Now the other, inadequately protected. It's what I feared. It's why I stopped by."

He had been more than willing to spell out the vast conspiracy he saw under way and the *Tribune* was delighted to feature it. The story caught the fancy of the wire services and readers around the nation and eventually those abroad were following the sinuous path of Glockner's theory. Mason and his shady mentor Parker had patiently arranged the transfer of the Ford portrait of Bridget from the museum, replacing it with a copy, then staged a discovery in New Jersey. They would have been tempted to do the same with the other Fords in the museum, but they had not mastered the problem involved in such lucrative coincidences occurring swiftly enough for them to profit by them. The portrait of Margaret Sinclair proved irresistible as a second strike.

"You think Parker and Mason stole it?"

"The police, of course, will have to determine that."

"But isn't that what you're saying?"

"I am just calling attention to certain facts."

"What good does it do them? They can't auction this portrait."

Glockner lay a fat finger alongside his pudgy nose. "There is an underground market."

Was there no longer a limit to what newspapers could print? The damning statements were all carefully enclosed in quotation marks and attributed to Professor Gearhart Glockner, art historian at Hathaway Hall in Indiana and a renowned expert on the work of Clayton Ford. The reporters had hurried to George Frederick Mason.

"I will not dignify such nonsense with a comment."

"It's all false?"

"I have stopped beating my wife, I no longer lie, I have not betrayed my country within the past six months. Do you have any other questions?"

"Will you sue Glockner?"

"I am sure that under appropriate psychiatric care Professor Glockner can return to society, if not as a productive member, at least as a harmless one."

"Wow," said a reporter.

"Indeed," said George Frederick Mason.

All in all, Maud felt uncomfortable with her allies. This attempt to commune with Margaret's spirit by coming to Fairview had met with only limited success. When she was lying in the chapel with Matthew beside her, she would be more accessible, Maud was sure of it. Father Dowling's friend in Rome had been encouraging.

"Would it help if you went over?"

"That's his suggestion."

"Then you must go. Of course the foundation would send you."

He hadn't agreed but he hadn't said no either. Maud began to make inquiries at travel agencies.

At the house she went upstairs in the hope of finding Peggy at work on foundation business, but she was disappointed.

49

If her parents had let her keep the painting in her room, if Professor Glockner and Mason had not made such a fuss over it, if she had listened to her father and locked it up somewhere . . .

If lots of things hadn't happened, things would be different. That was called a tautology in Philosophy 101. Peggy was stunned into silence by the theft of the painting and listened with amazement to the things her father and Professor Glockner said to the police, to reporters, to one another. Their outrage seemed wholly unrelated to what she felt. When Agnes Lamb, the black detective, talked to her, there wasn't much Peggy could say. She was still bruised from finding out about Joel's wife and daughter. She would gladly give up the painting for that not to be true.

Margaret should not have given her the painting. It was too valuable, too much of a responsibility. It had been such a sweet thing to do, but it was trouble to give it to her. What had been the alternative? Giving it to the museum? It should have been left where it had always hung, in Fairview. There were other paintings in the house; the portrait would have been safe there. The will had called

275

attention to it, and what had been meant only as a touching gift became something worth millions.

These crazy events had the welcome effect of preventing her from thinking about Joel. That was over, she told herself. It was not meant to be. But when she had to try to put him from her mind, her heart ached and tears filled her eyes.

Peggy found it easier to talk about Joel with Bridget Pincus, maybe because the old woman seemed only half interested in the subject, although she was happy to have Peggy visit her.

"I fell in love with him before I knew he'd been married."

"Thank God you found out in time."

"In time for what?"

"Isn't the boy a Catholic? Of course if he isn't a Catholic, that's another matter. The Church might not recognize his previous marriage."

"He's applied for an annulment."

"There you are, then."

"He has a wife and daughter and wants the Church to say he was never really married. Isn't that dreadful?"

"Does the wife want an annulment?"

Peggy realized she didn't know. Would it make any difference to her if it was a mutual wish, both Joel and his wife wanting to be told that they had never been married at all, despite their daughter? What was the daughter supposed to make of that when she was old enough to wonder?

"How old are you, child?" Bridget asked her.

"Child! I'm twenty-three."

Bridget pushed back to take another look at her. "People don't grow up as fast as they used to. Margaret Sinclair was two years a widow when she was your age. I myself had two children and another on the way when I was twenty-three. But it isn't done like that now. Probably just as well. Look at what happened to your young man."

"He's not my young man."

"You should get married."

She wanted to protest that she was only twenty-three. "Lester isn't married."

"Lester!" That was all, but it seemed answer enough. Bridget took hold of Peggy's arm. "Don't tell me you're interested in him."

Lester? Good Lord. "He's not my type."

276

"He's a good boy and a relative and all that, but God knows he's no prize in the marriage department. No ambition, no sense of humor. Thin hair."

"Joel Cleary has thin hair too."

But Bridget wasn't listening. "Clayton Ford had a head of hair, he did."

"Tell me about those days."

"There isn't anything to tell."

"Tell me about the kissing."

"What! Did I ever say anything about kissing? That is a terrible thing to say about a young woman."

"You wrote all about it in your diary."

"I did not."

"I could bring you copies."

Bridget turned her head away and threw up her hands. "Please. Memories are bad enough, I don't want to see what I wrote when I was a silly young girl."

"Margaret did the kissing and you did the counting."

"Oh, that's the way it was, was it?"

"Wasn't it?"

Bridget put on her playful expression. "It's not the sort of thing a lady talks about."

"Oh, come on! Things were the same then as now. Old pictures make women look all bundled up and aloof as if they would die rather than show a little leg, but you can't tell me it was like that when you were posing in the barn for Clayton Ford."

"What on earth are you saying?"

"He fell in love with Margaret, didn't he?"

"Clayton Ford was the kind of man who fell in love with every woman he met."

"Then he must have fallen in love with you as well."

"And what if he did?"

"Are you blushing?"

It was terrible to tease an old woman this way, but Peggy was amazed that someone as old as Bridget could still blush about something that had happened nearly three-quarters of a century ago.

"I thought I asked you not to read my diary any more."

"There's a big fuss about the painting Ford did of you. I told you

Margaret gave me the one he did of her? It's been stolen. Maybe yours was too. It was in the Fox River Museum and . . ."

"Museum!"

"Margaret loaned them all her Fords, except her own portrait. I showed you that clipping of the discovery of the original of your portrait in New Jersey. That means the painting in the museum is a copy. One of my former professors is accusing George Frederick Mason of stealing the original."

"And losing it in New Jersey?"

"He thinks when it's sold Mason will share in the profits."

"That ought to buy him a cigar."

"Bridget, I won't tell you what your portrait is now worth."

"As I remember, the Sinclairs gave him five hundred dollars for Margaret's. Can you imagine? All that money for daubing oil paint on canvas. He did mine for free though."

"As a present?"

"I guess."

"For whom?"

"I don't know. The Sinclairs hired him."

"At auction your portrait would bring several million dollars."

"Don't lie to an old lady. I suppose you think I'm gone in the head and you can tell me anything." She kept her eyes on Peggy. "Just make sure you don't tell such nonsense to Lester."

There seemed little point in persuading Bridget of the value of her portrait. Nor was Bridget as struck as Peggy was by the fact that one of the nurses at Riverside had attended Margaret Sinclair during her final months. Honora would sit on the bed and visit. She was there when Peggy told Bridget Lester ought to claim that the portrait Clayton Ford had done of her belonged to the Pincus family.

"I will not! I never heard such nonsense. Why should it? If they want a picture of me, there are plenty of photographs. And you can bet they're all put away in attics, if they've been kept at all."

"Lester is Bridget's grandson," Peggy explained to Honora.

"Oh."

"This young lady is involved in a tragic love affair, nurse. She's in love with a man who already has a wife and child."

"Bridget!" Peggy felt betrayed.

"Oh, it's all right for you to tease me and make fun of me in front of the nurse as long as two don't play the game, is that it?"

278

Peggy went to the old woman and put her arms about her.

Conversations with Bridget had sent her back to the earliest entries in Margaret's diary, but there were only the most fleeting references to the time before the wedding trip itself. Writing of Bridget's behavior with Hans, she compared it to "her boldness with C that started it all." Like a scholar with his manuscript, Peggy was now sufficiently expert in her great-grandmother's diary to read that C as Clayton and the passage as a reference to Bridget's manner with the painter.

"My boldness!" Bridget said. "Well, she had a nerve, didn't she? She was the one about to be married, not me. And I wasn't the one he was sweet on anyhow."

Peggy wondered if she should be shocked by the suggestion that Margaret had "been bold" with an artist just weeks before her marriage to Matthew Sinclair.

"What did being bold amount to?"

"Nothing. The whole thing amounted to nothing."

"Including the kisses he gave you?"

"Gave me! Oh, girl, you've got it all wrong indeed."

Earlier, Peggy had been amused at the thought of the artist stealing kisses from the maid while employed to paint her mistress's portrait.

"Then you were counting kisses he gave Margaret?"

"She asked me to. It was like a little game. Teasing him. You know."

Reading the two diaries made it difficult to think of the time they were written as one in which young women were china dolls, naive, repressed, reduced to blushing silence in the presence of a man. Margaret and Bridget had acted as she and Michele might have in similar circumstances. They would have had to overcome the awkwardness of their ages, but Peggy suspected that Bridget and Margaret were more at ease with a man than she and Michele might have been. This realization made it difficult to regard the kissing as on a nice antiseptic plane, a peck on the cheek, lips proffered and swiftly withdrawn at the touch of his lips, a children's game. But Bridget had been counting, and that made it sound like a game.

"I'm surprised they let you be alone with him."

"Alone! The both of us were there."

"Well, you were some chaperone, weren't you?"

Bridget refused to say more. Why should she agree to be scolded about events seventy-some years ago?

Reading Margaret's diary was especially poignant after the theft of the portrait. Perhaps it was her own mood that enabled her to pick up a thread she had not noticed before, perhaps it was talking with Bridget and realizing Margaret had been a woman of flesh and blood. Well, here she was on her wedding trip. It had been a bad crossing and the entries made it clear that nothing much of a marital sort had occurred on the high seas. Peggy began with the Naples entries. There ought to have been at least some coded reference to the first successful lovemaking of Margaret and Matthew Sinclair. If there was, it eluded her.

Italy is like a palette, colorful, smudged, a pile of shapes, clouds build right on up out of hills of stone. It needs an artist as it needs sun to be seen. But Oh the noise of Naples as we were driven up from the dock, urchins running alongside, hands out, dirty hopeful faces and then narrow streets no wider than paths lined with buildings that seem anchored to one another with lines of washing, people everywhere, shouting, talking, smiling, laughing, singing, young women haughty as they go by the men who quite openly insult them but all in the most good natured way. This is where C should be, Bridget said, and I wish he was, said I.

Leaving the carriage at the station I looked up at what I first thought was only cloud and it was cloud but cloud exhaled from a huge black mountain hunched up to the sky and then I realized, Vesuvius. It sits up there over the city, over the bay, over all these laughing shouting happy angry people, a malevolent presence, the promise of death and they live like that always. As do we, M said, the most solemn remark I have ever heard him make. He has so little to make him happy, poor man, but goes on accepting the sentence we passed on one another. My God how I have wronged him.

Brazen Bridget asked today if all was right and of course I did not answer but why would she ask if it were? There is a story of a mule left halfway between two piles of hay who starved of indecision. The daytime I can enjoy, more than enjoy, Italy is so gay. On the train we had oranges and grapes and M drank wine but I didn't tho Bridget teased and then she had half a glass, bold as that. My illness is not always feigned now; I pretend to be well because M returns to the thought that I must see a doctor. A doctor! Jesus, Mary, and Joseph, have mercy on me.

Thus the newly wed Margaret Sinclair on the train to Salerno. From there they were driven up the winding coastal road, their destination Amalfi, but fated, or doomed, to stop at Maiori on a whim. The entries were often forced, as if Margaret were determined to write prettily. But for whom did she write?

M asks to read what I write and Bridget offers to show him her diary and alone with her I scolded her and she said she wasn't ashamed. But she should have been from the page or two I read when she pushed the book under my nose. I keep this because it's a way to be busy, an excuse in the evening, after supper, when we're alone. Last night while I wrote he went outside and from the balcony I saw him down below on the narrow road that goes toward the town. I put on a robe and stayed on the balcony, looking out at the water, a great round moon so close I felt I might reach out and touch it and stars by the millions winking into life. Then I noticed M across the road sitting on the stone ledge looking down at the castle that sits right in the water.

There was something so sad in the scene, the bride alone on the balcony, the groom alone on the road below, both looking out to sea. It did not sound like a happy honeymoon to Peggy. Would Margaret have alluded to any intimacy after he came up to her? If the diary was oblique it was not inhibited. But not only were there no shy references to married love, there were remarks that suggested the couple had not yet consummated their love when they arrived at Maiori.

He is angry and has a right to be not that he shows it he is the soul of patience on the outside but he obviously did not think it would be like this. Neither did I. Dear God, I wanted so to marry him, to sail away, to begin all over again. It is possible to begin again. God is merciful. That was my intention. But now . . .

The entry stopped, the pen trailing away. Matthew insisted that she see a doctor and she refused, her case strengthened when it appeared no doctor in Maiori spoke English. Margaret and Bridget huddled in the bathroom together while Matthew spoke soothingly through the locked door and said they would forget all about the doctor, he was only thinking of her, the whole journey was spoiled by her being out of sorts.

Out of sorts! Bridget squeezed my hand as I cried and I thought we have more in common the two of us than I have with M but then Bridget must know what the problem is.

"What was the problem between Margaret and Matthew?" Peggy asked the old woman, shielding her eyes from the sun as they sat on the patio of the nursing home.

"I don't know what you mean."

"She writes of it in her diary."

"I think you make these things up."

"I'll show you."

"I don't want to see it. Why do you keep at it, child? It was a thousand years ago, they're both dead. Let them rest in peace."

"They didn't have much peace together."

"You don't know what it was like. A young woman, suddenly married, then off to foreign places, tossed about at sea, it was exciting but it was frightening too and she got off her feed, that's all it was."

"Bridget, did they sleep together?"

"What a thing to ask! Of course they slept together."

"I know they shared a room and a bed but did they make love?"

"Glory be to God! Do you think I hid under the bed?"

"You must have known or guessed. Did she ever say anything?"

"Did she ever tell me what she did with her man beneath the covers? I should say she did not. What kind of a person do you think Margaret Sinclair was? Even then, quite young, she was a lady, a beautiful thing. In Italy the men couldn't keep their eyes off her."

"I don't see any indication that they ever had sex together."

"Good God, what a way to put it."

"Well, I don't think they did."

"You don't, eh?"

"No."

"Well, my girl, if they didn't where did all you Sinclairs come from?"

Bridget might have looked more triumphant than she did. Her

remark was the definitive answer, of course, and Peggy felt like a fool. She had been so busy looking for the wife to emerge from the virginal diarist that she had forgotten the essential fact. Margaret had returned a widow and pregnant from Italy and from her son Henry all the rest of them had come.

Was it really odd that there wasn't a clue to the time or times that presented the opportunity for Margaret to conceive a child?

Although Bridget usually had the television on when Peggy came to see her, the old woman seemed unaware of all the fuss over the stolen portrait of Margaret. Her own had somehow found its way to New Jersey and after years and years had been discovered, causing Professor Glockner to make terrible charges against the director of the Fox River Museum. But that had been nothing to what he said when the portrait of Margaret was stolen. When would they have realized the painting was gone if he hadn't come to the house that day and insisted on studying it? Since then, in the newspapers, on television, local and national, he had made his wild accusations, absolutely convinced he was right and not even Amos Cadbury could stop him.

"Would you speak to him, Peggy? I am not his lawyer and cannot of course volunteer legal advice but he is opening himself to a devastating libel suit unless he knows something he isn't telling."

"He won't listen to me."

"Please, try. I know he believes what he's saying, but he offers no evidence. And if Mason is guilty, and I don't for a moment say he is, these wild charges are gaining sympathy for him."

She promised and tried to reach him at his motel but the phone rang and rang. She called again and asked the clerk but he just told her to keep trying the room. Professor Glockner's car was in the parking lot. The poor man. His vacation had been ruined. His lifetime study, the work of Clayton Ford, seemed snatched from his grasp and turned into the sensational fare of newspaper stories. She would telephone him again that evening. Meanwhile she had come to talk with Bridget in an effort to understand a few weeks spent in Italy seventy-five years before. The remark that squelched her questions seemed nonetheless to justify her curiosity. She and the rest of the Sinclair family had derived from the lovemaking of Margaret and Matthew in their room in that cliffside hotel on the Amalfi coast.

Bridget asked what time it was and then in a panic asked to be taken to her room. There they watched her afternoon soap, Bridget participating in the melodrama, booing villains, warning heroines of imminent danger, the ridiculous story as real as anything else in her life now.

Her mother came out the front door when Peggy drove in and stood waiting for her, an odd expression on her face.

"Have you heard about Professor Glockner?

"Heard what?"

She took her daughter's hand. "He's dead. He was found in his room at the motel."

"Oh, how awful." She thought of the overweight, overexcited little man. "All this excitement and hurrying about."

"Peggy, he was shot."

Her father drove up then and hurried toward them. He seemed relieved to see that Peggy had already been told.

"Well, they got him," he said, grim-faced.

"They?"

"He said it himself. This wasn't just a lost painting. He wouldn't keep quiet so they shut his mouth."

"Oh, Dennis," her mother said, rejecting this interpretation. Peggy felt that she had entered the world of Bridget Pincus's soap.

50

Painful as Peggy's reaction was when she heard of his marriage, Joel Cleary understood. He would have felt the same way if their roles were reversed. How could he explain to her that he had married while he was in law school, had a daughter, and later divorced? Divorced, too, active voice, not *been* divorced. He had initiated the case. So he hadn't told Peggy, and that had been stupid, he saw that now. He had informed Amos Cadbury before he joined the firm and while the founding father had clearly disapproved, he took it to be extenuating that Joel intended to apply for an annulment.

"Ah."

"I'm told I have a good chance."

A slight frown came and went on Mr. Cadbury's chiseled face. "Such a petition used to take years."

Joel relaxed when it was clear that Mr. Cadbury did not intend to ask him the grounds on which he would appeal for annulment. They were very difficult to explain, another reason he had not told Peggy about Anne. It had been hard enough when eventually he talked with a canon lawyer.

285

"The marriage was consummated?" Monsignor Looney's office was not unlike Amos Cadbury's. Joel had half expected to meet in a sacristy.

"We have a daughter."

"I see."

Joel managed to give the good monsignor a version of Anne's reaction after the baby came. She had married in order to have a child and now she had one and that was it, she wanted no more.

"She wished to use contraceptives?" Monsignor Looney leaned toward Joel as he asked this question. Joel suspected what might be coming. He had heard it before, from a theologian at Notre Dame, a breezy man who kept rubbing his hand over his face as he talked.

"Your marriage is fruitful, you have a child, so there's no problem."

He meant in the use of contraceptives. If that had been the problem, Joel would have taken this dubious advice, but the problem was that Anne had had enough of sex. It had fulfilled its function, she had her child. And that is how she thought of Thea, as her child. Anne apparently regarded him as the female of certain insect species regards the male who expires when copulation is accomplished.

Women can get a little nutty after having a baby, he knew that, and at first he discounted what Anne said, pale against the pale sheets of the hospital bed, holding the baby, saying things she might have rehearsed. But she came home and months passed and every effort to resume marital relations brought forth a repetition of her declaration. She had married him in order to become a mother.

"Why didn't you try a sperm bank?"

"I wanted to know who the father was."

"I could have been the donor."

She thought about it. "It's too late now."

She was serious. Neither anger nor joking, not patience or threats, altered her. To marry without the intention to have marital relations might provide grounds for an annulment, but how could you say a marriage had never existed when it was entered into in order to have a child?

Monsignor Looney nodded. "Let me think about it."

He had gone to Looney only after he met Peggy and the prospect of having now what he had thought he would have with Anne

286

presented itself. Mr. Cadbury had never asked how the annulment procedures were going. Joel hadn't started them. Anne and Thea were in South Bend, he was in Fox River, it seemed that he would no more wish to marry again than Anne would. And staying active made celibacy possible, lots of tennis and golf, swimming several times a week, work, work, work. Interesting work, like helping Mr. Cadbury with the Sinclair estate. And meeting Peggy.

When they had watched baseball in his apartment, having popcorn and beer, Joel resolved never to lay a hand on her until he told her about Anne. But all he had to do was imagine telling her to know what the result would be. The more he got to know Peggy, the surer he was that she would drop him immediately, no matter how difficult it might be. Perhaps if they were lovers . . . In a motel in Indiana, with malice aforethought, he had made love to her. The day he got back he went to see Monsignor Looney. Meanwhile Peggy learned about his marriage and the result was far worse than if he had told her.

She refused his calls. Father Dowling was sympathetic.

"I was the one who told her, Joel. It was clear she didn't know."

"I'd give anything now if I had told her." He didn't blame Dowling. It wasn't slander to tell a young woman the man she was going with had a wife and child in South Bend. "Father, explain to her that I've applied for an annulment."

"Who did you talk with?"

"Monsignor Looney."

"I know him."

Joel told Amos Cadbury too. He felt he owed him that. The old man would not like the thought that a married junior partner was wooing a Sinclair. Father Dowling said he would tell Peggy. It didn't matter.

"Can they annul a daughter?" she asked when he got through to her on the phone and blurted out that he was seeking an annulment.

She hung up but her question was like a knife in his chest. But what else would she think? He was a man who wanted to pretend he had no child, that's how she thought of it. But when he went to South Bend to see Thea he had difficulty thinking of himself as her father. Anne was scrupulous in letting him see Thea but of course that was part of the divorce and her income depended on it. Joel felt he understood better what was happening when he saw *Great Expectations* on television. But Peggy would think he was trying to pretend

Thea did not exist. Joel had the sinking feeling that, even if he did get an annulment, Peggy would not see him again.

So find another girl, the world is full of them, isn't it? Yes and no. He dated other girls, he even tried an affair, but that only worsened matters. He did not want to become what Peggy apparently already thought he was. He could not get her out of his mind.

He began to follow her, feeling like an idiot. What would she think if she knew he would drive out to Fairview to see if her car was there and then park down the road in the hope of seeing her when she drove out the gate? When the portrait was stolen, Joel thought at first he must have been parked up the street while it was going on, but he had only come later, after Peggy returned from the meeting at the museum he and Mr. Cadbury had talked of beforehand. He knew of her visits to Riverside and learned the reason from Mr. Cadbury, who had it from Maud Sinclair.

"The woman who was Margaret Sinclair's maid years ago is a resident there. The one whose portrait is causing all this fuss."

Mr. Cadbury accepted Maud's theory that Bridget's family had sold the portrait, that that was how it had ended up in New Jersey.

"When was the copy made?"

He was remarkably uncurious. There were, of course, many explanations. An owner could have commissioned the copy, Margaret could have acquired the copy as she had acquired genuine Ford landscapes. Whatever records of those purchases there had ever been were no more. Amos Cadbury considered Professor Glockner a man out of control, in the grips of a theory, out for revenge.

"I don't intend to become his instrument, Joel. Nor shall I permit the Sinclairs to do so." He looked away. "Those with whom I have influence, that is."

That Peggy would take the trouble to visit the old woman in the rest home endeared her to him more. Peggy's interest in her great-grandmother's fateful marriage, the death of her newlywed husband in Italy during the honeymoon, seemed marvelously right after Anne's cold eugenics. Babies are part of families and families exfoliate through time, mysteriously producing and uniting persons who are unintelligible apart from these relations. He followed her home the day her parents came out to meet her. Later he realized they were telling her about the death of Professor Glockner.

51

Honora was ready to leave half an hour before her shift was up and Gloria didn't like it, but Honora hardly noticed. Sitting on the bed, listening to Peggy Sinclair talk to Lester's grandmother, Honora had felt that she was an intruder, but she could not tear herself away, not after she learned of the theft of Margaret Sinclair's portrait.

The memories came unbidden but once they began she encouraged them, replaying in her mind those times when she and Lester would lie in her bed at Fairview and talk about stealing the portrait of Margaret that hung on the wall of her room. Of course she had never imagined it was anything but a game, a way for lovers to while away the languorous time after lovemaking.

Finally her shift was done and she hurried out to her car. On the radio, a professor was being interviewed. She had heard him before. He accused people in New Jersey and New York of stealing the portrait. "The same crowd who staged the discovery of the Ford portrait a week ago." Honora followed the man intently, his account pushing from her mind what had occurred to her in Bridget Pincus's room when she listened to Peggy Sinclair tell the old woman of the theft of the portrait of Margaret Sinclair. Why did she hope the professor was wrong? But then an announcer was explaining that they had just been listening to Professor Gearhart Glockner, whose body was found in the Waterbed Motel just hours ago.

The parking lot was across the street from the building that housed the Fox River Historical Society. Honora parked her car facing the street and remained behind the wheel looking across at the window of Lester's office. He had been so cold to her on the telephone, there had been nothing at all of the tone that had always thrilled her, the voice of a man whose interest in the woman to whom he was speaking was unmistakable. No man had ever spoken to her as Lester had. No other man had ever loved her. Before Lester, she had never gone to bed with a man. Even if that was all there was, their relationship a secret to the world, but still going on, she would have been happy. But Lester had said things that could only have meant that they were in a first phase of their love. There would be something more later. When his ship came in. Had his ship come in?

She pushed open the door of the car, put one foot out, and hesitated. The fear of being rebuffed immobilized her. What he had said on the phone depressed her so, but it had not been definitive. Wisdom suggested that she stay away, wait for him to come to her, not force herself on him. All that was true enough, but now there was a new factor, the stolen portrait of Margaret.

She got out, closed the door, and walked swiftly across the street. As she approached the door, she looked at her watch. It was almost closing time. What if the door was locked? Her pace quickened, but when she pushed against the door, it gave and she was in the vestibule. Through the next set of doors was the turnstile through which visitors went, being automatically counted as they pushed through. What was a busy day? Twenty-five visitors, Lester had told her, except when schools were in session and whole classes came. Honora could not have said whether he thought that twenty-five a large or a small number. It seemed ridiculous to Honora. No wonder the turnstile squeaked.

Lester was not at the desk behind the counter where he spent much of the day. The door of his office was open but the light was not on. Of course there were hours of daylight left.

Honora eased the inner doors shut behind her and, as she had done before, following Lester, went around the turnstile. He did not want to count himself each time he came and went during the day. Honora had not wanted to make any noise. She had decided that she would pretend this was a spur-of-the-moment visit meant to surprise him.

There was no one else in the large room filled with display cases and various mementos of the past effectively on view. Honora crept toward the open door of Lester's office, a smile fixed on her face. But when she stepped into the doorway, ready to cry, "Surprise!" she found that the office was empty.

She swallowed her disappointment, letting the false smile die, and went in. He must be in the rest room in back. She went behind his desk, pulled out the chair, and sat. She would be waiting here for him when he returned. And then she saw the painting.

It was propped against the wall as if meant to be viewed from the chair she sat in. The familiar countenance that had looked down on her when she attended to Margaret Sinclair observed her here without surprise. Honora felt herself adopting the attitude conveyed by the expression in the painting—hopeful, innocent, naive. She was so absorbed in the portrait she was not immediately aware of Lester standing in the doorway.

"So you stole it after all." The words came forth bright and easy, the way they had when they lay on her bed and concocted plans. Lester stood in the doorway, dressed all in black as he had been when he visited her at Fairview.

"I wish you hadn't come here, Honora."

He shut the door behind him, looked thoughtful for a moment, then came purposefully across the office toward her.

(52)

"When will they stop saying these dreadful things about you?" Miss Knutsen asked, looking at him with large, unfocused eyes. He had not realized she wore contacts. She wore nothing else. She had come to sit for him and within minutes of disrobing was in bed with him. How sweetly the afternoon had passed.

"Sticks and stones," George Frederick Mason said, groping on the floor beside the bed for his shorts.

"I don't know how you do it."

His left hand found her bare thigh and he gave it a pinch. She squealed but seemed to be offering him the smooth expanse for another pinch. He patted her bottom instead.

In bed with Miss Knutsen. It fitted too well into the mad pattern his life had assumed since first he practiced to deceive. Had the thought ever occurred to him before his fall, he would have expected resistance, the need for a long campaign, promises, the expenditure of oodles of money and, in the end, disappointment in success. Not a bit of it. She was a spanking pagan of a girl, as quick as an imagined Lalage to respond to his overtures. Out of the office, into the car, up

292

to his apartment and into bed, bang, bang, that's how easy it had been. And now, with a sheet pulled over their nakedness, they were stuck with one another.

"I never trusted Glockner," she mused, staring at the ceiling.

"Oh?"

"Why does he hate you so?"

"Envy, I suppose."

"Exactly. That's just what it is." She rolled on her side, the sheet fell away, and her great pendulant breasts put him in mind of a Flemish painting. "I told you he tried to pump me."

"Watch your language."

"Oh, George." She tugged at the sheet, then let it go when she noticed his expression. She reached out, put her hand behind his head, and drew him to her. She knew all about him now, at least in the bed department. Nuzzling into her sweet warm flesh seemed what he had always wanted.

"Tell me about Glockner," he murmured, cradled in her arms, his lips moving against her.

"Why do people wear dark glasses indoors? There's something shifty about that, isn't there? It's hiding something. Talking with him was always like addressing a mirror. I mean, I could see myself, not his eyes." She shuddered.

He traced the line of her body, his hand following the great scoop beneath the ribs which flared magnificently into her smooth, smooth thigh. This was the way Mohammedans imagined heaven, a literal Song of Songs. Comfort me with apples. He said it aloud. And she did.

They got back to the subject of Glockner some minutes later, Mason sitting up now, his head against a propped-up pillow, Miss Knutsen with her head on his chest.

Although Glockner had guessed rather well what had happened, it became a preposterous series of events as he expressed it. It was preposterous, far more so than Gearhart's version allowed, but how could he guess that Mason, from being the lone perpetrator of the theft, had become its victim before he evolved into a partner? Partner. All he had was the word of Parker that he would share in the proceeds. It would be public knowledge how much the painting brought, but what way in the world did he have to enforce the agreement? Parker could play dumb, ignore him, give him nothing, and he would be helpless. Of course he could threaten to expose the whole thing, but that would entail confessing his own turpitude and all would hinge on Parker's belief that George Frederick Mason would pull his whole career down on his head in order to include Parker in the debacle. It was more likely that the body of George Frederick Mason would be found floating in the Fox River. Parker played for keeps.

The fear that he might weather this storm and profit nothing from it made him reckless, enabled him, in fact, to weather it. It lent a note of madness to events. How else could he airily dismiss questions the mere posing of which a few weeks ago would have undone him? It helped that Glockner made his case so badly. The first time he accused Mason of stealing a Ford portrait he had been flanked by Maud and Peggy Sinclair, Father Dowling and Tuttle, Bunny and Octavio Salazar, a citizens' posse come to hear the sheriff accused of malfeasance. But Glockner had quickly turned himself into a lone gunman, shooting wildly about in the middle of Main Street, attracting attention and incredulity.

Mason lay abed, running a hand distractedly through Miss Knutsen's hair, recalling the events of the past weeks which, familiar as they were, still retained the aura of a bad dream.

"He told me I'd be called to testify," Miss Knutsen murmured.

"I suppose you would be if anything came of it."

"The time he came when you were away and the painting was in storage, that's what he was babbling about yesterday on the phone."

"What an imagination the man has. Can you imagine a lawyer leading him on about what he didn't see? All you'd have to say is that the painting was always there on my wall."

"Where was it?"

The flat denial that the painting had ever been off his wall was in his mouth before he stopped. He had become so used to meeting the truth with lies that the bland claim of the contradictory opposite of what had happened was the easiest course. If there was no way to test opposing statements they could oppose one another to a fare-thee-well and it was his word against Glockner's. But Miss Knutsen was something else altogether.

"I took it to New York to sell it."

He held her as she laughed, loving the soprano lilt of her laughter,

294

bell-like, upper register, helpless. Sometimes truth is the best lie of all.

When she subsided, he slapped her bottom, rolled her away, and swung his legs over the side of the bed. He found his shorts with his foot, lifted them with his prehensile toes, and tugged them on.

"I can offer you dinner if you'll take potluck."

"I never do drugs."

She skipped into the bathroom carrying armsful of clothing. Drugs? He could believe anything of Miss Knutsen after their session in bed. Looking at the tangled arena of passion, his breath caught at the improbable fun of it all. Miss Knutsen, imagine. But he doubted this could have happened before the upsetting events of the past few weeks. It was part of the general falling apart of his life. Could he ever return to the *status quo ante*? Even the successful fending off of Glockner would leave him tainted by the accusation. The virus of doubt would have been introduced. And in any case, the Fords would be removed from the museum and his post become a nullity.

He made beef stroganoff and a huge salad. They ate it with the television on, they might have been married, shoveling food into their mouths, eyeing the screen. That was how they learned that Gearhart Glockner was dead.

"You're my alibi," Mason said to Miss Knutsen.

She looked at him pop-eyed. "What do you mean?"

"We were in bed together at the time of the crime."

"You wouldn't tell!"

Where had the insouciant sensualist gone? Miss Knutsen was back in a bourgeois world that frowned on taking one's pleasure where it could be found, denying no chance for dalliance, gathering rosebuds while ye may. "I am joking, my dear. Do you think I'll need an alibi?"

She calmed down, but he sensed that Miss Knutsen would be a slender reed on which to lean if it ever came to that. There was no way in the world she would deny under oath that the painting had been missing from his office. She could testify that it had been, and for how long. In bed she had connected its absence with his New York trip. Frailty, thy name is Miss Knutsen.

But he kissed her affectionately good night when she left, urbane, sophisticated, a quick roll in the hay, but still friends, it's the way of the world, drive safely, my dear. He closed the door on her parting laughter and was immediately engulfed in a huge sadness.

He went into the kitchen and splashed bourbon over ice, three ounces, and drank it pacing through the apartment. Gearhart dead. Killed, apparently. Since Gearhart had all but accused his old friend Mason of stealing the Ford portrait Margaret Sinclair had left to Peggy to avoid having to point out the infallible mark of a Ford portrait, it might seem that he had shot his old friend. He could have used the pistol in his office.

Of course Mason knew better. It had been Parker. Call Glockner nuts, he had nothing on Parker, the greedy bastard. He already had one portrait worth millions, yet he had to steal another. Glockner was right in one thing, the Sinclairs were insane to hang such a valuable painting in their house, particularly while all the publicity about Ford paintings filled the air. They might just as well have advertised for a thief. If Parker could arrange for a copy of Bridget to be made as quickly as he had, it would have been child's play to send hired thugs to Fox River for the portrait of Margaret Sinclair. And, later, to shut up Gearhart.

These past days had been a comic opera, the part Mason played incredible and flamboyant, but ultimately unreal. It was as if, win or lose, he was playing with Monopoly money. In his mind, he was able to see his career in the balance, possible ruin on all sides, but it was in his mind, after all, and thus by definition unreal. The theft of the Margaret portrait brought into his immediate neighborhood forces he had imagined to be at Parker's disposal, a surgical strike of laughably minimal risk, toting a picture out of a private home. Neighbors in subsequent news broadcasts thought they had seen a van and men in overalls. There was a suggestion of Laurel and Hardy, but George Frederick Mason was not deceived. He had fallen in with ruthless men and more than his career was at risk.

Miss Knutsen took his mind off his worries, at the museum, more importantly in his apartment. Don't overdo, he told himself, but when alone he drank too much, and she seemed the safer of two debauches. So it was that she had been with him, enjoying postcoital television, when the news came that the body of Glockner had been found in his motel room.

Shot. Suicide? For an hour after the first announcement, after Miss Knutsen had left, it was possible to nurse the hope—and how

296

welcome would have been the notion of a despairing Glockner putting an end to his own self-induced misery—but then came the truth. Glockner had been shot. Local police were pursuing clues. The ten o'clock news had just finished when Maud telephoned.

"Have you heard the dreadful news about Gearhart Glockner?"

"The poor fellow."

"I want you to know that I never believed a word he said against you."

"I appreciate that."

"You should have threatened to sue."

"No need for that now, Maud."

"It's good to hear you in such fine spirits."

Mason glanced at his drink and smiled. He thanked Maud, replaced the phone, and settled down before the set, remote control in hand, as if he were keeping a vigil. It has been called a mark of genius to be able to keep two unrelated thoughts simultaneously before the mind, but it did not take genius to recognize that the theft of the Ford portrait and the shooting of Glockner were related. The fool had named not only Mason but also Parker and Marjorie, he had maligned the New York art world, he had in effect set himself up. But how dumb was Parker? A finger is pointed at him in Fox River, Illinois, and a few days later, the accuser is shot dead. Even local police would consider the possibility of a link.

When his doorbell rang he sat still. Why should he answer? He was half in the bag already and had no desire to see anyone. It was bad enough that any idiot could interrupt him simply by dialing a telephone number, but it was too much to be at the beck and call of anyone capable of pressing a door button. He carried his glass with him when he tiptoed to the door and looked out the little peeking hole.

A stranger. No, Mason had seem him before, at the museum. A policeman. He was wearing a tweed jacket despite the August heat. He shifted and Mason saw a black woman. What the hell? He hurried to the kitchen, dumped the bourbon down the sink, stopped at the bathroom and gargled quickly, and was back to the door when the bell rang for the third time.

"George Frederick Mason?"

"That's right."

"Director of the Fox River Museum?"

"We've met before. What's your name?"

A wallet was produced and opened to display a badge. "Horvath. This is Detective Lamb. Could we come in?"

Was it imagination that the living room smelled like a distillery? Well, why the hell shouldn't he have a drink if he wanted one? Horvath and his companion knew nothing of his resolution to quit. A relaxing drink at day's end, nothing could be more natural.

"I was just about to have a drink," he said cheerily.

"Go ahead. I see you're watching the news."

Mason turned as if surprised to see the television on. "I was looking for something to watch. Unsuccessfully. Television," he said with disgust.

They came with him to the kitchen. He used the glass he had just emptied. Did they notice the ice cubes still unmelted in the sink? He opened the bourbon quickly to counteract the smell rising from the drain. Horvath watched as Mason poured.

"Care for one?"

"Can't."

"Coke?"

"Thanks."

Detective Lamb refused a soda. It lent her a certain moral authority when they returned to the living room.

"I wondered if you had heard of the shooting of Professor Glockner."

"The poor fellow."

"When did you last see him?"

"On television? Constantly. Not in person of late. We'd had a bit of a falling out."

"That's pretty mild, isn't it? He's been accusing you of grand larceny."

"He was a bit cracked, you know."

"When did you leave your office today?"

He gave it some thought. "I came home early."

"Having left when?"

"I don't think it was three o'clock."

"Where did you go?"

"Here."

"You came directly here from the museum?"

"That's right."

298

"What is that, about a ten, fifteen-minute drive?"

"That's right."

"And you've been here ever since?"

"Right here."

"Mr. Mason, if someone were to doubt that you came home directly from your office and haven't left since, what could you say that would dispel this doubt?"

"Why should I bother to?"

"Is there anyone who could vouch for your being here all that time?"

The naked vision of Miss Knutsen formed in his mind and he was half tempted to engage in a little masculine confiding with Horvath, but chivalry was not dead, not in the heart of George Frederick Mason it wasn't. How weak his drink seemed when he sipped it. And then he remembered Maud's call.

"Maud Sinclair. I talked to her tonight."

"What time?"

He thought. The news was just about to come on. "Ten o'clock."

"You spoke to her on the phone?"

"That's right."

"Did you call her?"

Mason gave Horvath a look. "No. She called me."

"Do you know the Waterbed Motel?"

"I've heard of it. I don't know it."

"It's where your friend Professor Glockner was found dead."

"I understand that."

"You could have been there and back any number of times between three o'clock and ten."

"Oh, for God's sake."

"Surely you weren't indifferent to the things he was saying about you."

"Listen, if you can imagine me doing such a thing you're in the wrong line of work."

"No one saw you there, of course."

"I'm not surprised."

"But we seldom have that solid a base to work on. You did have motivation. I think anyone would agree that Glockner had tested your patience. You had opportunity."

"Opportunity!"

"Do you own any firearms?"

Images of blunderbusses, bazookas, and howitzers formed in his mind. "Oh, come on."

"Do you have a handgun registered in your name?" Horvath said. The two of them took turns, like parts of a chorus.

"Yes, I own a pistol. It's in my desk at the museum."

"What kind is it?"

"A pistol. I don't know the make."

Agnes rattled off a number. "Is that the registration number?"

"Look, half the time I can't remember my Social Security number. What's the point of this?"

"A gun was found in Glockner's room, on the floor, kicked under the bed."

"We think it's yours," Horvath said. What an unreadable face the man had. Was he serious?

"That's impossible." Mason looked back and forth between the two of them. "Not that it matters."

"Oh?"

"Someone was with me here, until almost ten o'clock."

"Who?"

In the circumstances he had no choice. The questioning had become uncomfortable. He had to spill the beans.

"Hazel Knutsen."

"We'll check it out," Horvath said after a moment.

"Don't leave town."

Mason stared at Agnes Lamb. She seemed to be serious.

(53)

Peggy Sinclair's calm reaction to the loss of Margaret's portrait surprised Roger Dowling, but when he found her hard at work at Fairview the morning after the murder of Gearhart Glockner his first thought was that she could not have heard the news. But she had.

"I called my roommate Michele to tell her but she had already heard it on the radio."

"He certainly turned himself into national news."

"We always made fun of him," she said sadly. "It was hard not to."

"I don't blame him for getting excited about the theft of the portrait."

"Margaret couldn't know how valuable her picture was, Father. She wouldn't have given it to me if she had. Still, she wanted me to have it and I hope I get it back but not because it's worth a lot of money. It's only worth a lot of money if you sell it and I wouldn't. I still have her diary, anyway."

"Was the painting insured?"

"I don't know. Who would have thought it needed it? I'm sure it'll come back. Once I had a car stolen and they found it."

Father Dowling looked at the wall where the portrait had hung. Poor Margaret, she could never have imagined that her collection of Ford paintings would cause such trouble.

"I remember it hanging there, Peggy," Father Dowling said. "It drew the eye, particularly when you realized that the young woman in it and the old lady you were talking with were one and the same."

"Eve in the Garden, she called herself."

"She said that?" Meaning sinless?

"Once she called it 'Before the Fall.' That was the most painful way to think of it, I suppose. Her life was divided into two very unequal parts by what happened to Matthew in Maiori."

"I've spoken to a friend in Rome about what would be involved in shipping his remains to the States. The consulate has experience with Americans who die while visiting Italy and are taken home immediately by relatives but not with a body involving an interval of . . . how long is it?"

"Seventy-five years? A little more."

"If it can be done at all, it will take time."

"It seems a shame to move him after all those years but it's even worse to have him lying there as if we're ignoring him. How I wish I'd asked Margaret why she didn't have her husband brought home."

"At the time of his death, I'm sure that would have been extremely difficult to do. And she would have had to make all the arrangements herself, wouldn't she?"

"There was just herself and Bridget. A man came down from the embassy in Rome and helped."

"Are you still poring over those diaries?"

"They fascinate me, Father."

"Don't overdo it."

"But you read them yourself."

Indeed he had, and he had learned things it might not be well for Peggy to know. Pinkie, alternately forthcoming and closemouthed, might have been luring Peggy on.

A call came for Peggy while he was still there and he left the room for a time. The subject of Joel Cleary did not come up between them and he supposed Peggy must half blame him for what had happened. Joel had indeed applied for an annulment and, the way things had changed in such matters, he might very well get one. Looney apparently was encouraging Joel to think his prospects were good.

302

"Guess who that was?" Peggy said brightly when he returned.

"I'm sure I'd be wrong."

"Lester Pincus! He's been studying Bridget's diary and wants to talk to me. Father, I am going to tell him I think his family owns Bridget's portrait."

"The copy or the original?"

"The original! Clayton Ford painted Bridget as a gift to her. I wouldn't be surprised if Lester has figured that out."

"When will you see him?"

"Oh, not until this afternoon."

That afternoon Roger Dowling asked Marie Murkin if she would like to come visit the residents of Riverside.

"What on earth for?"

Marie was genuinely put out by the half-teasing suggestion. Did she fear that one day she too would live in a rest home?

"Maybe you should keep an eye on things here. I'm going to look in on Bridget Pincus."

"I don't even know the woman."

"If anything comes up, you can reach me there."

"What would I say to her?"

"Marie, you wouldn't get a word in edgewise."

Pinkie seemed happy to see him and willing enough to return to the subject of Clayton Ford and those long-ago days when Bridget and Margaret had taken turns sitting for the artist. He supposed the family would have been wary of letting an artist loose among them, but Bridget as chaperone did not suggest the fear was excessive.

"How old was Ford then?"

"He was thirty if he was a day but he acted like a much younger man. The way he dressed. He had no beard or mustache, which was a rarity then, and he wore a wide-brimmed hat when he painted, indoors or out, it was like a rabbit's foot to him, his lucky hat. It looked as painted as the canvas." Bridget's frown gave way to a smile. "Talked a mile a minute, to entertain you while you sat, but you couldn't smile or laugh, you had to hold the pose and all the while Margaret would be there. He insisted he was painting me nude though I was dressed as full as you please." Bridget did laugh then

303

and her eyes might have been seeing things that had long since ceased to be.

"How long did it take, having your portraits painted?"

"Weeks longer than he said it would, we seemed to be at it most of the summer. Oh, it was an experience. When we weren't with him we were talking about him. I remember daydreaming that when he left he would take me with him. What an age that is, Father. They shouldn't have let us out of their sight. I said that to young Peggy and she laughed but no one can tell me young women are better running around loose and independent as they do now. It's asking for trouble."

Roger Dowling thought of Joel Cleary and Peggy. There was something in what the old woman said, perhaps, but were people ever safe from themselves?

"Lead us not into temptation, isn't that it, Father?"

"She was expecting when she married Matthew Sinclair, wasn't she, Bridget?"

"Why would you say a thing like that!"

"They were married in August. Her baby was born in January."

"That doesn't prove a thing."

"Then it isn't true?"

Bridget looked half wildly around the room, then rolled toward him. "Don't tell Peggy, Father. Don't tell any of them. What difference does it make now?"

Bridget had the knack of the very old to see human weakness in perspective. He assured her he would keep Margaret's secret.

"It must have been exciting for you to sail off to Europe with them, young as you were."

"Do you know, I hadn't any memory at all of coming this way as a child, though how I could forget I don't know. The ocean! What a great frightening thing it was to stand on deck and look as far as the eye could see and there was only water and sky, day after day."

"Did any of you speak Italian?"

"Mr. Sinclair had some, less than he thought. I think they took advantage of him, but he was proud of it nonetheless."

"I used to visit Italy fairly often." When he was on the marriage tribunal, referrals to Rome were commonplace.

"How could you stand it?"

He laughed. "You didn't like it?"

"Well, imagine, not knowing a word of the language, a servant to the two of them. After Clayton Ford, he was dull as a stick." She rolled her eyes.

Gloria looked in, her mouth an O of surprise. "Your program is on, Bridget!"

A click of the remote control remedied that. Father Dowling rose, blessed the old lady who even as she bowed kept an eye on the TV screen, and took his leave. Gloria looked as if she would have liked to stay behind to watch the soap with Bridget.

"Is Honora working today?" he asked Gloria when they reached the nurses' station.

"She was supposed to. She hasn't come in for two days and doesn't answer her phone at home." Gloria's tone altered. "That's not like her, Father Dowling. When she says she's coming in, she comes in."

54

Phil Keegan went to the Waterbed Motel with Cy and Agnes, wanting to see for himself this latest in the events that, in his own mind, he thought of as the Sinclair troubles. It had been one damned thing after another since Margaret Sinclair died and he was sick and tired of it. Robertson continued to express fear that the family would blame all its troubles on the Fox River police.

"Troubles? They're all going to be millionaires many times over and most of them already are."

"I've spoken with Dr. Pippen," Robertson said, frowning at his captain of detectives. "If we followed her advice, we'd bring charges against the nurse who attended Mrs. Sinclair."

"Maybe you should mention that to the prosecutor."

Robertson's eye drifted to the window. "I did talk to Grady. He feels it would be difficult to phrase the charge, legally. I would have thought negligence obvious from what Monique Pippen tells me. I trust that girl."

Keegan's hand went to the pocket in which he carried his cigars, but he did not take one out. How could he tell the chief to keep his nose out of police business? Robertson seemed to think they owed the Sinclairs an apology because the chef at Fairview had committed suicide. Keegan found such sessions with Robertson worse because he himself was still bothered by the death of Regis Factor.

"Who the hell called 911?" he asked Cy.

"A man."

"The only man at Fairview was Regis Factor, right?"

"That's right."

"Are you saying he made the phone call himself?"

Cy didn't answer that. Why should he? It was not impossible that the man had decided to kill himself, called in to make sure his act would not go unnoticed, then went ahead with it. Maybe the phone call gave added motivation. Otherwise he would have had to explain that he had changed his mind since the call.

Meanwhile the Sinclairs were all over the front page, first talking about contesting old Margaret's will, then all friends again when they decided they still owned paintings in the Fox River Museum supposedly worth megamillions. Those damned paintings were no end of trouble, particularly when the mad professor from Indiana blew into town and began holding news conferences right and left. Keegan frankly couldn't keep up with it. A Ford painting was discovered in New Jersey, making one in the Fox River Museum a copy rather than an original, and Glockner all but accused Mason of stealing it, entering into a conspiracy with shady types in the East. If they ever determined whether a crime had been committed it would be a question whose jurisdiction it was in.

But there was no doubt that the theft of Margaret Sinclair's portrait was the job of the Fox River police.

"Mason," Agnes said, when Keegan sat down with her and Cy.

"There was going to be a showdown with the portrait of Margaret Sinclair. Mason would point out how he knew it was authentic and the copy wasn't."

"Like the big scene in 'Gunsmoke,' two men in a dusty street, only one can survive."

Of course Agnes had been mocking the inflated way Glockner spoke of the painting. But now Glockner was dead.

"Find the weapon?"

It was bagged, a nice little .38. The chances of there being prints on it were nil, of course, but Cy would check the registration. Keegan went on to St. Hilary's where Marie entertained him while they waited for Roger Dowling to return.

"He's at the Riverside. That's a home for the aged."

"Making an application for you?"

"That's not funny!"

"I'm about ready for the funny farm myself."

"Joking about things like that is in very bad taste, Philip, and you know it. Those are real people over there who have done nothing worse than stay alive so they've been abandoned by their relatives and left to stare at the walls or one another . . ." She ran out of air, she was so excited.

"I've never been there."

"Neither have I!" She said it as if she were denying an accusation. Phil gave up. He missed his dear departed wife but he was damned if he would ever understand women. Monique Pippen, Agnes Lamb, even Marie Murkin half the time. The rest of the time she was the sanest person, male or female, he knew, but she was obviously in an irrational phase at the moment.

"I'll wait in the study."

"Take a beer with you."

He got comfortable, lit a cigar, took a deep drink from his glass, and looked around at all the books. Four walls of them, not counting the piles on the desk, beside the chairs, on the floor. Phil tried to imagine himself in such a setting. It was what he had wanted as a kid, to be a priest. He had entered Quigley and started on the long road to the priesthood, but Latin had tripped him up. He just could not get the hang of it and in those days you couldn't be a priest unless you knew Latin. The Mass, the breviary, the ritual, everything was in Latin. Nowadays, and Roger vouched for this, there were ordained priests who didn't understand a word of Latin.

"You were born too soon, Phil."

"Maybe I should reapply."

"Holy Apostles Seminary in Cromwell, Connecticut, specializes in late vocations."

"No thanks."

"Why not, Phil?"

"I might end up with a housekeeper like Marie Murkin."

The kitchen door slammed. Phil had been sure Marie was tuned in out there, she usually was.

308

Roger was preoccupied when he got home, but Marie's dinner occupied them and not much was said until they adjourned to the study.

"You haven't anything on Honora Brady, have you, Phil?"

"The nurse who looked after Margaret Sinclair? Don't you start on me, Roger."

"What do you mean?"

"Pippen convinced Robertson we ought to prosecute her for negligence."

"She hasn't been seen for a few days, Phil. She didn't come to work."

Phil picked up the phone and called downtown but as luck would have it Peanuts Pianone answered.

"You still on duty, Peanuts?"

"What can I do for you, Captain?"

"Check and see if Missing Persons has anything on Honora Brady. You want me to spell that?" Peanuts said nothing, so Keegan spelled it, slowly. "She's a nurse."

"I know. I tailed her."

"You did! What the hell for?"

"I was with Tuttle. He got the plate number of the guy she goes with. Want me to get that?"

Keegan told him to get it and call when he had it. When he put down the phone, he looked at Roger Dowling. "I ought to take Peanuts off my payroll and have Tuttle put him on his."

"Tuttle must be prospering."

"The two of them followed Honora and some guy around and Peanuts will check out the license plate of his car. It's something, anyway."

During the ball game, Keegan found himself unable to forget the murder at the Waterbed Motel. He had confidence in Cy and Agnes, to put it mildly, but maybe he should have skipped the Cubs game and pitched in. God knows Robertson would be all over him tomorrow, wanting someone arrested, indicted, and hanged by nightfall.

He was interrupted twice during the game. The first time, Cy called to say that they had visited Mason but he had an alibi.

"He says he brought his secretary home. The time he says they were together covers when Glockner got it."

"You talk to her?"

"Agnes wants to know if we can wait until morning."

"What if he's lying?"

"The maintenance man saw him arrive with a woman. But he doesn't know how long she stayed."

"Maybe he didn't see Mason go out either."

"Maybe."

"Tomorrow's fine, Cy."

"Right."

No sooner had he passed this on to Roger than Peanuts called.

"That car she was in? It belongs to a guy named Lester Pincus. You want me to spell that?"

Phil had him spell it, and repeated the letters aloud. As he did so, Roger Dowling sat forward, and then he was on his feet.

"We better use your car, Phil."

"Where do you want to go?"

"The Fox River Historical Society."

55

Joel Cleary received a call from Monsignor Looney telling him that, while a definite decision was still far from a sure thing, Monsignor Looney thought Joel had reason to hope for an affirmative judgment from the tribunal.

"What I'm saying," Monsignor Looney said, "the reason I'm calling, is to tell you not to do anything now that might tip the scales against you."

"Do? I don't understand."

"I'll be blunt. Don't contract a civil marriage. Be patient."

Looney went on and Joel listened patiently because what the monsignor had said at the beginning of the call was such incredibly good news. People as often as not apply for annulments when something new is on the horizon, that is when they want to get rid of the old. Monsignor Looney understood that, but presuming on the favorable judgment of the tribunal was a very unwise thing to do.

If Joel had never before felt the layman's distaste for legal niceties, he felt it then. Looney was talking about the trick Anne had played on him, using him as a stud and then putting him out to

311

pasture, he was talking of what he might have with Peggy Sinclair, what Joel felt he deserved to have, and to hear it expressed in terms of licitness and irregularity, not to mention sin, made him want to roar into the phone to stop the monsignorial flow. But if legalities did not matter to him he would not have consulted Looney in the first place.

"Thanks for calling, Monsignor."

"And don't make any announcements. Better yet, don't tell anyone. Except, of course . . . Well, I'll say no more."

Monsignor Looney sounded as if he dealt out annulments from his personal largess, as a governor might stay an execution by fiat. You have been tried and convicted by a jury of your peers, you have been sentenced to die and the date of execution set, but I have decided to pardon you. Just like that. Annoying as Looney was, he represented the Church and if the Church said no marriage had been contracted between Anne Margaret Dudek and Joel Francis Cleary then, by God, no marriage had ever been contracted, and he was free.

He understood Monsignor Looney to mean that it was all right for him to tell Peggy, though Joel had never mentioned her, had never suggested that his application had anything to do with the desire to marry. He didn't like the implication that he was a predictable instance of a type. But the annoyance was scarcely skin deep when he thought of telling Peggy.

But how? When? Where?

To hell with calculations. He picked up the phone and called Peggy's home, counting off an even dozen rings before he gave up. He cleaned off his desk, went out to his car, and headed for Fairview. He had as good a chance of running into her there as anywhere else. As he drove, he prayed that she would be there, that she would listen to him, that when she heard his news, things would be different, would be as they had been before the motel in Indiana. Oh God, he was willing to wait, he was willing to beg, only let her be there. He told God to let it be a sign that He approved of it that Peggy would be at Fairview when he got there. An annulment would be a kind of divine endorsement, so all he was asking for was an installment on it.

He was fifty yards short of the entrance to the estate when Peggy drove out. She turned in his direction and he watched her coming, saw her face behind the windshield grow more and more distinct, wanted to surprise the expression with which she drove. He was so

312

absorbed in this answer to his prayer that he just watched her go by without doing a thing to attract her attention. Actually, his foot had stomped on the gas because he had to go in the drive at Fairview to turn around and follow her.

By the time he had done that, her car was out of sight on the undulating, twisting county road. Joel controlled his urge to put the gas pedal to the floor and went after her at judicious speed. Chances were that she was on the way home and if he lost her he could find her there. But within a minute he had her in sight and a good thing too. She took a left and headed toward town.

From then on there was no chance that he could lose her. He settled back and told himself that he was driving toward a moment in his life after which nothing would be the same again. If he understood, even sympathized with, Peggy's reaction to learning of his marriage, he also knew that her reaction was in proportion to what she felt for him. How wonderful it had been simply to be with her, lying around, shooting the bull. Her way of looking at things was antic and interesting, she had a capacity for both fun and seriousness, and dear God how wonderful to hold her in his arms. What had happened with Anne had been so unsuspected. There had been nothing to warn him about what lay ahead. He could not believe that he was destined for another disaster now. Peggy had to welcome the news he had gotten from Monsignor Looney.

It was an odd hour of day for her to be going downtown. What few stores were left would be closing. Signal lights were still set for maximum traffic, although there were few cars on the street. He paced himself so that they were an intersection apart. Wherever she was going, he did not want her to realize he was following her until they got there.

When she pulled to the curb, it surprised him. He drove on by to the intersection, where a red light waited obligingly for him. In the rearview mirror, he saw her hop out of her car and enter a building. One-way streets and the traffic lights made it difficult for him to get back to where Peggy had parked and he got antsy, fearing her car would be gone, but it was there. He swung into the parking lot across the street and turned off his engine. He had no idea what was in the building she had parked in front of. He decided he would wait for her to come out, ready to jump out of his car and cross the street as soon as she appeared. There was no way she could avoid hearing what he had to say, even if he had to say it right there on the sidewalk.

He sat in his car rehearsing the scene. He mustn't put her on the spot or make it seem that he expected some immediate answer from her. The thing was, she had to know what, if Monsignor Looney was right, was very likely to happen. Should he even make it sound only probable? Maybe it would be better simply to tell her the annulment had gone through.

No. He had lied to her once, in a way, by not telling her about Anne and Thea. From now on, he would be honest and straightforward, his speech yes, yes, and no, no.

Fifteen minutes went by, then half an hour, and the summer twilight came on: not darkness yet, that was quite a way off, but a general dimming as the sun, long since out of sight downtown, continued westward. The lights in the building across the street had been on and with twilight they grew brighter. Suddenly they went off.

Joel sat forward, puzzled. Peggy's car was still parked at the curb in front of the building. Whatever the place was, she seemed to have stayed until closing time. He became tense. At any moment, she would be coming out those doors. His fear now was that she would not be coming out alone.

But nobody came out. The lights were off, her car was still there. Joel began to feel like a damned fool. Had she come down here to meet somebody? He drove the thought away. He felt he knew enough about Peggy, tagging around after her the way he had been, so that if there was another guy, he would know about him. Nonetheless, the thought got to him. He pushed open the door, got out, and stood for a moment, stretching. Then he started across the street.

Fox River Historical Society? This was the legend lettered on the glass doors through which Peggy had gone forty-five minutes ago. It seemed an odd place to visit and an even odder one in which to stay after hours. The place was closed at five-thirty. That must have been when the lights went out. Joel put his hands to the window and tried to see inside. Nothing. The door, when he tried it, was locked. Someone had to have done that while he was parked across the street talking to himself.

There seemed little else he could do but return to his car and wait. Sooner or later, Peggy had to come out. Her parked car was the promise of that. Back behind the wheel, he started his engine and listened to the radio for a time, but there was nothing he wanted to listen to. More chatter about Glockner, the art professor who had been making life tough for Peggy and the rest of the Sinclairs. He turned it off, shut off the engine, and waited. He was hungry. He thought of popcorn and beer and smiled.

His patience ran out when dark deepened and the Fox River Historical Society looked as closed up as anything could. What in the hell was going on? He crossed the street again and rattled the locked doors, getting some satisfaction out of the noise he made. But nothing happened. He had not thought it would. He wondered if he should go around to the back of the building to see if there was another way in. But what if Peggy came out in the meanwhile and drove away? He would take that chance. If she left, he could assume she'd gone home and he would look for her there.

Between the entrance and the corner, a narrow passage ran toward an alley. As he went down it, Joel imagined what he would say to the arresting officer. Young attorney found skulking around historical society after hours. A light shone at the back of the building. Joel went toward it but it was set too high to see through. He crossed to the opposite side of the alley but that didn't help. Jumping up didn't either.

There was a door. He went to it and knocked. It was a metal door and pounding on it with the heel of his hand produced a satisfying bong. He paused and put his ear to the door, listening. Suddenly it opened and he pitched forward, losing his balance. And then the blow fell, sharp pain went through him like fire, there was a flash of light, and then he was falling, falling, falling.

56

It was difficult for Peggy not to think of Lester the way Bridget did, as a dull man in a dull job, fussing among artifacts of the past rather than living in the present. Unfair, no doubt, particularly when she considered her own interest in what Margaret and Matthew and Clayton Ford, to say nothing of Bridget, had been doing all those years ago. Nonetheless, although she was unconscious of it at the time, she drove to the Fox River Historical Society with a little smile on her lips, on her way to do a good deed. She might have been bequeathing Bridget's portrait to Lester rather than arguing that by all rights it belonged to the Pincus family.

"Why do you say that?" Lester's eyes seemed never to blink. His beard was trimmed, symmetrical on his symmetrical face. He himself might have been playing an historical figure rather than himself.

"The Sinclairs paid Clayton Ford to paint Margaret. They did not pay him for Bridget's picture."

"Because they didn't commission it."

"Right. So why did he do it?"

"Bridget was there as chaperone. I suppose he just decided to paint them both."

Lester did not welcome the subject as she had expected him to. Were only Sinclairs alive to the value of Ford paintings? That portrait of Bridget promised to bring millions. Peggy had no idea what Lester's financial situation was, but she would guess it to be modest. Nor did she know how many Pincuses might lay claim to any proceeds from the sale of the painting.

"Lester, do you have any idea what that portrait is worth?"

"It was owned by someone in New Jersey, wasn't it? And now a New York dealer has it."

"How did it get to New Jersey?"

"Good question. Obviously it wasn't thought to be as important as Margaret Sinclair's portrait."

There was an accusing tone in his voice and Peggy realized it was directed against her family. Well, he had a case, after all. How *had* the portrait of Bridget ended up in New Jersey so that it could be discovered by the New York dealer? Peggy conceded that it was a good question.

"You don't know the answer?"

"Do you?"

"I think so."

"Well, tell me, for heaven's sake."

She listened, fascinated by the intricate explanation Lester Pincus gave of what had been going on at the Fox River Museum as well as in New Jersey and New York. Peggy listened, an audience of one, to an obviously rehearsed account. After some time, Lester halted. It was time to close up. He locked the front doors, turned off the lights in the main exhibition rooms, and they adjourned to his office at the back of the building.

"It's the simplest explanation," he said, settling behind his desk. Peggy took the straight-back chair he indicated. She had come to condescend to Lester Pincus and was receiving a lecture instead. But she wouldn't have missed it for the world.

The simplest explanation was that, no matter who could rightfully claim ownership of Bridget's portrait, it had formed part of Margaret's Ford collection and it went with the landscapes when she loaned her collection to the museum.

"Holding back her own portrait, of course."

The records of the transfer were minimal. Even secretive. When the new director came in, he might very well have thought that they were part of the permanent collection. Lester opened a thick folder and found in it a clipping that he handed to her. It was from years ago, when George Frederick Mason arrived in Fox River as the new director of the museum. "I can tell you that the museum's Fords figured prominently in my decision to leave the New York art world for the Chicago area," Mason was quoted as saying. Lester wanted the clipping back. He replaced it in the folder and closed it.

"His predecessor did not hang my grandmother's portrait. I don't know why. Perhaps he didn't think the subject of the painting important enough."

"Oh, I'm sure that wasn't the reason."

"Sure? Why are you sure?"

"I mean I can't believe that any museum director would decide on such a basis."

"The basis that Bridget Doyle did not have the same social prominence as the other subjects of Ford portraits?"

"You know what I mean."

"I think I do."

"Please go on."

He sat back, steepled his fingers. He might have been a professor, a slim version of Gearhart Glockner. "Mason, for his own reasons, rescued Bridget from the vault, but hung her in his office, not in the gallery."

"I saw it there! Or at least a copy."

"You saw the original."

Lester, speaking with utter certainty, said that George Frederick Mason had taken the original of the portrait to New York and arranged for a copy to be made. The folder opened again. "I have here a record of his flights. I also have the UPS record of the arrival of the copy at his apartment. Subsequently, former associates of Mason's in the East staged a discovery. Bridget will be sold and Mason will share in the proceeds."

"Have you gone to the police with this?"

He smiled. "I have decided to keep matters in the private sector."

"Obviously you accept my point. Bridget's portrait belongs to you."

318

"I do not think of it as your point," he said frostily. "I have been proceeding on that assumption for some time."

From the museum came a rattling sound. Lester got up to investigate. Someone unwilling to believe that the historical society was closed.

"I am open eight hours a day. There were seven visitors today. The hours are plainly indicated on the door."

The noise stopped. Lester did not return to his seat behind the desk.

"I asked you here to enlist your help in the execution of my plan."

"Of course I'll help you, Lester. What you need is a lawyer. I've thought about this too. There must be a court order blocking the auction . . ."

"Shut up."

He did not raise his voice, but he was perfectly serious. Anger flared in Peggy. She wasn't used to being spoken to in that way, certainly not by the likes of Lester Pincus. In a microsecond the sympathy and solidarity she had felt for Lester were gone. Bridget was right. He was an odd man. Peggy rose to go. Lester's hand closed in a viselike grip on her upper arm and he forced her to sit down again. Anger gave way to apprehension. He went to the door and locked it.

"If you will look behind you, you will see a painting leaning against the wall."

The painting was on the floor, facing the wall, but Peggy recognized it immediately. She sprang to her feet and turned it around. The serene youthful face of Margaret Sinclair looked expectantly into the future. Peggy turned to Lester. He had once again taken his seat behind the desk, his hands flat on the closed folder before him.

"How did you get this?"

"Consider it on loan to the Fox River Historical Society. Unofficially, of course."

Peggy stared at him. Lester had broken into her parents' home and stolen a portrait worth millions, causing anguish and consternation to many. Why, think of poor Professor Glockner . . . Peggy was very conscious now of the locked door of the office.

"My proposition is a simple one. *Quid pro quo*. Margaret for Bridget."

"But I don't have Bridget!"

"But you have a plan to recover her, don't you? Lawyers, a court order stopping the auction, a judicial decision as to the ownership of the painting. These are things you can afford. I cannot."

Peggy nodded as he spoke. Promise him anything. Agree to hire a lawyer and get things under way. She had to get out of here. Thoughts were banging around in her head she did not want to consider, thoughts suggesting that Lester was far more involved in the events of the past weeks than she would ever have believed.

"All right. I'll do that."

"Good. I was sure I could count on you."

But he did not rise. Rather he leaned back in his chair as if to get more comfortable.

"This building has an interesting history. It is only fitting that a historical society should be housed in a building with history, isn't it? This was once a bank, a very secure bank. Day-to-day transactions took place on the street floor. The main exhibition room was once a very busy place. We are sitting in what was then the president's office. Directly below this is a vault."

There were sounds again, different sounds, closer, an odd metallic bonging. Lester sat forward, frowning, head cocked, listening. The sound did not stop.

"Excuse me," he said, rising, rounding his desk and going to the door.

He let himself out, closed the door, and Peggy heard the sound of the key turning in the lock. She looked wildly around. There was a window but its sill was above her head. And then her eyes swung to the phone on the desk. She ran to it, snatched it up and put it to her ear, her finger already punching buttons. It was her parents' telephone number that sprang to her fingertips and she waited for the ringing to begin. Had she ever noticed before the odd little noises before the connection was made? As if from another dimension, scarcely audible conversations came over the wire. The phone began to ring. It rang and rang. Why didn't someone answer? Please let someone answer.

But she couldn't wait. She slammed down the phone. What was the emergency number? Her mind was a blank. And then she had it. She punched it out, and again there was a whir of electronic transactions before the ringing began.

"Overseas operator, can I help you?"

"Overseas operator!"

"Can I help you?"

"Yes! What's the number of police emergency?"

There was a reproachful silence on the line. "This is the overseas operator, ma'am. If you want directory assistance, you must . . ."

Peggy slammed down the phone and punched 0. She had never felt so useless in her life. She was locked in a room with a telephone, she had to get through to someone before Lester came back, and she could not remember the damned number she should call. There was something weirdly wrong with Lester and she had to get out of here.

"Op-er-a-tor."

The voice spoke in her ear at the same time that she heard the sound of the door being unlocked. Lester let himself in, saw what she was doing, and rushed toward her, grabbing the telephone and slammed it down in its cradle. Peggy scooted around him and ran to the door. She pulled it open and stopped. Joel Cleary lay on the floor outside the door, on his back, staring upward, blood running from a cut on his head. As she knelt to help him, Lester grabbed her arm and tried to jerk her back into the room. Peggy, enraged, turned on him and began to beat him with her fists. She felt filled with the strength of mothers who lift automobiles off their injured children. She felt that she could beat the hell out of Lester Pincus.

She was wrong. He began to hit her with his fists and she was forced to use her hands to fend off his blows. This did not stop Lester from hitting her viciously again and again on her raised arms. The pain was unlike anything she had ever felt. She cried out, pleading with him to stop.

Eventually he did. He had to catch his breath from the exertion of beating her.

"Very well. I want you to take this young man by the ankles. I will take him under the arms. We are going to carry him downstairs."

"What have you done to him? Do you know who this is?"

"I suspect he followed you here. Doubtless he is the one who rattled the front door. He came around to the back where he pounded on the alley door. Take his ankles."

"What's downstairs?"

"A vault. As I told you, this was once a bank."

57

Thank God Phil did not demand an explanation before running out to his car. Roger Dowling was right behind him. He slipped into the passenger seat and fought impatience as Phil fished out his keys, looked for the ignition key, inserted it, and started the engine. They were rolling downtown before Phil asked.

"Why the Fox River Historical Society?"

"A hunch. No, it's more than that."

But how to say it without sounding a little crazy? Honora had been missing for several days and they had just learned that she had been going with Lester Pincus. The cool, bearded director of the Fox River Historical Society was nobody's idea of a menacing man, perhaps, but the connection with Honora had started Roger Dowling's mind going. A bearded man had been in the house the day Margaret died and they had all assumed it was Terence. Whatever significance there was in that, Regis Factor, the pathetic chef enamored of Honora, had died in a bizarre way that Monique Pippen at least refused to believe was suicide.

All wildly speculative, of course, but there was more. Roger picked up Phil's cellular phone and asked the operator to put through a call to the Dennis Sinclair home. The phone was answered on the second ring.

"Yes?

"Mrs. Sinclair, this is Father Roger Dowling. Is Peggy there?"

"Oh, Father, I hoped it was Peggy calling. She hasn't come home yet and nobody answers at Fairview. Have you any idea where she might have gone?"

"Yes. I'll call you back shortly. Good-bye."

Phil took his cigar out of his mouth. "I'm beginning to get the picture."

The historical society was locked up, the building dark. The street was empty except for a car parked in front.

"That's her car, Phil. I'm sure of it."

Phil was on the radio, calling in any patrols in the area. Roger Dowling got out of the car and looked across the street. There was one car in the lot there. Phil went across the street but in a minute hurried back.

"That vehicle doesn't have the license tag Peanuts gave me." Phil looked at the darkened building, just as a patrol car came squealing around the corner. Phil waved it to a stop and went to the driver's door.

"Go around behind the building. Make sure nobody leaves." He turned to Roger Dowling. "If the building isn't empty already."

Another patrol car had arrived when Phil was checking the locked front door.

"Two young women are missing, Phil," Roger Dowling said.

Phil's hesitation was gone. He summoned two officers and told them to break open the door. For a moment, Roger Dowling thought they were going to refuse, but then there was the sound of breaking glass, one of the officers reached through the shattered door, depressed the bar, and the door was pulled open. Father Dowling went inside on Phil Keegan's heels.

"I've been here before, Phil," he said, pushing through the turnstile and moving swiftly through the main exhibition room. Any number of people could have been there in the darkened room and he would not have seen them. He was headed for Lester's office.

The door of the office was open, the light on, but it was empty. And then he saw Margaret Sinclair's portrait propped against the wall. Any doubt that might have remained in his mind was gone.

"Margaret Sinclair," he said to Phil beside him. Phil turned and shouted.

"Find out if anyone is in this building. And turn on those lights out there."

There were half a dozen uniformed police in the building now. The ceiling lights in the exhibition room went on. Father Dowling turned in the other direction, toward the staircase. He was well down the stairs before he realized Phil was not with him.

Descending the stairs into darkness, light left behind above, he narrowed his eyes. He heard a sound below. A whimper. He was about to call out to Phil when he decided not to alert whoever waited below. Swiftly and as silently as he could he moved down into the darkness.

The whimpering, if that was what it was, had stopped. At the bottom of the stairs, Father Dowling waited, trying to accustom his eyes to the darkness. He put out his hand, in search of a light switch. Suddenly his wrist was grasped and he was pulled violently into deeper blackness, stumbling along, unable to stop himself, his wrist caught in a grip that seemed capable of snapping it if he did not allow himself to be dragged away from the foot of the stairs.

His progress was halted, he felt himself slammed against a wall, and then there was the sound of a door opening, as if with a great effort, and he was shoved and kicked into a deeper darkness.

58

In the office, Phil Keegan got on the phone and called downtown.

"Get hold of Cy Horvath and have him get down to the Fox River Historical Society right away."

He slammed down the phone and turned to find a man standing in the office doorway. He wore a beard; his eyes sparked behind his glasses.

"What in hell are you doing in my office? What's the meaning of all these policemen?"

"Who are you?"

"Who am I? Who are you? How did you get in here?"

The man's indignation did not ring true to Phil, and a good thing. He was in a hell of a spot, having broken into the building without a warrant, cops scurrying all over the place in search of what? The man walked into the office, but Phil's eye was caught by the portrait propped against the wall.

"I am Captain Philip Keegan. Where did you get that painting?"

"Did you break in here to ask me that?"

"Where were you when we broke in?"

"Show me some identification."

Phil was sure the guy was faking now. His museum was crawling with uniformed police, and he wanted ID. Phil pushed past the man into the hall. When he came to the darkened stairway, he turned. The bearded man had come with him.

"What's down there?"

"A basement."

"Where's the light?"

"Look, whoever you are, I am not going to take any further part in whatever is going on here."

"Where are you going?"

The man glared at him. "I would like to call the police, but I suppose in this town that makes no sense."

"Don't leave."

"You can't prevent me from leaving."

"Where's Honora Brady?" That got his attention. "Where is Peggy Sinclair?"

"Where? How should I know?"

"What's a painting worth a fortune doing in your office?"

An officer came, looked down the stairs, found and flicked on the light. The director's reaction decided Phil. He said to the officer, "Go get Father Dowling. We're going downstairs."

"Where is he?"

"Isn't he out in the main room?"

The officer's expression was blank. He shook his head. Pincus turned and ran toward a large metal door.

"Get him," Keegan barked. "Then bring him downstairs."

And he hurried down the stairway. The vault door drew him but when he got to it, it appeared to be locked. He put his ear against it. Nothing. At the top of the stairs, Pincus was struggling in the grip of several officers.

"Bring him down here!"

Pincus was brought unceremoniously down between two officers, his feet never touching the stairs.

"Open this vault, Pincus."

Pincus kicked out at him but Phil got out of range. "Open this goddamn door or we'll use you as a battering ram."

Pincus's arm was twisted high behind his back and he yelped in pain. He was brought to the door, bent over, his head almost banging into it. His hand lifted and began to turn the dial.

When the heavy door was pulled open and light fell into the vault, the first thing Phil Keegan saw was Roger Dowling sprawled across the floor. Keegan rushed in and that was when he saw the others.

After the police left, Mason went to the kitchen and splashed more bourbon over the melting ice in his glass. How in the name of God had his gun ended up in Glockner's room in the Waterbed Motel? Obviously it was meant to point the finger of suspicion at him. Stirring his drink with his finger, he thought he knew exactly what had happened.

Gearhart—the idiot!—had asked for what happened to him, hurling accusations at Gabbiano and Parker as well as Mason, charging theft and fraud, demanding that something be done. Something had been done, all right. Gearhart had been silenced. And with Mason's gun. That was meant to keep the matter local.

Two things loomed large in George Frederick Mason's mind. First, he must let Hazel know that her vouching for the time they had been together was essential. Second, he would go to his office, no matter the lateness of the hour, and make certain that his gun was missing. He picked up the phone and dialed.

"You aren't serious," Hazel said in shocked tones. "You can't tell them about us."

"Hazel, you were at my apartment. That's all you have to say."

"No! I can't do that."

Was this the girl who had shucked her clothes and hopped into bed without so much as an *arrière pensée*? How, given her presumed lifestyle, could she possibly care if people learned they had gone to bed together? Yet here she was in a semi-panic at the very thought of discovery, as if a reputation for virtue meant as much to her as it would have meant to the late Margaret Sinclair.

"I will deny it if you tell," Hazel cried and slammed down the phone.

Her unexpected reaction puzzled him. He tried to discover in what he knew of her any clue to her unwillingness to admit they had been together in his apartment when Gearhart was killed. Surely, when she saw the police were serious, she would tell them the simple truth.

Although he'd only sipped it, he had finished his drink when the phone rang. It was Horvath.

"We talked to your secretary."

The fact that Horvath was telephoning seemed to tell the tale. Mason felt relieved. "Yes?"

"What do you think she said?"

"I know what she said."

"She didn't back you up, Mason. She's a loyal employee and would obviously do almost anything for you, but not this. At first she didn't know what the point of the question was."

"Lieutenant, I talked with her myself since you were here."

"The reason we took so long. The girl she said she was with? She was with her. We talked to her too."

"What girl!"

"The point is she wasn't with you."

"Oh, for heaven's sake."

"We'll see you in the morning."

After Horvath hung up Mason dressed, went out to his car, and drove to the museum, where he locked himself in his office. He sat at his desk, hands flat upon it, staring at the copy of Ford's portrait of Bridget Doyle. He told himself it was silly to think that even without Hazel's corroboration he could be convicted of a crime he had not committed. This was the land of the free and the home of the brave.

There were laws he had broken and others he had tried to break, he had stolen a picture and colluded to sell it, he had betrayed the public trust, of all that he was guilty, but fortunately it was not of that he was suspected. Nor was he likely to be, now that Glockner was gone. However, the great danger was that, accused of a crime he had not committed, those of which he was guilty would come to light. Perhaps, as part of the investigation, they would look into what were regarded as Glockner's wild charges. They need not be proven in order for it to be argued that they provided Mason with motive, and even a perfunctory look into his trips to New York could be ruinous, not to mention his telephone calls to the Virgin Islands. They might even turn up the cabbie in whose taxi he had left the painting! It was silly to think that Ginger and Marjorie, let alone Parker, would come to his defense. Mason sipped his drink from real need. Would he rather be hanged for the crime he did not commit or be ruined by those he had? It was not his idea of an attractive choice.

He had no way to prove to the satisfaction of the police that Hazel was with him and that he could not have killed Gearhart. He opened a drawer and was not surprised to find that his gun was missing. That removed his last hope. The gun used to kill Gearhart and found in his motel room was registered to George Frederick Mason. He closed the drawer. He could no longer ignore the hopelessness of his situation. They had killed Glockner but they would let the law and the courts take care of George Frederick Mason.

He wanted another drink but he wanted even more to spell out as clearly and as thoroughly as he could what really had happened. He owed it to himself to be the recording angel of these last crazy months. No one else knew the truth. He turned on his dictating machine, settled back, and began. At the beginning, when as the newly appointed director of the Fox River Museum he had found Bridget in the vault and brought her upstairs and hung her in his office.

For two and a half hours he talked, relieved to be confessing what he had done, what others had done, emphasizing the irony that after all his efforts he would gain absolutely nothing from them except an unjust accusation of murder. After he had finished, he poured two ounces of whiskey into a glass, drank it off, then lay his head on his desk and slept.

He came wildly awake with the ringing of his phone and at first had no idea where he was. He picked up the phone but before he could speak he heard Hazel say, "Fox River Museum, Dr. Mason's office." She was out of breath.

"Hazel, can you talk?"

"Let me catch my breath."

"Tell me what's happening."

Mason's hand went white as it gripped the receiver. The voice was Marjorie's! She was calling Hazel Hazel. But his former wife did not know Miss Knutsen.

"Are they still questioning him?" Marjorie chortled.

"Marjorie," Mason said. He had meant to roar, to make his voice resonate with indignation, with the sea of emotions this sudden epiphany churned up. But what emerged from his mouth was more of a bleat than a roar. Almost simultaneously he heard two phones go down. His own made a third. He pushed back from his desk, stood, and strode across his office to the door. He gave a mighty pull and felt his back go out. The door did not open. He had forgotten it was locked. A minute later, he hobbled into the outer office, but of course there was no trace of Hazel.

He looked wildly around, pain shooting through his back, then went to the desk and touched the phone. It was still warm from Hazel's hand.

He felt at once very drunk and very clearheaded. He returned to his office, bent slightly forward to ease the pain in his back, opened his briefcase and put a bottle of bourbon and a half-full bottle of gin in it, then snapped it shut. He gave the office a valedictory look, then walked with what dignity he could muster through Miss Knutsen's office, down the corridors of the museum, and out the front door. Guido the guard saluted in a half-mocking, half-serious way and George Frederick Mason returned it solemnly. He felt like Nixon going out to the helicopter for the last time.

Traffic roared along the river road which was spanned by a beautiful arched pedestrian bridge encaged in sparkling mesh lest some despondent soul decide to involve his hurrying co-citizens in a suicidal leap. He gripped the mesh with one hand, the other holding the handle of his briefcase, and looked down at the flow of cars. *I had not thought death had undone so many.* With unwonted lucidity he saw the pointlessness of it all, hurry, hurry, hurry, and to what avail? We're always hurrying on from where we are to somewhere else until the hurrying stops. What would a life look like if its journeys large and small were traced upon the globe? He imagined a celestial pencil tracing his own erratic route of late. One swooping line would represent his trip to New York only a few weeks ago, another his agonized return. God would know that he and Hazel had gone to his apartment for a tumble in the hay while Glockner was being despatched to that bourne from which no traveler returns. He knew, Hazel knew, but if God and Hazel remained silent, how could anyone else know? They could listen to the tape he had left behind.

On the far side of the bridge was an odd-shaped island of grass formed by the coming together of roadways. A single red maple stood in stunted defiance of the noise and noxious fumes that swirled around it, there were hardy bushes of the kind that flourish in adversity, there was a bench. On this he sat, his briefcase beside him. As he had suspected, the bench afforded him a view of the museum, the great concrete plaza before it, the glass doors giving the world back to itself, the flags of the state of Illinois and of the United States whipping in the wind. There was the stage on which to strut and fret an hour and then be heard no more. What did it all mean? What the hell did it all mean?

Marjorie's voice on the phone revealed what it seemed now he had always known. Hazel Knutsen had been a Trojan horse, an agent of the enemy placed at his right hand the better to betray him. If there were any room for doubt he might have gotten out her dossier and seen what truths and lies were in it. She had been with him less than two months, showing up miraculously when old Mrs. Fluty was struck down by a hit-and-run driver. He had not yet posted the position when Hazel came to apply for it. She had heard through the grapevine of the opening. One glance and he knew he would hire her. Had Parker gotten rid of Mrs. Fluty to create the vacancy? Mason could easily believe it. He knew now that he had been playing a part written for him by Parker and Marjorie.

He could almost hear Marjorie and Parker dreaming of getting hold of one of the Fox River Fords, just one, and it would make their fortune once and for all. Both had known him in the past but ignored him for years, almost as if that had been the unconscious beginning of the conspiracy. How had they secured Hazel's aid? There were so many ways he did not care to count them: money, sex, vanity, revenge . . .

332

But why should he care what her petty motives were? She had been more observant than he had imagined and when he went off to New York intent on looking up Parker, Parker already knew he was on his way. They knew his hotel, Ginger lay in wait for him, intercepting him in the lobby, working the carefully planned shared-taxi routine like a consummate actress. All he had to do was review the conversation in the gym to see now how odd an exchange it had been. He had thought he was about to use Parker, but Parker already had the portrait, thanks to Ginger.

Sipping from the bottle of bourbon, he wondered if any passengers hurtling by so much as noticed the well-dressed, elegant man swilling booze on a bench three hours shy of noon. Who could suspect that he was a tragic figure? But it was not tragedy in which he was caught up, it was farce, a bedroom farce at that. At his age he was to be undone by his *cojones*, like a boy in heat. How pathetic the way he had swept up Hazel and hurried away with her to his bed, as if he were in control of the situation. Stunting away beneath the sheets, he was providing her, and all his enemies great and small, with an unexpected trump. They could kill Glockner and bring suspicion on him. It no longer seemed absurd that he should be thought a murderer.

From where he sat, he saw the police arrive. Horvath and Lamb got out of their car and approached their mirrored images in the great glass doors of the museum entrance. They had come for him. Well, all they needed to know was on his dictating machine.

He left his briefcase and the bottle with what little bourbon remained in it on the bench. When he crossed the narrow feeder street by which cars entered the pell-mell traffic of Cavil Boulevard, he looked straight ahead, ignoring the squeal of brakes, the horns, the angry shouts. He made it to the other side, where the spangled brown surface of the Fox River moved indecisively southward.

60

Roger Dowling swam back to consciousness and the insistent voice of Phil Keegan. He managed to sit up. Someone found a light switch inside the vault and turned it on. Gasps were audible. Honora was propped against a wall, staring sightlessly ahead, her penciled eyebrows smudged. Roger Dowling knelt beside her and gave her conditional absolution, then went to where Peggy and Joel Cleary were being attended to by paramedics. Joel's head wound was severe and he had not regained consciousness. Peggy put out her hand to touch Joel and then her arm slid around his shoulders and she leaned over him, holding him tightly, weeping. This did not deter Roger Dowling from giving the last rites to Joel. Then he got out of the way. The vault was crowded now. Monique Pippen appeared in the doorway and was directed to Honora's body. Father Dowling rose and made his way out of the vault, but before he could reach the stairway, his knees buckled and he sank once more into unconsciousness.

*   *   *

"You're lucky it's not your funeral tomorrow too," Marie Murkin said. In robe and slippers, the convalescent pastor of St. Hilary's sat in his study two days later. He had just informed Marie that he would indeed say Honora Brady's funeral mass the following morning.

"Better not, Roger," Phil said. "With that bandage on your head, people will think it's an eastern rite."

"I feel wonderful."

Except for the ache in his head and the worse ache in his heart when he thought of poor Honora Brady. How long had Lester meant to keep her body there in the vault? He could imagine that door being opened years from now and four skeletons found within. Edgar Allan Poe would have approved. Phil was telling him how everything was falling into place.

"A voice expert matches the nine-one-one call from Fairview the night Regis Factor died with Lester Pincus's voice."

Roger Dowling picked up his pipe, then put it down again.

"Regis, Honora Brady. Professor Glockner." Phil was ticking them off on his fingers.

"Glockner?"

"It's all connected with those portraits. Margaret Sinclair, his grandmother. Don't ask me to explain."

"A jury might."

"Don't worry about the jury."

Roger Dowling closed his eyes, remembering Glockner. He opened his eyes. "I would like to hear the tape Mason made."

"It's just babble."

But later Cy Horvath came and told him what was on the tape. "All the things he said he did? That's what he was worried about, but who knew? No one thought Mason killed Glockner, but we let him think he needed an alibi. That's my fault, Father. He was at his place with his secretary and she denied it, but we knew she was there. I should have told him."

"His gun?"

Cy shrugged.

"What does his secretary say now?"

"She's gone back to New York. Anyway, Mason's her alibi if she needed one."

335

"Phil adds Glockner to Lester Pincus's list."

"Where did he get the gun?"

Pudge Hanrahan reminded his former colleagues that there had been a break-in at the museum. Nothing taken, some minor vandalism, but not to the artworks. Nothing had been reported missing.

"Mason must've forgot his gun," Pudge said.

The tape made it clear that Mason had set forces in play over which he had no control. His finger may not have been on the trigger of his gun when it killed Glockner, but the director had recognized his own guilt. And so for the time they left it. Lester Pincus was indicted for the murders of Honora Brady and Regis Factor. The prosecutor was content with those charges.

When Roger Dowling went to see Bridget he was undecided whether he should tell her about Lester, but Gloria had already passed on the sad news. Bridget sat in her bed, rosary in hand, the television silenced.

"Before my programs come on I used to write in my diary."

"Where is it?"

"It went out with the rest of the trash. It was that diary that put thoughts in the boy's head. He wanted the Pincus family to be as important as the Sinclairs! He put my diaries in his silly museum and then he wanted my portrait too."

Roger Dowling said nothing. Maud Sinclair now agreed with Peggy that Clayton Ford had done the portrait as a gift for Bridget and it belonged to her.

"It's worth a fortune, Bridget."

"Oh good. I'll buy a new nightie."

Her family would benefit from this unlooked-for bonanza, except Lester of course. Money had not been his goal, apparently, and now, thanks to his crimes, the Pincus name was indeed a household word in Fox River.

George Frederick Mason drifted out of the picture as his lifeless body had drifted down the Fox River until it attracted the horrified attention of some boys in Elgin. It did not seem right to Roger Dowling that Gearhart Glockner was put in escrow, unaccounted for.

"I've spoken to Mr. Cadbury," Peggy told him the following day, after Honora's funeral. "He got a court order to stop the auction in New York. We're going to get that picture back."

"For whom?"

"For the museum," Maud said. "That's where Margaret intended it should be. We Sinclairs have all the paintings we need."

Terence found this hard, particularly after the decision about Bridget's portrait. "Maud, you can't just speak for the family."

"Don't be greedy."

"Do you know what inheritance tax amounts to?" He was growing a beard again; somehow it made him look balder.

"Shall we talk of the money you borrowed from Margaret, Terence? We could ask the others whether they think you should be made to pay that back."

Maud shook her head sadly as she told Father Dowling the story. Terence would be a millionaire after taxes but he found it difficult to be satisfied with this. Maud did agree to consider Tuttle's fee a family expense.

"How's Joel?" Roger Dowling asked Peggy.

"He'll live."

"Europe still on?"

"I can hardly wait."

He would be in Italy at the same time and they arranged to meet. Archbishop Corbett had called to say that the consulate in Naples was surprisingly optimistic about the chance of bringing the remains of Matthew Sinclair to the chapel at Fairview.

"Is there any need for me to come over?"

"His optimism is based on my assurance that the Sinclairs are very generous people."

"Ah."

337

Epilogue

The leaves of the great plane trees along the Tiber rustled in the warm breeze, tourists landed each day at Fiumicino, the Via della Conciliazione and Piazza San Pietro were crowded.

"The last time I was here I was wearing a backpack," Peggy said. "Does a Protestant need a visa?"

Michele's hairdo attracted as much attention as her leather mini-skirt. Their driver ogled his passengers as he put their luggage on the curb, great liquid eyes mirroring his sensual soul. Lust gave way to greed when Michele drew out a large note. They spared the driver the dramatic search for change and picked up their bags.

The hotel was in the shadow of the Vatican and full of Germans. The dining room was on the roof and at breakfast the great dome of St. Peter's seemed close enough to touch. After two days of churchy stuff Michele insisted they enjoy a little *dolce vita* and asked advice of the man at the desk. They took a cab to the Via Veneto, looked into several clubs, but ended up having a beer at a sidewalk table.

"I feel as if I offered to sell my soul and no one made a bid," Michele said.

338

"But you didn't want to go into any of those places."

"Did you?"

"No."

"Maybe we'll get picked up."

They were just as likely to be cast in a movie. They went to an American film dubbed into Italian but the fun ran out after twenty minutes and they took the metro back to the hotel. A week in Rome had seemed ridiculously brief when they planned the trip, but now Peggy wondered what they would do until they got on the train for Sorrento.

One morning, thanks to an invitation wangled by Father Dowling, they attended the Pope's private mass.

"Does this make me a nun?" Michele wondered, when she put the mantilla over her Brillo hairdo.

But they were both impressed to be there and afterward had their pictures taken with the Holy Father. Michele said she would send a copy to Phonsie.

Peggy laughed. "Maybe I'll send one to Leon."

References to Hathaway Hall reminded them that was what they had in common, the capital on which they continued to draw. There was something valedictory about this European trip together. Michele said she had gotten out of Toledo just in time. After repudiating the advances of a married suitor, she had been confronted by the wife and called every name in the book.

"Keeping a straight face was the problem. Peggy, I was flattered! I kept thinking, I'm involved in a *drama*. This is real life. I put it in my novel."

Michele was glad to get away. She worried that her parents believed the irate wife rather than their innocent daughter. Now that they were together in Europe, Peggy half wished she were alone. In her mind's eye there had formed the image of taking the same room in Maiori her great-grandparents had occupied, sitting on the balcony and reading Margaret's diary. She had the superstitious certainty than in those circumstances she would know exactly what had happened on that stormy night in 1912. She was not certain it would work if Michele were there.

"What's the latest on Joel?" Michele asked when they were on their way to Naples.

"I wondered when you'd ask."

"What's the answer?"

"He may get an annulment."

Michele wrinkled her nose. "I thought he was already divorced."

"He is."

"So what's an annulment?"

"Think of it as a Catholic divorce."

"Then what?"

"Then what what?"

"Won't that give you a green light?"

"I'll let you know."

Michele was not put off easily, but Peggy managed to get off with a few lies. Rattling along on the train toward Naples, she remembered how much it had hurt her to learn that Joel had been married. Why hadn't he told her? She wondered if she was as displeased as she pretended by his wanting an annulment. Would his marriage be any less dead if it wasn't annuled? It seemed that only Catholics think marriage is indissoluble anymore, because it is a sacrament. If the Church said no marriage existed, despite appearances, somebody had goofed, and what seemed to have happened really hadn't.

Peggy tried to wave the thoughts away but an on-limits Joel was harder to forget. She remembered their times together, playing tennis, watching ball games, eating popcorn. And she remembered too the motel room in Ohio where she had given herself to him and he had called her his wife. That's how she'd thought of it too. A private marriage ceremony.

At O'Hare, waiting for her flight to be called, she had been paged. "Would Peggy Sinclair please pick up a courtesy phone?" It was repeated several times before she picked up the phone. It was Joel.

"I had to hear your voice again."

"Joel, I'll be late for my plane."

"You have an hour and a half."

"Michele is waiting for me."

"So am I."

"Okay. I've got to go."

"Peggy." His voice became a whisper. "Please let things be as they were."

"Coming from you, that's strange advice." Even as the words issued from her mouth she would have given anything to recall them. Why did she want to hurt him?

340

"Joel, I'm sorry."

"Sure." An intake of breath, and then in an arch tone, "Dare I hope?"

She laughed. He must be reading Trollope, an author she had urged on him.

"Ask me after I come back from Europe."

"When the hell will that be?"

"Halloween."

"Trick or treat?"

So they had each said something stupid on that occasion. Rocking along in the train to Naples, Peggy developed the case against Joel Cleary. He was a Catholic, of a sort, but she had no idea what his conception of life was. He would practice law to earn money to do what? He already had a wife and child and had walked away from them, presumably because he found marriage confining. She had not wanted to hear the sordid details. The acrid smoke from Michele's Italian cigarette snapped her back to the present.

"Let me have one of those."

"You don't smoke."

"Neither do you."

"I'm on vacation." She handed the package to Peggy. "I've been thinking of your great-grandparents."

Peggy said nothing. She had given Michele the right to her secrets, God knows they talked about everything. But what would Michele say if she told her, "I've been thinking of your novel." She said it.

"So am I."

"What do you mean?"

Michele meant that the mystery of human life is inexhaustible.

At Maiori, they found the Norman castle but the hotel on the cliff side of the road was not the Paradiso Peggy had read about in Margaret's diary. The woman at the desk spoke English with careful accuracy. Paradiso? There was no such hotel now certainly. Their room in any case overlooked the sea and on the balcony, looking down on the castle, Peggy felt that she had entered the pages of her great-grandmother's diary. They sat on the balcony and had one of the awful cigarettes.

"Matthew went out on the balcony to have his cigar."

"How long had they been married when they stayed here?"

"Maybe three weeks."

"Did Ford paint her portrait before or after the honeymoon?"

341

"Oh, before. I don't think she ever saw him again."

The two men in her life ceased to exist for Margaret when she was twenty-one.

When they went downstairs the proprietor, a tall man with luxuriant growths of red hair in his large ears, asked Peggy why she had inquired about the Paradiso.

"My great-grandparents stayed in that hotel a very long time ago."

"But *this* is the hotel." He waved his arm. "It has changed, yes, but it is the same. It has been called Il Sole since it was remodeled."

So she had reached the aim of her pilgrimage after all. In this hotel her grandfather had been conceived, assuring that the Sinclair family would continue despite the death of Matthew.

"Why here?" Michele asked. "It might have happened on shipboard, in England, on the way here."

No need to tell Michele of how indisposed Margaret had been on the ocean crossing. It wasn't simply that no entry mentioned lovemaking; their contents seemed to exclude the possibility. No, it had to have happened in Maiori, Peggy was sure of it. And none too soon.

Peggy went down to the town alone, found the church with the many-colored tile dome, climbed to the cemetery and found, after a twenty-minute search, the grave of Matthew Sinclair. The cemetery was a city of miniature churches and chapels lining the narrow avenues. Photographs of the deceased, fresh and fading flowers, the song of birds and the slanting afternoon sun deprived the scene of melancholy. Matthew lay in a miniature replica of the church with the tiled dome, a legend above the sealed door. *Matthew Sinclair. 1889–1912. Requiescant in Pace.* Peggy stood there, her mind a blank, and when she said a prayer it seemed a small thing to do after having come so far. She was glad she had seen where Matthew had lain for all these years. If Father Dowling was right, the next time she visited Matthew would be at Fairview. Did it really matter if his remains were left here until Judgment Day? It mattered to Maud.

That night in bed she read in Margaret's diary.

The storm outside was terrible, with lightning and a howling wind. Suddenly the doors of the little balcony blew open and the drapes and curtains danced into the room. I fell back and Matthew gave me a glance, then walked through the waving curtains and outside. The shuttered doors swung out and were banging against

342

something. I waited for the storm to be shut out of the room, for the doors to be closed, for Matthew to return. It was several minutes before I went to see what was taking so long. He wasn't there! He wasn't on the balcony! Rain and wind and the terrible noise, it was so difficult to see, but then, gripping the railing, I looked down. He lay below. Dear God! It was a moment before I understood. Then I screamed, screamed more loudly than the storm itself, I was screaming when I ran back into the room and then Bridget came. We went out on the balcony together and I showed her where Matthew had fallen.

When she first read that account, Peggy saw only the most freakish accident. A young husband anxious to calm his distraught bride, forgetting how small the balcony was, had rushed into a storm, continued on over the railing and fallen to his death. Peggy wondered why Margaret wrote as if they had been awake already, aware of the storm, and were only affected by it when the balcony doors blew open. This was in the wee hours of the morning. Bridget's diary put it between two and three. Had they been awake? Had they been making love? Had that perhaps been the occasion when Margaret conceived? As always when she read the diary, her thoughts turned on how easily the rest of them might never have been if Margaret had not become pregnant on her honeymoon.

Peggy turned to a photocopy of Bridget's entry.

She woke me in the middle of the night, howling like a banshee, howling like the storm that was on that night and by the time I got there she was out in the hall and others were stirring, wakened by her wailing like a lost soul and I pulled her into the room and she led me out to the balcony, and pointed down. I pulled her back into the room, we were holding hands, facing one another, and she just stared at me as if she was going mad, and I couldn't get my hands free and then others came into the room and calmed us. By then I was making as much noise as she was.

Peggy slipped out of bed and stood on the balcony, looking out at the sea spangled with reflected stars. The heavens were all around her, ink-black, stippled with sharp points of light. How easily she might never have been born. Her parents might never have been born, and the same of theirs. However many billion people lived

343

upon the earth, each one was a statistical improbability. The marvelous thing was that each person was intended, chosen out of billions upon billions of possibilities, against all the odds, because they were meant to be.

Michele frowned over a notebook in which she had been writing daily since they left New York. Would some descendant be reading her words a century from now, perhaps come here to the Amalfi coast to do so? Peggy opened Margaret's diary and read the entries written here. They differed from earlier entries only in that they did not seem to exclude the possibility that the young couple had consummated their marriage at last in this place.

An hour after they turned off the lights, Peggy still lay awake, listening to the ceaseless roll of the sea below, imagining Bridget and Margaret here all those years ago. Matthew was more difficult to imagine now that she had visited his grave. It was far easier to form a mental picture of Clayton Ford.

All three were in paradise now but once long ago Margaret and Matthew had been here in the Paradiso, apparently on the brink of a lifetime of happiness. And then it had all gone wrong. They had quarreled. Bridget's diary as well as her old woman's memories made that inescapable. Adam and Eve before the fall. But there had been no serpent to tempt them. What a contrast with the happy memories of sitting for Clayton Ford in the barn at Fairview.

It was then that the unsettling thought first occurred to her, a thought she found impossible to dismiss once it came, perhaps because she felt she had been suppressing it for weeks. Of course it was crazy, the kind of thing you think when you can't sleep. It was like imagining that she hadn't been born after all, that none of the Sinclairs had been. How could they be Sinclairs if the child Margaret bore was Clayton Ford's and not Matthew Sinclair's?

What is real and what unreal? It had been a summer when the work of dead painters had been valued in millions, yet copies of them could deceive all but the very few. What if the Sinclair family, all of Margaret's descendants, were not what they seemed, not Sinclairs at all, but the progeny of Clayton Ford?

Peggy got out of bed and went out onto the balcony, but she stayed back from the railing. The thought that they had all descended from Clayton Ford rather than Matthew Sinclair filled her with vertigo. Doubt once admitted was difficult to expel. Could either possibility

344

be proved now? Peggy did not see how. That so much of the family's prospects were tied up with the Ford paintings collected by Margaret seemed steeped in ambiguity.

Joel's deception, if that was what it was, seemed less wicked as she stood there on the balcony, looking out to sea, the scene Margaret Sinclair had regarded all those years ago. With child. But whose child?

St. Cecilia lay on her side, facing away from them, her hair swept up to reveal the marks on her neck representing the unsuccessful attempts to behead her. They had returned to Rome to find a note from Father Dowling telling them he was in town. Peggy surprised herself by her reaction, telephoning him immediately. After lunch, Michele left them to go shopping and Father Dowling and Peggy strolled through Trastevere to Santa Cecilia.

"The patroness of music."

"Because she ended on a sad note?"

She winced as she said it. Outside they sat on a low wall.

"How was Maiori?"

"I wish I hadn't gone."

"Margaret would have approved."

His eyes lifted to the tower he had pointed out as an early medieval structure. Telling him of the thoughts she had had on the balcony in Maiori was like going to confession. Priests are meant to receive confidences. If he found it too fanciful, he did not show it. Peggy developed her troubling hypothesis as they walked the narrow streets of Trastevere. Finally, she made the point as sharply as she could.

"What if we're all descended from Clayton Ford rather than Matthew Sinclair?"

"What if everything in the world just doubled in size?" He looked at her. "That's something else you couldn't prove one way or the other."

"But what I said could be true!"

"Or it could be false."

"I have to know."

"Why?"

"I have to know who I am."

"You're looking in the wrong direction."

"I thought I could talk with you about this."

"We're talking, Peggy, and I'm saying it doesn't matter."

"You can't mean that."

"I never knew my grandfather, let alone my great-grandfather. I have no idea what they were like or where they lived."

"Haven't you ever wanted to know about them?"

He didn't answer. He didn't have to. Peggy did not know whether she admired his indifference or thought less of him for it.

"Are you going to look for the grave of Clayton Ford?"

She looked at him for a moment, then looked away. "I don't know."

He talked then, slowly, looking for the words, and she listened. He was trying to tell her life isn't a research project. Our task is not to discover our objective self, who we are independently of what we do. Did it really matter who fathered Margaret Sinclair's child?

"Are you going to tell your parents this? Or Maud?"

She thought about it, then shook her head slowly. "I guess not."

"Peggy, there are people who wonder whether Shakespeare wrote Shakespeare."

"Did he?"

"Whoever wrote the plays is Shakespeare so far as I'm concerned."

They emerged onto a busy street, into which traffic flowed over a bridge, and he led her to a sidewalk table where he ordered coffee.

"Thanks, Father. For listening."

"Maybe you could find out for sure, Peggy. Track down Clayton Ford's descendants, get a biogeneticist to check you all out . . . ."

"He didn't have any descendants. Except maybe us."

"Joel Cleary was granted an annulment."

"Really?"

He shook a packet of sugar, tore off a corner, and poured it into his coffee. "He asked me to tell you."

Peggy was in the tub when the phone in the room rang. Michele got it and a moment later pounded on the door.

"It's for you. Long distance. The States."

"Who is it?"

"Get out here!"

Wrapped in a towel, dripping wet, she took the phone and turned away so Michele would not see her idiotic smile.

"Joel?"

346